SURPRISE

"We'll [...] "They'll be coming [...] ng down in the opp [...] run into each othe[...]

The elevator door opened, and there were four of Kolya's guys in it. They looked at me with that look of stupid surprise that I have seen so many times—that look that says that the last thought they'll ever have in their life is wrong. For an instant, they wonder how this happened, and they wonder how they will get out of this bizarre, unexpected situation. They never, in that instant, actually believe they are going to die. And while, in that instant, they are wondering those things, I raise the gauss pistol and shoot them.

Snap, snap, snap, snap.

First I shoot the guy in front, who actually has his pistol drawn. Then I shoot the one in the far right corner, so he can't use the body of the guy in front of him for cover while he draws his gun. Then I shoot the guy in front of him, because he's in my sight. Then I shoot the last guy, in the corner to my left.

"Get in," I said, and I stepped into the elevator. Marfoglia and the boy had become statues, staring at the interior of the elevator, and the little Varoki girl in my arms began making a *"ooo"*-ing sound.

"Get in, Goddamnit!" I shouted, and the two of them almost jumped into the elevator.

BAEN BOOKS by
FRANK CHADWICK

How Dark the World Becomes

The Forever Engine

For a complete list of Baen books and to purchase these titles in e-book format, please go to www.baen.com.

HOW DARK THE WORLD BECOMES

FRANK CHADWICK

How Dark the World Becomes

This is a work of fiction. All the characters and events portrayed in this book are fictional, and any resemblance to real people or incidents is purely coincidental.

A Baen Book

Baen Publishing Enterprises
P.O. Box 1403
Riverdale, NY 10471
www.baen.com

ISBN: 978-1-4767-3626-6

Cover art by David Seely

First paperback printing, February 2014

Library of Congress Control Number: 2012043560

Distributed by Simon & Schuster
1230 Avenue of the Americas
New York, NY 10020

Pages by Joy Freeman (www.pagesbyjoy.com)
Printed in the United States of America

For Barraki and Tweezaa.
You know who you are.

||||||||||||||||||||||||||||||||||||||||||||||||

ACKNOWLEDGMENTS

Thanks first of all to my many friends and colleagues who read the work and offered both insightful criticism and generous encouragement, but particularly to Jake and Beth Strangeway, Don Perrin, and Bart Palamaro, one of the best editors I've ever worked with. Thanks also to everyone at the Greater Lehigh Valley Writer's Group, especially my critique group pals, for making an inescapably lonely occupation a little less so.

Finally, thanks to the whole gang at Baen Books, but especially to Gray Rinehart, Toni Weisskopf, and Edith Maor—who gives great line-by-line.

There is something in the human spirit that will survive and prevail, there is a tiny and brilliant light in the heart of man that will not go out no matter how dark the world becomes.

—Leo Tolstoy

HOW DARK THE WORLD BECOMES

Arrie...Arrie was something else: an iridescent-skinned lizard, a bit over two meters tall, wearing bell-bottoms, a tie-dyed tee shirt, and rose-tinted granny glasses. Pretty odd getup for a Human these days, let alone a Varoki, but Kako Arrakatlak—Arrie to his pals—was deep into that whole retro–Haight-Ashbury scene. I figured that was how he romanticized mainlining Laugh. Well, that was his business.

His shining hairless head looked small on that long body, and, if you weren't used to looking at Varoki, there were things just *wrong* with it: the ears as big as your hands—leaf-like, delicate, and constantly moving—the narrow, slitted eyes, broad, flat nose, and the big brow ridges that made his forehead look smaller than it was, made him look stupid—which he was not.

He had me listening to his latest "classical music" acquisition. I could have told him Yanni being dead a little over a century don't make his stuff classical, but when your best customer wants to impress you with how hip he is to *Terrakultur*, you don't spit in his eye; you sit there and you listen to the overproduced, soulless crap as if it meant something. The color and pattern of the walls around us changed in time with the music, the smart surface keyed into the audio data stream, and Arrie had his system rigged to look like a back-projected psychedelic light show. Only thing missing was a lava lamp.

Finally it was over, and Arrie took a slow, gurgling pull on his water pipe, ears quivering, smiling in dreamy pleasure. He held the mouthpiece in his long, bony lizard fingers—too long for the number of joints, so they looked awkward and graceful at the same time, like spider legs.

"Beautiful, Sasha, you agree?"

"A remarkable piece of music," I answered honestly, feeling no need to share the precise remark I had in mind.

"Do you know why I find your music—Human music—so fascinating? Because it is a window to your souls, and your souls are amazing!

"We found you—what?—less than seventy standard years ago, and already Human composers, architects, designers are everywhere. Your music and visual arts have thrown the aesthetic sensibility of the *Cottohazz* into turmoil. But this other side of you—this delicious, savage darkness ... Your soldiers are the most feared in the *Cottohazz*, second only perhaps to the Zaschaan. And Humans are taking over organized crime everywhere. You are such *brilliant* criminals!"

"Well, now you're makin' me blush," I said. I shifted

my weight and put my left arm up on the back of the couch, and my jacket fell open a little to show the chrome-plated automatic in the shoulder holster. I hardly ever wear the damned thing, but Arrie gets a kick out if it, and what the hell—a little theater never hurts. "So if we're so smart, how come you guys own everything?"

He smiled and tilted his head to the side a bit, the equivalent of a shrug.

"Give yourselves time, Sasha."

"*Oh, tha's good advice, Massa Arrie,*" I drawled. "*Meantime, we jes' keep choppin' cotton.*"

He smiled again, knowing enough Human history to appreciate the reference. Like I said—very into *Terrakultur*. He took another slow pull on the pipe and studied me, ears twitching playfully. Arrie likes to play the fool, but he has to stretch his acting chops to do it.

"Speaking of brilliant criminals," he said, "how is Mr. Markov these days?"

"Still a homicidal sociopath. How's *your* boss?"

He laughed—that creepy barking honk of a lizard laugh, ears fluttering like butterfly wings.

"Still far away, and not very interested in me—the best sort of boss."

"Amen to that, brother." I didn't know a lot about Arrie's organization, except he liked to refer to it as his Brotherhood. I figure he picked that up from *Terrakultur* as well, even though no Human criminal I knew of had used that term for maybe a century.

"Speaking of business," I said, "you got something for me."

He rose, unfolding like a pocket stiletto, and glided

to a small table—rattan and wood, simple but elegant. It looked like Sung Dynasty to me—reproduction, of course, but a nice one. I used to be a second-story guy, and you can't make money at that without an appraiser's eye.

He opened a black lacquered box on top of the table, took out a neat stack of *Cotto* flexichips bundled together with plastic, and tossed it lightly across the room to me. I caught it with my left hand and put it in my jacket pocket without counting—I trusted Arrie, and besides, if it was short, I knew where he lived.

"Tell me," he said, his eyes more serious, "how confident are you and Mr. Markov in the continued... reliability of your supply."

"If there's a problem, I don't know about it. Hell, Kolya wants me to lean on you to up your volume."

"Interesting," Arrie said thoughtfully, his ears open but folded slightly back—alert but cautious. "Mr. Markov tells you to encourage me to increase my purchases, but you choose not to. Why?" He walked back and settled into his formachair, waiting patiently for an answer while it readjusted to his shape.

It was a good question. I just wasn't sure he was going to like the answer.

The thing Arrie and Kolya Markov have in common is both of them are dangerous enough to get me killed, but that's about the extent of the similarity. The big difference—aside from the whole lizard thing—is I figure the worst move I can make with Kolya is to tell him the unvarnished truth; the worst move I can make with Arrie is to bullshit him.

"Well, I see it like this. We get pretty good cover from your people up the food chain, but sooner or later, enough high-end leather-heads are going to get themselves dead on Laugh, there's going to be serious heat, more serious than you're going to want to handle. On that day, as we like to say, the shit hits the fan, and I figure *all* the shit is likely to hit *our* fan. You're gonna walk away clean, Arrie, and just find yourself another hobby, while we're gonna be up to our ears in Co-Gozhak provosts."

I took a chance, calling him and the other Varoki *leather-heads*, and his ears had folded tightly back against his head when I did, but he'd relaxed into a smile by the end of my little speech. If you insult someone, they may not love you for it, but they'll give you points for honesty—that's kind of a cross-cultural truism.

"Did you share this insight with Mr. Markov?"

"Sure, for what it's worth. Kolya fought on Nishtaaka, so he says he's not afraid of the Co-Gozhak."

"Markov fought in the Nishtaaka campaign?" Arrie asked, his ears fanning wide again.

"Yeah, so what? Yesterday's news. It's not like he was the only guy there."

He shook his head and drew on the pipe, his ears settling back.

"Sasha, Sasha," he said, taking the pipe from his mouth and waving it at me like a scolding finger. "You are too hard on your friends. Veterans of Nishtaaka speak with admiration of the two Human rogue brigades they fought there."

"Nobody ever said Kolya didn't have steel teeth," I answered, and Arrie nodded his agreement.

"So what do you plan to do, my friend?" he asked, and the pipe went back into his mouth, eyes narrow and unreadable, ears motionless. Of course, he hadn't said I was wrong. One of the things I like about Arrie is he doesn't waste your time denying the obvious.

"Don't know yet," I answered truthfully.

He leaned his head back and studied me for a moment in unguarded curiosity.

"Then why share this with me?"

"I knew it would entertain you."

For a second he said nothing, and then he broke into laughter.

That same creepy honking laughter.

It was a good question, though. What *was* I going to do? I thought about it as the teardrop-shaped auto-cab hissed out into the Riverside Traffic Trench and insinuated itself into the tail-end tatters of the evening commute.

"Clear top," I commanded. The roof went transparent and I leaned back, taking in the view up the canyon walls, stars twinkling in the narrow ribbon of black sky way up at the top, kilometers overhead, like a diamond necklace hopelessly beyond reach. Glowing traffic ramps snaked up the sides of the canyon, linking apartment blocks and crowded market clusters, hanging from the canyon walls like glass and concrete moss. The leather-heads had a name for the city, something that translated as Capital of Peezgtaan—about as creative a name as they ever thought of. Humans came up with our own name, and now that's what everyone called it, even the leather-heads: Crack City.

Climb all the way up to the top of the Crack, climb all the way up and walk on the surface of Peezgtaan, and you die in maybe a minute, your lungs failing in near-vacuum, the yellow-orange light of Prime burning your skin off. But way down here, down at the bottom of the Crack, people can live. All kinds of people: leather-heads like Arrie, Humans like me.

At least until the shit hits the fan.

TWO

The autocab dropped me at the edge of the Human Quarter. You couldn't see the stars from down there; open space out in the canyon went at too much of a premium. The Quarter lurked under rock, back in the honeycomb of dark tunnels and crumbling chambers that made up most of the low-rent space in Crack City. A lot of those old chambers were left from the ice mining that made the Peezgtaan Eco-form possible, way back before we'd even heard of the *Cottohazz*—the Stellar Commonwealth.

My office was on the second floor of a commercial block facing Planck Plaza. I got there half an hour before my people showed up. Somebody had stuck a flyer to the front door of the building—an announcement for a meeting of the Society of Human Progress down at St. Mike's tomorrow evening, along with a list of speakers and the Society's e-nexus code. I crumpled it up and threw it into a trash tub. It's not that I'm against progress; I just don't have a lot of patience for talk. You want to make the world a better place? Fine. Just *do* it, okay? Tell me about it when you're done.

I unlocked the office, fired up the samovar, and took a look around. The furniture's all composite of one sort or another. The outer office had my admin's desk—with a built-in viewer screen—half a dozen chairs for waiting clients, and a little kitchenette with the samovar for tea and a nuker to heat soup and sandwiches. I had a couple framed prints on the wall—Earth landscapes, very soothing.

My inner office was pretty much the same, but with a bathroom and shower instead of the kitchenette, and a sofa in place of half the chairs. The furniture was sturdy and in good condition, but I'd gotten it here and there over the years, so it was all different styles and colors. The office was clean, but it wasn't expensive looking, and that was deliberate. I guess you'd call it austere, if you were being polite, and—without making too much of this—I'm a guy you probably want to be polite to.

Through the window, I watched Planck Plaza below. It was never very bright, even during the brief daylight out in the canyon. They had rigged up a lot of polished metal mirrors and cut some shafts through the rock to let natural light into the Quarter during the day, but there were five major levels up above us that each took some of the light, so there wasn't much left for us. There was artificial lighting, too; power was cheap—it was the fixtures and cables and stuff that ran to money, and were always burning out, and never got fixed in less than a couple months. But even with just the feeble glow from the light tunnels, Planck Plaza was kind of nice around midday. Half a dozen food vendors usually showed up, and lots of working folks met here, to eat lunch or just stroll around and talk. Nice.

At night it was dark, though—dark and dirty and empty.

Henry showed up first, along with his two top people. They crossed the plaza and entered the front of the building. After a couple minutes, they showed up in the office.

"Boss," Henry said in greeting, and he and his two lieutenants nodded.

"Tea's fresh," I said, and waved to the outer office.

"I'll get it," Phil Gillman—inevitably known as Phil the Gil—the youngest of the three, volunteered. Henry settled his short, thick body into a chair across the desk. Henry was built like a linebacker, but I'd seen him move when he had to, and he was fast—really fast. Big Meg Stanker, his other lieutenant, crossed her arms and leaned against the wall. Meg was taller than any of us, and looked like she lifted weights as a hobby—which she used to. Phil the Gil was tall as well, but skinny, frail-looking next to the other two.

"How'd things go with Arrie?" Henry asked.

"Pretty good."

"He gonna up his order?"

I shook my head. Henry frowned a little at that, and then settled back in his chair when Phil gave him a glass of tea.

Henry was smart, and he was loyal, and he was level-headed. He wasn't any crazier about peddling Laugh than I was, but what Kolya wanted, Kolya usually got, or there was trouble. Henry knew it, and so did I.

"You make any progress on that special deal we were talking about?" I asked.

"Yeah, actually."

"Really?" I asked, and he nodded.

"Looks like it might work out. I think I got a guy. I'll know more in a couple days." He smiled.

Now, that was good news. Henry and I were working on an e-snap data-mining project, without Kolya knowing about it. Two of the big Varoki merchant houses—AZ Simki-Traak and AZ Kagataan—had hub offices on Peezgtaan, and with round trip transmission times of weeks between different worlds, they kept most of the proprietary stuff their techies had to reference in the float memory of their central e-synaptic core. Henry had figured out a way—in theory—we could tap into it and sell it to their competition. Lining up the inside guy was actually the hard part.

Of course, if either the Varoki conglomerate we were planning to mine or Kolya found out what we were up to, we'd be dead a lot quicker than with the Laugh business. But potentially it was a whole lot of money . . . and clean money.

Well, cleaner than Laugh.

"How big a fortune we gotta pay this guy?" I asked.

His smile got broader and he shook his head.

"Less than we figured—a lot less. The guy's in the wrong social club or something—I didn't follow all of that—but he got passed over for promotion one too many times. He's in this as much for the pain as the payoff."

That I wasn't so crazy about; people out for revenge

get stupid. Greed—in moderation—is a more reliable motivation. Still, it wasn't like we had a lot of candidates to pick from.

We made small talk for a while, waiting for Ricky Lee, my number-three guy, to show up. Big Meg showed us new pictures of her youngest daughter. Cute kid, maybe turn into a real beauty some day.

"Good thing she takes after her old man," Phil joked, and for a second Big Meg looked like she wanted to hit him, but then she grinned, which was good. I wouldn't want Big Meg to hit me.

"They're coming," Henry said, looking over my shoulder. He stood up and leaned over the desk to watch. I turned the swivel chair and saw Ricky and three other guys walking across the plaza. They were horsing around and laughing. *There,* I thought to myself, *is a guy who thinks he has the world by its ass.*

"You're gonna have to do something about him," Henry said softly, just for me to hear.

"Yup," I answered.

But what?

Ricky came from what most people would call a difficult background. Around here that was pretty common, one way or another, but in Ricky's case it had left more of a mark. His father, Andy, was first generation—like most of ours—but Andy had come out as a kid, the son of a lab tech or something, not that it mattered. He hadn't adapted very well to the collapse of his comfortable, well-planned life when the Varoki pharmaceutical house that relocated all the Human workers to Peezgtaan went belly-up. Andy's family disintegrated, his father—Ricky's grandfather— drank himself to death, and Andy grew up to be a bitter, pissed-off man. He took his bitterness out on his wife at first, and later on his two kids. One of the kids died; the other one—Ricky—survived.

When Ricky first came to work for me, he was probably the most loyal guy I ever had on the payroll. He couldn't do enough. He looked up to me, like a father, I guess. Problem was, his father was a grade-A son of a bitch, and Ricky had hated him, so he ended up hating me, too. It was weird. Every time I gave him more responsibility, or encouragement, or support, he soured on me a little more. Maybe he only understood a good beating, but I think he'd have hated me just as much for that.

He had a problem with authority—obviously—but not one like I'd ever seen before. Right now, I figured Ricky wasn't my guy anymore; he was probably Kolya's, and he'd be loyal to Kolya right up until the time Kolya was actually his direct boss. Then, little by little, Ricky would start hating him.

I wasn't really sure what to do about Ricky. Since Kolya was looking after him now, my options were somewhat limited. And there was this thing with my conscience. Of course, if *I* were ever out of the way—a morbid thought—he'd be Kolya's problem, and Kolya wouldn't have any trouble figuring out what to do. He'd just kill him.

There are advantages to being a homicidal sociopath.

It didn't take them long to file in. Ricky had been growing a goatee, which I thought looked stupid, and tonight he had brought an extra guy along—fellow named Saito, one of his mid-level muscle guys.

"This is a closed meeting, Ricky. You know that," I said.

He smirked to his three stooges and shrugged.

"Saito's moving up. Thought he should see what goes on."

I just looked at him. Five seconds was about all it took.

"Okay! Okay! Saito, take a walk and we'll see you later."

Not that anything we were going over was top secret; it was just the principle of the thing. Ricky was always pushing like that, either trying to see if he could get away with something, or trying to provoke a reaction, I wasn't really sure which. But it was a pain in the ass—that much I was sure of.

Ricky nodded to the Hawker 10 in my shoulder holster.

"You're carrying that antique hand cannon, so you musta' seen Arrie. He upping his order?"

"That's between me and Kolya," I answered.

"Yeah, well, Kolya ain't gonna like it much if he don't."

"Never mind what Kolya likes. You better just focus on what *I* like. Did you get your payment over to the clinic for this cycle?"

He shrugged. "Not yet. Why the hell do we skim so much for the clinic, anyway?"

"Because I *say* so, Goddamnit!" I exploded and hit my desk with my fist hard enough that it jumped and sloshed tea out of the glasses sitting on it.

I took a deep breath and leaned back. Always pushing, always arguing every stinking point, always trying to provoke a reaction—and I'd let him get to me. I hate losing control like that; it's a sign of weakness. Ricky just settled back in his chair, a scowl replacing his smirk.

"You get your cash over to Doc Zhan tomorrow morning, and you add four percent to it this cycle, as a late charge," I said, pointing at him for emphasis. "You understand?"

He started to open his mouth, but then he clammed up and nodded.

The rest of the meeting was pretty subdued. We covered all the boring business stuff you have to keep a handle on. Personnel issues. Security. Revenue. Receipts from the Lotto and the Bank were the main revenue items—numbers and loan-sharking they used to call it. We also got a cut from all of the fences, and we had interests in about a dozen legitimate local businesses as well, but most of those were pretty much break-even propositions. Lotto and the Bank—that was the real money, always had been. And now Laugh. Kolya cooked it and we sold it, mostly through Arrie, although we had a couple other Varoki contacts that did a little business. Laugh was a Varoki-specific drug, which made it perfect for us—the Varoki had all the money, and our people didn't get hurt. But anyone who thought it could go on like this was nuts, and Kolya was at the top of that particular list.

He'd fought the *Cottohazz* before, and for him, Five Races be damned—there was only one race in the *Cottohazz* that meant anything: leather-heads. If Laugh messed them up and eventually killed them, then that was just a bonus as far as Kolya was concerned. Me, I'm a businessman, not a revolutionary.

It was past quarter-night—about hour 25 of the 28-hour Peezgtaan day—when we broke up and I sent them on home.

"I got an autocab pickup wired. You need a ride?"

Ricky asked. Maybe he'd decided he'd gone a little far and wanted to mend some fences. I thought about it, but I shook my head.

"No, thanks. I'm gonna walk."

He looked relieved. The small talk in the cab probably would have sucked.

THREE

I walked along the irregular archipelago of yellow islands cast by the overhead lights that were still working. I stepped over or around the sleeping drunks and addicts, took in the smell of rotting garbage, illegal cooking-fire smoke, urine and shit and vomit and people way too long without a bath. I listened to the background noise of techscreech booming from big speakers in bars, to laughter, angry curses, and coughing—always coughing. I nodded to the whores and hustlers and club bouncers, said hi to those I knew by name, but I kept going.

Whenever I started feeling sorry for myself—and I was armed, like I was that night—I'd take a walk down there. Even armed, I'd stick to the main thoroughfares. There were too many people with nothing to lose for anyone not in an armored vehicle to feel really safe, unless they had nothing to lose either. I walked down there to remind myself how most people lived at the bottom of the Crack, in the Human Quarter. That I sometimes needed reminding is, I think, evidence of a flawed character.

They lived without the certainty of the next meal, or the security of a safe domicile. They lived without the means of protecting their property, and so they lived without property. They lived in constant danger of injury and disease, and without the means of coping with either. All life leads to death, one way or another, but for them, the progress was visible, palpable. Their journey was a crippling, disfiguring death march, losing bits of themselves along the way—tooth, finger, eye . . . hope, self-respect, sanity.

And most of them lived without love, because loving someone, and being loved in return, carries with it an obligation on which they could not deliver, and the inability to provide for the people you love is the most soul-crushing burden of all. People—a lot of the good ones, anyway—willingly lived an empty, loveless existence in preference to acquiring that obligation, and failing.

There was a lot of excitement and optimism back on Earth when we made first contact with the Five Intelligent Races of the *Cottohazz*: the turning point in man's history, the dawn of a remarkable new age—you know. It all seems pretty naïve, looking back at it now, but how were they supposed to know? Races with the wisdom to travel the stars surely would have worked out all those little things like wealth and distribution of resources.

And the guys in charge had. They surely had.

Depending on your point of view, my condo was either a luxury suite or a hole in the wall. Since I'm second-generation Crack Trash, I called it luxury. Once upon a time a lot of folks did. It was in the old *Traak-Amahaat Gor*, a high-end residential complex built originally for the Varoki executives of a long-bankrupt pharmaceutical conglomerate. Like a lot of Varoki buildings from around first-contact time, it looked like a gigantic clay pot that somehow just hadn't worked out right. No matter how many times somebody told me it was supposed to look that way, it never looked good, and the green-black grime that seven or eight decades of airborne mold had left on it didn't help. Only the thought of a whole bunch of rich folks living in it could have made it attractive, and they were long gone.

The complex was sort of a landmark, a border-crossing checkpoint. It hadn't been part of the Human Quarter originally, but times change. Now it was fair warning that Varoki passing the foam-stone buttresses of this massive beehive-ugly insult to architecture were leaving civilization and entering the land of desperate, dangerous savages. But as long as they stood in the lee of the *Traak-Amahaat Gor*, they weren't quite there yet. Young leather-heads looking for thrills would hang around the complex and gaze into the depths of the Quarter, breathe in its sour but seductive aromas, listen to the distant tinny music of anarchy, and savor the danger-juice humming in their blood. Later they would dream about what adventures they would have experienced, if only they could have found the courage to cross that invisible threshold.

"Jo-Jo. Arriving alone," I announced to my front door. Jo-Jo was my home security command code for the day. The laser scanner did a quick once-over, my door swung open with a soft chime, and I walked into the wonderfully rich odor of jambalaya.

There aren't a lot of things better than jambalaya, in my opinion, especially with a full-bodied red—it doesn't have to be expensive, just a good working guy's table wine. I'm not sure how good you'd consider our local hydroponic red; we don't call it "Piss-Can Special Reserve" for nothing. But Cinti's jambalaya was damned good—almost as good as mine—and she'd made it special for me, which was nice.

My condo was a corner unit, with no windows—but there's not much to see anyway. The walls were original stone on two sides and low-density feldspar aggregate foam on the other two. I'd added paneling to those two foam-stone walls—well, composite armor, actually. The condo itself was four rooms—kitchen, den, master bedroom, and a small guest bedroom that did double duty as a home office. A small bath was off the den and a bigger one off the master bedroom, but big is relative; two people had trouble moving around in there at the same time. The open area in the bedroom wasn't much, either, because we'd put in a couple walk-in closets.

Cinti and I had painted broad, diagonal swaths of color on the walls—warm browns and dark reds—to damp down the paleo-industrial look of the place, and tie in to the big Persian carpet in the den. Maybe it wasn't much, but I liked it. The whole thing was maybe 100 square meters.

We'd been together for six years. Sometimes it seemed like just a couple months; other times, it seemed as if we'd always been together. She'd been Jim Donahue's girl when I first met her. Donahue ran most of the action in my part of the Quarter, and I sort of worked for him. It wasn't as organized back then as it is now, but he was definitely higher up the pecking order than I was. Cinti and I hit it off right away—probably because of jazz, blues, and *jonque*. I loved them all, and she had this amazing vocal range and a smoky, sexy voice that melted my heart one minute and set me on fire the next. At first we were just pals, but Cinti's a hot-blooded Brazilian, and my blood was plenty hot too. It helped that Jim was a pig.

I'm not sure I'd have been able to work out the plan without her on the inside, but we did it, and I brought down Jim and took over most of his operation. Kolya was moving on a couple other old-timers at the same time, and so he and I ended up working together—Sasha and Kolya, the two young Ukies who shook everything apart, then put it all back together again, only better than before.

Cinti and I were going to open an upscale *jonque* club. She'd sing, maybe manage it even, but there'd never been quite enough money to do it the way we wanted to. Ricky was right about one thing; the clinic was a money sink. But when Big Meg's delivery had gone bad on her youngest daughter, it was Doc Zhan who saved both their lives. What's that worth?

So, yeah, the clinic cost money. It cost Cinti and me something else, too. There hadn't been a lot of good evenings lately. This was turning into the best one we'd had in a long time. She'd been moody a lot lately, so her smiling and joking over dinner made it seem like old times. Cinti looked really good, too. She wore a pale yellow knit top that didn't leave much to the imagination, and the color suited her, set off her olive-colored skin, dark eyes, and black curls.

She really did look sensational.

❖   ❖   ❖

I lay on my back afterwards, all but spent and enjoying the feeling. Cinti curled up in the crook of my arm, her fingers playing with the hair on my chest. After a few minutes, she shifted and then kissed me on the cheek.

"Gotta pee," she said and slid off the bed and padded across the carpet to the bathroom, her hips swaying from side to side to the rhythm of a samba in my head, and I smiled. She closed the door behind her, and I heard the lock click.

Did you ever wonder why new stuff always sells better than the old, proven stuff? Why the pitch in sales and entertainment and—just about everything—is always about what's *new new new?* You'd think that once we found stuff we liked, we'd stick with it. But whenever somebody says "new," or we see something that looks different, or sounds different, or smells different, right away it's got our undivided attention. Maybe you think that's because we're all idiots, with short attention spans and no common sense, but you're wrong. It's because of survival genetics.

Back when our ancestors were hunters and gatherers, maybe not even smart enough to talk to each other, the environment was pretty monotonous most of the time. If something new happened—the grass moved, the smell of the air changed, birds started singing, birds *stopped* singing—those guys either gave that their absolute, undivided attention, and I mean right *now*, or they didn't make it into our gene pool, 'cause they got eaten.

Cinti had never locked the bathroom door before.

The adrenaline surge made my scalp tingle as I rolled over to my left and pulled open the drawer of the night table. That's where I always kept a loaded H&K 13mm AutoMag, but tonight it wasn't there.

"Shit!" I said, and I heard the door to Cinti's walk-in closet open behind me. I looked up and saw Ricky's reflection in the mirror as he brought his gauss pistol up. I could hardly recognize him, except by his stupid goatee. Christ! How tough did he think I was? He was wearing full body armor and a visored helmet, with V.I. goggles underneath. This was definitely overkill for one unarmed naked guy in bed—and it pissed me off.

I rolled forward as his pistol fired—a series of four quick soft snaps—and I felt the burn as a flechette cut a furrow across my left shoulder blade. The rest of the burst blew up the lamp on the night table and plunged the room into darkness. For a half second, as I hit the floor beside the bed, I thought the darkness was an improvement, but then I remembered the V.I. goggles under the clear bulletproof visor. I grabbed a shoe, threw it at the mirror on the wall, and got lucky. It shattered, so at least he'd have to come around the bed to see me. I reached for another shoe—anything—and my fingers closed on the leather of the shoulder holster I'd dropped by the bed.

I pulled out the Hawker 10mm—for whatever good it would do me. No telling how good Ricky's body armor was, but some grades I don't think even the sabot round for the Hawker would punch. As it was, all I was loaded with were plain old flat-head slugs for target practice. They'd hardly leave a bruise through armor.

He was walking now. Any second he'd be around the bed, and that would be it.

Or maybe not.

Maybe he'd overthought this whole thing, or maybe he'd let his hatred overpower his common sense. Vision-intensification goggles? Like he planned to put out the lights and then "stalk" me in the dark, toy with me—first terrify me, then kill me. He should have just shot me.

"Jo-Jo! Evac!" I shouted. Evac was notification that I needed to get out—probably because of a fire or something like that—and to turn on the emergency lighting. The evac lights were set low around the room—so they'd be below smoke level—and they shined up. They came on, and Ricky's V.I. goggles must have immediately whited out.

Now, if Ricky were smart, he'd have waited in his bulletproof shell for the two or three seconds it would take for the goggles to reset to the new ambient light level, but I didn't figure it that way. I sat up, bringing the Hawker up in both hands, and sure enough, he pushed his helmet visor up to pull off the goggles. You gotta love a guy like that. I shot him once, in the eye—the Hawker sounding like a bomb going off after Ricky's quiet gauss pistol—and he fell down. He didn't stagger, or stand in frozen shock for a moment; he just collapsed in a heap, like a marionette that someone had cut the strings on. Once he was down, he twitched a little, but I think it was involuntary—I'd guess he was dead before he hit the floor.

I stood up and looked at him to make sure. There was a lot of blood on his face, but he was resting on his back, and all the extra blood had run back into the helmet, so there wasn't much of a mess on the carpet. That was pretty considerate of him.

I sat back down on the floor by the bed, grabbed

the little wastebasket with pictures of elephants on it, and threw up into it. Then I had to put the wastebasket down before I dropped it, because I was shaking uncontrollably.

I sat there awhile until the shaking mostly stopped, and as I did, I felt blood trickle down my back. I'd forgotten that the stupid son of a bitch had shot me.

"Jo-Jo. Secure."

The lights went out, except for a little ribbon of light coming from under the bathroom door. *Cinti*. Now what the hell was I going to do with her?

I pulled on my slacks, turned on the overhead light, and got a towel out of a drawer in the bed pedestal. I wrapped it around my shoulder and back, mostly to keep from getting blood all over, and sat down on the bed.

"*Honey?*" I called, "have you seen my H&K? I can't find it out here."

No answer. I waited a minute or two.

"*Sweetie?* Are you okay in there? You been in there a real long time. Come on out, why don't you?"

"You're gonna kill me," she said at last, her voice trembling with fear, and I could tell she was crying.

"Aw, c'mon, Sugar. Let's not argue over who's trying to kill who," I answered.

I could hear her sobbing now, and all of a sudden I felt bad. That was *Cinti* in there. Six years of my life, really the six best. Hell, I wasn't going to kill her, but she didn't know that, and that last smart remark was nothing but torture.

"Cinti, you ever know me to kill two people in the same night? Think about it. It's too messy."

I let her think about it for a while.

"*Cinti?*"

"Yeah?"

"If I want to kill you, I can just come in there and kill you. You're not good enough, even with the H&K, to stop me, and you know it. Your backstairs boyfriend was a professional killer in body armor, he took me by surprise and unarmed, and he's out here getting stiff. So how well do you think *you'll* do? Now toss the damned pistol out before I get angry."

The door opened a crack, and she tossed out the heavy automatic. Cinti wasn't stupid. I got up and picked it up and slipped the Hawker into the pocket of my slacks. The H&K was a real hand cannon, and it was . . . persuasive; people take one look at it and start babbling. The door opened again, and she stuck her head out, eyes wide, makeup smeared by tears. She looked at Ricky's body on the floor and started crying again.

"Let's go out in the living room," I said. "We're going to sit for a while, and you're going to tell me everything. And I mean everything. Then you're going to take a couple thousand in cash, and one suitcase of clothes, and disappear."

"How do I know you won't just kill me?"

"Cinti, if you've got a better offer, go ahead and take it."

She went out into the living room. Before I joined her, I triggered my embedded comm link and squinted up Henry's number from my autolist.

"*Yeah, boss,*" he answered inside my head.

"Cleanup in Aisle One."

"*On my way.*"

FOUR

Henry and I cleaned up the apartment ourselves. He took care of Ricky's body, and I packed Cinti off on the up-canyon red-eye maglev an hour before dawn, with a couple thousand in her pocket, as promised. One of Henry's guys was with her, to make sure she showed up at Karla Bell's place in Manaklak Bay. Karla owed me from a while back, and I lined up a singing slot at her jazz club for Cinti. Karla would put her up and make sure she stayed put. I was doing Karla as much of a favor as she was doing me; Cinti really was that good. Maybe if I'd opened the club we'd talked about, things would have been different.

Water under the bridge.

Later that morning I sat in my office, tried to figure my next move, and didn't get anywhere useful.

The story Cinti had told made ugly sense, ugly enough I believed it. Much as Ricky had it in for me, and much as Cinti made his dick stand up and salute, I thought Cinti was too smart to have gone along with this move if it was just Ricky on his own, and I was right. Kolya was behind it. That much Cinti knew, but not much more than that.

I figured maybe Kolya wouldn't have tried moving against me, either, but he was always quick to recognize a fleeting opportunity. Ricky was ready to do the deed today; no telling how he'd feel next week. But why let him go after me at all? Was he that pissed off about me dragging my feet on the Laugh? Maybe. But that couldn't be all of it.

Ricky would be easier to control than I was, he must have figured, and Kolya would get a bigger slice of my action. Ricky was tough enough to keep the crew together, but he'd still need Kolya behind him. I wouldn't be surprised if he also figured that Ricky wouldn't inspire a lot of loyalty, and Kolya could play that to his advantage, too.

Not that I'd been exactly a champ at inspiring loyalty lately, either. Even Henry had started wondering what the hell my problem was, although seeing Ricky dead on the bedroom floor had settled some of his worries. But Cinti...

That was the big question I'd needed answered: *why?*

The reason was simple. She saw a showdown coming between Kolya and me, if not today, then tomorrow, or next week, or next cycle, or whenever, but it was coming. When it came, she needed to be on the winning side if she wanted to survive. In addition to everything else, Cinti was a survivor, and one smart lady. She'd bet on me over Jim Donahue six years ago. Now her money was on Kolya. That was fairly discouraging.

How much would Kolya know I knew? If I knew he was behind the killing—and he knew that I knew—he'd figure his hand was forced and he'd have to keep going. I wasn't sure I could convince him that I *didn't* know he was behind it. Kolya wasn't stupid, and he knew I wasn't stupid. So how stupid could the two of us *pretend* to be to keep the peace?

I really didn't want a war with Kolya, not right now. Henry was ready, which was unusual for him. Normally, he was a pretty cautious guy, but I think he was just losing patience. "We gotta shit or get off the pot," he'd said earlier this morning, before he went home. But Kolya had more guys than we did, and the hard truth was he was tougher than me, so there was a good chance we'd lose, and second prize in this war wasn't going to be all that great.

To be honest, I wasn't crazy about winning, either. I didn't want Kolya's job. That was probably the root of my real problem. Once I'd be in charge, the killing would just have started. I'd have to keep killing people, just to let the guys know I'm capable and willing. And lots of the guys were thick enough that I'd have to do it fairly frequently, lest they forget. Who but a homicidal sociopath would *want* that job?

And that brought me to something that had been bothering me. I was beginning to wonder if I'd misplaced my soul.

What are we? Is our soul what we are deep down inside, or is it what we do? That's the question.

I never took any pride in what I was born—or any shame, either, and it seems to me that people who do are pretty much losers. Pride and shame have to do with *your* accomplishments, not somebody else's, so knowing that my great-great-great-grandfather helped defend Moscow against the Nazis is interesting, but it's not something I'm proud of, because *I* didn't do it.

Sooner or later everyone ends up doing something they're ashamed of but takes consolation in the fact that "deep down inside" they're a good person. They just did this bad thing out of unfortunate necessity, but they didn't really want to, so it wasn't as bad. Their urge was to do good, and so the existence of that urge proves they *are* good, even while they were pushing people into boxcars—or selling drugs.

Right?

If so, I guess I'm supposed to be ashamed of the things I want to do, can't help wanting to do, was born wanting to do, but *don't* do, since I know they're wrong. Because if good urges mean you're good, even though you do bad things, then bad urges must mean you're bad, even though you do good things.

But I don't know. If I feel the urge to bang a friend's wife, but choose not to, am I supposed to be ashamed of the urge, or proud of the choice? You can't have it both ways. In which of those two things—urge or choice—does my soul reside?

I was still gathering that wool when Mrs. Laubach, my admin, knocked and stuck her head in.

"Sasha, I know you said you didn't want to be disturbed..."

"It's okay, Sophie, what's up?"

"There's a lady here to see you, and she had this." She waddled over—Sophie was only a meter and a half tall, and a good 100 kilos if she was a gram—and put a metallic business card on my desk. It was from Arrie's art gallery, his front business.

"Lady? As in *Human* lady?"

"Yeah, Human lady. She says it's very important."

"Hmm. Is she good-looking? I'm kinda in the market."

"I suppose. Not really your type, though."

"That figures. Well, hell. I'm not getting anything else done. Let's see what Arrie's friend wants. I sure don't need to piss *him* off right now. Oh, and Sophie, one more thing. I want you to take the rest of the day off. In fact, take the rest of the week off, with pay."

I opened the bottom drawer, opened the flat safe, and counted out a week's salary from the emergency fund. It didn't seem like a lot when I got done, so I counted out another week's worth. When I handed the flexichips to her, she just looked at them for a moment.

"It's really bad, isn't it?" she asked.

"Sophie, I've lived through a lot worse. But if there's a . . . you know . . . disagreement, I don't want you to get hurt. So take some time with your old man. It's just a precaution. You know how careful I am."

She wasn't buying it, but some things aren't meant to be bought—they're just the things you say so you don't have to talk about ugly stuff that won't get any less ugly for talking about it.

"Check the wire for messages every day, if you would," I asked.

"Sure."

"I'm expecting word on about a dozen clerical jobs up-canyon. Could really mean something for a couple families. You've got the names."

"Sure."

"And tell the cleaning crew not to come in, okay? Okay. So, I guess show in Miss Sunshine, or whatever the hell her name is."

"Marfoglia, her card says." She handed that to me and then waddled back out. This card was also metallic—a silvery gray—and expensive-looking, with engraving that glowed reddish gold when the light hit it right.

MARRISSA MARFOGLIA, PhD.

MARKET CONSULTANT.

Not Market*ing* Consultant. I wondered what the difference was. Probably an extra zero at the end of the paycheck. The door opened again and I looked up.

Quite a consultant. She looked like she'd been airbrushed into an ad for some obscenely expensive perfume. Her black pumps probably cost about what I'd just given Sophie, and the gray pinstriped suit was so well tailored it followed every curve of her body without a fold or wrinkle, and without looking like it was tight anywhere. Her blond hair was pulled back in a smooth, simple bun, and she was wearing makeup, but not too much. She was one hot number, if you were into that whole cold steel robot look.

Lots of guys were.

She looked around my office, and I could see that it wasn't what she'd been expecting. God knows what that was, but whatever it was, this wasn't it.

"I don't really know if there's anything you can do to help me, but Mr. Arrakatlak insisted that I speak with you."

"Have a seat," I offered.

She sat down, a little heavily, the only indication from her movements she wasn't from around here. I guessed she was Earth-born, so carrying around five or six more kilos than she was used to. Most folks you could tell from their gait, but she had the sort of graceful walk people—some people—spent a lot of money to have their kids taught. She put her small briefcase in her lap and studied me for a moment.

"Mr. Naradnyo, what *exactly* is it that you do?"

I just looked at her for a second or two before I answered.

"I do a lot of things . . . *exactly*. What is it you need done?"

"It says on your door that this is an employment agency. I don't need an employment agent."

"It doesn't just *say* it on the door; this *is* an employment agency," I answered, starting to get irritated. Some people think they'll have an advantage in negotiations if they start by making the other person uncomfortable or self-conscious, and that's what she was trying here. I had a few things on my plate that morning, like figuring out how I was going to get to tomorrow morning alive, and this Marfoglia person was starting to wear thin after about one minute. That did not bode well for a successful professional relationship.

"Look, lady," I said, "I'm going to take a wild guess here and theorize that what you want done—it looked at from a particularly narrow-minded perspective—might not be considered entirely legal. That being the case, you can't go someplace that has what you need stenciled on the door, 'cause those people will call the Munies as soon as you leave just to protect their licenses. So what the hell difference does it make what's on my door?"

For an instant, I fantasized she'd storm away in a huff and leave me to my melancholy brooding, but no such luck. Instead, she looked down at her briefcase and nodded.

"Yes, of course. You're right."

"I won't kill anyone," I said.

She looked up, a little surprised but not really shocked.

"I wasn't going to ask you to."

"Good."

"You've never killed anyone?" she asked after a moment, her curiosity getting the better of her.

Boy, what a day to get asked that question, huh?

"I'm not in the mood," I answered, and that was the truth. I was tired of hurting people.

"I need passage off Peezgtaan and to Akaampta for four people: myself, two companions, and a . . . security specialist. A bodyguard, I suppose. Mr. Arrakatlak said that you could provide us with such a person, someone who is trustworthy."

She pronounced the planet names like a leather-head, with clicks instead of the velar phonemes—*Peezg!aan* and *A!aampta*. Actually, since they are Varoki names, I guess if you wanted to be fair you'd say *we* use velar phonemes instead of clicks.

How many guys even know what a velar phoneme is, I wondered?

"Private charter or commercial?" It made a huge difference in price.

"Oh . . . commercial," she answered. Okay, so we weren't talking the *mega-buckage* range.

"Awake or asleep?" That was another big price break, although I was pretty sure I knew the answer to that one.

"I think that, for security reasons, we'd need to avoid cold sleep."

"I'll need the biometrics before I can do anything," I said.

She nodded, reached into her briefcase, and pulled out a data tab. I opened the channel on my desk reader, she thumbed the data tab to transmit, and everything started to make sense. Lifting four people off-planet—why had Arrie tried to fob this job off on me? He could snap his fingers (well, actually, he physically *couldn't* snap his fingers, which was a serious limitation to his beat persona, but if he could have . . .) and get jump tickets for four people.

But it wasn't four *Human* people. One Human—female, 52 kilos, United States of North America citizen, Earth permanent resident. One Varoki—male, 77 kilos, uPeezgtaan citizen and permanent resident. One Varoki—male, 92 kilos, uKa-Maat citizen, Akaampta permanent resident. One Human—gender, mass, citizenship, and residency to be provided. That would be the bodyguard.

Marfoglia sounded like a North American, although she looked more Scandinavian. The look could be cosmetic alterations, or it could be Northeast U.S. old money genes, hard to tell. Either way it meant buckage. The citizenship and residency of the other two were probably phony

I leaned back in the chair, locked my fingers behind my head, and studied the fine cracks in my ceiling for a moment. I felt a burning sensation where Ricky's flechette had torn across my shoulder blade, just the reminder I needed that life was becoming more . . . interesting.

Interesting indeed. Two leather-heads so hot that none of Arrie's contacts would handle them. Maybe it was political. Politics always messes up business. Pass them off to Sasha, who doesn't know anything about leather-head politics, or care a mouse's fart, and if everything ends in gunfire and blood, Arrie's still clean. And alive. You had to hand it to the guy.

"Mr. Arrakatlak said to tell you that he would be very grateful if you could help with this. *Very* grateful. He told me to emphasize that." Her voice was businesslike, very controlled, but under it I sensed desperation. She and her leather-head pals were in deep trouble. They had come to the end of the line, and I was it, and they were probably hot as hell and bringing all that heat with them. I wasn't sure Arrie was capable of being grateful enough to make this worth my while.

"Are you and Mr. Arrakatlak...business associates?" she asked after a moment. Of course, etiquette prevented me from saying we were, because that would mean Arrie was crooked. She probably already knew, or at least suspected, that, but it wasn't for me to confirm it.

"Arrie and I are kind of friends," I answered.

"What exactly does that mean, 'kind of' friends'?"

"Well, if something really horrible were to happen to me, Arrie would feel bad, and if he were the one who actually did it to me, he'd feel even worse."

"You must have wonderful friends," she said, and a bit of her distaste seeped through the professional façade.

"Not really." I stayed leaning back in my chair, studying the ceiling, but I needed a couple more pieces of the puzzle.

"I've got some questions. Don't bullshit me. Your friends are hot. Both of them? Or just one?"

"Both," she answered reluctantly.

"How about you? Hot?"

She shook her head.

"Are people going to look for you as a lead to your friends?"

She shook her head again. That made sense. It's probably why they were using a Human as a go-between.

"Their comm implants are disabled, right?"

"They have no communication implants," she answered, "so there won't be a problem with remote tracking."

Really? Leather-heads with no comm implants? Who were these guys?

"There are two more things," she added. I looked at her without sitting back up.

"First, Mr. Arrakatlak asked that you not contact him directly. He said that it would be dangerous."

"Yeah? Then how am I supposed to know you really came from him?"

"He gave me a code word, which he said would make that clear to you."

That was interesting. Arrie and I didn't have a code word worked out. What was she trying to sell?

"Okay," I said with a shrug. "What's the code word?"

"Yanni."

I laughed.

"Does it mean something?" she asked.

"Yeah. Okay, you're from Arrie. What was thing two?"

"Mr. Arrakatlak suggested—no, he was quite insistent—that a Mr. Markov not be told any of this."

I laughed again, but with less humor. I laughed because sometimes things just get so completely hopelessly fouled up that the only thing you can do is laugh. And yet...

And yet, there is an enormously liberating sensation which comes with the realization that you are completely screwed. When all roads lead to pretty much the same place, why not take the one with the best view? And if this particular road was a thumb in Kolya's eye, I was in the mood. I sat back up.

"Okay. Forty-five thousand, and I'll need all of it tomorrow morning."

"Half tomorrow and half when we are ready to depart," she said.

I laughed again.

"How about this instead? Nothing tomorrow, nothing on departure, and you take your business to the next guy on your list."

She looked down for a moment, and I was afraid that she was going to turn on the water, but when she looked back up, it was with barely controlled rage.

"And what if your arrangements fall through? Are we supposed to just *trust* you to return the money?"

"What difference does it make?" I asked. "Lady, if my *arrangements* fall through, money's going to be the least of your worries. Am I right?"

Of course I was right.

FIVE

I loved sitting by the windows at H'Tank's Six-Star Club. I didn't get by there as often as I liked, and it was usually night when I did, so seeing the Crack in daylight—or at least the mid-morning twilight—was a special treat. H'Tank's was five levels up from the river—about 150 meters. The club was mostly back in the interior of the canyon wall, of course, but the window tables were in a bay that hung out over the river, and the windows wrapped around the bay, top and bottom—it wasn't the best place to eat if you suffered from vertigo.

Peezgtaan is a fair-sized planet, but the only habitable part is the Crack, a canyon that makes the Grand Canyon back on Earth, and even the Coprates Rift Valley on Mars, look like little ditches. The Crack's over two thousand kilometers long, and almost twenty kilometers deep. With the surface nearly a vacuum, there wasn't any wind or weather to cause erosion, so living in the bottom of a rock-walled canyon wasn't as dangerous as it would have been other places. Most of the rocks that were going to fall already fell about a hundred thousand years ago. Of course, it would be a death trap if the planet was still seismically active, but Peezgtaan was old, so old its core was as cold as a woman's feet.

Don't get me wrong, women's hearts come in all different temperatures, from cool to sizzling; but their feet are all cold enough to leave scar tissue. Why is that?

I was so wrapped up in the view, I didn't hear her come up until she cleared her throat.

"Dr. Marfoglia. Have a seat." I snapped my fingers and across the room the waiter's head came up.

"The *g* is silent in my name, and do people really still snap their fingers for service here?" she said as she sat down.

"I do."

She sounded irritated. Hard telling if it was from me snapping my fingers or from her having to fork over 45,000 *Cottos*. She had a small leather case that she put in her lap.

"Is it in there?" I asked.

"Yes," she said as she took a menu from the waiter and frowned at its thickness.

"Flip to the back page," I advised.

"I think I can decide for myself."

I shrugged and looked out the window.

"Oh," she said as she realized that most of the menu was for non-Human consumption.

"Six-Star Lounge isn't its rating. Its cuisine serves the races of all six home stars. Sol is the last page."

There were five intelligent races before they found us. We made it six, and we've been stuck at six ever since. The Varoki were the first race—that we knew of—to get to the stars, the ones that first contacted all the rest of us, and they didn't come along with guns or threats or anything. They shared power and knowledge. They shared markets. They helped everyone out. They backed most of the deep space survey missions to potentially habitable worlds, and when somebody found a world with protein chains compatible with one of the other six races, they even brokered the territorial swaps and resettlement. Advancing the interests of all six races of the *Cottohazz*, that's all they wanted. But somehow they always ended up on top. Pretty smart.

A century or so ago, when there was all this talk about alien invasions and interplanetary wars, who knew it would be just too damned expensive? Not that common sense always stopped people from killing each other, but out here the bottom-line meat-heads were pretty firmly in charge.

The biggest section of the menu, the first eight pages, was devoted to the star Akatu— which meant Varoki cuisine. Then there were three pages of Katami food followed by two each for the Trand and Buran. Humans got one page, at the end, right across from the one page of Zaschaan black and green sewage noodles—at least that's what they smelled like. This shows you exactly where we stood in the pecking order.

All the food proteins grown on Peezgtaan were poisonous to Humans, but that was the story everywhere we'd been. The other races had found a world or two where the proteins were compatible with their body chemistry—or they'd forced the issue, like the Varoki had here on Peezgtaan—but we'd come up dry. Even on Bronstein's World, the biggest Human extra-solar colony, all the Human-edible protein was vegetable-based and grown hydroponically, just like here in the Crack.

I glanced around the dining room. H'Tank's was an inn at a crossroads, and the roads led everywhere—to every race, world, occupation, and greed-fueled dream in the *Cottohazz*. This is where people met to figure out how to steal stuff: politicians the next election and the corporate types everything else. Guys like me were pikers.

Most of the tables had two or three customers, almost all of them Varoki. Eight excited, chattering Katami crowded around a six-top, feathery cranial membranes flaring and swaying with nervous energy, like a jungle bird's crest. The oxygen mix was a bit rich for them here. A table back in the corner had two big, sour-looking Zaschaan, troweling some kind of baby-shit-brown sludge into their lower mouths while a middle-aged Varoki, smelling of money and desperation at the same time, made his animated pitch to them, ears fluttering almost as much as the Katami's crests. The Katami were obviously visitors from off-planet; the Zaschaan looked like they'd been here awhile—just the way they weren't very interested in what was going on around them. Travelers—even Zaschaan—are usually more engaged with their surroundings. There were uniforms here and there—mostly private security outfits. There were more and more of those around these days.

There were also a couple Human customers scattered here and there. Of course, the entire service staff was Human—fashionable *and* cheap was a hard combination to beat.

The waiter came back. Marfoglia ordered a tofu and green salad. I had the hutsul omelet, egg whites only, with soy nuts, and Thai chili sauce on the side. One nice thing about the Crack being half-full of bullet-headed Ukrainians was that you found hutsul cuisine all over the place.

Another nice thing about it was me, although opinions on that vary.

Once the waiter left, I nodded to the leather case. "I'll take that now," I said.

She looked around the dining room and frowned. "Don't you want to do some sort of . . . I don't know . . ."

"Secret transfer?" I whispered, leaning forward. She colored with embarrassment and irritation, and pushed the leather case across to me. I put it on the table, on the side closest to the window, where it was in plain sight, but nobody could get to it except over me.

"Aren't you going to count it?" she asked.

"Why? Can't your bank count?"

That got me a much deeper, angry frown.

"That's interesting," I said. "When you scowl like that, it makes you look heavy . . . sort of jowly in the face."

And that earned me a look of pure hatred, but it was all in her eyes, not in her mouth anymore.

I love to annoy assholes. Provided they aren't armed, of course. That would be stupid.

The conversation sort of died out after that, which was fine by me. I was here for the cash, the food, and the view out the bay windows anyway. After a few minutes, the waiter brought our meals and I dug in.

"Now that you have the money, how soon can you make the travel arrangements?" she asked.

"Already done," I answered between bites of omelet.

"Done?" she asked, lowering her fork. "What do you mean?"

"There's no direct jump to Akaampta for three weeks," I started.

"Three *weeks*?" she said, her voice rising. "That's too long!"

"Hey, quiet down," I said, motioning her to lower her voice. "You're gonna have half the people in the restaurant interested in your trip."

She looked around and then leaned forward.

"That's too long," she whispered.

I laughed.

"Yeah, I figured. I can get you off-planet in six days. Better?"

She nodded and sat back in her chair, her composure returning.

"Like I was saying, there's no *direct* jump to Akaampta for three weeks, but there's a jump to Seewauk and a connecting jump from there to Akaampta."

I sketched out the itinerary for her. The deep-space jumps between stars are pretty quick; it's moving around in orbital space that takes time. In six days, the four of them would lift to high orbit and board the shuttle that would take them out to the system's main gas giant, where the C-lighter—the jump ship—was in a parking orbit. The gas giant was critical to in-system travel—the Newton tugs use it to replace reaction mass burned to move the C-lighters in and out of gravity wells, and the shuttles do the same for the round-trip burns to and from Peezgtaan. The C-lighter uses the gas giant's gravity source as a J-space vector terminus—sort of a big astrogation beacon. Stars stand out better, but shuttles and Newton tugs can't refuel at a star.

At the gas giant they'd transfer passengers and cargo to the C-lighter, a Newton tug would accelerate it out of the gas giant's gravity well, and then it would make the jump to Seewauk. The shuttle ride out to the C-lighter would take twelve days, then the better part of two days for the C-lighter to get clear of the gas giant's gravity well, a quick fall through J-space to an empty intermediary system, a day to recharge the jump capacitors, a second jump to the Seewauk system, and then two days in to the gas giant.

There was actually a fully staffed orbital station there, since it was a fairly common jump nexus, and there were layover quarters for people making connections. The schedule showed three days there at Seewauk, then board a connecting C-lighter for the jump to Akaampta. With the jump and everything else, say four more days to the gas giant in Akaampta system, and then a fourteen-day shuttle glide to Akaampta itself.

"So that's over thirty days' travel time, but it gets you out of here as quick as I can manage," I finished. "It will take a couple days to get the travel documents dummied up—I don't imagine your friends will be traveling on their own passports, and I'm getting one for you as well. I'll need pictures and retina scans tomorrow or the day after."

"Why for me?" she asked. "I told you I'm not wanted for anything."

"I know. Just a feeling. The more we cover your tracks, the better off you are."

She accepted that.

"What about the bodyguard?" she asked. "When can I meet him?"

"When I pick him...or her. Or would you object to a female security specialist?"

She shook her head. I gave her a line about how it was better to wait until the last minute to hook her up with a guard—less chance of a leak. But the truth was, at that time I wasn't sure who to send. I didn't have that many good shooters, and it was looking like I might need all of them. Of course, this might be more of a babysitting job than anything else. I had a couple younger guys without a lot of experience, but pretty levelheaded—they'd cover all the basics and wouldn't do anything stupid. Yeah, maybe one of them.

She snapped her fingers in front of my face. I jumped a bit, and it was my turn to scowl at her.

"Wherever you were, it wasn't here," she said.

"Thinking about taking a couple days and going fishing up-canyon," I lied. I've never gone fishing in my life. Among other things, the fish here aren't edible by Humans.

"Want to go fishing?" I asked.

She shook her head, frowning a little in distaste. No surprise there; I doubted that her wardrobe included the proper ensemble to wear while gutting and scaling a half-dozen long-jaws.

"No, I won't go fishing with you. And don't get any other ideas, either."

"Ideas?"

"Yes," she answered, her jaw firmly set. "I've already been through my 'bad boy' phase." She almost spat it out, and being the careful student of the Human condition that I am, I'd say as much of the contempt in her voice was for herself as for me.

It made up my mind on one score, though: I'd send Paolo Riks as her bodyguard. When a woman tells you this emphatically that she's over her "bad boy" phase, she either *really* is or she *really* isn't. Either way, some young hotshot making a pass at her could end up in disaster. Paolo wasn't going to make a pass—he liked guys.

I wasn't crazy about a sit-down with Kolya, but if I had to do it, a public place was good as any, and Quann's was the best. The place was usually crowded, between the bar and the supper crowd, and everyone knew everyone else, so it was hard for our guys to start trouble. Besides, Jerry Lopez tended bar nights, and he always took good care of me. I'd gotten him the job, and I tipped good, so he kept a bottle of orange food color under the bar for me. I always ordered bar scotch and seltzer. Jerry poured it real weak, and added a drop of food color to make it look stiff. Because of Jerry, I could match drinks with anybody all night long and keep my wits about me.

Hey, any edge you can get, take it.

I'd spent most of the previous afternoon—after the Marfoglia meeting—with Henry, making sure we'd drug plenty of brush over our tracks on the Ricky business. *Maskirovka*, they used to say in the old days. First we decided what we would have done if he'd really just vanished, and then we did all those things. That was a lot of work, and it might all be for nothing if Kolya decided to move anyway, but most times you live by covering every bet, not by figuring which bet is smartest and just covering that—which is why so many geniuses die young.

I wasn't used to going to bed alone, and I wasn't sleeping all that well. Cinti always made breakfast and so it took me a long time to find everything in the kitchen that morning, and between that and sleep deprivation, I was in a real scratchy mood by the time I got to the office. Sophie's abandoned desk didn't improve my mood much, nor did the arrival about half an hour later of Henry, with Archie Nakamura in tow.

"Archie says he wanted to talk," Henry explained, "and I figured I'd tag along. You want me to wait outside?"

"Nah," I said. "This isn't hush-hush business, is it? How you been, Archie?"

We shook hands and he flopped into a chair, the way he always did, like he was double-jointed all over. I guess you'd say that Archie and I were peers, both mentally penciled in on Kolya's organizational chart as captains. Archie handled most of the business in the far west side of the Quarter, and he had some action in a couple Varoki neighborhoods, too. I knew he gave Kolya a bigger cut of his revenue than I did, which made him Kolya's guy in my book. Vassalage is vassalage, and you can look it up.

Archie was relaxed and smiling. A smiling thief is never to be trusted, which is why I make it a habit to smile as little as possible. Archie, on the other hand, always smiled, and today I smiled back—I was only scowling on the inside.

"You mind if I smoke?" he asked and offered me a cigar from his plastic humidor.

"Go ahead." But I waved off the cigar. "You know them things are gonna kill ya, Archie."

"Well, it's damned sure something will. May as well be something I like." It was hard logic to argue with.

For most of my life, all I ever smoked was the local weed, just like Archie. That's all there was. Braka, they call it. It's got something like nicotine in it, something that jingles you, and that was enough. Then when I hit some cash one time, I sprang for an imported cigar, shipped all the way from Earth.

Perfect.

Everything about it was perfect: the little brown wood humidor it came in, the way the leaf was rolled around it just so, even the cigar band was perfect. I lingered over that cigar for probably two or three hours, and never had to relight it once. It burned smooth and even and cool, and the flavor just got richer the longer it burned; it never got that sour taste the cheap local cigars did down toward the bottom.

Perfect.

But it ruined me for the local weed, and I couldn't afford to smoke imported cigars for the rest of my life, so I just quit.

We talked about this and that for a while. He asked where Ricky was; I said he'd apparently split, but maybe the provosts had picked him up—nobody knew for sure. We were firewalling all his operations so they'd be hard to come back on, even if he talked. They could pick up a couple of the guys, but the banks were safe and we'd moved a couple Lotto counting rooms to new locations. His two top guys—the first ones the provosts might pick up—we'd already pulled out of the loop and put up in safe houses for a while, just till things cooled down.

He nodded in approval. If it occurred to him that this also took Kolya's two most likely allies inside my organization out of circulation, he didn't let on.

After a while, he got up to leave. But before he walked out, as if he almost forgot but remembered just in time, he said, "Oh, yeah. Kolya's got dinner reservations at Quann's for tonight. Wants all us captains there. You know, if you can make it. No business, just social. Says we don't get together enough anymore. You be there?"

"Sure," I said. "Sounds great."

Sure. Great.

So there I was, sitting to Kolya's right, with Archie across the table, Bear Bernardini to my right, and the other four "captains" filling the eight-top. If Archie was in Kolya's pocket, Bear was stuck up his asshole.

Kolya was in a good mood, laughing and joking with the guys. Kolya's a little shorter than me, with a thick dark moustache and thicker, coarse, straight hair, clipped short on the sides and combed back off his forehead. His hairline made his forehead look low, which suggested a sluggish mind, but one look at his eyes and you knew better. His eyes told you he was always measuring, weighing, calculating. Everything was carefully assessed and then filed away. But at the same time, there was this playfulness in his eyes that let you know he was having a great time sizing you up, deciding what he was going to do about you. It made it hard to hate him—this unmeasured joy he took in his life. That's probably another reason I didn't want a war. No doubt about it, Kolya was a monster without conscience or mercy, but I liked him. What does that tell you about me?

I figured Ricky would be the main topic of conversation, but he wasn't. While we were waiting for our drinks, Kolya mentioned that Archie had filled him in on what we were doing about Ricky's "disappearance," and it sounded okay to him. Had we heard anything from him? Nope. Just weird, he said, but he may have been thinking that Ricky had lost his nerve and just left. Not likely, but not impossible, either. To work, *Maskirovka* doesn't need to persuade, only confuse.

Our drinks came, along with a shaker of coarse ground pepper. Kolya dumped pepper in his double vodka—Cossack style—and threw it back in one gulp.

"Some broad named Marfoglia stop by your office the other day?" Kolya asked, seemingly out of the blue.

"Good-looking coppery blonde, green eyes, great set of legs, and dressed like a million *Cottos*?" I asked.

"Yeah, that's her."

"Nope. Ain't seen nobody like that," I answered, and Archie laughed so hard beer came out of his nose. I grinned over at him, but watched for Kolya's reaction out of the corner of my eye. I'd been caught flat-footed, and when I am, I always admit the little thing to cover the big thing—that's another side of *maskirovka*.

"Why?" I asked.

"She came to see me this afternoon," Kolya answered. I nodded.

"She came to me, what? Couple days ago," I improvised. "Stuck-up pain in the ass—definitely not my type...one of those ice queens you like so much. I gave her your name. What did she want?"

Kolya was looking at me, frowning, but in thought, not suspicion. I'd known him long enough to know when he's trying to figure out what's going on, as opposed to trying to figure out how he should kill you.

"It's complicated," he answered.

I turned to Bear Bernardini to my right.

"That means he hasn't figured out how to nail her yet." The rest of the table burst into laughter at that one—because only the truth is really funny.

She *was* Kolya's type: distant, self-assured, and very controlled—the conservative tailored suits, the perfect hair and makeup. Something about that combination turned him on. But when he was done with them, they were never as confident or self-assured, ever again, and I think that turned him on even more. There was something fetishistic about it, this need to deface a particular sort of beauty, something like an urge to break a delicate piece of porcelain.

But it wasn't my problem. I wasn't sure quite what she'd said to Kolya, or why, but whatever it was, it had probably screwed me—and maybe screwed me to death. So she'd decided to get in bed with this monster herself, and whatever happened to her there wasn't any skin off me.

I took a big drink of my scotch and grimaced, but right away shot Archie a big grin to cover it up. For the first time in years Jerry Lopez had made my drink full strength—stiffer even, maybe a double. What the hell was he thinking? I looked over at the bar, and he was polishing a glass, looking down. He glanced up, saw me looking at him, and made eye contact for a couple seconds. No apology, no smile, just a serious look for a moment, and then he went back to polishing the glass.

When birds stop singing...

I pretended to take another sip of my scotch. My lips started to tingle. The scotch was spiked with something, no question, and Jerry—bless his soul—had done the only thing he could to alert me.

Had Kolya poisoned me? Probably not. You poison someone in a restaurant, the public health guys start asking questions. More likely it was a drug to make me seem drunk—then haul me out of here and finish me someplace else. I wondered how many of the other captains were in on this? Maybe just Archie... otherwise why make things so complicated?

Kolya leaned over toward me and smiled.

"Good to see you, pal," he said. He'd said that when I first got there, but it had been jovial, public. This was private and, I thought, a little wistful. "Long time," he added, and nodded. "We used to get together all the time, you know? Hardly at all anymore. What happened?"

"Yeah, those were pretty good days," I agreed. "You know... once we got our asses out of the gutter and started making some buckage."

He laughed and nodded.

"Yeah, sure. But you know, even the gutter wasn't as bad as it could have been for a couple *bezprizornyi* like us. We covered each other's backs in those days."

"Kept each other alive more than once," I agreed, but felt the familiar flush of guilt that thinking about the old days always brought. Sure, we'd covered each other's backs. Sure.

Maybe it was the drug working, but I started feeling blue, or maybe just sentimental. On one hand, Kolya was a rabid dog, but on the other, he was my oldest friend. And the truth was we'd made a good team because we were two of a kind—twin sons of different parents. Had we both changed so much since then? Had he gotten crazier? Had I found a conscience? Or were we still two of a kind, and all my angst just so much self indulgent bullshit?

Now we sat over a drink, just like we had a thousand times before, and I knew it was the last time we'd ever do it, as long as we lived. It made me feel sad, even as my lips tingled from the drug Kolya had used to make it easier to murder me.

"What happened?" he asked again. He wanted an answer, was even a little desperate for one, maybe because if he didn't get it right now, the odds were he never would.

I shrugged and shook my head.

"Hell, Kolya, who knows? You get busy with one thing or the other, business, the lady...guess I won't have that distraction anymore. You knew Cinti split, right?" Then I frowned and looked down, as if something just occurred to me, and then I looked back up at Kolya.

"Hey, you don't think...Cinti and *Ricky*?" But then I shook my head and looked away. "Nah."

But I'd seen a moment of uncertainty in Kolya's eyes, and that happens about as often as Ukraine wins the World Cup—which still hasn't happened in my lifetime. Kolya knew Ricky had a thing for Cinti, and so now he was thinking maybe they did go off together—who knows? And if so, maybe slipping a mickey to old Sasha was contraindicated. Not that he could take it back now, but if I kept him mentally off balance, even a little, maybe I could wiggle out of this alive.

So I played along, horsed around with the other guys, even had a chance to pour some of my drink on the floor once when I was facing Bear and he was looking away. I only pretended to drink, but I was starting to feel distant and weak anyway, just from that first gulp.

"You okay, Sasha?" Kolya asked after a while.

"Yeah . . . maybe shouldna' skipped lunch, huh? I guess I gotta hit th' head."

I got unsteadily to my feet and had to grab the chair back to steady myself.

"Sasha, you're turning into a lightweight," one of the guys shouted, and there was laughter all around. I smiled drunkenly and gave them the finger.

"Bear, why don't you go with him?" Kolya said. "Make sure he doesn't hurt himself."

"Sure," Bear said and stood up beside me and slapped my shoulder fondly. "C'mon pal."

So Bear was part of it.

We walked back toward the bathrooms, and I didn't have to act much to look groggy. My knees were starting to buckle under me, and I had to concentrate on where I was walking. There was a little hallway leading to the bathrooms, out of the line of sight of the dining room, and I stopped there by the two doorways to the heads, leaning against the wall.

"Wha' d'you guys slip me, Bear?" I asked.

"What do you mean, Sasha?"

"C'mon. 'Sall over, I know that. Jus' bu'iness. So wha'd you slip me?"

He looked ashamed.

"I don't know. One of those stoopie drugs or something. Kolya said you'd be easier to handle . . . I'm sorry, Sasha. Just how it is."

Nobody ever saw the trick punch coming, and messed up as I was, it still caught Bear hard enough to take the wind out of him. Then I grabbed him by the Adam's apple, thumb and fingers on either side, inside the throat tendons, and pushed all the way back behind the windpipe, and that paralyzed him. I kicked open the door to the ladies' room, pulled him in, and looked around.

Someone was coming out of a stall, so I gave Bear a big kiss on the lips, looked back at her, and yelled, "Hey! Can we get some privacy here?"

She hurried out, and I locked the door behind her with my left hand. I still had Bear by the throat with my right, no air getting to his lungs; he'd already turned bright red, and now the red was shifting to purple. He stopped struggling after a few more seconds, and then slowly slid down the wall to the floor. I held him for a full minute after that—never trust a thief. When I let him go, he still had a pulse, but he was definitely in dreamland.

I'd picked the ladies' room because it had a window overlooking the alley; the men's room was an interior room, a closed box. But when I started over to the window, I fell on my ass halfway there. I was in pretty rocky shape, but I got back up using the sink for support. Three of me looked back from the mirror, all soft and glowy.

I got to the window and cranked it open, but I wasn't sure if I could even crawl out. My legs had no strength left. The alley was four meters down—I sure couldn't climb down. I could fall down, but then what, even assuming I didn't split my head open or break a leg? How far was I going to get? I wasn't armed, of course. Not polite to come to a sit-down packing. Only one thing to do.

I pulled off my sport coat, wadded it up, and threw it as far out into the alley as I could, out in the splash of yellow-orange light from the windows in the delivery entrances. Then I went back and got in one of the stalls, crouched up on the toilet seat, and braced myself against the wall. I was light-headed, so I kept my head as low between my legs as I could and still keep my balance; this wasn't going to work if I passed out and fell on the floor. It probably wasn't going to work anyway, but it was as good a plan as I could come up with on such short notice. I didn't latch the stall door—that would be a giveaway. I just leaned as far over to the right side as I could, out of the direct line of sight.

After what seemed like an hour—but was probably only five or ten minutes—there was pounding on the door, lots of swearing, and eventually somebody tripped the lock with a hard key from the outside. I could hear Kolya, Archie, and the others raising hell, but the sound had a distant, hollow quality, as if it came from the other end of a long hallway. It went on for a long time, between swearing at the open window, swearing at my sport coat out in the alley, swearing at each other, swearing at Bear, getting him conscious and moving, and then getting everyone chasing after me. Eventually they went away and it was quiet, except for the rhythmic pounding of blood in my ears.

Now what? I could still hardly move. I wasn't sure I could even get down off the goddamned toilet without falling on my face. Then the door to the head opened, someone came in, and started looking in the stalls, one at a time. There were only three stalls, and I was on the end closest to the inside wall. He got to mine last, slowly pushed open the door, looked in, and laughed.

"Man," Henry said, "I know people who would kill for a picture of this."

Much later, people would look back on "The Quann Sit-Down" and say that it was the second most amazing escape of my life. I think taking out Ricky was really the most amazing, but for some reason, nobody talks about that. Instead, they talk about Quann's . . . and the other.

It's creepy to hear people talk about you like that, as if you're a character in history, even if luck and circumstance make it turn out that—you know—you are. It's especially weird if you know all you did was squat on a toilet seat and try like hell not to fall off.

I often wonder how many of the "amazing" things in history really just involved the equivalent of someone squatting on a toilet seat and not falling off.

SEVEN

Bernie the Rat. What a name, huh? You gotta love a guy who calls himself a rat. He was wearing gray silk pinstripe slacks—banker pants, he called them—with red suspenders, just like the big shots. The look was...not spoiled, exactly, but certainly altered by the faded yellow and red "Gearloose Star Tour" tee shirt, some *mechnod* band that that been popular on Terra maybe a decade ago.

Bernie was mostly bald, but with a faint shadow of fuzz cut so close you couldn't really tell where the skin started and the hair stopped. That and the wrinkled face and deep-set eyes made him look older than I remembered, old enough that he was starting to look young again, like a baby.

Bernie had been an old-school *shtarker*, back when the world was younger, but he gave it up to run a fence and sell information. He had a reputation among the old guys as about the toughest son of a bitch in the Quarter, and he probably could have run the place if he'd worked hard enough at it, but instead he walked away. He told me once he just got tired of all the violence. I can relate.

One thing's for sure, he's still a wiry little son of a bitch, and impossible to kill—enough people have tried. After a while, they just get tired of hunting him, because once he goes to ground in the Quarter, forget it, and then he starts ratting out all *your* secrets. Everybody's got 'em, and Bernie the Rat knows most of them.

I've never tried to kill him. I think it would be like burning a book because you don't like what it says, and I'm not much into book burning.

"So, Bernie, you find out anything about two leather-heads trying to get off-planet?"

"Ooo. Very interesting. There's this hot babe that Kolya wants to poke, she's looking for a way off for 'em."

"Yeah, that much I know. But who are they?"

He shook his head and frowned.

"Who are they . . . don't know. But I think they got something to do with that shooting, up-canyon. Very woird. Very weird."

I'd heard there had been some high-level leather-head gunned down, but I hadn't paid much attention to the details. Arrie was right about that—didn't give a mouse fart about leather-head politics, no matter how violent it got. It wasn't just a species thing—they really do own everything, and much as I like Arrie, in a cautious, eyes-open kind of way, *they're* the problem for us down here in the Quarter. So when bosses start killing each other, smart slaves just look the other way.

"I heard a little about the shooting," I said, "but educate me."

"Okay. Sure. Leather-head with *serious* buckage—I'm talking stinking rich, like in the top ten of the *e-Varokiim*—named Sarro e-Traak, him and his driver got shot dead in his limo. Secure parking facility, all closed up. Very weird. Couple other leather-head bystanders killed at the scene. First reports were they were provosts, but not so. Just rubberneckers—wrong place, wrong time. Rumors like that . . . big guy gets shot, everybody starts grabbin' for their ass and getting the information fucked up, you know?"

I nodded.

"So big hunt going on, 'cause his little kids were with him. No sign of them yet, but they're dead, too. At first Munies thought the Human bodyguard—guy named Bony Jones—was on the inside, maybe lined the whole thing up, 'cause he was missing from the scene, but they found him dead the next day."

"Maybe he *was* on the take and his partners did him," I offered, but Bernie shook his head.

"Don't think so. Don't think so. Ballistics on the slugs in him matched those in e-Traak, and Bony's blood was at the scene, so it looks like he 'died of wounds sustained,' as they say. Haven't found the bodies of the kids yet, but give it a day or two. I figure the killers took the kids' bodies and hid them, 'cause long as there's a chance they're still alive, the Munies will make finding the kids the top priority, and every Munie looking for the kids is one less looking for the silencers. But the kids are dead."

"Any reason to think the bodyguard was on the inside, other than going missing?"

"Just that he's Human." He looked at me as if that was supposed to be significant, and when I shrugged, he shook his head.

"You don't know about the e-Traak fortune? Sasha, Sasha . . . you gotta pay more attention. E-Traak family money was behind AZ Tissopharm—the big chemical outfit that brought all us Human workers here forty years ago and then pulled the plug on the operation, left us scratching dirt with the chickens. I don't even know what the guy was doing on-planet—usually I hear he stays a dozen or so light-years away. It's not exactly healthy for him here."

No, apparently not.

I'd heard the name e-Traak before, but I didn't get the association until Bernie filled in the blank. Over a hundred thousand Human workers had been brought here to open the big pharmaceutical operation based on the native Peezgtaan mold spores that were supposed to revolutionize Varoki medicine. The company went bust, but everyone here had return-passage bonds to Earth as part of their contracts. Then it turned out the bonding company was bust, too. In both cases, e-Traak family money had been behind the companies, and in both cases they'd gotten their money out before the collapse.

And if that sounds as if it should be illegal in any sort of system that's fair, then maybe you'll understand why folks around here don't have much love for the *Cottohazz* anymore. Too many bony lizard thumbs on the scales of justice.

"Okay. So what do the two flight-prone leather-heads have to do with all this?" I asked.

He nodded rapidly, as if he were a bloodhound who'd picked up the scent again.

"Ballistics at the scene makes it two shooters, one for e-Traak and one for his driver. There's also something weird about the weapons they were using—haven't been able to find out the details yet, but it's got the provosts sure these guys are real special killers. Connect the dots. A couple silencers get brought in from off-planet—real pros, good enough to penetrate a secure facility and take out old Sarro, his kids, driver, body-guard, and anyone standing around watching. Anyway, they do the deed. What comes next? Time to leave."

Maybe. But something just didn't add up.

"We know the kids aren't kidnapped?" I asked.

He nodded.

"Only fools are positive, but I'd say ninety percent. Blood of one of the kids was on Jones *and* at the original scene. Besides, no percentage in keeping them alive. This is a very, *very* rich family, Sasha. You never, ever kidnap kids from families this rich, because all that buys you is a life of running, and a very ugly end. If you're going to fuck with them at all, better kill 'em and be done with it."

"The family won't do the same if the kids are dead?"

"No. No. You're a hopeless romantic, Sasha, God love you. But the truth is, it ain't a very romantic world."

I already had that much figured out. But hell, everyone was a romantic compared to Bernie—with the possible exception of Kolya.

"See, with the kids dead, it's easier to disappear," he went on. "No contact for the ransom transfer, no buckage to trace, not as many leads without the kids to help. Kidnapping is a humiliation, and that you have to deal with if you want to stay on top. You know? But death...death is just a tragedy, and tragedies you endure, with dignity. Besides, now that the kids are gone, somebody else in the family inherits all that buckage. Very consoling. Very consoling."

Bernie had given me part of the puzzle, but not a part that helped with my immediate problems all that much. I was holed up in a little flat in a building Henry owned. Shower, kitchenette, foldie-bed, and a desk with a viewer was about all there was. In a funny kind of way, I liked it. It was basic, and right now, basic was good. My environment was stripped down to bare essentials, uncluttered, and that helped my thinking. If you don't think that your environment shapes the pattern of your thinking, you don't know much.

If I was careful—and I was—I could still move around a bit during the day, like to find Bernie. I just dressed like a gutter bum, and nobody looked twice. I kind of liked the sense of freedom that gave me, but I wasn't stupid enough to press my luck.

"So what's our move, boss?" Henry asked as I poured him hot tea.

Where would I be without his guy? He could have just stood back and watched, or could have turned me over to Kolya, but he'd gotten me out of Quann's without anyone recognizing me, and gotten me here to this place, where I'd been able to sleep off the drug. Why? I'd asked him.

"Maybe I don't want your job any more than you want Kolya's," he'd answered.

Yeah, maybe not. But I doubted that either one of us could afford the luxury of that choice much longer.

Kolya had scoured the city for me all last night. He'd regroup today, think things over, but he'd start beating the bush tomorrow at the latest. Beating the bush meant hurting my people, so what was our move?

"We punch," I answered. "But if we punch now, we're punching blind. We aren't strong enough to punch everywhere, so we have to look for a soft spot. There's something with these two leather-head silencers that's mixed up with all this, but I can't make it out. We've got to make somebody talk to us, and right now—tonight."

"Archie?" Howard asked.

"No. Too hard to get to. Archie, Bear . . . everybody's going to be bunkered up."

"Okay, so who then?"

The "glass" on the balcony sliding door was actually a high-density synthetic, but that was pretty standard on these upscale lease units, and my ultrasonic cutter went right through it. I reached in the hole and undid the latch, and then slid the door open, slow but steady. I hadn't done any of this second-story stuff in quite a few years, but I was surprised how it all still seemed like second nature. I always used to cable down along the rock borders between units, like I did tonight, but—being young, dumb, and full of cum—I used to wear a parasail and just exit off the balcony instead of climbing back up. With all the weird crosscurrents, I was lucky I never broke my neck. This trip, I planned to use the elevator when I was done.

I was in a breakfast nook off the kitchen. Not big, but nice: pale carpet, off-white walls and ceiling, two paintings on the walls, one nice abstract statue on a shelf. Tasteful, but my appraiser's eye told me there was nothing here I'd risk a jump off the balcony for—the real artistry was in the arrangement. The carpet wasn't thick, but there was something so perfectly cushioned about it that it felt like the floor wasn't hard and solid underneath. I looked around—its simple elegance whispered luxury and major buckage, and with a sixth-level bay balcony view of the canyon, the apartment itself was worth a hundred times whatever stuff was in it.

There was movement in the next room. I drew the gauss pistol and stepped back to blend into the shadow of the drapes by the sliding door.

She came into the dark room—alert and curious but not, as near as I could tell, alarmed. There was a little draft from the door, and she went to close it. It was only when she saw the fifteen-centimeter circular hole cut in the glass that alarms started going off in her head, but it was way too late by then. Before she could react, I had my left arm around her neck and shoulder, hand clamped over her mouth, and the muzzle of the pistol pressed against her right temple. She froze, but I could feel the sweat break out on her face.

"No sound," I said in a low whisper. "You understand?"

She nodded quickly.

"They're here?"

She didn't respond for a second or two, so I moved the muzzle of the pistol forward from her temple and let it rest in her eye socket. She tried to turn away but I held her in place.

"They're here?" I repeated insistently, and she nodded.

"What room?" I loosened the grip on her mouth. If she was going to scream, she'd start with a big gulp of air, and that's all the further she'd get.

"Please don't kill them," she whispered. "Just let them go, *please.*"

"Lady, I don't know what that son of a bitch Arrie told you about me, but here's the deal: I'm not smuggling a couple of paid silencers off this or any other rock—not when they knocked off a guy so big they're going to have half the provosts this side of Terraspace looking for them." I didn't bother to add *"and not when they got some little kids' blood on their hands,"* because that was personal, not professional.

"I don't know why you double-crossed me with Kolya," I went on, "and I don't really care. I figure you're just following somebody's orders, and that's who's on my hit parade. The two leather-heads in the next room are as good a place to start as any. Either way, their murdering days are over."

It felt like she was going to faint in my arms, but I held her up and pushed the pistol against her head harder.

"Now, which room?"

"They're not the killers," she whispered.

"No? Then who the hell are they?" But then the light came on in my brain like a magnesium flare at midnight, and I knew the answer before she said it.

"The children."

She was pretty shaken up, so I let her sit at the dining table while I drew tea from her samovar. She'd been ready for bed when I made my entrance—hair down, no makeup, slippers and a big fuzzy white robe. I had to hand it to her, she regained her composure pretty quickly, since a few minutes before she must have figured she was just a second or two from a flechette in the brain. Hell, she got points in my book just for not wetting herself when I grabbed her from behind in the dark—lots of tough guys I know would have.

After I brought two tall glasses of tea over to the table she told me the whole, lousy story.

She'd been on Peezgtaan on a consulting gig, but not for the e-Traak family; it was for the Bureau of Economic Culture—something about the spiraling cost of importing fine art from Earth, alternate sources of supply, that sort of stuff. The fact that there is a prevalent mindset which considers art a commodity—like bauxite ore—is interesting, but I won't go there right now. She'd been done with the assignment when the assassinations took place. During her survey work, Arrie had met her, in his capacity as a gallery owner and importer, and now he'd contacted her to help get the survivors off planet.

What survivors?

The driver and the father were down at the scene, as reported. The bodyguard took out both of the primary assassins—the two "bystanders"—but he took two bullets himself, and they were both Poisoned Pills—lead-lined composite hollow points with polonium kickers—which meant that the bad guys were very, very bad. That must have been the odd thing about their weapons Bernie had gotten wind of but hadn't been able to nail down. No wonder.

Huh! I knew something Bernie didn't. Now, there was one for the record books.

One of the bullets in Jones had first gone through the open palm of the little boy—fortunately without encountering enough resistance to dump its poison—which accounted for his blood being on Jones and at the scene. Figuring that the primaries were not the only things to worry about, Jones got the two kids to Arrie before he died.

Why go to Arrie?

Because the primaries had had Co-Gozhak provost credentials. There was no way for the bodyguard to tell if they were genuine or not, but even if they were stolen or forgeries, if they were good enough to get them into a secure facility, then that probably meant at least a contact on the inside. That made it hard telling who was really clean and who wasn't, or from how high up the mountain the boulder had started rolling—and so that's when the smart move was to go below the sensor horizon, to crooks.

This guy Bony Jones, the bodyguard, figured all that out, and made the right move, with two radio-active cocktails spreading through his system, eating his organs up from inside. Knowing they were in for a real painful, ugly death, most guys would have just started looking for a lifetime supply of happy-drugs. Jones didn't. He did the job, right up to the end. I wished I'd known him when he was still breathing.

"First thing," I said, "this means the biometrics are wrong for the jump tickets."

She nodded.

"We figured two children would trigger any data mines they had running, but two adults wouldn't. The gender change for the girl wouldn't really matter. Since the children are lighter than the reservation, there's no problem with the physics, and a last-minute bribe should fix the administrative difficulties."

Sure. Just like I was doing with the bodyguard biometrics—you can always ratchet them down.

"Okay, but you should have trusted me on that one. I'm going to have to scramble to get the phony passports changed in time. Now, what about the thing with Kolya?"

"Mr. Markov? After you and I talked—the evening after I gave you the money—Mr. Arrakatlak found out that Mr. Markov had discovered that I was helping the children. Mr. Arrakatlak already suspected that Markov was in the employ of the assassins. We—Mr. Arrakatlak and I—decided that the only thing to do was for me to go to Markov and ask him to arrange the escape."

"And this actually made *sense* to you?" I asked.

"Yes, of course," she answered impatiently, becoming more confident as the shock wore off, confident enough that some of her hostility was beginning to resurface. "Mr. Markov already knows I am part of the escape, but he doesn't know that I know that he knows . . . You understand?"

I nodded, doubtfully.

"He thinks I came to him by chance, and that he's the one who's arranging everything, so he stopped looking for us, and for anyone helping us. He knows he can take the children as soon as we show up to leave planet. So I gave him Bronstein's World as a destination, because I knew there would be no shuttle for the Bronstein C-lighter until several days after the Akaampta departure. With luck, we should be gone before he realizes anything is wrong."

I thought about that for a couple seconds. Two things occurred to me.

First thing, she wasn't afraid of me anymore. She wasn't trying to convince me that she'd actually done this thing—only that it was a good idea. So she was probably telling the truth.

Second thing was, much as I hated to admit it, this was actually an okay plan, or would be under most circumstances. It was a very gutsy move, but that's what made it work. Kolya would never think that this pale and pampered thoroughbred with a PhD in something or other would walk right into the lion's den unless she was as clueless as she looked. Pretty smart.

"Except for the part about not telling me," I said. "Why didn't you *tell* me?"

"We couldn't right away. Mr. Arrakatlak found out that Mr. Markov has a data mine on your comm link, and there was no one at your office. Then you disappeared. I thought you were dead, but Mr. Arrakatlak said to wait, and that you would turn up."

Now it was starting to smell like bullshit. A mine? Surgically implanted comm links like I have are all but impossible to mine, even with nanos, since you need to have someone physically close enough . . . like Cinti. Shit! Cinti could have planted nanos while I was sleeping. And, sentimental fool that I was, I'd figured she really *had* told me everything.

It occurred to me that if I didn't start getting smarter here, and really quickly, I was going to die. At least Kolya couldn't trace me through my link. Nobody could, data mine or not, unless I told somebody right where I was over an open circuit. I had too many dummy repeaters squirreled away in different parts of the city and all my signals went through them. Even if somebody was smart enough to backtrace all the electronic blind alleys to pinpoint a transmission—and I didn't know of anyone working for Kolya that smart—by the time they did it I'd be long gone.

"Okay, but how did Arrie find out about the mine?" I demanded.

She shrugged, and I could tell it had never even occurred to her to ask. This was all black arts stuff to her, and one magic trick seemed as difficult or as easy as the next. But how the hell *did* Arrie find out about a comm mine that Kolya had planted on me? I was sure Arrie didn't have Kolya's organization penetrated—he was an operator, but on his own side of the divide, not on the Human side. I was his link to Kolya's organization. Right?

But at the moment, I had bigger concerns. This changed everything, and I had to figure out the new patterns here—and quickly.

First things first. I triggered my embedded comm link and called Henry. He was waiting, of course; he was back in one of the under-the-rock plazas that adjoined the inside face of Marfoglia's living complex, watching the entrances.

"Yeah," he answered inside my head.

"Hey, what's new?"

"Not much," he answered. *"You?"*

"Nuthin' worth mentioning, except I'm gonna bow out on dinner later. I think I got some bad curry at lunch."

"You gotta watch that subcontinent stuff, boss. It'll eat your guts out."

I laughed.

"Yeah, but this was Thai, so go figure. See you later."

I broke the connection. Marfoglia was looking at me with a mix of curiosity and disdain.

"Breaking a date with a girlfriend?" she asked.

"For you? In your dreams," I answered. "That was my number-two guy. 'Bad curry' is my code phrase for compromised communications.

"We're going to have to move you and the kids. Right now," I added.

"They're sleeping."

"Then wake them up," I answered. "They aren't safe here anymore, and neither are you."

"But Mr. Arrakatlak—"

"*Fuck Arrie!*" I shouted, and she jumped in surprise.

"Arrie doesn't know shit! He sure as hell doesn't know Kolya Markov. All this double-cross pretend-your're-hiring Kolya ying-yang might work most of the time. But Kolya's tried to kill me twice in the last three days, and I've gotten away twice, and when things start going that bad, Kolya goes into Operating Mode B, which is *No Loose Ends*.

"So wake the kids up."

After about ten minutes, she came back with the two little Varoki. They were wearing purple silk robes, with Chinese characters embroidered on them in gold. Arrie was right about that—it really was pretty amazing how *Terrakultur* had grabbed hold of the imagination of the *Cottohazz*, especially the wealthy Varoki.

The Varoki are hairless—eyelashes don't count as far as I'm concerned—and for us hair styles are a big clue to gender. But if you're around them enough, you start noticing other gender differences, things like proportion of hips to shoulders, prominence of the jawline, that sort of thing, even in little squirts like these two. Early physical and emotional development isn't that different from Humans, either. The boy was older, maybe early teens, on the verge of adolescence, with his left hand in a clear bandage case. The girl was a couple years younger, about twenty centimeters shorter. Both of them were very frightened, but the boy was trying hard not to show it. His ears were trembling with the effort to keep them from folding tight back against his head. I was glad their last bodyguard had been Human; that would help.

"Hello," I said. "My name is Sasha, and I'm going to keep you safe and get you back to your family. Do you understand?"

The boy nodded, but the girl looked to Marfoglia, who translated in what sounded to me like perfect aGavoosh—clicks and glottal stops like a native. The girl not speaking English was a problem; we'd need to work out some simple words so she and I could communicate in an emergency. Well, I had a couple words of aGavoosh, and it wouldn't kill me to learn a little more.

"What are your names?" I asked.

"Barraki," the boy answered.

The girl must have figured out the question from his answer, because she said, "Tweezaa."

I held out my hands.

"Take my hands," I said. The boy took my left hand right away. The girl looked at Marfoglia, who said another couple words in aGavoosh and nodded, and then the girl reluctantly took my right hand.

"Barraki. Tweezaa. I'm not just something you see and hear. I'm something you can touch. I want you to feel my skin, how warm my hand is, and remember how it feels, so you'll remember I'm real. And remember I'm going to get you home safely." I squeezed their long, bony little hands, and Marfoglia translated, but the girl looked away and said something softly.

"What did she say?" I asked.

"She said, 'There is no home,'" Marfoglia answered, and her voice had a catch in it.

The funny thing is, I don't even remember deciding to go along as their bodyguard. I just knew I was. And all of a sudden, a lot of things started looking clearer. There just might be a way out of this mess for all of us.

Have you every noticed how often happy thoughts like that come right before a disaster?

My comm link tingled behind my left ear. Then it stopped. Then five seconds later it tingled again, and stopped.

"We've got company," I told the three of them.

I expected more of an argument. When I told Marfoglia she had thirty seconds to grab the passports and identification we'd need, she did it almost that fast. She started to say something about getting dressed before we left, but she looked at me and something she saw in my face made her shut up—it was probably the fear. If I was afraid, she better be too. And believe me, I was.

We were out into the hallway in under sixty seconds. I'd studied the floor plans before I broke in, so I knew there was a stairwell at the end of the hall—the far end, of course, on the other side of the elevator foyer.

"Tell the girl I'm going to carry her and it will be okay," I ordered. Marfoglia told the little girl—I couldn't remember her name. Her eyes, already big with fright, got bigger and her ears flared out in alarm. She shook her head and reached out to Marfoglia.

"I'll carry her," she said, but that would just slow us up.

"Sorry, little girl," I said, and scooped her up as I started to run. "Haul ass, you two!" I ordered over my shoulder. The girl gave a little cry when I picked her up, and held her arms stiff across her body, keeping them between us, but she didn't cry or struggle, so I was okay with that.

We got to the stairwell before there was any activity from the elevators. I was there first, but Marfoglia and the boy were close behind me, and I closed the fire door behind us—no way to lock it, of course.

"Up," I ordered, and started taking the stairs two at a time, still carrying the little girl.

"Wait!" Marfoglia shouted from behind me. "That's the wrong way!" Her voice carried and echoed up and down the concrete and stone stairwell.

I stopped, turned around, and put my finger to my lips.

"*Quiet!*" I ordered, but softly. "Sound carries a long way in here. The right way may be full of bad guys, so just shut up and follow me." While we were talking, I shifted the girl from my right arm to my left and pulled the gauss pistol out of the pocket of my slacks. She started to make an "*ooo*"-ing sound—not really crying, but getting warmed up for it. I looked at her and shook my head. *Not now, little girl. Cry later.*

She stopped making the sound, but then she kicked me in the stomach—not hard enough to really hurt, just enough to let me know that she was really frustrated with the travel arrangements. Lack of a common language is really no barrier to communication, provided your message is sufficiently emphatic. Despite the situation, I'd probably have laughed, but it just would have pissed her off more, and I had a feeling that this was a lady you crossed at your peril.

I started running up the stairs two at a time again and went up four levels before I stopped. I was panting for breath by then, and told myself it was just because I was carrying the girl. The boy in his black pajamas and purple Chinese silk robe was right beside me by then, watching me to see what we'd do next, and Marfoglia wasn't far behind him.

"We'll take the elevator here," I said. "They'll be coming up to your floor, we'll be going down in the opposite direction—no chance we'll run into each other." The boy looked at me as if I were a genius. Really it was just common sense—foolproof, actually. I mean, think about it. They're coming from ground level up to her floor. Once we get above their floor, we'll be taking an elevator down ... well you get the idea. There's no way we could run into any of them—absolutely no way.

The elevator door opened, and there were four of Kolya's guys in it. They looked at me with that look of stupid surprise that I have seen so many times—that look that says that the last thought they'll ever have in their life is wrong. For an instant, they wonder what will come next. For an instant, they wonder how this happened, and they wonder how they will get out of this bizarre, unexpected situation. They never, in that instant, actually believe they are going to die. And while, in that instant, they are wondering all of those things, I raise the gauss pistol and shoot them.

Snap, snap, snap, snap.

First I shoot the guy in front, who actually has his pistol drawn. Then I shoot the one in the far right corner, so he can't use the body of the guy in front of him for cover while he draws his gun. Then I shoot the guy in front of him, because he's in my sight. Then I shoot the last guy, in the corner to my left. He's actually starting to reach for his gun when I shoot him.

I shoot each of them once, in the head, and they fall down.

"Get in," I said, and I stepped into the elevator, being careful not to trip on a still-twitching body. Marfoglia and the boy had become statues, staring at the interior of the elevator, and the little Varoki girl in my arm began making that *"ooo"*-ing sound again. The first scent of ozone from my gauss pistol was already overpowered by the coppery smell of freshly spilled blood.

"Get in, Goddamnit!" I shouted, and the two of them almost jumped into the elevator.

They jumped in because they were afraid of me. I did this thing to protect them, to save their lives, and then they followed my orders because they were afraid I would kill them next. They knew I did it to save them, and it didn't matter. They couldn't have done it—no *normal* person could have done it—no matter how good the reason, or just the cause. I had become a monster to them.

That was okay. It would make the job easier. Right?

"They don't eat a lot," Marfoglia said almost apologetically, as Big Meg looked through the bag of groceries.

"No wonder," she answered. "My brats wouldn't, either, if you fed them snails and goose liver."

"No, that's all Varoki food," Marfoglia answered. She was dressed in a pair of slacks and a man's shirt, both way too big, but on short notice it was the best we could organize.

"Yeah, it's Varoki rich grown-up food. Kids don't like this stuff. *Eddy!*"

"Yeah, babe," her husband, Eddy, answered, already getting up from his chair because he knew the sound of a work order when he heard one.

"Run down to the Waadi-mart and get a box of redroot porridge. What do you kids like on your porridge?"

"Brown sugar," the boy—Barraki—answered at once, and Big Meg snorted in disdain.

"In your dreams, buddy boy!" she answered with a laugh. Human-compatible proteins are poisonous to Varoki, but they have no problem with our carbohydrates—unless you consider refined sugar hitting the bloodstream as alcohol a problem. Brown sugar on his porridge would have left him drunk on his ass. "He try this scam on you?" Meg asked Merfoglia, and she shook her head. No, he'd probably been in shock when he got to her place. Now he was coming out of his shell.

Meg rattled off a short, sharp string of aGavoosh to Barraki, which I didn't catch any of except *shaashka*, which I knew was a small burrowing animal transplanted here from Hazz'Akatu, the Varoki home world—known for stealing food and being hard to catch. We'd probably say *weasel boy*. Funny, it never occurred to me how similar my name was to that animal's until just then.

The girl—Tweezaa—giggled when she heard Meg

chew out her brother in aGavoosh. Barraki just smiled shyly and looked down, ears fluttering gently while a soft iridescent blush spread over his neck and face, and all of a sudden he wasn't just some victim anymore—he was a smart kid, full of mischief, and I started liking the little weasel boy.

Marfoglia didn't react at all, and didn't look at me when I spoke. Pretending I wasn't actually there was, I suppose, her way of not dealing with what she'd seen in the apartment building. She hadn't spoken to me since getting into the elevator. When I told her to do something, she'd do it, but she wouldn't look directly at me. She'd look off to the side while she was listening, as if the voice were coming from inside her own head, not from the thing standing next to her.

The kids were getting over it a lot quicker—they'd actually seen more killing in the last week than Marfoglia had in her whole life, and they'd seen what happened when you didn't take down the bad guys quickly enough—no more father. Maybe next time no more brother, no more sister. The kids would be okay with me a lot sooner than Marfoglia would, which was fine. This wasn't a popularity contest; all I needed her to do was follow orders.

Once Eddy got back, the two kids started putting away porridge as if they hadn't eaten in a week. Meg's two older kids had already made friends, at least with Barraki. Tweezaa not speaking English meant it would take longer with her—maybe ten or twenty minutes. Meg's kids probably spoke more aZmataan than any of us—because they hung out with local Varoki kids, and most Varoki on Peezgtaan were originally uZmataanki—but Tweezaa only spoke aGavoosh.

aZmataan is a regional dialect on Hazz'Akatu, the Varoki home world, a national language, actually—but I didn't know much Varoki history, and nothing from before space travel. All I knew was that aGavoosh was the official language of Varoki government and commerce, kind of like Mandarin was the court language of old China, even though a dozen or more different languages were spoken by the common folk.

The e-Traak were not common folk—definitely Mandarins.

With Eddie, Marfoglia, and the kids in the kitchen, Meg and I checked security. Her townhouse was at the end of a dead-end cul-de-sac, and she had two guys with thud guns down front and a light man—a high-energy-laser sniper—covering them from a second-story window. She had three or four more guys hanging around to relieve the others or back them up, as needed, and when we first came in I'd spotted a case of Mamba anti-vehicle rocket launchers stashed in the coat closet in the front hall. If Kolya wanted to make a fight of it here, he'd better bring a combat platoon with him—a dozen thugs wasn't going to cut it.

Once Henry and Phil showed up, Meg and I led them into her den and closed the door. We pulled chairs up around her card table and I looked at the three of them in turn, trying to get a feel for how much steel they had left. This was a tough spot. You could argue about whose fault it was we were in it, but that didn't matter. What mattered was how well these three could stand up under the shit storm that was coming.

"So, Kolya's got a mine on your internals," Henry started. "That's not good."

"Not *that* good, no," I agreed. "But I've been going over everything I've said over the wire since this whole thing with Ricky started, and I think we're in good shape. I'm careful about anything over the wire anyway. Never thought I'd have a mine myself, but you never know about the guy at the other end."

Henry nodded. Loose lips crash ships.

"The thing is," I went on, "if I stop using the comm altogether, Kolya's going to smell a rat. So we need to work out what we're going to say. It has to be believable, but keep Kolya making wrong moves for the next couple of days. Once I'm gone, the equation here changes."

"You sure about this, boss?" Meg asked. "The leaving, I mean. I think we can win this war—on the ground. Kolya's got a lot of guns, but we've got friends everywhere, even inside his organization. The only reason half of his people are with him at all is they're sure he's going to win, quickly. If we go to the 'safes,' hang tough, keep him from grabbing the quick win—and *bleed* him—his organization starts to crack, and then all bets are off."

I nodded.

"You're right, Meg. And if Plan A doesn't work, we'll go to ground and fight it out. Well, keep fighting it out, since we're doing everything we can to make it look like that anyway. Hell, you've got the best head for tactics in the Quarter, and I think that if it comes to a hard fight, we've got a real good chance to win."

I wasn't nearly as confident of that as I sounded, but sometimes you have to fib a little bit to keep your people from getting depressed. Depression lowers brain function, and I needed everyone's brain at 100 percent.

"But what's winning going to cost us?" I asked. "We can't take everyone to the safe houses. We can't hide all of our people, all of their families. *That's* where Kolya will hit us. So maybe we'll win, but it's gonna cost—and it'll cost more than I'm willing to pay... at least if there's another way. And I think there is.

"The way to take the heat off of the organization is to remove me from the equation. Once I'm gone, Kolya's mind is going to be on me, not you. That's when Henry steps up, takes over, and makes peace with Kolya. Everything we do between now and then is a setup to let you guys make peace when I'm gone, and that's how we play it."

"What makes you think this thing between you and Kolya is all personal, instead of just a business move?" Phil asked.

"Everything between me and Kolya is personal," I answered, and Henry nodded his agreement.

They sat in silence for a few seconds, chewing it over, but it wasn't anything we hadn't talked about already, one way or another.

"Okay," Henry finally said. "So, what line do we feed Kolya? You think I play at taking you prisoner and turning you over to him, but you engineer another amazing escape?"

"No. Kolya has an appreciation for loyalty—not for its own sake, but from a utilitarian point of view. If he thinks you double-crossed me while I was still your boss, he won't trust you not to double-cross him somewhere down the road. But if you're loyal to me *as boss*, as long as I *am* boss, and don't make peace until after I've run, he'll trust you to be loyal to him *as boss*. That's the key. You've got to convince him—with action—that your loyalty is to the position, not to the man.

"Beyond that, with Ricky gone, he doesn't have anyone inside the organization to take it over and keep it together. Phil's still a little young, and we know Kolya won't make Meg a captain."

It wasn't a coincidence that there were no female rankers in Kolya's organization.

Henry thought that over for a while, and then nodded in agreement.

"Okay. That's the way."

We worked out details for the next hour. We'd keep Marfoglia and the two kids at Meg's until it was time to leave. I'd rather have gotten them somewhere else, to reduce Meg's exposure, but somebody had to keep an eye on them to make sure they didn't do anything stupid.

Henry would come up with a schedule of comm chatter that might fool Kolya long enough for me and the kids to get off-planet in three days, and cover Henry's, Meg's, and Phil's collective backside at the same time. Meg would handle tactical security—getting everyone we could to the "safes," but also making sure we had eyes and ears where they counted.

At the same time, Phil and I would be the strike team—hitting them where it hurt most—silver and gold targets, primarily Archie and Bear's banks. Archie made a lot of his money from pimping, too, but we couldn't hit that side of the operation without hurting the girls, and we weren't going to do that; working for Archie was tough enough on them. But by hitting Archie and Bear's banks, we'd do two things.

First, hitting revenue made it look as if we were

in this for the long haul—a good message to send to the streets if we *did* have to go the distance, and good *maskirovka* if not.

Second, by hitting Kolya's allies, but not Kolya himself, we put pressure on him, but we didn't open any wounds—which would make it easier for Henry to make peace with him once I was gone.

Phil and I were doing it alone, without any other guns, because it cut the organization's exposure, and it reduced the chance of a leak. In operations like this, firepower means almost nothing; surprise is everything.

So when you've got a plan that good, what could possibly go wrong?

NINE

"We've got to stop meeting like this," I said to Doc Zhan. She took another stitch in my left arm—a bit more vigorously than she really had to, in my opinion. I guess I winced a bit, because Phil the Gil shifted from one foot to the other and then back again, like he needed to pee.

"Phil, do you need to go to the bathroom?" I asked.

"No, boss. I'm just—"

And then his eyes rolled up into his head and he fainted, hitting the floor with a solid thud. The Doc stopped stitching for a moment and we both just stared down at him, crumpled like a pile of dirty laundry. He hadn't wobbled or anything; he'd just gone down—thud.

"You think he's okay?" I asked.

"I've never thought he was okay," she said, and went back to stitching my arm.

"Does this hurt?" she asked as she took another stitch.

"No."

She took another quick, hard stitch and gave the surgical thread a tug to draw the wound closed. I sucked in a quick breath between clenched teeth.

"How about that?" she asked.

"Yeah, *that* hurt."

She smiled.

"You know, your bedside manner really sucks."

"You didn't always think so," she said without looking up, but the next stitch was gentle. Her long jet-black hair, shining in the UV antiseptic light, hid her face from me for a moment.

"Nope, guess not," I answered, and I sighed.

She looked up at me, but what was there to say? That I'd have been better off with her than Cinti? But without Cinti, I wouldn't have taken Jim Donahue's place, so there wouldn't have *been* a clinic for June to come and take over, and she'd probably still be doing meatball triage in a Co-Gozhak field hospital out in some godforsaken backwater.

Some *other* godforsaken backwater.

Water under the bridge.

"Did Markov's people do this?"

"Indirectly. We've been hitting banks. We hit one of Bernardini's—lifted a ton of *Cottos*—and then some son of a bitch sliced me as we were walking out. We checked for guns, but this little prick had a composite blade up his coat sleeve."

"Did you kill him?" she asked.

I shook my head.

"The Gil did—kept his wits, too. No wild gunplay, no retribution on the others standing around, just one quick, clean head shot before the guy could stick me again. I was proud of him."

She glanced down at Phil's crumpled form with a look of mixed surprise and approval, and then went back to my arm, using a surgical sponge to clean away some of the blood seeping from the wound. I had my shirt off, and she paused a minute to look at my left forearm, below the wound.

"Still got that stupid tattoo, I see. First time I met you, I had to stitch you up," she said softly.

"Yeah."

Nine years ago and a bunch of light-years away.

"I've got this feeling . . . ," she started, but she didn't finish the sentence. She just finished stitching the knife wound closed. June was smarter than ninety percent of the people on the planet; *she* knew I was leaving—one way or another.

"I'm taking off tomorrow," I said, answering the unspoken question. She didn't look up. "You know that if I stay here, he'll come after the clinic, to get at me."

She nodded.

"Just the clinic," I added. "He doesn't know about us . . . he can't. Everything between us was off-world, way back when, before you came here. There's no way he can know about us."

"You could have given him something to find out about," she said quietly, still not looking up. There was a hint of bitterness in her voice, but not much— mostly there was just resignation, because she knew I couldn't have come around, couldn't have given Kolya something to find out about, not while I was with Cinti—or with anyone else. Nope, not me.

I wonder if they have support groups for serial monogamists.

She sprayed a fast-set bandage on the wound, and

Phil started stirring on the floor. June glanced down at him, and before he opened his eyes, she leaned forward, grabbed my face in both hands, and kissed me hard on the lips. When she started to let go, I put my arms around her and pulled her close to me and kissed her back, long and hard.

Because she was right—this might be the last time we were ever going to see each other, and here she was, just stitching me up again, and it wasn't fair, but there it was.

The cigar smoke curling around Henry's face blended with the dark caramel of the bourbon as he took another sip, eyes closed in pleasure.

"Not bad," he allowed.

"If you like bourbon. Tastes like liquid candy to me."

"Kiss my ass," he answered, and then shook his head. "It's gonna be strange around here without you, you know?"

"Yeah. You be all right?"

He made a face.

"What? Without you here to get every psycho and dumb ass thug on the planet intent on killing us? Let me think . . . Yeah, I guess I'll be all right."

"Kiss *my* ass."

He chuckled in reply, and we sat in silence and drank for a while, bourbon and scotch, Henry and I.

"It's gonna be weird for me being . . . someplace else. You know?"

"Fish out of water? All that?" Henry asked.

"Yeah."

"Gotta make it work for you, that's all. I ever tell you about my grandiddie's grandiddie?"

"Nope."

"Way back when your great-great-grandiddie was eating boiled cabbage and screwing sheep in Ukraine, mine was fighting the Nazis."

"Yeah, I think the Ukies got the word there was a war going on, too. This musta been one of your white ancestors, right?"

"No, black. He was a flyer, and they hardly let any of them fight in the war, just one little unit. They escorted bombers over Germany. Lots of bombers got shot down, and the flight crews got put in Nazi POW compounds—*stalags*, they called 'em."

He took another sip of bourbon and smiled appreciatively.

"Just like you in the ladies' room at Quann's, their job was to escape, so they formed these escape committees. Nazis knew it, so they'd send in Germans who could speak English, pretending to be captured aircrews, trying to infiltrate the escape committees."

"That work?" I asked.

"Yeah, worked pretty good. Till some black dudes got there. Then all those southern white pecker-head bomber pilots put the black fighter pilots in charge of the escape committees. My great-great-grandiddie was one of them, shot down over Germany, escorting bombers. Know why they put 'em in charge?"

"They knew they weren't Germans." I said, and Henry nodded.

"Damn right, and that's the point: they made fish-out-of-water work for them."

I took a sip of scotch and thought about that for a while.

"Nice story. But given my complexion, I don't

think the whole Nazi POW camp thing's going to work for me."

"It's an analogy, dumbass."

"No kidding? Henry, how am I going to survive without you around?"

"Huh! Who says you're gonna?"

I tried not to brood about June during the maglev ride the next day. Brooding is dangerous when people are trying to kill you, and there was no guarantee that Kolya didn't have someone watching the trains. Watching wasn't the problem, of course—riding along joining the party was.

Our two compartment mates were Varoki, middle-aged annoying husband and bored wife, which from my point of view was a nice low-threat combination. Once we got moving I'd gone out into the corridor and planted two tiny remote eyes looking either way. They fed into the inside of my shades. Not reflector shades—that's too obvious—just standard polarizing wraparounds with a receiver for live feed. I could keep an eye on the approaches to the compartment from either direction, and for all anyone knew I was watching a dirty movie.

But nobody made a move, and after a while the brooding came back, because there was nothing I could do about June but brood. I was committed to a course of action and had to see it through—too many people's lives depended on it. After that, who knew?

It was the sight of the Needle that finally cleared my mind.

I'd seen Needles a half-dozen times, but I never got over the sight. Marfoglia was *blasé*, of course—the jaded traveler who's seen it all before—but the two kids and I couldn't take our eyes off it.

"Barraki, how many Needles have you ridden?" I asked.

He screwed his face up thinking, ears up and alert, and started ticking them off on his long fingers.

"Akaampta, Hazz'Akatu, Peezgtaan, Zissiwaa... mmm...and Tu'up! Yes. Those five, but I was very young when we visited Tu'up. I do not remember it very well. How many Needles have you ridden, Sasha?"

"Just two: this one and Nishtaaka."

"How many for you, Boti-Marr?" Barraki asked.

Boti-Marr, Aunt Marrissa, turned and smiled at him. It was one of those smiles that looked like she'd gone to school to learn how to do it—like she could smile that way even with a mouth full of sewage. I don't know about you, but I always get a warm, fuzzy feeling when someone smiles at me and I know they're at least as happy to see me as they would be to have a mouth full of sewage.

"I was just thinking about that," Marfoglia answered. "I've been on *both* of Earth's Needles, of course, since I'm from Earth. I've been up and down the Needle on Bronstein's World, the one here at Peezgtaan, Akaampta, Sha-shaa, and Eeee-ktaa. Now, which Needle on Hazz'Akatu did you ride? The Old Tower or the Merchant Gate?"

"Only the Merchant Gate," Barraki answered.

"I've heard that's the better one," she said. "The Tower is slower, and the compartments aren't nearly as nice."

I had a feeling that any compartment the e-Traak rode in would be pretty nice.

The maglev ride from Crack City to Needledown had taken most of the afternoon, even at a couple hundred klicks an hour through the near-vacuum on the surface. The Needle's at the equator—has to be—and the Crack's, you know, where it is, so there's no way to get the two any closer together.

By now we had a pretty spectacular view of the base of the Needle, only a couple kilometers away, with Prime setting to our left and casting impossibly long shadows across the dusty, barren rock flats that some long-dead Varoki snake-oil salesman had named the Sea of Welcome. The Needle glowed yellow-orange in the setting sun, a sparkling, impossibly thin thread stretching up to the heavens. Well, we could see it from a few kilometers away, so maybe not thin in an absolute sense, but compared to its length...

The massive laser domes to either side were visible as well, also glowing yellow-orange in the twilight. With no significant surface atmosphere to diffuse the light, sunset meant almost immediate darkness. When Prime disappeared below the horizon, the Needle stopped glowing at its base and disappeared, the darkness then shooting up its length, as if the Needle were a fuse to a celestial bomb, burning out before our eyes.

"Oooo!" I heard little Tweezaa say, and I nodded in agreement.

Oooo.

Mr. Hlontaa said something to Barraki in aGavoosh, Barraki answered fairly sharply, and Hlontaa actually bowed a little and said, "I beg your pardon. I forgot. I was just saying that the structures at the base of the Needle are gigawatt-range optic lasers."

I smiled to myself. Hlontaa and his spouse were

our Varoki compartment mates on the maglev, and once he'd found out that Barraki and Tweezaa were traveling with Human "servants," he'd started fawning over them. He was one of those guys with lots of opinions and no hesitation about sharing them with you. Out of politeness to me, Barraki made him say everything in English, as well as aGavoosh for Tweezaa.

Earlier, he'd shared some of his theories about Humans. He was very fond of us Humans, he'd assured us. He'd said that several times, I guess so we wouldn't forget, or get confused about it. We were very creative, he'd said, and quite intelligent, of course. But we just didn't put the same value on life as other races did.

Really?

Oh, yes. Obviously. Just look at the physical violence in every Human enclave in the *Cottohazz*, or the suicidal attacks Human military units are known for. Look at how the rogue brigades on Nishtaaka had fought until they were nearly annihilated. Humans clearly don't value their own lives the way other intelligent races value theirs.

"Have you considered the possibility that those soldiers on Nishtaaka were just very brave?" I'd asked.

No, it's something more than just that, he'd said. Humans live in the moment, slave to the impulse. That's why they are such good artists, but cannot control their violent urges—you have to agree with me on that point, don't you? Considering Human history?

I'd told him that I thought I was actually doing a pretty good job of controlling *my* violent urges, all things considered. Barraki, who had seen what results my violent urges could produce, giggled at that, which I thought was an interesting reaction. Hlontaa had lapsed into sullen silence for a while—catching up on his reading, he'd said.

After a while he'd snorted in disgust at what he saw, and then had turned back to us.

"Just look at this," he'd demanded, and pushed the viewer screen at me. It was an ad for a new Earth import holovid, called *Blood Vengeance of the Tong*. The video snip showed an actress I recognized from a couple of those Black Hand potboilers, held between two leering oriental dudes who looked as if they could snap her like a wishbone, if that's what they had on their minds. Her hair was wild and disheveled as she struggled between them, and the blouse of her Victorian costume was torn open, her heaving bosoms exposed. These Black Hand vids were definitely a guilty pleasure.

"What do you say about that?" he'd demanded.

I'd studied it for a moment longer and then nodded.

"Nice tits," I'd answered.

He'd sat back in disgust and kept scanning. Across from me Marfoglia had looked almost as disgusted. I just grinned.

Hollywood, Bollywood, and Hong Kong holovid pictures were a major Earth export, action-adventure yarns were as popular as they'd ever been, and there was this explosively popular subgenre of historical costume epics depicting a desperate struggle against a sinister secret society. They call them Black Hand vids because the first really successful ones were about the old Sicilian Black Hand. After that, they started cranking them out, and they all followed a pretty standard formula: hero or heroine falls afoul of evil secret society, then sixty minutes of chases, captures, menacing dialog, and gratuitous bodice ripping, concluding with a long bloody finale where the evil secret society is defeated.

Of course, you could only defeat the Black Hand so many times, so then there came all these other period costume pieces with reluctant heroes and beautiful, self-reliant women menaced by the Templars, Hashashins, Thugee, Ku Klux Klan, Bavarian Illuminati, and now the Chinese Tongs. They were in danger of exhausting the historic supply of secret societies, so they were also now remaking old Fu Manchu films and inventing secret cults in ancient civilizations for which they had few or no records either way—the streets of Aztec Tenochtitlan ran red with the blood of the sinister Tutuwaan.

Here's an interesting thing about those vids. Most of the Human folks I knew who watched them—at least the grown-ups—watched them as comedies. Sometimes Henry and I and a couple others would get together and put one on, drink some beers, and make up our own dialog. The late and unlamented Ricky had actually been pretty good at coming up with funny lines, interestingly enough. Of course, a lot of teenaged boys used the vids to jumpstart themselves into puberty. I'd smiled a bit to myself thinking about that.

Here's another interesting thing about them. I know this thing because I go way back with Pat Jarawandi, the regional manager for Cinestellaire A.G., the outfit that imports and distributes a bunch of these—I actually got him his first job there as a sales rep. The thing is, between seventy-five and eighty-five percent of the paid views of these things locally are by Varoki, not Humans. Figure that one out.

But then Hlontaa had found the news story on his hand viewer about the surge in murders in the Quarter over the last three days.

"And what about this?" he'd asked me. "All this violence in the Human Quarter—you can't just shrug that off, can you?"

Marfoglia looked at me coldly and nodded.

"Yes, what *do* you have to say about all those killings in the Quarter, Mr. Black?"

Mr. Black was my cover name—not very creative, but if you're going to lie, keep the lie simple, so you can remember it.

I shrugged.

"Oh!" I said. "Gee, I guess I *can* just shrug it off, after all."

Barraki giggled again.

"That's what I meant by no value on life. They're *your* people, and it means nothing to you," Hlontaa said in disgust.

"None of *my* people fell down. Not yet, anyway."

He looked at me in confusion, but Marfoglia knew what I meant, and the look of cold hostility momentarily left her face. Barraki didn't really understand what had just gone on, but he knew something had, and he wasn't giggling anymore.

Maybe Marfoglia had forgotten that those were real people back there—Big Meg and Henry, and Phil, and June—assuming she'd ever known. Or maybe she'd forgotten that this wasn't just about making clever conversation on the train—it was about killing, and maybe about getting killed.

She didn't know exactly what I'd had to do with the stuff in the news, since we'd kept her in the dark about the operation back there, our plans, and what I'd been doing with Phil the last couple days—but she had a few notions, and she'd figured to find out something by bringing it up, and maybe make me uncomfortable while she was at it. Instead, she was the one looking out the window and frowning. She didn't have any more answers about me, either, and the questions were just as dark as ever, and that was fine with me. She could stew about it all the way to Akaampta, as far as I was concerned.

She'd actually started talking to me again the day before. When the kids weren't around, she'd asked me why I'd killed all four of the men on the elevator.

"What should I have done?" I'd asked.

Take them prisoner. Disarm them.

"Yeah. Good plan. And if just one of them decides to be a hero, just one, there's two-way gunfire and the odds are we've got a dead kid. But suppose I disarm them. Then what?"

Leave them behind when we take the elevator.

"And they call Kolya on their comm links and tell him we're on the way down and which elevator we're in."

Oh.

Well, then take them with us.

"Sure. Eight of us packed cheek-to-jowl in one elevator, and me with the only gun. On the way down, a hero just reaches out and grabs one of the kids, and then what?"

No answer to that, of course. And the real truth is that you never get that far, because while you're standing there at the elevator door, trying to sort all of this out in your head, weighing the upside and downside of every possible course of action, one of Kolya's thugs just shoots you.

Now, with the Needle in sight, Hlontaa was giving Barraki and Tweezaa a science lecture on how the lasers lit the photo panels on the lift capsule, which provided power for the traction assembly, which walked the lift capsule up the Needle to orbit. Barraki had heard it all before, and Tweezaa wasn't listening, even to the aGavoosh version, but Hlontaa kept going. Some people love to hear themselves talk. Madame Hlontaa, I noticed, looked about as bored as Barraki and Tweezaa—she'd heard it all before, too.

The view on the way up to the Upstation is something you just never forget, and looking down at Peezgtaan's barren, meteor-pocked surface, was a reminder—if you needed one—of how precarious existence was down in the Crack. For the first half hour or so, you could even see the Crack, off in the distance. It didn't look like much from up here.

Without a Needle, nobody would ever have invested the buckage in eco-forming the Crack, but cheap transit to orbit, coupled with all those handy, exotic mold forms that had lain dormant in the ice down there for a couple million years, made Peezgtaan an economically viable world.

More viable for some than for others, but what's new about that?

Humans had come here forty years ago, a hundred thousand or so—including my mother and father—in freezer containers, brought in like any other cargo and thawed out to work for the new pharmaceutical conglomerate that was supposed to make everybody rich—great salary packages, great benefits, and bonded repatriation to Earth. Well, you already know how that worked out. So a generation later, there we were.

Why hadn't relief organizations on Earth stepped up to repatriate us? Because they'd already had their hands full. As bad as things were on Peezgtaan, they were worse on Earth. The Collective-wide crash of '75 hit Earth harder than most places, when its exports went into freefall and the interest rates on all those Varoki-underwritten developmental loans doubled in about six months. Couple that with back-to-back temperate zone droughts and a fresh-water shortage that had been building for a long time, that everyone figured the shiny new technology would fix but didn't, and things got pretty crazy for a while. The fresh-water shortage was the worst of it. In some places people killed for a drink of water, and nations went to war over watersheds and aquifers.

All four of the horsemen got in on the act eventually. There were even three or four nuclear exchanges—depending on whether you call a device that about a dozen whacked-out groups claimed credit for, delivered on a freighter to a port city of nine million people, part of a "nuclear exchange" or just an act of terror. I guess by then the distinctions were beginning to lose any meaning. Madness was the uniform of the day—madness and panic and rage.

So helping a hundred thousand folks on Peezgtaan with no ticket home was not exactly high on anyone's priority list. Just a year earlier, those people had been the lucky ones—travel, money, and adventure is a hard combination to top, so I guess there was probably some jealousy as well. When things went to hell out here, a lot of people back home probably thought, "Serves 'em right, running out on us."

Maybe the Peezgtaan Humans *had* been the lucky ones—we'd died by the hundreds, instead of by the millions. The green hills of Earth weren't as green as they'd once been, and maybe nobody back there gave a damn about what happened to us out here... but the Crack wasn't home. Earth was home, even if most of us alive now had never been there.

It's hard to think of any place as home if it's trying to kill you, and Peezgtaan would kill me or any other Human if it had the chance. So would every other world anyone in the *Cottohazz* had walked on, except Earth. Where there was native life, the protein chains were poisonous to us, and after a while it got to you. Even Bronstein's World, the largest Human extra-solar colony world, was having a hard time hanging on to its population. The best and brightest young people wanted to move back to Earth, and who could blame them? On most other worlds the Human enclaves were held in place by poverty as much as anything—poverty and inertia and an occasional dully glowing ember of stubbornness.

Living on an "alien world" sounded pretty romantic and exciting until you'd actually done it for a few years. Then it was just work—hard work.

All those early dreams of colonizing the stars had sort of taken it for granted that a world with life would be one we could sink roots into, one on which we could grow crops we could eat, hunt animals we could eat—if you were into that sort of thing—at least pick berries and nuts and eat them and not die. No such luck.

There's something very lonely about living in a galaxy that doesn't want you. In some ways it's worse than thinking you're the only ones there.

So there I was out of the Crack, but headed in the opposite direction from Earth, deeper into Varoki space. Akaampta was an "old world," colonized in the first wave of Varoki expansion over three hundred years ago, and close enough to a garden world, complete with Varoki-compatible proteins, that it hadn't required any eco-forming. What are the odds? Some guy once said it's smarter to be lucky than it's lucky to be smart. Boy, ain't that the truth? Akaampta's population was in the hundreds of millions now, and it had been politically independent since before Humans joined the *Cottohazz*.

So we were headed deep into the heart of the *Cottohazz*, and our first step was the ride up the tapering carbon nanotube Needle—really a bundle of nanotubes, a big vertical cable in permanent synchronous planetary orbit—SPO—over one spot in the equator, but reaching way past the SPO orbit track and tethered to a massive captive asteroid, far enough out it moved at escape velocity and would depart orbit if it weren't for the mass of the Needle holding it back; the centrifugal force of the asteroid trying to escape orbit held the Needle up and balanced the centripetal force of gravity trying to pull the whole thing down.

It's very creepy, at least to me, to think of that whole big thing—tethered asteroid, upstation complex, and long carbon nanotube ribbon down to the planetary surface—as a single structure in orbit, but it is. It's one big thing with its center of mass at the SPO altitude, going round and round, but at the same rotational rate as Peezgtaan does, so it never gets anywhere. As soon as the passenger capsule started up the ribbon, I'd turned to Baraki and said, "We're in orbit." Hlonta wanted to argue the point, but he lost. We *were* in orbit as soon as we became part of the mass of that one big structural system. We just needed to get to a different place in the system to do anything interesting, and at a fairly leisurely 200 klicks an hour, that would take a while. Rockets were an awfully expensive way to get to orbit; elevators are cheap, the ride's a lot more comfortable, and the view is spectacular.

After about half an hour, we overtook the terminator and Prime's yellow light momentarily flooded the interior of the compartment, until the windows polarized and damped it back down. By then we could see the shuttle, white and gleaming in reflected light—at first just the brightest star in the sky, but soon a recognizable shape.

From a distance, it looked more like a part from a machine—some sort of gear and axle assembly from a transmission—than a ship. There was a long, narrow spine not much more than a communications tube full of power cables and life-support conduits—and everything else was built onto that: fuel tanks and thrusters at the back, spherical command module way up front, couplings for big cargo modules along the spine behind Comm and forward of Drive, and in the middle of the ship, the two big counter-rotating wheels of the warm accommodations. It was so ugly it was beautiful, in a no-bullshit form-follows-function kind of way.

We'd spend the trip in the aft wheel; all the passengers would. Both wheels were over a hundred meters in radius, with the center hollow except for structural members and the access tubes up to the spine. Because of the artificial gravity generated by the centrifugal force of the rotating wheel, "up" was toward the spine and "down" toward the rim. The body of the wheel was about thirty or so meters thick, and the same width. Inside the wheel was divided into six decks, numbered from one, on the outside of the wheel, up to six closest to the spine. Gravity was noticeably weaker on Deck Six—where the luxury suites were—than on Deck One.

It was Varoki-built, like every other ship in the Peezgtaan system, but this was one of the newer shuttles that AZ Simki-Traak Trans-Stellar was flying, which meant it was mostly Human-designed. That was good news. Varoki-designed ships fly okay, but the accommodations are pretty lousy—not that Varoki don't care about comfort; they just don't have a knack for interior design, so the layouts make everyone—including them—claustrophobic and jumpy, and you're always cracking a shin or an elbow on some piece of shit housing sticking out where it shouldn't be. Varoki engineers don't know *Feng Shui* from *Dim Sum*.

One advantage to living on Peezgtaan was you didn't have to decompress going up the Needle. Spacecraft run on a low-pressure high-oxygen atmospheric mix, very similar to Peezgtaan's. But the higher up the Needle you get, the less you weigh, and the purser's staff came around and secured us in our seat harnesses about the time the kids started seeing how high they could jump. Once we got to the top, the seat harnesses became our transport slings, moving us along the magnetic tracks to the air locks and out into Peezgtaan Upstation. Most people have trouble moving around in zero gee, and if you let them try, you just have a mess, so better to relax and let the slings do the work. The staff had given each of us a vomit bag, and a couple of the passengers used them. I kind of enjoyed the feeling of weightlessness—like falling, but without the prospect of a sudden stop.

The last time I'd been up and down the Needle was almost ten years earlier. Upstation looked different now—kind of worn out. Somebody was skimping on maintenance—hopefully not the kind that mattered—and it had that run-down look that made you wonder if anyone gave a damn anymore. There was something else different—the big sign by the passenger in-processing gate read AZ Simki-Traak Trans-Stellar instead of Peezgtaan Planetary Authority, and the staff had AZSTTS (in the aGavoosh alphabet, of course) flashes on their jump suits. Another triumph for private enterprise, and some consultant like Marfoglia had probably cashed a six-figure check for coming up with the idea. Well, everyone's gotta make a living, and since we were traveling on phony docs, this was actually good news for us—security is always half-assed when the bottom-line meat-heads are in charge.

TEN

I woke up and could hear giggles. I blinked sleepily and looked around. Marfoglia was reading a book, but beyond her Barraki and Tweezaa were sticking their heads up and looking at me, and giggling.

"What's so funny?" I asked.

"You snore," Marfoglia answered without looking away from her book.

"Varoki don't snore?"

"Not like that, they don't," she answered, frowning. Barraki whispered something to Tweezaa—probably a translation—and they both giggled again.

"How much longer to burn's end?" I asked.

Marfoglia looked up at the chronometer on the ceiling—the opposite wall, actually.

"Seventeen minutes."

"Good." I yawned, stretched, and scratched my belly. "Let's talk."

Our cabin was like any other in the big wheel—well,

bigger and nicer than most, but functionally similar. As long as we were accelerating, "down" was toward the ass end of the shuttle, and the back wall of the cabin became the floor. There wasn't much furniture on it other than the acceleration couches, which the purser's staff had helped us into back in orbit, when we'd been at zero gee. All four of us had had some experience with weightlessness, but none of us were experts, so you relax and let the purser's staff move you around and strap you in. Then the long burn started to move us out to the gas giant. Once the burn was done, we'd be weightless again, but the big wheel would start up, and once it got up to revs, "down" would be toward the outside of the wheel, the normal orientation of the furniture secured to the cabin floor.

What would be the floor later was a bare wall right now, except for the furniture permanently affixed to it. There weren't a lot of unattached things, and no *heavy* unattached things, in a spacecraft.

I could have gotten used to the whole setup. The cabin made my condo back in the Crack look like a flophouse. There was a decanter of cold water and a drinking glass in secure sockets beside each of our couches, and just the way the light sparkled in the cut glass told me they weren't just plastic pieces of shit. Personal cut glass water decanters in case we got thirsty during the burn? I'd booked luxury accommodations—because it was Marfoglia's nickel— but I had no idea luxury accommodations were this... luxurious. Of course, when it came to my own experience with interstellar travel, all I had to compare this against was hot bunking with a bunch of bad-smelling Crack Trash grunts in a troop transport.

This was nicer.

The big wall screen—which right now was on the temporary ceiling, to encourage everyone to remain supine during the burn—showed the aft external view. It was partly obscured by the rocket flare, but you could see gray dead-looking Peezgtaan, already filling less than half the screen. They were piping in a violin concerto, and it went well with the view.

"Okay, here's the deal," I started. "We know somebody wants to . . . well, stop you two from getting home. They'll know there are four of us—two Human and two Varoki—and there won't be many travel groupings like that, so we'll be fairly obvious. What I did was make similar travel reservations on almost every ship leaving the system over the course of the next five weeks. Kolya doesn't have enough reliable people to put someone on every ship."

Marfoglia translated for Tweezaa, and then turned to me.

"Won't Markov know we're on this ship, once you aren't—active?"

I nodded.

"Sure. He may even have had eyes at Needledown, but it's too late for him to do anything about it. Unless he already has somebody on board—which means one of the passengers that came up the Needle with us—we're in pretty good shape. For now. We'll have some other issues to deal with later, but right now our biggest concern is someone hired by the assassins, on the shuttle, and interested in hurting us."

The "other issues" involved Kolya sending a message via the C-lighter's public data dump to our destination, for dissemination from there. He probably didn't have anyone on the shuttle, but every scheduled stop we made, our odds went down.

I let Marfoglia translate what I'd said, and watched the kids while she did. They were scared, but interested, too. Tweezaa's skin coloration was darker than Barraki's, and the iridescence seemed stronger, so sometimes when the light hit her just right, it was as if she were jewel-encrusted. There was something so serious, and so self-possessed about her, I'd started thinking of her as the Dark Princess.

My two charges—the Dark Princess and Weasel Boy.

"So what we're going to do," I went on, "is mingle, and try to find out as much as we can about the other passengers. In particular, we want to know if there were any last-minute changes in travel arrangements. Now, I don't want to minimize the danger, but someone is less likely to make a move against us while we're actually on the shuttle or the C-lighter."

"Why?" Barraki asked as Marfoglia translated.

"Well, they can't get away," I explained. "Any violence on a spacecraft and they just seal everybody up inside until they get to where they're going, and then the provosts come in and nobody leaves until they've figured everything out. Tough situation to wiggle out of, especially with so many security monitors on board.

"I'm more concerned about the layover in the Seewauk system. We'll be at Rakanka Highstation for a few days, and it's a big place—almost a small city—and security won't be as tight.

He nodded, but he didn't look completely convinced. Just as well. I didn't want them thinking there was no danger.

"That doesn't mean they *won't* try something on

board," I went on. "So although we'll be going out and mixing, I want us all to stay together, always in sight of everyone else. And I'll be armed."

Not very well armed, but they didn't need to know that. No spacecraft line allows anything more powerful than low-velocity slug-throwers—still lethal, of course, but not dangerous to the airtight hull. So it was my old Hawker 10 again. The H&K was in a cargo container someplace—even firing slugs, that cannon was dangerous to delicate things like spaceships. I had a little LeMatt 5mm automatic as a backup, and that was even less powerful than the Hawker. At least I could be fairly sure I wouldn't be up against anything heavier. Even security personnel—when there are any—don't carry anything heavier than that, which is why passengers aren't allowed to carry any body armor at all. Can't have troublemakers wandering around immune to the security guys, and anything that will punch body armor will let in hard vacuum.

Once we'd finished the maneuvering burn, the big wheels were spinning, and the steward's crew had reset the cabin furniture—and I'd tipped them—we explored the suite in its new horizontal orientation. It had a sitting room and kitchenette in the middle, one large bedroom to one side, and two smaller ones to the other. The stewards had put Marfoglia's and my luggage in the big one, the kids' in the two smaller ones, so the first thing we did was move everything around. The only door to the corridor outside—other than the one in the sitting room—was from one of the smaller bedrooms, so I took that one, Marfoglia the other small one, and the kids bunked together in the master room.

Over the next couple of days, we went to all the common meals, got to know the other passengers, and tried to figure out if any of them were Markov plants. To be honest, it was pretty boring work. People are interesting—Father Bill taught me that. Take the time to get to know them, and just about everyone you run into has a story that's worth hearing, and not just for its entertainment value. People go through life, they have their disasters and triumphs, no matter how big or how small, and they learn stuff along the way. Listen to them, and you can learn something about life, too.

Father Bill was the closest thing to a real father I could remember, and I didn't even meet him until I was sixteen, so I guess the damage was done by then. I'd already been living on the streets for nine years, the first six of them as part of a bezzie-pack, and although I'd developed scruples, I had no compunctions, if you understand the difference.

So Father Bill saw this wild, violent thing, and he liked me. Well, he liked almost everyone. Some people, when they say that, it means they like the *idea* of liking people, but that's all. Not Bill. He found people really interesting. He'd tell you all these interesting things about other people's background he'd found out, or about what they thought, and it was stuff that would never even occur to you until he told you, and then it really was amazing. He found everything about me amusing and intriguing and even admirable. I guess he taught me to see a bit of that in other people, too.

But the truth is, if you're looking for someone trying to kill you, insights about the meaning of life just don't hold your attention. And that tells you something about the meaning of life right there, if you think about it.

The shuttle had a capacity of 170 passengers, but there were probably only half that many on board—the travel business was in a slump lately. The passenger cabins were in the sternward wheel, along with the common spaces and dining. That way, passengers never had to go up to the spine and grapple with zero gee. The stewards lived forward, in the bow wheel. The flight crew had cabins in the bow wheel as well, and spent their off-duty time there. We passengers never saw any of the flight crew, only the stewards. That old Earth custom of VIP passengers dining at the captain's table was beginning to be observed on some of the classier routes—there's that *Terrakultur* thing again—but nobody was likely to call the Peezgtaan in-system shuttle a classy route.

Of the eighty or so passengers other than us, I'd guess that no more than a dozen were Human. Most of the rest were Varoki, but there was a solitary Trand, small and wrinkled and lonely looking, five Zaschaan, and the same gregarious group of eight Katami I'd seen at H'Tank's Six-Star Club—I guess it really is a small world. All we were missing was a couple Kuran witchlocks for a complete set of the six sentient races, but Kuran don't get out much, and that's fine by me.

Most of the passengers had reservations which predated the original killings—I knew this because I bribed the steward—so they were clear . . . unless Kolya had managed to pull the old swicheroo and at the last minute substitute a silencer for one of the legitimate passengers. I considered that unlikely—he'd have to not only find out this was our real flight, but he'd have to do it far enough ahead to set up the switch—which meant document work, research...it just sounded like too many moving parts to me.

Not that I ignored the possibility—I'd been ass-bitten by long shots too many times. But nobody seemed terribly suspicious, and—much more importantly in my experience—nobody seemed too terribly *non*-suspicious, either.

There was a Varoki security contractor who got really interested in me once he figured out I was the muscle for our little group, but it turned out he wanted to recruit me. Private security was getting to be a big growth industry, and hard-eyed Humans were the bodyguards of choice for the rich and powerful. Arrie was right about that—the Zaschaan might be bigger and tougher than us, but there was something sexy and cool about Human thugs that the Zacks could just never match. If you wanted to convince people that you were wealthy, influential, and sophisticated, you'd hire a dark elf as your exotic bodyguard, not some bugger-eating troll.

And why was private security getting more profitable? Because we lived in interesting times. Karl Marx dreamt of a day when government would wither because there was no further need for it. A lot of rich guys had the same dream and, unlike Marx, they were used to getting their way.

There were a couple other guns on board. One of the passengers was the Varoki *wattaak* from Peezgtaan—basically like a senator back in North Am. He had four security people: two Varoki and two Human, and I didn't know any of them, which was a good thing, because that meant they didn't know me.

Okay, civics lesson. The Wat was the upper house of the *Cottohazz's* assembly—one *wattaak* from each "nation" of the *Cottohazz*. Each home world, which means each of the six races, had twenty-seven nations, because that's how many national polities there were on Hazz'Akatu, the Varoki home world, when the *Cottohazz* had been formed—so everybody else also got twenty-seven, and how they made that work was their problem. From Hazz'Akatu there was uKa-Maat, uZ'mataan, uBakaa, and twenty-four other Varoki national governments I hadn't heard of or didn't remember. With all five of the original sentient races, there had been 135 *wattaaki* at first. When Terra joined, they added twenty-seven more—the United States of North America, the Western European Union, the United Arab Republic, the Republic of Canton, India, Russia, Brazil, and eighteen more, some of them pretty awkward political unions.

The colony worlds were usually part of a nation back on one of the home worlds, but at a certain point, some were recognized as separate nations, with their own *wattaak*. Our guy from Peezgtaan was the newest *wattaak*, and it brought the total number to 171. Peezgtaan had been an uZ'mtaanki colony originally, but we got our nationhood because we raised and sent troops—Human troops—to Nishtaaka, to help suppress the rogue mutiny. Since independence, all us Human Crack Trash had become uPeezgtaani citizens, which was probably an improvement over "stateless alien residents," which had been our previous status.

So now we had our own *wattaak*—Varoki, of course— his election campaign paid for by AZ Simki-Traak *Cottos*, all nice and legal. And in its small way, it was good for

Peezgtaan economically—it gave us another product to produce and export for hard currency: legislators.

They call it democracy, because there are no hereditary rulers, no kings, and everything is done according to laws passed by elected representatives. You can't inherit power, or titles, or political office. What you *can* inherit is money, and when a world like Terra, with about nine billion people on it, gets to elect just twenty-seven representatives, money shouts, and everything else murmurs. They call it democracy, but it's just a puppet show.

Mostly what we did on the shuttle was walk around the wheel, explore its different levels, and work out expediency plans. We poked around in closets and maintenance access bays, looking for places where a kid could hide from a grown-up, and we gave the places numbers. I learned the numbers, and a few other words, too, in aGavoosh, so if I needed to, I could tell Tweezaa where to hide.

My only bad scare with the kids came our fourth day out, when Barraki went missing one afternoon. We were all back in the cabin, and he must have slipped out when nobody was looking. I got the LeMatt automatic out and showed Marfoglia how to use it—how to put the safety on and off, how to reload, and had her dry fire it to see what the trigger pull was like. Then I told Marfoglia not to let Tweezaa out of her sight until I got back, strapped on the Hawker, and went looking for Barraki.

It didn't take long to find him; he hadn't really been trying to sneak around or hide his tracks. He was all the way down on the observation deck, looking out the big rear ports at Prime. It seemed to spin slowly around as the wheel turned. It wasn't much of a sun, this far out, but it was bigger than anything else in the sky.

I should have kicked his ass, but he was crying, and I just sat down next to him.

Yes, Varoki cry . . . sort of. No tears, but repetitive sobbing a lot like us. Most animals born live probably do something similar to get the breathing started, and the really smart species remember it and use it as a lament. Coming into this world is not for the faint of heart.

I figured he was crying because of his father being dead, but I was only half right. He looked over at me and then looked down and away.

"Why do you not hate me?" he demanded, his voice quivering.

"*Huh?*" I asked.

Normally I'm a little more articulate than that, but the question caught me flat-footed. *Hate him?*

"What the hell are you talking about?" I asked him. "Why would I hate you?"

"What we did to you. On Peezgtaan," he said.

"Did I miss something back there? I don't remember you doing anything that would even irritate me, let alone make me hate you."

"Not to you. I mean, to Humans. What my family did to your people on Peezgtaan. Why do you not hate me for that?"

He was serious, and he wanted a serious answer, not just some *hey, kid, don't worry about it* bullshit.

"Well, I look at it this way, sport," I said finally. "If I was going to hate someone for what was done forty years ago, it'd be someone a lot older than you."

He looked at me, and I could tell it wasn't enough of an answer for him. I held my open left hand out, palm facing him, fingers splayed.

"Here, spread your hand like this and match it up against mine," I told him. He did, and even though his hand was smaller in most respects, his fingers were longer. The hands were functionally the same—five digits, one of which was an opposable thumb—but the proportions were different, and the skin even more so.

"You got longer fingers than I do," I told him. "You want me to hate you for that?"

He frowned and shook his head.

"No, that would be stupid, wouldn't it?" I said. "Because you don't have any control over how long your fingers are. Well, connect the dots, Barraki."

"But it is not fair what happened," he insisted.

"No argument there, pal. It just wasn't on your watch."

"Someday it will be my watch. What then?" he asked.

"Well, then we'll see."

He looked out at the stars for a while before speaking again.

"My father...was very sad, since my mother died."

"How long ago was that?" I asked. I hadn't known his mother was dead, but I'd noticed she wasn't in the picture.

"Almost four years. He did a lot of things...I think because he was so sad. Then a year ago, he got better. He said there was a poison in our blood, but he was going to cure it. He worked hard on it. He had never worked before, but this last year he worked very hard. And he was happy. He was almost done. That is why we came to Peezgtaan, to finish the work."

"What was here? Some kind of medicine?" I asked. I wasn't really sure what that "poison in the blood" stuff meant. Barraki shook his head.

"No medicine. Just councilors—lawyer I think is the word. They were for the...mmm...I think the word is *faiths*?"

Faiths? That sounded religious, but no religion I know of uses lawyers to make the mumbo jumbo work. I shrugged and shook my head.

"They were for the money, to hold it," he said.

"*Trusts!*" I said. "Trust funds?"

He nodded. "Yes, that is the word."

"Your father was setting up some charitable trusts on Peezgtaan? Maybe to help poor people?"

It made sense. Rich playboy loses rich wife, goes into mourning, wonders about the meaning of life, decides to spend the rest of his life "doing good," or at least until he gets bored and decides that big-game hunting would be better. Not nice to think that of the dead, I know, but I've seen a lot of rich people sling hash in St. Mike's soup kitchen, and never for very long.

But Barraki was shaking his head.

"No, the trusts were for Tweezaa and me. He said they would take care of our education, and give us some money for a while, but then we would have to work, like everyone else."

Work?

The e-Traaks? One of the ten richest families in the *Cottohazz*? *Work?*

"Um...So, like, what was he doing with the family fortune?"

"He was giving it to the Humans on Peezgtaan,

to all of them. No, not giving. There was a different word...*entailing*? Do you know that word?"

"Sort of," I answered, but I still wasn't clear on this whole giving-away-the-fortune concept. "What do you mean by 'it'? As in entailing *it*?"

He looked at me, unsure what I was asking.

"Everything," he answered. "All of the family holdings. Well, there are private estates which are already entailed to others—he had no control over them. But the ownership in all the different companies, like this one—Simki-Traak. I think we own a lot of it, yes? I am not sure. But he had a plan; he told me all about it."

Barraki turned to face me now, and he was getting excited.

"There would be a big company, and it would own all of the other things, and every Human living on Peezgtaan today would have one share—just one share—and that's all the shares there would be. But you could never sell your share—that is what I think *entailed* meant. When you died, your share was gone, but all of your children would have a share of their own, and no one person could ever own more than one share. There were other things...I forget. But that was the main thing. He said that he had set it up so that only Peezgtaan Humans could ever own it. Ever."

He stopped then, and his enthusiasm faded.

"Then they killed him," he said.

What Barraki was talking about—what his dad had dreamed up—was revolutionary stuff. It would have shaken the Varoki establishment to its foundation, that's for sure, which was okay, I guess. But more importantly—at least to me—it would have given everyone on Peezgtaan a chance. No overnight millionaires—just a decent stake in the world around them. That was something to think about, wasn't it?

I put my arm around Barraki's shoulder. No wonder somebody killed his dad. And no wonder they wanted to kill him and his sister, too—the poison was gone from their blood.

A lot of my memories concerning the shuttle ride are missing in action, for reasons you'll understand later. The parts that remain are not necessarily the most important parts. Well, one of them is, but the other one is just a lunch, of all things—lunch with the Hlontaas.

I remember I didn't like how often Hlontaa shared meals with us, but that was because I didn't like the guy, not for any professional reason. I could have kept him away and cited security—used the power of the job to get something I wanted—but once you start down that road, it gets easier and easier to keep going, and pretty soon you're the manager of some city, screwing everyone who elected you just so you can line the pockets of your pals, who only pretend to like you anyway because you own the trough. No thanks.

So there we were. The tables were eight-tops, so it was the four of us, plus Hlontaa and Madame Hlontaa, and another Varoki couple, husband and wife, both councilors—lawyers—criminal prosecutors, as it turns out, from Akaampta. They had been on Peezgtaan as consultants, helping the Munies set up a new organized-crime task force.

That was kind of creepy.

Hlontaa was explaining one of his theories—this one about criminal justice—to the table in general, but mostly to the two prosecutors from Akaampta. He'd figured out that the reason there was so much Human crime on the jointly occupied worlds was that Humans placed this lower value on their lives—a recurring theme with him—and so normal deterrence didn't work. You needed harsher penalties for the same crime with Humans, just to get the same deterrent effect. He thought the death penalty was appropriate for a wide range of crimes—at least for Human offenders. Not because he didn't like Humans—he actually liked them very much, just ask him. But because he liked them, he understood them better than most Varoki, and once you understood them, you saw that they needed a firmer hand, for their own good.

I don't know much xeno-psychology, because I haven't had to interact with all the different races. I know that the Katami are very gregarious, more so than us. The Trand are as well, which is why it was so odd to see just one of them on the ship, and probably why he looked so unhappy. I don't know what's going on with the Kuran, and I don't particularly care. The two races of the *Cottohazz* I've bumped up against most are the Varoki and the Zaschaan, and psychologically, they're not that different from us. The Zaschaan tend to be cranky, but I know plenty of cranky Humans, too. Maybe the Zaschaan just don't bother to cover it up with a phony smile. The Varoki are a lot like us, and I think that, secretly, they'd like to be even more like us, which is odd, considering we're the ones inside the apple barrel.

I mention all of this by way of explanation as to

why the two Varoki prosecutors sort of studied their menus and blushed while Hlontaa was laying all this out, and when Varoki blush, with that iridescence skin tint, you can really see it. Barraki was blushing, too, but not the Dark Princess. I figured she had more sense than to be embarrassed by what some other fool was saying. *She* wasn't saying it, after all.

"Capital punishment is barbaric," I said while he was catching his breath. The whole table looked at me, and Marfoglia and Barraki looked particularly surprised. Barraki translated for Tweezaa, and she nodded and went back to looking around the club deck.

Hlontaa smiled condescendingly. "And yet so many Human nations use it," he said, as if that was some killer argument.

"Lots of Humans fart at the dinner table," I answered. "Doesn't mean I have to."

"Do you mean that in your...line of work," he said with obvious distaste, "you've never killed anyone?"

Marfoglia and Barraki got real interested in their own menus right about then.

"Yeah, I've killed people. It's not the same thing."

"No," he said sarcastically. "It never is."

I should probably mention that my confession that I'd killed someone didn't elicit much surprise from the two prosecutors, nor was it a damaging admission. Back in those days, the frontier planets were a bit like the old American wild west. Thug, private security specialist, and lawman were job titles, not distinct classes of people. There was a lot of the "It takes one to catch one" philosophy going around, so not only did people not look too closely at the criminal past of security specialists, there was a tacit assumption—even an expectation—that they had been on the wrong side of the law at one time or another, at least for Humans. Varoki were supposed to all be good little boys and girls.

"Just for the sake of argument," he said, "how is it different?"

"You shouldn't kill people for points," I answered.

"Points?" he repeated. "You mean like in a game?"

I looked up at him.

"No. Like in an argument. It's wrong to kill people to make a point. People are more important than points."

"But most important points people try to make are *about* people," he said.

"My point exactly," I answered, and went back to the menu. The chicken *katsu* was sounding pretty good, but there was this Paleo Special—flame roasted on a spit and guaranteed to have the authentic flavor of prehistoric Terran mastodon. It was soy protein, of course, but it was based on the flavor of some genetically reconstructed meat.

"That does not even make sense," he said.

"Huh?" I asked, my mind still on genetically reconstructed mastodon meat.

"Capital punishment is not about making a point," he said.

"*All* punishment is about making a point," I answered. "Don't do that, or *this* will happen to you."

"Deterrence, yes. But there is retribution, also."

"Revenge. Sure. But that's just a different point, one you make to yourself. You chopped my hand off, but I got even, so there. But since that doesn't get you back your hand, all you've done is make a point."

"And I suppose you've never killed someone to make a point—or to get even?" he demanded.

I sat and thought about that for a while, mentally going through the list. After about half a minute he started to look uncomfortable.

"Well?"

"I'm thinking," I answered. I didn't want to lie.

"How many people have you killed?" Marfoglia asked quietly, speaking for the first time, her brow wrinkled in concern. I looked at her. Not that it was any of her business . . . well, I guess it was, come to think of it. Her life was pretty much in my hands, so I suppose she had a right to know how bloody those hands were.

"Eleven that I'm sure of," I answered, and it was interesting to see four pairs of adult Varoki ears fold up and back in perfect unison, like a ballet.

"Three of them were in combat, when I was in uniform. As to Mr. Hlontaa's previous question, the answer is, once. Back in my very brief army career, a sniper shot two of my squadies. We nailed him with a frag missile, and when we went out to collect his weapon, he was still alive. He might have made it, too, but I shot him. That was actually the first person I ever killed—that I know of, anyway. You know, you throw a lot of energy downrange in a firefight, and who the hell knows where it all ends up? But other than that guy—which I am ashamed of to this day—I've never killed anyone to make a point, or to get even."

Marfoglia had a confused, conflicted look. She was doing the math and realizing that she'd witnessed half of those eight non-military killings. The killings had horrified her, but they'd also saved her life. Hlontaa just looked skeptical.

"So, I suppose that the other eight, when you were

not in uniform, were all self-defense?" he asked, his ears relaxing and unfolding again.

And that showed how full of shit Hlontaa really was. He only asked about the eight people I'd killed after the military, as if killing three men while in uniform was the most natural thing in the world.

Most guys in a war survive—even most guys on the losing side make it through in one piece, so anyone can do the math and figure out that most people in uniform don't actually kill anybody. Now add in the fact that most people who do get killed are killed by big fire-support systems, not AWiGs—*Assholes With Guns*. Almost everyone I knew who went through an actual shooting war—and I knew some guys who were in special operations and right in the thickest part of the shit—never killed anyone.

I killed three, and Hlontaa didn't even know enough to find that unusual or interesting.

Were the eight others all in self-defense? I shook my head.

"Nope. Some were, but not all of them."

"Really? Well, other than self-defense, or 'making a point,' what reason is there to kill someone?" he demanded, and then he got a strange look, almost frightened. "You do not mean you kill for . . . for pleasure, do you?"

I laughed.

"No. Other than that first time, I've only killed people to stop them from doing things I didn't want them to do. Mostly, the thing I didn't want them to do was to kill *me*, and I guess that counts as self-defense, huh? But there are other things."

"For example," he said.

"For example, and pertinent to my current employment, I will kill anyone trying to hurt these two kids," I said, and gestured to Barraki and Tweezaa, "not because the killers are bad people—although I assume they're probably pretty bad—and not as an object lesson to others, but just to stop them from hurting the kids."

Hlontaa looked at me for a while, thinking that over.

"So, if the government kills a killer, does that not prevent him from killing again?" he asked.

This was getting to be a stupid argument, and I went back to the menu.

"Lock 'em up," I said. "That'll stop 'em, too. I'd do it myself, but I don't carry a detention center around with me. So, what do you think, Dr. Scarlet?" I asked Marfoglia, using her cover name. "Chicken *katsu* or Paleo Special?"

"I've heard the Paleo Special is very interesting," she said, cool and chic again, her composure having returned.

Interesting, huh? Okay.

Chicken *katsu* it was.

I don't believe in God, not in any traditional sense— some old guy with a beard sitting in the clouds, looking down on all of us? Yeah, right. I have to say, though, sometimes it's as if *someone* is listening, someone with a very twisted sense of humor, or irony, or something, because it seems like whenever you lay out some fundamental element of your life's philosophy, as soon as you're sure you've got something important figured out about yourself, right away something happens to test it. Test it good and hard. This test was the second thing I remember.

The morning of the seventh day out, the cabin reader's message light was on. I keyed the screen and saw there was a recorded incoming message waiting, with an attached video feed. It was addressed to Sam Black, my cover identity.

The sender was Kolya Markov.

ELEVEN

Marfoglia insisted on watching the message. She was right—it concerned her as much as it did me. We took it in my bedroom, and closed the door so neither of the kids would hear whatever it was Kolya had to tell us.

"Hey, Sasha," Kolya started with a smile. "Long time no see—now maybe even longer, what with you leaving and all. I just wanted to get this to you before you got to the lighter. Somebody sent me a recording—no idea who. I'm turning it over to the Munies, of course— evidence and all. But since it's about a friend of yours, I though you should know. Terrible thing, just terrible." He frowned and shook his head in sympathy. "I'm sending a copy along. Give my regards to the blonde."

He grinned, winked, and reached forward, and then the screen went blank.

The recording was appended to the message, but I had to trigger the viewer in order to see it. For several long seconds I just sat there, staring at the blank screen, afraid to play it. Finally, my hands shaking, I keyed the playback.

It was June.

A jumpsuited man, his face covered by a mask, sat on the bed in a shabby room somewhere, and June was naked, crumpled at his feet. He reached down, grabbed her hair, and used it to pull her up, so she was looking at the camera. She was badly beaten—one eye swollen shut, nose broken—and spattered with blood. Her hair was tangled, wet with sweat and plastered to her head. She was conscious, but listless, drained, dead-eyed. This wasn't the start of something, it was the end.

My hand fluttered by the console, wanting to shut off the playback, as if this were happening as I watched, and I could stop it if I just stopped the vision of it, but I let it play, because I had to. There was no sound on the recording, but I could hear whimpering, and I realized that it was me. Big tough guy. I felt a hand on my shoulder, and I shrugged it away.

The masked man lifted the gauss pistol in his right hand, put it against her temple, and fired, and then fired again and again and again, even though she was dead after the first shot. I sat there, wincing at the savage ruin that every shot caused, shuddering in pain and horror, tears running down my face, powerless to do anything but watch. Then the screen went black, but the vision of her bloody, eyeless death mask remained, burned into my consciousness, is still there right now, crisp and vivid and awful.

Do you know the worst moment of your life—the absolute lowest, darkest point? I do.

After a while I looked over to Marfoglia, and she was lying on the floor, gasping for breath. I hadn't shrugged her away; I'd elbowed her in the solar plexus hard enough to double her over. She'd tried to comfort me, and I'd done this to her. She looked up at me, fear and pain and confusion all mixed up together in her eyes, and I just stared at her. Maybe I should have said something, but what was there to say? *Sorry?*

If I had words that could change anything, I'd have used them to bring June back.

For the better part of a day I stayed in my bedroom with the door locked and the lights out. I sat in the chair and didn't get up from it except to go to the bathroom. I didn't eat—wasn't hungry. I probably dozed a bit sitting there, I don't remember for sure. The one thing I did before withdrawing into that shell was to send a two-word message to Henry.

You probably figure that all through that day I relived every moment with June, but I don't think I did. Mostly my mind was blank, empty, black. I just shut down for a while, like a machine that overheated. But you can't shut down forever. Well . . . you can, but that doesn't fix anything, either.

> The Moving Finger writes; and, having writ,
> Moves on: nor all your Piety nor Wit
> Shall lure it back to cancel half a Line,
> Nor all your Tears wash out a Word of it.

Boy, ain't that the truth?

When I finally breached containment, Marfoglia and the kids were sitting down to breakfast. They'd probably had all of the meals delivered while I was mourning—if that's what it was I was doing. They looked up at me, kind of shy and embarrassed.

"I wasn't sure if you'd want anything, but I ordered you some breakfast," Marfoglia said, and looked back down at her own meal.

"Thanks. I'm hungry." I sat down and lifted the heavy plastic lid off the plate—hutsul omelet, egg whites only, with soy nuts, and Thai chili sauce on the side. For some reason, it got me all choked up, I guess because it was such an unexpected act of consideration—unexpected and undeserved. I didn't say anything—wasn't sure I could without making a fool of myself, so I just started eating.

"Sasha, we are sorry your friend died," Barraki said. "Boti-Marr told us, and Tweezaa and I are very sorry."

I nodded without looking up at first, but then I looked at them. Their father had been murdered in front of them, horrible people were trying to kill them, and they were sorry for *me*. They at least deserved to see my face.

"That means a lot to me, Barraki. And Tweezaa. I mean it." My voice was hoarse, but I got it out. "Now eat. You probably haven't been out of the cabin in over a day, have you? We'll get some exercise today, get out and see people, and see if there's any part of the shuttle we haven't explored. Okay?"

He smiled and nodded, and translated for Tweezaa. She listened to him, but her eyes stayed on me, studying me the whole time, frowning slightly in concentration. When he was finished, she thought for a second or two and then nodded—agreement? Approval? Hard to tell with her, but she went back to her breakfast and ate faster than usual.

After the meal, while the kids were getting dressed, I started for my own bedroom to shower and change, but Marfoglia stopped me.

"Do you have to send a message to Mr. Washington?"

"Henry? I already did, yesterday. Short and to the point."

She shook her head and looked down.

"So now there'll be more killing," she said sadly. "And what will it prove? What will it change?"

It was the sort of pretty little speech—that world-weary, what's-the-point-in-going-on? bullshit—that always pisses me off.

"Lady, you don't know a goddamned thing about me. You want to know what I told Henry? Two words: make peace."

She looked at me for a moment, surprised, and then shook here head.

"But...but how can you possibly...after he did... *that*?"

"How can I...? A second ago it was, '*Oh, when will the violence end?*' Then I tell you, and you say, '*So soon?*' Make up your fucking mind!"

I stormed away and pulled my bedroom door shut behind me, before we ended up screaming at each other, which would have been bad for the kids'—the *other* kids'—morale. I found myself muttering under my breath as I got the shower fired up, and then I shook my head and actually smiled a little.

My world would never be the same again, but come hell or high water, I could apparently count on Marfoglia to take my mind off my troubles by making me so goddamned mad I wanted to bite steel nails in half.

But much later that night, after I turned in, I dreamed about an omelet—a hutsul omelet, egg whites only, with soy nuts, and Thai chili sauce on the side.

What kind of nutcase dreams about an omelet?

TWELVE

You could see the *K'Pook*—the C-lighter we were going to take to Seewauk—off and on for several hours, growing larger in the aft vistaports on the observation deck. You only saw it off and on, because the shuttle had its ass pointed almost right at it and was still making deceleration burns and little course corrections to intersect its orbit around the gas giant.

The *K'Pook*'s configuration wasn't that different from the shuttle, except it was bigger, and instead of conventional thrusters in back, it had the glowing, sparkling, spiderweb tracery of the J-field generator. Other than that, it had its own big wheels for passengers and crew, and then long, angular cargo modules coupled to the central spine fore and aft of the wheel, with a command module out front. A Newton tug hovered nearby, to shift cargo modules back and forth and then to break the *K'Pook* out of its parking orbit when the time came.

Our shuttle had four or five cargo modules to add to the C-lighter's load, and it would take some modules back to Peezgtaan as well. We'd transfer over first in a jolly boat, and then the tug would deal with the cargo transfers while we were getting settled. We'd already gotten our cabin assignments on the *K'Pook*, and the four of us had pored over her deck plans so we knew where we were going in case we got separated. I'd already picked out a couple places that looked like low-traffic areas with possible hides, and we had given code names to them—those were our rally points in case something went wrong.

Security talk still frightened Barraki and Tweezaa, but they were interested in it as well, and having a plan they were part of made it—well, maybe a bit of an adventure. Of course, it was an adventure that had already gotten their father killed right in front of them, so it wasn't exactly big fun. But it was exciting, that's for sure, and having an active role to play made them feel less like helpless victims.

My main concern was that there were passengers already on board the C-lighter, through passengers from someplace else and headed toward Akaampta, like us. The odds of them being—by coincidence—part of whatever outfit was after Barraki and Tweezaa were very long. A more likely danger was that whoever was after us could have gotten a tight-beam message to someone on the C-lighter—passenger or crew—and made a deal of some kind. That was still a long shot, since it meant knowing who to contact and how, but it wasn't quite as remote.

My biggest immediate worry was the time from when we got on the little jolly boat that would take us over to the *K'Pook* to the time we'd be in our new cabins. I'd had to pack the Hawker and LeMatt in our luggage and turn it over to the purser's staff, and until I got them unpacked over there, I'd feel naked. If *I* were going to hit us, this was exactly when I'd do it.

My worries were unfounded, as it turned out, and I wouldn't even have mentioned all of this except it's important for you to remember that, even when nothing bad was happening, we were always on edge, always waiting for the other shoe to drop. Constant tension can wear you down after a while. That, I suppose, is the edge that a professional has.

Well, "professional" sounds kind of pretentious, doesn't it? Let's say that it's something you learn from experience, that this is going to go on a long time, and that if you let yourself get lulled into a sense of routine by the constancy of danger, you are asking to get killed. My staying alert, staying constantly attuned to the smallest changes in the environment, would make a real difference later in our journey, and save lives—just not as many as I'd have liked.

One of the first things I did when we got settled on the *K'Pook* was strike up an acquaintance with the chief purser, Walter Wu. Walter was an interesting guy. He was trained as a quantum physicist and here he was, chief purser on a C-lighter, making sure meals got served on time and everybody had clean linen. Father Bill taught me that you can learn something interesting from almost anybody, and that you can't always anticipate what that might be. I figured I might learn something about physics from Walter; instead, I learned about intellectual property law.

That's okay. A guy in my line of work can never know too much about the law.

I made it a point to introduce myself to Walter because I needed a favor. Not a big favor, at least in terms of what *he* had to put out, but it could make a big difference to *us*. I'm getting ahead of myself, but since the favor ended up not being that important, I'll satisfy your curiosity and then we can move on.

Communication is at the speed of travel or the speed of light, whichever is faster. You can jump objects with their own J-field generators between stars, and that beats light speed, so every ship has a burst transmitter, and when it jumps into a new system, it executes a data dump that updates the local databases. The point is, there's no way to "phone ahead," so when you get to where you have to make a travel connection, seats are first come, first served. The C-lighter we'd be connecting to in the Seewauk system was called *Brukata*, and there was no way of knowing how many berths would be open.

So when the time came, I wanted to be able to suggest to my friend Walter that when we emerged from J-space in the Seewauk system, he transmit our request for reservations, then go have a cup of tea, come back, and transmit everyone else's. Nothing really illegal about it, just a favor for a friend. I'd even buy the tea for him—slip him a hundred-chip and expect him to keep the change.

That would come later, and it did, and he was happy to do it. But in the meantime, I got to know the story of a physicist who had become the manager of a moving hotel. That's how Walter said it, and in terms of a skill set, that was pretty much it in a nutshell, but it was more than just that, wasn't it? It was physics, and it was happening all around him.

Walter got his education at the High-Energy Physics Institute in Beijing, which is in China back on Earth. He did a spell at a lab in Switzerland, too, but his project funding got cut, and he was out of a job. You'd think a guy trained in quantum physics could get a job busting up atoms almost anywhere, especially since all communication and most macro-commerce in the *Cottohazz* relies on space travel. Turns out, you'd be wrong. There's actually very little demand—on Earth—for experimental physicists.

"How can that be?" I asked after I'd known him a couple days. "I mean, damned near everything relies on moving stuff from world to world, and—correct me if I'm wrong on this—physics is kinda important to that, isn't it?"

He'd laughed. We were down on the observation deck, which was a lot like the O-deck on the shuttle—but with a lower ceiling and generally not as nice, at least to my eye. *K'Pook* was Varoki-designed, top to bottom, and it was already making me a little jumpy. Marfoglia and the kids were with us, but Barraki and Tweezaa were over by the clear rear wall, looking back along the length of the ship at the sparkling J-field generator. The Newton tug had already cut us loose, and we were coasting to the jump point. Marfoglia was sitting with Walter and me, but reading—her preferred way of avoiding the need to interact with me.

"Yes, physics is important," Walter answered. "But you can't count electrons in your backyard. That takes money, and it's hard to spend money if you can't make money in return.

"Back when Terra joined the *Cottohazz*, the price for membership was to buy into its IP—intellectual property—covenants. We figured it would get us access to an amazing body of knowledge—and it did, but it turns out we can look, but we can't touch. All the J-space physics is intellectual property of the people that came up with it—or rather the big mercantile houses that own it, since the patents have all been bought up. Even the early quantum tunneling research we Humans had already done—the precursor work to J-space physics—was covered, since the Varoki had done it earlier. *Cottohazz* IP laws don't recognize coincidental discovery, and there's no expiration date when it becomes public domain.

"It's all called 'foundation knowledge,' and any out-growth of proprietary foundation knowledge becomes the property of the underlying patent holder."

"So, if you come up with a better mousetrap," I said, "the guy already making mousetraps owns it?"

He nodded.

"Well, that sucks!"

He nodded again, and looked out the observation port at the stars twinkling in the distance. What was it I'd thought looking up at the stars back on Peezgtaan? A diamond necklace hopelessly out of reach? But Walter could actually have reached out and grabbed hold of it—except it was against the rules. So he went to work on a C-lighter, because it was as close as he could come to touching those stars.

And sometimes I think I've got it hard.

Later that day, when we were getting close to the jump point, I had a funny thought, and I looked Walter up again.

"Walter, all this J-space 'foundation knowledge' stuff—who owns it?"

"Varoki trading houses—the big families, *e-Varokiim*," he answered, and shrugged.

"Yeah, but which ones? Do you know?"

He scratched his head and frowned in thought.

"Well, it's a bit complicated," he started, "since there were parallel research lines and different discoveries that seemed unrelated at first but ended up as converging research paths. As I understand it, it's all rolled into a big patent cluster that's jointly owned by seven or eight Varoki merchant houses."

"Are the e-Traak one of them?" I asked, and I tried to keep the excitement out of my voice.

"Of course. Simki-Traak's one of the main interstellar players, based mostly on the patents owned by the e-Traak."

"What if those patents somehow got into Human hands?" I asked. "Ownership, I mean?"

He just looked at me for a couple seconds, and then shrugged.

"I have no idea. I mean, I can't imagine it happening, unless they sold them, and . . . they'd *never* do that. I don't know how the law would shake out on it, but it would change everything," he said. Then his eyes wandered a bit, thinking about it, and he repeated "everything," but more softly.

Yeah. *Everything*.

We made the jump to the Seewauk system without incident. Well, there are no real opportunities for "incidents" in J-space; you just fall into a sparkling well of light, and then you come out the other end. You feel a little sick, you break out in a sweat, the ship warms up a bit, but that's it. No time passes in the ship; one moment you're one place, the next moment you're someplace else. Walter says they know that no time passes—as opposed to us just being asleep or something—because of some radioactive decay stuff that's over my head, but I trust him on that.

Time passes outside the ship, though—a few hours, a few days, depending on how far you're jumping and whether you're jumping across the axis of galactic movement or along it—and with or against the "current." Why different times? I don't know. Walter doesn't know, and he's honest enough to admit it. I've asked other rocket-science guys, and some of them start mumbling about relativistic effects and the elasticity of time, but I can tell bullshit when I hear it. Bottom line is nobody really knows why.

Do you find that kind of spooky? I sure do.

That's one of the reasons—maybe the big reason, the jumps are to and from the outer parts of stellar systems. Given the fact that time gets a little variable in jump, and interstellar astrogation is as much art as science, you don't want to be coming out anywhere near an inhabited world—if you're off a bit, you can make life real ugly real quick for a whole lot of people. You also don't want to come out in the middle of any drifting space junk. Since about ninety-nine point nine nine percent of the matter in a star system is concentrated on the plain of the ecliptic, you always come out above or below it. Even so, there's always a trace residue of molecular hydrogen in the space you suddenly occupy; that's why everything—including you—heats up a little.

They say it's safer than taking an auto cab. Sure. What did you expect them to say?

The astrogator must have been pretty good, because we came out in spectacular visual range of Rakanka, the system's gas giant, and with a residual vector pretty close to right on the money. Looking at Rakanka's pink and blue and green atmosphere reminded me of one of Arrie's tie-dyed tee shirts, and I felt a sharp pang of loneliness.

I might never see Arrie again. June and Father Bill were gone forever, and I might never see Henry or Big Meg or Phil the Gil, or anybody else I'd ever cared about, ever again. There was a whole big galaxy out there—at least what the *Cottohazz* had explored of it—and I guess it was full of great stuff, you know? But I wondered if I'd ever again eat an omelet at H'Tank's, hanging out over the river rapids 150 meters below.

There have got to be places a whole lot better than the Crack, but there can't be any place quite like it, and I was missing it.

I guess I was still thinking hard about the Crack when Marfoglia came up beside me, because I didn't notice her until she cleared her throat.

"Oh, sorry," I said. "Thinking about old friends."

She nodded.

"I just wanted to say how sorry I was about...your friend. And what I said afterward," she said.

"Water under the bridge," I answered. "'Grieve—but live.' That's what Father Bill would have said—did say quite a few times. You never knew Father Bill."

"He started the soup kitchen at St. Michael's, didn't he? There's a privately funded bronze bust of him at the Municipal Center," she said, and then she looked at me, brow compressed in thought. "Did...*you* fund that bust?"

"Yup. Bill saw something in me...something nobody else did."

"What?"

"Value."

She looked at me oddly for a moment, thinking that over. "How did he die?" she asked.

"Rapid Onset ATZL."

"The degenerative nerve disease? You know, they have a new drug that's supposed to do wonders on those nerve diseases. Maybe you haven't heard about it out here."

"Neurocine," I said.

She looked surprised, but nodded.

"It was in trial stage when he started showing symptoms. I found out about it. It took some doing, but I got some. Cost a fortune, but I didn't mind. I'd have paid anything to keep him around. The son of a bitch wouldn't take it. Know why? It cost too much for just one man, that's what he said. He said, 'Sasha, if you care about me, you'll take the money for this medicine and spend it for everyone else down here, to make them healthy.'"

Her eyes got wide for a moment as the pieces fell into place.

"The clinic?" she asked. I nodded. She thought about that for a while.

"He must have been quite a man," she said.

"Oh, he was that. I never heard him raise his voice once, all the years I knew him. Never saw him even mildly irritated. I saw him sad a few times, but mostly he was...blissful. Even right at the very end."

"Like St. Francis," she said.

I laughed.

"Yeah. Except Bill really *could* fly."

She looked at me, confused.

"Before he was a priest, he was a mike trooper," I explained. "Five combat jumps from orbit! Step out of a ship with nothing between you and reentry burn-up but a couple meters of composite foam, some stupid little guidance rocket, and a parasail. You know what that takes? If you do, you're one up on me. I can't even imagine it. *Five* jump stars! No idea how many training descents he made. He told me once, as he was getting ready for a descent he noticed he kept looking up instead of down, and he figured that was a sign he was supposed to get into a different line of work.

"So, yeah, quite a guy. But not *exactly* like St. Francis, was he?"

An hour later I was still looking at that big tie-dyed soccer ball floating in space when Walter found me, his face a mixture of excitement and fear.

"What's up, pal?" I asked.

He looked around to make sure nobody was in hearing range and then leaned close to whisper in my ear.

"You're going to have a longer layover at Rakanka Highstation than you thought."

"What? The *Brukata*'s already booked?" I asked.

He shook his head and wiped perspiration from his forehead with a trembling hand.

"No. *Brukata*'s been blown up."

THIRTEEN

Eighteen hours later, the Newton tug docked with us. Eighteen hours is a long time when you know something pretty bad has happened, but you don't know exactly what or why. Eventually Walter got the go-ahead to tell the rest of the passengers, but from the way the crew was acting—all jumpy and weird— they'd already figured out that something was up. The word was that *Brukata* had sustained major damage (he didn't use the expression "blown up" this time) and that it appeared to be the result of sabotage.

I passed Hlontaa in a companionway and he didn't say anything to me, but he looked at me with one of those half-smug, half-phony-sad "I told you so what do you expect from people like you it's not your fault it's just what you are" sort of looks that, if I weren't on the job, if I didn't have two little kids to think about, just might have gotten him the beating of his life. Instead, I continued to successfully control my violent urges.

Everyone—not just Hlontaa—assumed that the sabotage was by Human terrorists. They were probably right. First question a provost on a case will ask himself is "Who's got a motive?" Who's got a motive to go around blowing stuff up? Probably the people who are stuck with the shittiest end of the stick. It was like some sick experiment: show people paradise, then lock them out, and see what happens.

Speaking philosophically, of course. On a real-world level, if I could get my hands on the knuckleheads who blew the *Brukata*, they'd never blow another ship.

One hour post-docking, the purser's staff had all the stateroom furniture secured, we were all strapped into our "wall" couches, the big wheel was locked down, and the tug started its long burn to slow us to orbital velocity.

By then we could see Rakanka Highstation in the monitor, a silvery gray collection of components, none of which looked as if they exactly matched. That's what happens when you keep adding shit to an orbital station over the course of eighty years.

The main structural component was the spine, and it pointed straight "down" toward Rakanka. There were a couple different sets of counter-rotating wheels, as well as a bunch of non-moving structures, including big photovoltaic power panels, and some things that looked like the components of a gigantic virtual sensor array.

Brukata was in a parking orbit a couple klicks away. Even at a distance, you could tell she was hurt bad, her spine bent—probably broken—the big wheels no longer aligned, the J-field generator black and dead. There was some floating junk in between *Brukata* and Rakanka Highstation—you could see it sparkle now and then as the pieces slowly tumbled and caught bits

of starlight or the colored glow of Rakanka itself—
which suggested they'd moved the wreck away from
the station after the explosion.

I would have, too. Lightning hardly ever strikes the
same place twice, but when it does—well, the second
time you get hit, you feel like a real idiot.

There was a Co-Gozhak cruiser in a close parking
orbit to the station, with most of its orange-and-
black-striped troop pods detached—they were stuck
to the station like tumors. The station was going to
be crawling with Co-Gozhak combat infantry, probably
in a really bad mood and inclined to look up every
arriving passenger's ass with a proctoscope.

"What happens now?" Marfoglia asked. She and
both of the kids were looking at me, and the kids—
who, unlike Marfoglia, seemed capable of feeling
and expressing emotions other than indifference and
anger—were frightened.

"Plan B," I answered. "Rakanka High will be thick
with security now, and our travel documents won't
fool them."

"Because we aren't in their database," Marfoglia
said, and I nodded. She wasn't stupid.

"That's right. Those aren't corporate stiffs over there
now; those are real professionals. And we're four people
who aren't in their database . . . *anywhere*. Fortunately,
none of us—so far as we know—are actually wanted
for anything under our real identities, so we go with
Plan B: when all else fails, tell the truth.

"We'll show our real papers, and tell them we're
under 'travel covers' to get Barraki and Tweezaa home.
The *e-Varokiim* do it all the time. The covers, we
say, are partly to avoid publicity, but mostly because

we're worried about another attempt on their lives. The murder itself will have been in the flash dump from *K'Pook* when we broke J-space, so they'll have that much in their database already."

"But the travel covers—don't the legal ones have to be registered with the authorities?" she asked.

"Sure, but bureaucracy grinds slow sometimes, especially on a backwater like the Crack. It's easy to figure that the cover registration didn't make it to the *K'Pook*'s data dump—some asshole forgot to forward the right form or something. Happens all the time. The important thing is, everything else lines up right in their database. Remember, they aren't looking for *us*; they're looking for saboteurs. They're concerned about threats; we'll just be anomalies."

To be honest, I wasn't as confident of all this as I sounded, but it was important that they be confident, because I figured I was a lot better actor than they were. The worst thing they could do was look nervous. Of course, I couldn't tell them that, because that *would* make them nervous.

I was plenty nervous, myself. If the plan to kill the two kids really did trace back to someone inside the Co-Gozhak provost corps, there might be a data dump with the ship listing Tweezaa and Barraki as fugitives.

Or maybe not, since that would get them publicly into custody, and from there it would be tough to touch them. Well, not tough to touch them, but tough to do it without ramifications. How concerned were these guys about ramifications? If they really were imbedded in the Co-Gozhak, probably very concerned.

So a more dangerous possibility was that the data dump just had us listed as "persons of interest." Then

they'd let us go on our way, but quietly inform somebody somewhere where we were, and then silencers
would start to show up.

I did the only reasonable thing under the circumstances. I took a nap.

The jolly boat off-loaded us at a fairly small cargo
bay, the magnetic harnesses took us to an elevator, and
that took us down to the body of one of the wheels,
where there was gravity and we could unharness. Then
we had to thread our way down a corridor to screening.

The first things I noticed, once we got out of the
elevator, were the big, grim-looking Zaschaan in the
mottled gray fatigues of Co-Gozhak dirt soldiers.
We passengers were in a line down the middle of
the corridor, and there were Zaschaan on either
side, every ten meters or so. They weren't packing
polite crowd-control weapons, either; they had room
sweepers—selective fire 31mm "thud guns." Not even
the Zaschan were nuts enough to load sabot or HX
grenades inside a pressure hull, so that meant either
flexible baton rounds or multi-flechette canister, and,
knowing Zaschaan, my money was on the canister. If
these assholes started shooting in this corridor, as full
as it was, in about twenty seconds anyone who wasn't
dead would be up to their knees in blood.

I'll say one thing about using Zaschaan troopers
as hall monitors—nobody tried to jump the line, and
whatever bitching there was, it was subdued. The line
was moving pretty slowly, and it gave me time to try
to remember some of my pigeon Szawa. I was seven
or eight years rusty, and even when I was using it
regularly there weren't a lot of subjects that I could

converse about. Fortunately, there weren't a lot of subjects which interested the average Zaschaan grunt. The next trooper on my right looked more bored than pissed off—and since those are usually the only two moods you get to choose between with these guys, I figured I had a winner.

"Hey, Corporal," I said in Szawa, letting him know that I was enough on the ball to read the rank brassard on his shoulder. He looked at me—he had to look down a little—and I gestured at him and another of the soldiers.

"Where the monkey grunts? Shit duty like this—job for them."

Of course, I didn't say monkey—I used the name of a small hairy animal from the Zaschaan home world known as a high-strung troublemaker, but monkey's a close-enough translation. *Monkey grunt* was Zaschaan slang for Human soldiers.

They say that the development of intelligence in a species is tied to communication, and I believe it. I don't think it's a coincidence that every intelligent species we know of has remarkably sophisticated facial expressions, provided you know how to read them. For a moment, the Zaschaan corporal looked like he wanted to spit. Instead, he belched—a low, smelly rumble of disdain—from his lower mouth, and then spoke from the upper one.

"Fuck you, monkey boy," he answered, in the high-pitched nasal voice that always comes as a surprise at first, issuing from that massive body. But he was still bored rather than pissed off, so I grinned at him and shook my head.

"Zack corporal too big—hurt my ass."

That got a rumbling grunt of a laugh from his lower mouth, and it tickled his curiosity a little, too.

"Where you learn Szawa?" he asked.

I held my right arm across my chest as if it were a rifle at port arms, my index and middle fingers extended like a two-barreled pistol. That was the Co-Gozhak tactical hand signal for an armed soldier. He nodded, but his eyes narrowed a little.

"Which side?"

I laughed, because it was a stupid question.

"The one talks to Zacks in Szawa instead of pointy light."

Pointy light—laser fire—was more Zack soldier slang. He relaxed a little and nodded.

"Monkey grunts got sent away," he said, finally answering my original question.

"Lucky bastards," I said. He looked at me without nodding.

"Maybe not so lucky," he answered. "Couple monkey grunts the ones that blew up the C-lighter. Maybe more of them knew about it, but didn't say anything. Maybe whole cohort goes some place dark, gets talked to long time. *Long* fucking time."

Oh, great.

It had been almost ten years since two Human Co-Gozhak brigades mutinied and went rogue on Nishtaaka, but nobody in uniform had forgotten. Since then, almost all Co-Gozhak combat brigades had been made up of cohorts from different races, even though that made logistics and medical support a bitch, and unit coopera-tion . . . well . . . spotty. The thought that another Human cohort might have gone bad was just the sort of thing to drive the *Cottohazz*'s military brass ape shit. Any local commander's first instinct would be to come down as hard as he could, as quickly as he could, just to cover his ass to the guys upstairs. It would go hard on the six hundred or so guys in the cohort, not because they'd done anything, but just because some dickless asshole would think he had to "take decisive action"—and nobody who mattered was going to shed any tears over a couple hundred monkey grunts.

"Anybody hurt on the C-lighter?" I asked.

He nodded.

"Maybe dozen ship crew, three monkey grunts, and five brothers. All dead."

Brothers—what Zaschaan dirt soldiers call the others in their cohort.

The line had been moving a step every now and then, and I'd edged a little past him. The gap had opened ahead of me and it was time to move along, catch up with Marfoglia and the two kids, who I saw were watching me carry on a Szawa conversation with the corporal in openmouthed surprise. We were also almost to the end of the line, to the interview rooms.

"What's your name?" I asked him.

"Brollo Kootlun· ah Kap," he answered. "You?"

"Aleksandr Sergeyevich Naradnyo," I answered, like him using my patronymic. I couldn't remember the last time I had. "My brothers call me Sasha," I added. I didn't offer my hand—Zaschaan don't particularly like being touched.

"Sorry for your brothers, Brollo," I said, and I meant it. It's not like soldiers have a really great life or anything, and these were just five guys doing their job—five big, ugly, cranky guys, to be sure, but that wasn't a capital offense last time I checked.

He nodded, and I walked ahead.

"Hey, fuck you, monkey boy," he called after me, and it was about as friendly as Zaschaan get.

Without looking back, I patted the top of my head three times with my open right hand, another tactical hand signal—*take cover* in a combat situation, but between soldiers out of combat it just meant *keep your head down, pal.*

I heard another rumble of laughter.

"Where did you learn their language?" Marfoglia demanded when I caught up.

"I'll tell you when I know you better. Look sharp— showtime."

The door to one of the screening rooms opened and the Zaschaan senior sergeant at the head of the line waved us in. There was a Human seated at the table, wearing the black and red uniform of a Co-Gozhak provost corps captain, with two gold crescent-shaped gorgets dangling from chains around his neck.

"I have all of our travel documents," Marfoglia said in her cold, authoritative voice, with just the right touch of bitchy boredom. She was perfect—that's the virtue of typecasting. When she handed over two sets of documents for each of us, the Human provo captain looked up, interested. His gorgets made a faint jingling sound as he reached for the documents.

"I am escorting the two e-Traak heirs home," she went on. "Mr. Naradnyo is our security coordinator. These are our travel covers."

Also very good—a minimum of words. Never explain anything until they ask for an explanation. Otherwise you look as if you've got a story all cooked up you're dying to tell—which, of course, you do, and you are.

The captain hand-scanned the codes on the documents, looked at his viewer for a moment, and then nodded and handed the documents back to Marfoglia.

"Very well, Dr. Marfoglia. We're sorry for the inconvenience. We're bringing a replacement vessel here, but it won't be available for another eight days, I'm afraid. Of course, I will make sure that your party has priority reservations for Akaampta, but beyond that, I'm afraid there isn't anything I can do to expedite your travel."

Of course, of all the things it was possible for the captain to have said, this was the one that we had never anticipated. Marfoglia hesitated.

"The travel cover... it's in your database. Correct?" she asked.

He looked back down at his viewer and nodded.

"Yes. Everything is in order."

"I only ask...," she said, stumbling, not quite sure what to say. "There was a problem earlier..."

He shrugged.

"Perhaps a cross-referencing error," he offered. "It seems to have been corrected."

I fought down the urge to vault over the desk and look at the damned viewer myself, but Marfoglia snapped out of her momentary paralysis and recovered like a pro, taking the documents from the captain and dropping them into her briefcase in one motion. She said, "Come, children," in aGavoosh, and four pairs of wobbly knees carried us through the door.

"That was lucky," Marfoglia whispered to me, once we were out into the corridor. I just looked at her.

Lucky?

We were dead.

FOURTEEN

Whenever I have a very big problem to solve, I find it helps to lay it out as clearly as possible, so I can see what I have going for me and what obstacles are in my way. Also, it gives me something to do in lieu of hyperventilating.

Okay. We were on an orbital station light-years from any of my friends or contacts. Both our real and cover identities were in the security database, associated with each other, and somebody with access to that database wanted us dead—and had the resources to make that happen. We were sitting ducks at Rakanka High, and it's a safe bet that whoever was coming to kill us would show up before our ride did.

See? When you lay it out that way, it gets very simple, and the solution becomes obvious.

"What do you mean, *obvious*?" Marfoglia demanded.

"Well," I explained, "obviously we can't stay here and wait until the replacement C-lighter arrives, so we have to leave. Obviously we can't leave as passengers, because our identities are compromised, so we have to leave as cargo. Obviously, we are not—legally speaking—cargo, so we have to find someone with a flexible approach to the law, and who is leaving in the next couple of days."

"And going to Akaampta," she added, but I shook my head.

"Let's don't complicate things. Our immediate problem is staying alive, not getting to Akaampta. I don't care where they're going, as long as it's away from here."

She was annoyed—nothing new there—and my explanation didn't do much to reduce her irritation level. Instead she took a few paces back and forth, thinking it over, looking for a different way out.

"Where are you even going to find someone?" she demanded.

I just looked at her. We were on an orbital station that was a jump transit hub. About a dozen commercial ships coasted in nearby parking orbits, and only half of them had major line logos painted on the sides. Commercial ships don't make any money just hanging around, so they were all going someplace, and independents always need extra cash. The difficult part was going to be approaching them in such a way that they didn't think we were Co-Gozhak spooks trying to trap them into an illegal move so the *Cottohazz* could impound their ship. That part would be a delicate dance number, but *finding* them was going to be ridiculously easy.

"And how do you know which ones are honest captains who would turn us in to the authorities instead of taking a bribe?"

"The honest ones have already lost their ships," I answered. "If they've got a mortgage, they'll take the money."

More nervous pacing back and forth. Finally she stopped, her back to me and her arms folded, looking at the wall viewer with Rakanka filling the image. There was a big storm down there, one of those gas giant meta-storms visible from space, with an eye thousands of kilometers across. I thought she was looking at it, but I guess she was just trying to gather herself for what came next.

"How are we going to pay them?" she asked.

"*We?*" I asked. "Are you pregnant, or do you have a mouse in your pocket?"

She turned to look at me, anger on her face, but something else, too, something the anger was meant to cover. Panic?

"I paid you up front, and I had to pay Markov a deposit as well. All I have left is about four thousand *Cottos*."

"What do you mean, all *you* have left? Those kids..."

No, come to think of it, those kids might be rich beyond any mortal's dreams of avarice, but they were just kids. They had no access to bank accounts or stock portfolios. So they were all traveling on Marfoglia's cash, and she was just visiting on Peezgtaan, so probably wouldn't have had all of her assets available. She'd had a fair chunk of change, but I'd taken forty-five thousand of it, no telling how much Kolya had taken, so she'd gone through a nice little fortune in the past few weeks, and now she was down to her last couple grand.

"How long have you known those kids?" I asked.

"I never met them until Mr. Arrakatlak contacted me, the day I came to you," she answered.

"What did Arrie promise you?"

"Nothing," she answered, and I could see she was telling the truth. No pledge from Arrie and no family member to promise her reimbursement when and if she got the kids home safe.

"Then why?" I asked.

"I'll tell you when I know you better," she answered defiantly.

Touché.

Now this was an interesting situation, and one of considerable ethical complexity. My agreement was to get them safely to Akaampta, for which we had agreed to a price and an itinerary. The itinerary was broken—or rather sticking to it would likely get us all killed—and the client did not have sufficient resources to adjust the travel arrangements. Under the circumstances, was I obligated to stay with them until the silencers showed up and killed us all? Or could I, in good conscience, simply refund the unearned part of my fee and walk away? This was, after all, a business deal, not a suicide pact.

Not that I considered walking away. It was just, on a theoretical level, an interesting ethical problem. But on a practical level . . .

"Okay, here's the deal," I said. "From now on, we travel on my nickel, and at the end of the trip, I will be fully reimbursed—*by you*—plus an additional fifteen percent of whatever my out-of-pocket comes to. Is this acceptable?"

She looked surprised, but nodded quickly. I wasn't rich by any means, but since I was relocating, I was liquid—everything carried along in the form of bearer bonds and cash—and cash opens doors.

"You understand that if the e-Traaks stiff you, it's not my problem, right? *You* still owe me."

She nodded again.

As I think back on it now, I don't really have a good explanation for why I didn't consider leaving them. I didn't leave, and perhaps that's what's important—the choice I made. But it's interesting that I felt no urge to do otherwise.

At least *I* think it's interesting. Of course, I find everything about myself interesting. We each think we're the most fascinating person in the world, but we can't all be, can we?

The only sushi bar on Rakanka Highstation was about as good as you'd imagine, considering it was nearly a hundred straight-line light-years from any place where Human-edible fish swam. Since room on the station was limited, and there were only so many Humans around anyway, the sushi bar doubled as a veggie burger joint. You want fries with your *unagi*? No problem.

The menu was almost all Human-specific. Most restaurants have a couple dishes available for other races, just to cater to mixed parties, and this was no exception, but the clientele was overwhelmingly Terran. I looked around and the only non-Humans in sight were Barraki and Tweezaa—sitting with Marfoglia two tables away and eating some kind of fried brown starchy stuff—and a pair of Zack dirt soldiers with slung thud guns, standing outside the dining area but keeping a grim eye on everything going on inside. It was a Human gathering place, and Humans were the problem, so keep an eye on them.

Everyone in the restaurant was aware of the two Zacks, and everyone knew why they were there, so the food was seasoned with resentment, and just a touch of fear. But the patrons also stole occasional glances at their fellow diners, and wondered. The young man and woman leaning together, their heads almost touching—were they lovers, or anarchists figuring out what to bomb next? The two families having a boisterous dinner—were the noisy kids just a cover, a distraction?

Suspicion is a disease, and once it infects a community, the suspicion becomes the reality. Once you start thinking that the parents *might* be using their children as a cover, then whether those particular parents are or aren't, you hate them anyway, just for being *capable* of it.

Well, the good news was that it rendered us real conspirators fairly inconspicuous. I pow-wowed over beer and *tofu katsu* with the master and mate of a Terran registry freighter called the *Long Shot* out of Bronstein's World and inbound for K'Tok. K'Tok wasn't Akaampta, but it was in the right direction, and only one jump away for anything with a good set of legs on it—maybe two jumps if we weren't as picky about what we flew on.

There were Varoki independents in-station as well, but I thought I'd have better luck with the Humans. Although I'd told Marfoglia that independents were all a bit crooked, that wasn't really true. It *was* true for most Human captains, though, for a couple reasons. First, being a little bit shady had become an element

of Human pride out here. We might be at the bottom
of the pecking order when it came to most things,
but by God we could steal with the best of them.
Second reason kind of went along with that: it was
harder to make it on the level as a Human-mastered
ship, because everyone else in the *Cottohazz* figured
you were a crook anyway, so it was okay to screw you
every chance they got, just to stay even.

So we sat there and talked. Actually, the mate
and I talked; the captain just shoveled down the
tofu katsu as if he hadn't eaten in a week, and he
was skinny enough he might not have. His hair was
dark and straight, thinning on top, and there was an
Asian cast to his features, with mischief lines around
his eyes. The mate had introduced him as Joe Lee
Ping. The mate—guy named Jim Turncrank—was short
and stocky, with hard eyes and an unsmiling mouth
that told me the best thing you could say about his
life was that he'd made it this far. If he'd had any
joy in recent memory, he hid it well, and nobody
hides it *that* well. The captain of the *Long Shot* was
the opposite. He wasn't just enjoying the *tofu katsu*,
he was savoring it, relishing it, thinking hard about
how good it was as he chewed, so he'd be sure to
remember it later. I liked him right away. Here was
a guy knew how to live.

I laid out our problem, giving them as much truth
as I felt comfortable with. I didn't want to make a
big deal about the Co-Gozhak maybe being after us,
in case that scared them away, but I had to explain
that I figured there was a guy inside leaking to his
pals outside, which was why we needed to stay below
the sensor horizon. I also let them know the general

situation with the kids, but didn't tell them their real name; a name as big as e-Traak would scare too many people away—probably scare away everyone with any sense.

I got done, and the whole time it was as if the captain was in a different world, or at least at a different table. But when Turncrank looked at him, something passed between them—not a yes, but not quite a no, either.

Turncrank settled back in his chair, took a pull on his beer, and looked me over.

"So, what's *your* story? You're, like, Russian, huh?"

"Ukrainian . . . or my parents were. I'm second generation Crack Trash—don't even speak the old lingo, except a few dirty words. No story really worth telling. I ran some rackets back in the Crack, but I had a . . . a falling out with senior management, so figured it was time to move on. This gig came along and I took it. Not sure it was the best move I ever made, but sometimes the timing forces your hand."

The captain was watching me now as he continued to chew, and he nodded and grunted his agreement with that.

"So that's it?" Turncrank asked. "You're just some small-time crook from Peezgtaan? You act like you've been around, and there's talk about some guy shooting the shit with Zack dirt soldiers like he was their brother. That wouldn't be you, would it?"

So they'd done at least a little homework.

"Yeah. I soldiered a bit ten years back."

"Where?" he asked.

"Nishtaaka," I answered, and his eyes narrowed in suspicion and disbelief. The captain grinned and shook his head, looking down at the food, as if I'd been caught in some kind of lie.

"Every swinging dick from here to Sol claims they were on Nishtaaka," Turncrank said, scowling. "Thing is, I *was* there, and I don't remember you."

"Lotta people went to Nishtaaka," I said, but he shook his head.

"Lots of guys went, but not that many came back, and after the surrender they kept all of us in a processing compound for seven weeks before they shipped us out—those they pardoned. I figure I know about everyone still alive from the Ram and Gray Phantom brigades, at least by sight."

"Never said I was in one of the rogue brigades."

"Then what the hell . . . ?"

"A.C.G.," I answered. "Third Cohort, Peezgtaan Loyal Volunteers—The Piss-Can Rangers to our friends."

The captain's eyes got a little bigger, and he glanced at his mate, as if expecting trouble. A.C.G. was short for *Attatti Cottohazz Gozhakampta*—Co-Gozhak Reserves.

"So it's probably just as well we didn't run into each other," I added, and smiled.

Turncrank's face remained a sour, but otherwise expressionless, mask. There was silence for maybe ten seconds, and then he spoke.

"You guys sucked."

"So I've heard it said."

"Where were you?"

"We went in behind the Zacks at Sikander's Mountain. Then they shifted us over to the Garden. Mostly I pushed 'bots, while we had some. Resupply was all screwed up anyway, so once you guys broke the Needle, and everyone ran out of 'bots to push, the leather-heads pushed us—foot patrols, sensor sweeps, you know."

"Yeah, you're breaking my heart." After a moment he asked, "Kill anyone?"

I looked him in the eye and nodded.

He thought for a while and then shifted uncomfortably in his chair, scowling.

"I don't know," he said finally. "You're pretty damned chummy with leather-heads and Zacks."

He wanted me to say something then—deny it, justify it, something—but I didn't. After a moment his scowl turned into a puzzled frown and he shook his head.

"Well, maybe if you were a spook, you'd be telling us how much you hated them," he admitted reluctantly. "Maybe you're for real. *Maybe*. But maybe you're just a real smart liar. If I hadn't told you I was with the Rams on Nishtaaka, how do I know you wouldn't have stuck with some kind of story about being a rogue brigade hero?"

So I rolled up my sleeve and showed him the Piss-Can Rangers tattoo on my left forearm, right below the bandage from the knife wound.

"I don't got a Ram Brigade tattoo hidden away anywhere, but since I'm not about to do a striptease, you're just gonna have to take my word for it."

The captain laughed then, and even Turncrank grunted what might have been something a little like a laugh. Marfoglia and the two kids looked over, but without any alarm. Obviously things were going well.

The captain leaned over and slapped my shoulder with more force than I'd have thought a skinny guy like him would have.

"You have a sense of humor, Sasha Naradnyo. I like that. And I think you have been here and there. I tell you the truth, were it simply you we would have nothing to do with you, but the children ... not even the Co-Gozhak use children as agents. You and your people are welcome to share our voyage."

"Ah, shit," Turncrank said in resignation.

"Pay him no heed," the captain said, and smiled. "He is not nearly as ferocious as he pretends. And speaking of ferocity ... your lady has that appearance."

"Yeah, and appearances aren't always deceiving. She's not my lady, though. I'm between ladies right now."

"Oh. I sense the last one may have hurt you."

"She tried to murder me."

"Ah, yes. Very bad for relationship."

Marfoglia and the kids joined us after that, and we actually had a pretty nice dinner. Captain Ping started talking like an old-time pirate and made Marfoglia and the kids laugh—me, too, once in a while—and if Turncrank wasn't the happiest guy in the world, at least he wasn't looking for a fight. He didn't say much, but he kept glancing at Marfoglia now and then, when she was looking away. I looked at her and tried to see her through a stranger's eyes, through the eyes of someone who hadn't had to put up with her bullshit for the last couple weeks, and she looked pretty good. But looks aren't everything.

I'd been keeping an eye on the restaurant clientele all through the meeting so far, and there was one guy I was pretty sure was watching us. He was an older guy, balding, overweight, and sitting by himself. He was taking his time over his food, stretching the meal out, and he was interested in everyone in the restaurant—except for us. He kept looking around, studying everyone, but he was careful never to look at our table, and he'd never looked at Marfoglia and the kids when they were at a separate table, either.

When birds stop singing...

"So, you were in the Garden?" Turncrank asked after a while.

"Yeah," I answered. "Almost two hundred days."

"The Garden?" Marfoglia asked, having overheard us. "That sounds nice."

Turncrank and I both laughed, and Marfoglia colored a bit, her eyebrows coming together in irritation.

"Yeah," I agreed. "Nishtaaka's a really swell place. Bare-ass granite mountains that stick up almost out of the atmosphere, poles under a hundred meters of ice— that's where most of the water's locked up—lots of arid plains nobody's gotten around to looking at real close, and a so-called habitable tropical zone that's all overcooked sand or low-lying marsh. They call the biggest marsh the Garden, because they have a sense of humor."

"Only place I ever been," Turncrank said, nodding "where you can be up to your waist in swamp water and have dust blowing in your eyes."

"It's got bugs the size of your thumb," I added, holding up my thumb as a visual aid to the kids, whose eyes were locked on us, "that Human blood's poisonous to, and they bite you anyway, just out of spite."

"Damn!" he said. "Yeah, I'd just about forgotten about the bugs. Thanks for refreshing *that* memory."

We looked at each other for a moment, and then he held up his beer mug. I clinked it with mine, and we drank to Nishtaaka and made our separate peace.

"So, what made the likes of you volunteer?" Captain Joe asked.

"What else?" I answered. "A judge. They had me on three counts of burglary, and he suggested that a stint in the defense corps might be preferable to six years in detention."

"I've heard the really good burglars never get caught," Marfoglia said coolly, and the captain and Turncrank both laughed.

"Good? I was an artist," I answered. "My fence just got greedy, did some stupid things, got caught, and rolled over on a bunch of us to keep himself out of detention. Otherwise, they'd have never caught me. I did over twenty jobs, some of them very high end, and never once tripped an alarm, never once showed up on vid or saw an awake person. I never even carried a weapon, back in those days. That's probably why the judge gave me an out. Nonviolent offender."

"In retrospect, that doesn't seem to have been a very sound decision on his part," she offered dryly. The captain and Turncrank laughed again, good and loud.

"Yeah, well. Hindsight's 20-20," I answered, and I grinned myself. Why not? We were alive and free, our bellies were full, and we were shipping out with the Pirate Cap'n Joe Lee Ping on the morning tide. *Argh.*

So like I said—and despite the verbal sparring—not a bad dinner at all.

Until Rosen showed up.

Rosen was in his thirties, tall, and too handsome, if you know what I mean. I took one look at him and felt like I'd known him forever. He was one of those guys who acts his way through life, all passion and intensity and self-importance on the outside, and on the inside an insecure little punk. You've probably known dozens of them. He had one of those superior smirks that right away makes you want to just take a poke at him. The lady with him—I found out later her name was Abby—was short, slender, with fair skin but dark hair. I'd say she was about ten years younger than he was—not quite old enough to have figured him out yet, but give her a couple of years and she'd dust his ass—or end up running the show. She had that look of real smarts, real determination, and a hard edge in her eyes I liked right away. She was the real thing, and the bulge under her jacket meant she was packing heat.

My kind of gal.

They came in past the two Zacks, looked around, and then headed for our table. Turncrank saw them coming, and his face didn't change, but he kept his eyes on them as they crossed the room.

"Captain Ping, Jim Turncrank! Hey, *great* to see you!" Rosen gushed when they got to the table, and he laid it on just thick enough that you knew he didn't mean it. Then he looked at me and grinned.

"So, you must be Sasha. Or is it Sam Black today? I don't want to blow your cover or anything." Then he and his woman laughed. He scanned the table and as his eyes settled on the two kids for a moment, just for that moment the smile left his face and I saw something dark and hard. Then his eyes moved on and the phony smile returned

"Well, gotta run, folks. Just wanted to stop and say hi," he said. "Oh, and Kolya sends his regards," he added, looking at me, and then he made a pistol from his hand, pointed the barrel at me, and made the thumb/hammer go back and forth a couple times, all the while smirking as if this was a great big joke. He and his lady started to leave, but when they were a dozen steps away he paused, glanced back at us, and had a short talk with her. Then they hurried off in different directions.

I looked over, and the kids were confused, not sure whether to be scared or not. I made a sour face.

"What an asshole, huh?" I said, and Barraki smiled nervously.

"You a friend of Kolya Markov's?" Turncrank asked.

"Not so much these days."

He nodded and exchanged a look with the captain.

"Well, Rosen is," Turncrank said. "That's his name, Clyde Rosen. He's also the only other real Nishtaaka rogue veteran around here . . . and he's more than just that. I'm not sure how much more, but he's hit me up a couple times to join some underground army he claims to have. The war's definitely not over for him, and I wouldn't be surprised if he had something to do with the *Brukata* thing. I don't know why the provosts haven't rounded him up yet."

"So you're saying we should be careful," I said.

Captain Joe gave me a fond smile.

"He only means we would appreciate your fares in advance."

FIFTEEN

Once we had the kids in bed, I went into my room and got the little LeMatt 5mm automatic from my room safe, along with the three autoinjector units I kept for occasions like this. I slipped the autoinjectors into the right pocket of my slacks and the LeMatt in the left. Then I went back into the main room and looked around. There was a wall mirror that would do the trick. I moved a chair over to the entryway and got up on it, took out my pocketknife, and sawed a square opening in the overhead acoustic tile.

"What are you *doing*?" Marfoglia demanded.

"I'll show you in a minute."

"You can't *do* that...we don't *own* this suite."

"Gee, then I guess you won't get your security deposit back," I answered, and I kept sawing. Once I had a hole wide enough for the mirror frame, I cut a smaller one about thirty centimeters farther away from the door. I took a stylus out of my pocket and

171

wrapped the wire frame hanger around it twice. I put the bottom of the mirror frame up into the big hole, then pushed the stylus up through the small hole, turned it sideways inside, and had a solid suspension point. That held the mirror almost flush with the ceiling, but tilted down a bit facing the door. I carved on the big hole a little and adjusted the wire hanger so the mirror was at an angle to the side.

I got down and moved the chair back inside the lounge area, off to the side so it wasn't directly visible to the door. All the time Marfoglia stared at me as if I was crazy, still angry that I was doing all this damage, but curious, too. I waved her over and had her sit in the chair.

"Can you see the door in the mirror from here?" I asked.

She shook her head, so we slid the chair to the side until she could. Then I knelt down beside her, took the LeMatt out of my pocket, and put it in her hand. Once again I showed her how to take the safety off and put it back on, how to release the magazine and put in a new one, and I gave her one more magazine. If it actually came to shooting, she'd never get a chance to reload, but I figured having it might make her feel better.

While I was explaining all of this, her anger went away and I could see she was getting scared. That was okay.

"Now, here's the deal," I said. "I've got to go out and take care of something, because if I don't, we aren't getting out of here alive. You understand?"

She nodded hesitantly.

"Okay. When I'm gone, lock the door behind me. If somebody knocks, don't go look through the peep lens to see who it is, because they will shoot you through the door. Don't even answer the knock; just sit here. If they come through the door, they'll have to break it. You'll see them briefly in the mirror. Shoot them as they come around the corner. If they're dressed as housekeeping, or the purser, or the provosts, *shoot them*. Housekeeping, or the purser, or the provosts won't break down the door; they'll use the station's central grid to override the lock. Do you understand?"

She nodded jerkily, eyes now wide with fear.

"If the door opens without a knock, and it's not me, *shoot them*. It means I'm dead and they have my key. Anyone with legitimate access to the central grid will knock and identify themselves before entering. Do you understand?"

She nodded again.

"If it's me and there's anyone with me, *shoot them*, no matter what I say. *No matter what I say.* If I'm in the way, shoot me first, and then shoot them. Do you understand that?"

"I . . . I don't know if I can do that," she said.

"Sure you can. You probably wanted to a dozen times already."

I expected a smile from her there, but didn't get one.

"Look, if I'm with someone, and you don't shoot, you're not saving my life, 'cause they're going to kill me anyway, and then you. You have to understand that. They are going to *kill* both of us to get to those two kids in the other room, and then they're going to kill them. I'm going to do what I can to stop that, but if I fail, then you and this pistol are all that's going to be left between those kids and death, so you *have to shoot*.

"The big mistake people make is thinking that just pointing the gun at someone will be enough, that then they'll drop their weapons and do whatever you say; but they won't. Trust me, they won't. If you just point it at them, they will *kill* you, and then they will *kill* Barraki and Tweezaa. Do you understand that?"

She looked terrified now, and I half expected her to start crying, but she didn't. She nodded.

"What if... what if there are a lot of them?" she asked, her voice trembling.

"Well—no way to sugarcoat this. If there are more than one or two of them, you're probably going to die. The real question is what you want the last act of your life to be. Do you want to die sitting in a chair doing nothing? Or do you want to take as many of those murdering cocksuckers with you as you can? Me, I'm inclined toward option two, if for no other reason than you never know—you *might* get lucky, and even when you go down, you might hurt them enough that they leave the kids alone. But you can't get lucky unless you give yourself the chance to, and you can't do that unless you *shoot*.

"People say, 'You'll do that over my dead body.' This might be where you find out what that means."

And you find out how much of you is real and how much is just good intentions, I thought, but there was no reason to say that.

She looked down at the pistol in her hand, took a deep breath, and then nodded.

"You have to go?" she whispered without looking up.

"Yup," I answered and stood up. "Gotta go now. As soon as I'm gone, clean up all that broken tile. If they come, and they see the tile, they'll look up and see the mirror and you. Otherwise, they'll be focused at eye level and below, and you'll have a little edge. Okay?"

She nodded.

"Okay," I went on. "If I come back, it will probably be in less than an hour, but if it takes longer, don't freak out. There's no script for stuff like this; I'm making it up as I go, so don't take anything for granted."

That was really all, but for some reason it didn't seem like enough.

"If I don't come back, try to get to the *Long Shot*. I think you'll be safe with Ping. There's about twenty thousand in bearer drafts in the lining of my black carryall. You'll need that. Well . . . good luck."

She nodded, still without looking up, and I left. As I walked down the corridor outside, though, I heard the door open behind me, and she called after me, "Please come back safely, Mr. Naradnyo."

Well, that was the plan.

I had scoped out the security camera coverage a couple times already—force of habit—and I'd checked it again on our way back from the restaurant. There was heavy coverage in all the commercial spaces, with wide-angle full-spectrum lenses, but in the residential areas the coverage was token at best—cheap little cameras with lots of dead spaces, not that tough to slip past or fox if one of your resume entries reads "cat burglar." Of course, there were no public security cameras inside anyone's residence, nor were there public cameras covering the doorways. If you wanted to record your visitors, you could put in your own outside security camera. Rosen, of course, didn't have one—not even a hidden one, and I know how to find those. It made sense. Any recordings he made of visitors could be grabbed up in a search; if you're in the revolution business, it's probably better to not have any records like that lying around.

I took a deep breath and reminded myself that the people on the other side of this door were intent on murdering two children, and that they would certainly succeed in doing so unless I stopped them right here. *Harden your heart, Sasha.*

I knocked on the stateroom door, and I could hear a brief, muffled conversation inside. I almost started laughing. Anyone who thinks you have to be a genius to outsmart the provosts for a couple years has a very idealized view of law enforcement. Of course, if this guy really was in as deep as Turncrank suspected, then sooner or later even the provosts would catch up with him, but later didn't fit my schedule.

And even if Rosen was a total idiot, that didn't mean he couldn't pull the trigger on Barraki and Tweezaa. In fact, it sort of helped in a way. Smarter revolutionaries would be able to figure out something that might actually make a difference; it took morons to kill little kids for lack of a better idea. People have this notion that really smart people are the dangerous ones, but that's not always the case.

The door opened after a minute, and Rosen smiled when he saw me.

"What kept you?" he said, as if this was his plan all along.

"We alone?" I asked, and he nodded. *Lie number one.* I had the silencer clipped onto the Hawker, and I raised it and pushed it into his midsection. His composure slipped for a moment, but then he smiled again.

"No need for that, friend," he said.

"I'm not your friend, so cut the crap and back up." I answered, pushing him back into the room and closing and locking the door behind me. The layout was the same as our suite, except it was a one-bedroom unit, which simplified things. The closed bedroom door was to the right, so I turned him with his back to it and lined myself up so his head was between me and the peep lens. He was about my height, which was convenient.

"Gun," I demanded. He looked at me for a moment, then shrugged, reached into his waistband in back, and brought out a gauss pistol and handed it to me: Zaschaan-made, judging from the runes on the frame, but with a Human-friendly custom grip. Nice long-barrel job like Ricky used to use—had used to try to kill me, come to think of it. It fired 4.4x30mm smart-head flechettes. The nose stayed hard to punch through thin metal or composites, but deformed against liquid or soft tissue, so it would mushroom and tumble inside of you. I put the Hawker away, thumbed the selector on the gauss pistol to *burst*, and pointed it at him.

"Three steps straight back," I ordered, and he did it.

"You want me to put my hands up?" he asked with a smirk. I didn't bother to answer.

"What's it going to take to make you leave us alone?" I asked, although I was pretty sure I already knew the answer.

"Just walk away," he said. "There's no need for you or Dr. Marfoglia to get hurt."

"No, the kids, too. Barraki and Tweezaa."

He shook his head and looked away, and almost smirked again, as if amazed at how naïve I was. One thing was sure, he was way too cocky for me to have the only live gun in the room. *Carefully, Sasha. Very carefully.*

"We'll pay you," he said. "Kolya said you were a criminal. All criminals have a price. What's yours?"

There was that name again—*Kolya.*

Not that I even considered selling the kids out, but I could tell he was lying now. *Lie number two.* The only payoff he had in mind for me and Marfoglia was a forty-four-thirty flechette. If you're ready to kill a couple innocent kids—whether for money or for the revolution—what's a couple adults, more or less?

"There's no way I can get you to leave those two kids alone?"

"Not unless you kill me," he said defiantly, and he sort of smiled, knowing I wouldn't call his bluff. To this day, I have no idea what made him think that.

I raised the pistol and aimed it at his forehead, and his eyes got really big.

"No, wait!" he cried out, and he dove to the side, which is exactly what I needed him to do. I fired a six-round burst through where his head used to be and got a really nice grouping around the peep lens in the bedroom door. There was a heavy thud from the other room and Rosen got an odd, panicked look on his face.

"Abby?" he said. "*Abby?*" he shouted, desperation in his voice.

"Abby ain't there," I told him. "You're on your own now, pal. No backup, just you and me. Now, tell me about Kolya Markov."

"You *killed* Abby?" he demanded. He looked around the room, eyes wild, as if he didn't recognize where he was. He ran his hands frantically up into his hair, and then started sobbing.

"No, no, no . . . ," he wailed, shaking his head.

I don't get it.

Do people like him think that they're the only *real* people in the world? They make these cold, emotionless plans to kill people, maybe hundreds, even thousands of people, as if their victims were just characters on the vid, and then congratulate themselves on how dedicated, or farsighted, or iron-willed, or whatever the fuck they think they are, they are. But when somebody *they* know falls down, that's different. That matters! All of a sudden, it's all that matters.

He was starting to get hysterical, so I put a six-round burst into his foot to bring him back to reality. He fell to the floor, writhing in pain, and I took the opportunity to stick my head into the bedroom and make sure of Abby. She had her own gauss pistol in her hand, but I hadn't given her the chance to use it. Abby had been looking though the peep lens when I fired, and the light composite material of the door had shredded and come away in big chunks when the flechette burst had ripped through it, but I could still recognize her from her clothes. I closed my eyes for a second to blot out the sight.

Willing, enthusiastic child killers, I reminded myself. Not really my kind of gal after all.

Careful not to step in any of the blood, I came back to where Rosen was writhing on the floor. I sat in one of the chairs by the coffee table, took out the three autoinjectors, and picked out the anti-shock/doper combo. It would deaden his pain enough to make him lucid, and the doper would loosen his tongue. It wasn't a magic truth drug, but lying would take an effort. I leaned over and injected him in the neck. It took effect almost immediately. He relaxed a little, opened his eyes, looked around, and then slowly sat up.

"Is she ... ?"

"She's lying down," I said.

He sat there on the floor, still kind of crying, but groggy as well, looking around in a daze.

"Is that my toe?" he asked, pointing to a bloody lump on the carpet. I looked at it.

"One of them," I answered. "Now tell me about Kolya Markov."

Still disoriented, he looked around for a second, swallowed, and then nodded.

"Kolya and I knew each other from the Ram Brigade, on Nishtaaka. He was a ferocious fighter, terrifying sometimes."

Yeah, tell me about it.

"We were in different cohorts, so I never knew what happened to him. After the brigade laid down its arms, most of us took the pardons and went home. In my heart, though, I never gave up. A lot of us didn't. The day is coming when—"

"Yeah, yeah," I interrupted. *"Kolya."*

He nodded. "I heard from him again about a year ago. We had gotten covert access to some of the sealed AZ Tissopharm records, and there were some patents. One of them was for an addictive designer euphoric, Varoki-specific ..."

"Laugh," I said, and he nodded.

"Yes! That's what Kolya decided we should call it. We had the molecular formula, and he already had an underground resistance organization on Peezgtaan, so we decided that was the best place to start distributing it, since it had been developed there. Sort of poetic."

"An underground resistance organization?" I repeated. He nodded.

Well, Kolya always had a creative way of looking at things.

"What better way to fund our operation than with a drug we could sell to the Varoki?" Rosen added, and smiled.

"Let me get this right," I said. "Kolya Markov was actually *financing* your operations out here by selling Laugh?"

"Well, we didn't have positive revenue flow yet. We were still putting a lot of money into getting the production labs on line, and he didn't have the distribution operation up and running—there were a lot of difficulties, things you probably wouldn't understand. But eventually it will fund our revolution."

Riiight.

"He knew I was based here for the better part of the year," Rosen continued. "As soon as the *K'Pook* broke J-space, I got a flash transmission through the station's public comm center. It was in a plain language code, of course, but Kolya alerted us to the fact that the Tissopharm heirs were on the *K'Pook*, with a woman and a man—a criminal named Sasha—and it was our chance to strike back at the *e-Varokiim.*"

Strike back?

"They're *kids,*" I said.

"Nits breed lice," he answered, which didn't mean shit to me—are nits like little lice or something?—except that it didn't look like I was going to change his mind about this, especially since I'd killed his lady love.

"So, did you blow the *Brukata*?"

"Yes. We'd been planning a move like this for some time."

"You did this just to slow us down?" I demanded. That seemed unlikely.

"No. Your arrival was coincidental. We did it to draw *KKa-117* here."

Varoki never used to name their commercial ships, but they picked up the habit from us—*Terrakultur* on the march. They still don't name their warships. *KKa-117* was the Co-Gozhak cruiser in close orbit.

"Why?" I demanded. He just smiled.

Oh, great! They were going to take out a cruiser. And then what? I doubt he'd thought much further, but I knew I didn't want to be anywhere near when *that* shit hit the fan.

"How many people you got here on the station?" I asked. "Other than the bald guy in the sushi bar."

He looked startled that I'd made his man, but he bristled to cover it.

"Dozens!" he answered. "And if you kill me, they'll hunt you down and kill you, no matter where you go. But..." The wheels were starting to turn in his head—I could almost hear them grinding and whirring. He licked his lips and went on. "I...I can see now that you're not going to give in on this. There's been enough Humans killing Humans, and I have more important work to see to."

He looked over at the bedroom door, and I thought he was going to start crying again, but he didn't.

"Let's just call a truce, before anyone else gets killed. You, Dr. Marfoglia...even the two Varoki... can all just walk away.

Lie number three.

SIXTEEN

I knocked on the door, opened it with my key, and called inside, "It's me, and I'm alone." I came in and looked up at the mirror. Marfoglia was sitting in the chair, the LeMatt in both hands and aimed at the doorway. I closed the door behind me and locked it, and then turned to look up into the mirror again.

"It's okay. It's all done. I'm back, I'm alone, and you can put the gun down."

She was still holding it up in both hands, but she was trembling now.

"Okay, safety on. Remember how I showed you? Is the safety on? Check the safety: the little button on the hammer."

She looked at the pistol then, tried to put the safety on, but she started shaking uncontrollably and the pistol fell out of her hands onto the carpet. I walked in, picked it up, put on the safety, and lowered the

183

hammer. Then I looked at her. She'd buried her face in her hands and was shuddering violently.

I knelt down in front of her.

"It's okay. You did fine. We're—"

I reached out to pat her shoulder, and when I touched her, she popped me in the mouth with her fist, really hard, almost put me back on my ass. Then she started flailing wildly at me, sobbing hysterically, and I just brought my forearms up to cover my face and let her go, taking it on my arms and shoulders.

This was a situation I'd never encountered before, and I was kind of at a loss, so I guess my plan—if I really had one—was to hope she got tired quickly. In the old stories, sometimes the hero puts a hysterical dame out with a clean clip to the jaw. That never entered my mind—and besides, the one time I ever hit someone on the jaw with my fist, they ended up needing dental work, and I *really* hurt my hand.

Fortunately, my "plan" worked, and in a minute she sort of collapsed back into the chair, hands covering her face again, and sobbing. The door to the kids' bedroom opened and Barraki stuck his head out, eyes wide. I turned to him, but I didn't make any effort to get him to go away. If I did, he'd just wonder what was going on, and probably be more frightened than by the truth, so I motioned him over.

"Boti-Marr had a bad scare," I told him, "but she'll be okay. Come here and give her a hug."

I figured she wouldn't pop *him* in the mouth. I could already feel my own lip starting to swell up.

He came over and hugged her, and she sat up to hug him back, wiping away some tears.

"Help me get her to her bedroom?" I asked him.

"No," she said, still crying, but not as hard. "I'm okay."

We helped her anyway, one of us on each side, got her to her bed, and then she curled up on her side in a ball, on top of the covers, still crying softly. I put a spread over her, and we left her alone. I closed the door to her room behind us, and Barraki looked up at me.

"What frightened her so much?" he asked.

"Everything. I guess it all just built up to the point that it boiled over there for a minute. You know, she gives this impression of being tough and cool and always in control. I just figured something out about her: it's all a bluff."

"A bluff?" he asked, unfamiliar with the word.

I nodded. "An act, for you and your sister. She's . . . you know . . . an economic consultant, for cryin' out loud. A high-end, jump-set executive. She's no more used to all this shooting and running than you two are. So she's in way over her head, and I guess she's just been hanging on by her fingernails all this time. Why? Because you two needed her to. She's all you guys have got right now."

"We have you, too, Sasha."

That kind of caught me by surprise, and for a moment there I had a hard time finding my voice. I put my arm around his shoulder.

"That's right, pal. You got me, too."

We moved over to the *Long Shot* at about three in the morning. Of course, time of day didn't mean much on the station, except in a pretty arbitrary sense, but the kids were tired anyway, especially after all the excitement, so even the zero gee of the station's central shaft and the cargo level wasn't the novelty it had been earlier. Turncrank met us, floating at the cargo lock.

"Interesting news just up on the feed," he said by way of greeting. "Seems Rosen killed his girlfriend and then shot himself. A lot."

I didn't say anything. The two kids looked at me, eyes wide, but Marfoglia just kept looking down. She'd hardly spoken—to either me or the kids—since I got her up. I'd started packing for her, but she'd wordlessly taken over and finished.

Turncrank shrugged. "Don't guess anyone in charge is going to ask many questions or shed many tears over him. Let's get you squared away."

Turncrank helped us herd our floating luggage down the passageway to our cramped sleeping quarters— nothing like the suite on *K'Pook* or the shuttle, just four bunks and some lockers for our personal gear. *Long Shot* didn't have a wheel, but the crew quarters and common areas were in a spin capsule that would deploy once we were under way. Gravity wasn't a needless frill on a working ship, unless you considered bone density and cardiovascular health frills.

The bunks weren't set up for acceleration, so Turncrank took us to the control deck afterward and helped strap us in to four temporary acceleration couches on the rear wall of the small bridge. He especially helped Marfoglia, but he didn't make eye contact, and he didn't cross any lines. It's funny where you find gentlemen.

Captain Ping was already floating by the control consoles. Turncrank joined him when he was done with us, and they did the long preflight check. They were serious about it, and they did it as if they'd never done one before—strictly by the numbers, no fooling around, no shortcuts. You never know how professional people are until you see them at work. These two guys knew their business.

Beside me, Marfoglia leaned over and spoke softly, so that no one else could hear.

"In your entire life, Mr. Naradnyo, how many people have you killed?"

"Thirteen," I answered after a moment.

I wasn't expecting what came next. She gently patted my arm with her hand, a gesture of sympathy and understanding.

"Thank you, Sasha," she said, "for taking care of us."

I almost made a smart remark about the paycheck being all the thanks I needed, but a smart remark would have tasted strange in my mouth that morning, so I didn't say anything.

"Rakanka Prox, this is Stingray-Kilo-Oakum-zero-one-seven-seven-one-niner requesting scheduled release," Ping said to his embedded comm link. We couldn't hear the answer, but Ping nodded.

"Seven-seven-one-niner, thank you, Rakanka Prox. Magnetic couplings are all locked in the off position. Awaiting out-vector."

We felt the gentle acceleration as Rakanka Proximity Control used the station's servo bumpers to nudge *Long Shot* away from the cargo bay.

"Seven-seven-one-niner, thank you, Rankanka Prox. I show three-zero meters separation. Do you confirm?... Roger. Bringing up ACTs...ACTs on line. Five second ACT burn...now."

We felt another gentle acceleration as Ping used

the *Long Shot*'s attitude-control thrusters to speed us up a bit. He couldn't use the main thruster until we were a lot farther away from the station. Unlike the C-lighters of the big commercial lines, *Long Shot* had its own maneuvering drive and didn't use a Newton tug. It made it less efficient on the high-traffic runs, but a lot more versatile in the less developed systems, where there might not always be a Newton tug handy.

Ping put our forward view on the big screen, and we watched as we coasted past the *K'Pook* in its parking orbit.

"That is the ship you came in on?" Ping asked. "How was the service on the uBakaa, Incorporated line?"

"It's a Simki-Traak ship," I said. uBakaa was one of the Varoki nations, not a corporation.

"uBakaa, AZ Simki-Traak, it is all the same," he practically spat. "Don't believe me? Try pulling an inspection from an uBakai picket boat when you are running cargo in competition with AZ Simki-Traak Trans-Stellar—see how confused their database can get all of a sudden—and how long you will wait in orbit while they straighten it out."

Turncrank grunted in agreement and nodded. I just settled back in the couch. Who ever said the market was free, competition was fair, or government was honest? Not me, that's for sure. I glanced over at Barraki, though, and his eyes had gotten a bit bigger. It's a creepy feeling to hear someone who doesn't know who you are talk, even indirectly, about your family, and maybe say some ugly things you don't know anything about. He looked over at me, a question in his eyes. I just shrugged. Who the hell knows?

About twenty minutes later we coasted across the

control boundary between Rakanka Proximity and Rakanka Orbital and got the go-ahead to make our primary acceleration burn.

"Ita mai, Rakanka-Bat," Ping said into his comm link to the Varoki proximity controller—*see you later.*

Rules were rules: all traffic instructions and replies had to be in the ship's official language. Once we were past the control boundary, though, there was no rule against being friendly. The logic behind the language rule was sound. It was safer to make sure the controllers were fluent in the six official aerospace languages of the *Cottohazz* than it was to count on every single starship crew knowing another language well enough to take detailed maneuvering instructions. At least that was the theory. I'd heard that a few East Asian captains might have been more understandable in aGavoosh than English, but if so, Ping wasn't one of them.

Ping started the burn, and the orientation of the cabin seemed to change, the way it always did when you went from zero gee to one gee. Now we were on the "floor" and both Ping and Turncrank were on acceleration couches slung from the "ceiling" about two meters above us, with an access ladder between them on the "wall." The hatch we'd entered was now on the "floor" to our right.

Actually, we were pulling more than a gee. Not two gees, but I'd guess something like a gee and a quarter or more—not enough to be painful, but enough that you didn't feel like getting up and dancing.

"Very sorry for the extra weight," Ping said from above us. He unstrapped and leaned over the edge of his couch to look down at us. "We have a tight

jump window. We are carrying relief supplies—a lot
of medicine and some hydroponic seed proteins—for
K'Tok, and the government people are anxious to get
them there ASAP. That's why we got the contract
instead of one of the big carriers—we can get them
there quicker."

"Is your ship faster, Captain Ping?" Barraki asked.

"*Argh*, it's not speed we have, boyo," he answered,
reverting to his gravelly pirate voice, "it's what I'd call
a creative approach to astrogation. We'll not be going
deep out-orbit to escape Rakanka's gravity well. Instead,
we'll be making the jump from the L-1 Lagrange point.
That'll cut five score hours off our transit time—five
score hours be four days, lad."

"What's a Lagrange point?" Barraki asked.

"They be the places in a multi-body system where
the gravitational attractions of the different bodies
balance each other, giving you a stable orbit. It's the
L-1 point that's important; that's the place between
two planets where the gravities actually cancel each
other out, leaving a near-perfect zero-gee point," Ping
answered.

"How many large moons does Rakanka have?" I
asked. You need moons with fairly substantial gravity
to get a useable L-1 point near a large gas giant.

"Well, I suppose that depends on what you mean
by large," he answered, and gave us a big, toothy grin.
"Rakanka has no stable L-1 Lagrange point, as such.
But it happens there are two small moons coming
into close conjunction, and we think they'll give us
enough gravity for a useable jump point."

We think?

The gas giant Rakanka, two moons, and the residual

gravity of Seewauk, the system primary—unless I was mistaken, that made this a four-body math problem, and as far as I knew, there wasn't a reliable solution to the four-body problem, no matter how hot your computers were, and I said as much.

"Aye, that be so," Ping the pirate answered, nodding thoughtfully. "But that's why we have the best gravitometer money can buy."

Turncrank laughed at that, which wasn't encouraging. Ping frowned at him and then turned back to us.

"Pay no attention to that lubber. Belike, the computers will get us close enough, and the gravitometer won't let us go into the hole unless we're in the green . . . or a little in the yellow." He grinned again and shrugged.

"And this saves us a king's ransom in reaction mass," he added. "All them gas scoopers back at Rakanka are Katami-owned boats, and Katami are terrible thieves—steal the coins off a dead man's eyes, they will." He looked at Tweezaa, repeated it in aGavoosh, and pointed to his eyes with his two index fingers while making what I guess was supposed to be a dead man's face—his eyes crossed and tongue hanging out of the side of his mouth. Tweezaa giggled.

We were the only passengers on this trip, and Ping and Turncrank were the entire ship's complement—it doesn't take many hands to run a commercial vessel. Ping was the master, which meant pilot, astrogator, and business manager. Turncrank, the mate, was cargo master and system technician. In practice, both of them could handle each other's jobs, but you needed two guys so you could spell each other at the controls—that way both guys could catch some sleep and some one-gee time in the spin habitat.

There was a common room in the spin capsule, with repeaters of the important sensors, so everybody could get together for meals once in a while. First night out all six of us ate together. Turns out Ping was the cook as well as the captain, and he served a pretty good curry. Even Barraki and Tweezaa liked it, although the curry sauce was on a different protein filet for them. I don't know how Ping knew the curry would go with that type of Varoki meat substitute—not from tasting it himself, that's for sure.

When we were done eating, and the small talk had died down a bit, Captain Ping looked across at Marfoglia.

"So, there's something I've been meaning to ask you," he said, in his "normal" voice, not Pirate Joe's.

"What's that?"

"I know what a market*ing* consultant does, but what does a *market* consultant do?"

She shrugged at first, not out of confusion, I thought, so much as dismissal, as if it wasn't a very important thing.

"I explain how markets work," she said. "That's all."

"Okay," Ping said. "Explain how markets work."

"Really?" she asked.

"Yes, why not?" he answered, and then lapsed into his Cap'n Ping pirate voice. "*Argh*, but make it simple, for I be a simple man." Then he winked at Barraki, who giggled in reply.

"Of course you are," she said skeptically. "Very well. It's not hard to keep it simple, because it really is. Suppose you've got three farmers. One has an apple orchard, one has a peach orchard, and one has an orange grove. They all work just as hard, all have pretty much the same kind of land, each grows a quantity of fruit. But they get tired of eating the same fruit all the time, so they get together and trade fruit with each other. That's a market."

"And?" Ping asked.

"That's pretty much it," she answered. "There are things that can distort the market—maybe one farmer is better at bargaining, maybe one has a poor crop, but if everything's equal, when the market gets done, every farmer ends up with the same number of apples, oranges, and peaches as every other farmer."

"*Argh*, efficient allocation of resources," Ping said, still in his pirate voice, but she shook her head.

"No, not necessarily. That's not what a market does."

"But you said—"

"—that the farmers all end up with the same amount of fruit. Right. *That's* what a market does: it levels. And that's *all* it does. It's pretty good at leveling, but that's not the same thing as efficiency."

"Aye, but in the long run...," he started, but she was shaking her head. She wasn't kidding around anymore, either; he had her pretty solidly locked into PhD mode.

"The market can't read a calendar; it doesn't know long run from short run. It has no mind of its own—it's just the economic manifestation of a universal tendency toward stasis in systems. One room has oxygen, the next room is a vacuum. Open the door between them and the pressure equalizes. That's not necessarily the most efficient way to allocate the oxygen, especially if the original single-room pressure was sufficient to sustain Human life and the new ambient pressure isn't, but that's how nature works; it levels."

"So you're not one to hold with... *the invisible hand?*" Ping asked, leaning forward and saying it slowly, as if it were a secret organization of assassins.

She chuckled.

"Poor old Adam Smith. He's probably the most widely quoted economist in history whom hardly anyone has actually read. *The Wealth of Nations* runs to hundreds of pages, and all anyone knows about it is that it talks about the invisible hand. How much does he talk about it, Captain Ping? Do you know?"

He shook his head.

"Once," she answered. "In the entire *Wealth of Nations*, he mentions the invisible hand exactly *once*. One of the bedrock theses of the work—the concept that labor is the basis of any economic system, not a transactional commodity within it—is always ignored by people who want to make workers interchangeable consumable units, like ingots of steel. Instead, they invoke 'The Invisible Hand' as if it's an incantation, calling forth the blessings of the Archangel Adam Smith. No, I don't believe in the invisible hand, not the way some economists do."

"Aye," Ping said after a moment, "well, forget the invisible hand, then. But the way people respond—your three farmers—that's resource allocation, ain't it?"

She nodded. "Absolutely. But who says the way they respond is efficient?"

"Well, if not, someone else comes along and takes over their farm."

She smiled, but shook her head.

"You'd think so, but their efficiency is only related

to meeting the demands of the market, and my point is that the demands of the market itself are not necessarily efficient. Let me give you an example. We came to Rakanka from Peezgtaan—the capital city actually, what they call Crack City. Do you know how many Humans died of deficiency diseases last year in Crack City?"

He shrugged. How would he know? She turned to me.

"Mr. Naradnyo?" she asked.

"I don't know . . . a lot."

"About six hundred urban poor Humans died from deficiency-related diseases last year," she answered, "or a dietary deficiency was a significant complicating issue in their health collapse."

"Six *hundred*? That many?" the captain asked, the pirate gone from his voice.

She nodded.

"They should be mass synthesizing Human-specific vitamins and dietary minerals," she went on, talking to everyone at the table, "enriching the soya paste that's the basis for most Human-consumed protein on Peezgtaan, but they aren't. But Human criminals *are* synthesizing Laugh." She turned to me. "Why is that, Mr. Naradnyo?"

That made me a bit uncomfortable, as you might imagine, and she must have seen it in my face. She frowned and shook her head impatiently.

"No, this isn't a moral question. I'm asking as an economist talking to someone who is an expert on the local economy. Why—economically—are suppliers synthesizing Laugh instead of Human vitamin complex?"

"'Cause that's where the money is."

"Yes, of course," she agreed, and nodded vigorously, looking around the table again. There were times when she might look like a fashion model, but that wasn't one of them. At that moment, there was nothing elegant or graceful about her mannerisms, nothing practiced about her speech. For a moment, she was an economics teacher, so absorbed by her subject that it made her geeky and almost likeable.

"Because that's where the money is," she repeated, sill nodding jerkily. "But does that make Laugh more useful than vitamins, just because it's what the money in the market is chasing? The argument that the market allocates resources efficiently presupposes that the distribution of money demand within the market is based on some rational, economically efficient model. But what if it's not? What if, for example, it's driven by an uncontrollable addiction?"

She looked around to let everyone think that over for a couple seconds before going on.

"Alternatively, what if half the money in a market is controlled by one man? That market is going to allocate a disproportionate amount of its resources to satisfying that one man's whims, isn't it? But what's efficient about that?"

"But eventually it gets leveled out, ain't that so?" the pirate captain asked.

"That's what markets do; they level," she answered, nodding again. "Here's the problem: how did one man get all that money to start with? Not from the market. Significant disparities in wealth are *never* the result of pure market forces—they are the result of market *distortions*, and you can't rely on market forces to level a non-market imbalance. If the market by itself could correct the imbalance, then the imbalance would not have developed in the first place, would it?"

"Well, you lost me there," he said. "Why can't it correct one that just, well...happens?"

"Because imbalances do not *just happen*; they are the result of structural constraints, either natural or artificial, which are beyond the ability of markets to change.

"Case in point: innovation. Every advanced society we know of has made the determination, for right or wrong, that the market itself does not sufficiently reward dramatic and costly innovations. Someone comes up with an innovation, they enjoy a transitory advantage, but the pressures of the market drive everyone else to adopt the same innovation as quickly as possible and re-level the field. If the innovation was particularly difficult or costly to develop—say a new drug—the original innovator's momentary advantage is not enough, it is argued, to justify the investment. So the market encourages many simple and inexpensive innovations, but discourages major leaps forward.

"Since societies prize major leaps forward, every advanced society we know of has adopted a series of intellectual property covenants which protect major innovations from the leveling effects of the marketplace. They prohibit anyone but the original innovator from using the innovation; they prohibit competition in that field as a reward for progress. The imbalance those laws create cannot be overcome by the market, because the market is specifically enjoined from doing so."

"So, you're saying intellectual property laws are bad because they short-circuit the market?" Ping asked.

"No, Captain. I'm saying a market is no more good or bad than is gravity. Both are morally neutral forces of nature, to be understood and utilized, not worshipped."

Ping lapsed into a thoughtful silence, and my mind

went to the short lesson I'd received on intellectual property law courtesy of Walter Wu. I guess I understood the whole "protect innovation" idea as a basis of intellectual property laws, but to my economically naïve brain it seemed like the *Cottohazz* had managed to screw things up with theirs. They had choked innovation off, not encouraged it. It wasn't hurting the *e-Varokiim*'s bank accounts, though.

"So how come I don't hear more economists talking like this?" I finally asked.

She shrugged languidly, and settled back in her chair, eyes half closed, and the teacher vanished.

"You'll never hear me talk like this to a client," she answered.

"So you're saying," I said, "that economic analysis is a commodity subject to market forces as well?"

She laughed, and I think it was the first time she'd laughed at something I said . . . other than in derision.

Nice laugh, actually.

Sixteen hours out from Rakanka Highstation we found Ping's elusive Lagrange point and made the jump—went "into the hole," as he said—and despite my doubts came out in the K'Tok system with a solid residual vector pointing us almost square at Mogo, the main system gas giant. We did a minor correction and a supplemental burn to speed us up, and then settled back to enjoy the glide in. We'd glide to Mogo, refuel by skimming the gas giant, and do an orbital transit and breakaway maneuver which would slingshot us in-system toward K'Tok.

The day after we broke into the K'Tok system I was down in our quarters with Barraki teaching him to play twenty-one. I was up about two hundred *Cottos*. Barraki didn't have any cash, but I figured his credit was good, and I was about to explain the vig to him when my embedded comm chimed softly in my head. I squinted, opened the line, and Turncrank's voice filled my head.

"Hey Naradnyo, you down there in the pod?"

"Yeah."

"Anybody with you?"

"Barraki. Why?"

"Maybe nothing, but both of you come on up to con. Dr. Marfoglia and the little girl are already here."

"What's up?" I asked.

"Oh . . . probably nothin'. But we may have to do a maneuvering burn sooner than we thought. Best if everyone's strapped in, and I'll need to secure the spin pod."

"Okay. On our way," I answered.

"We gotta head up to the control room. Lucky for you," I added to Barraki. "I'd have cleaned you out in another hour."

He giggled. "You think so, *Boti-Shaashka?*"

"*Uncle Woaool?* I'm gonna kick your ass from here to dirt-side for that!"

I grabbed for him, but he was too fast, trailing laughter out the door and up the access tunnel ladder. I took a look around the cabin before following him, and on a hunch grabbed my black carryall. Never can tell when you'll need a 10mm hand cannon, twenty large in bearer drafts, or a toothbrush. I pulled our travel documents out of the desk where Marfoglia kept them and dropped them in the carryall as well.

Why? To this day I can't tell you. I just did.

Marfoglia and Tweezaa were already strapped into their couches when I got there, and Barraki was fumbling with his straps. His couch was on the far right of the four and mine was on the far left, with Marfoglia and Tweezaa between us.

"Good thing for you we gotta do this maneuvering thing now," I told him. "Once it's done, though, your ass is mine."

He giggled again.

"Yeah, laugh while you can, weasel boy."

I stashed the carryall and then strapped myself in. Ping and Turncrank were both already strapped in and engaged in low conversation. I looked at Marfoglia, and she looked uneasy. I looked back at Ping and Turncrank and started feeling uneasy myself. There was something different about their attitude—not worried so much as preoccupied. They were absorbed in the details of the sensor feeds the same way I get absorbed by details whenever the birds stop singing.

"What's wrong?" I asked them.

"Um . . . we lost contact with K'Tok Orbital about forty minutes ago," Turncrank answered without looking up. "Not sure if it's a receiver problem at this end or transmitter problems there."

I'm no pilot, but I know that a failed communication link by itself wouldn't make anyone consider an unscheduled maneuvering burn when we were still nearly a day out from Mogo, so there had to be something else.

"And?" I said.

Ping and Turncrank exchanged a glance, and then Ping answered, and not in his pirate voice.

"And we've picked up some activity near Mogo— flickers of light and some interference across a lot of the EM spectrum. And no, we do not know what that means, but it is unusual."

"Flickers of light on the planet surface?" I asked. That sounded odd, but not that menacing. Mogo was a gas giant, after all. It's not as if anyone lived down there.

"No," Turncrank answered. "Out in nearby space. Close orbital, I think."

That meant nothing to me. Them either, apparently.

For the next three hours we coasted in toward Mogo, with nothing unusual on the sensors but no orbital nav beacon from Mogo and no answer to our requests at the top of each hour for a glide update from K'Tok Orbital. We talked a little, but not much. It started feeling spooky, as if we might be the only ones left alive in the whole system.

Ping and Turncrank had the long-range scope pointed at Mogo with the image on the big screen. All of us could see it, but it just looked like a gas giant. Mogo had a nice set of rings round it, and a yellow-green tint to its atmosphere, but nothing unusual.

Then we saw the flash.

"Oh, shit!" Turncrank said. Ping hadn't been looking at the screen, so his head snapped up from his monitor.

"What was it? I just got an EMP reading."

"A nuke!" Turncrank answered. "Look! Another one. We're coasting into the middle of a goddamned naval battle!"

A naval battle?

A naval battle with *whom*? There was only one navy—ours.

Right?

"Um...somebody's painting us," Turncrank said, his voice higher pitched, fear present but under control. "I'm locking down all the airtight doors."

I heard the hiss and solid clunk of the control room's door closing and securing beside me.

"Okay," Ping answered quickly, his hands flying across the control console. "Sending our recognition codes on every freq I can reach...NOW. *We are a civilian vessel, you fool! Stop painting us!*" he shouted, as if the other captain could hear through the better part of a light-second of vacuum.

"Painting us?" Marfoglia asked beside me in a frightened whisper, so the kids wouldn't hear.

"Target-acquisition radar," I answered, my mouth dry.

"I've got him on the CA radar," Turncrank said. "Oh...," he added quietly, his voice changed, tired and dead-sounding, "it's way too small to be a ship."

Ping looked at him, looked up at the screen, and then—suddenly calm—took a long, slow look around him at the control room of the *Long Shot*.

"I really love this ship," he said quietly, to no one in particular.

The screen went white. There was a simultaneous thunderous explosion that I felt as much as heard, and the ship rocked hard to the side, almost tearing my restraining straps off the acceleration couch. Then the control room went black as the power failed, and we were alone in the darkness, the only sounds being the tortured metallic groans of the *Long Shot* breaking up and the screams of its passengers and crew.

I'm not certain, but I think I must have been one of those screaming.

SEVENTEEN

Marfoglia was holding my hand in the darkness. Or I was holding hers. Who knows? At the moment you think you're facing death, you grab for life, wherever you can find it.

The worst of the metallic groaning had stopped, and I didn't hear any telltale hiss of escaping atmosphere, so that was good. The kids were both crying, but that meant they were alive, and Marfoglia was almost compulsively squeezing my hand, so she was, too.

"We should engage the auxiliary power, Jim," I heard Ping say. "Jim?"

No answer.

"Oh no," Ping said in the darkness.

"What's wrong?" I asked. That was a pretty bone-headed question under the circumstances, but Ping knew what I meant.

"Jim's hurt," he answered. "Unconscious, but he's alive. Hold on a second..."

Half a dozen dim emergency lights came on around the cabin. I looked over at Marfoglia and the kids first. Marfoglia was terrified but dry-eyed and keeping it together. Not sure where she got it, but she had some sand in her, that was for sure. I saw a cut on her forehead and some blood, but not a lot. A few small things floated free in the control room, things that had come loose in the explosion, and one must have clipped her. Beside her, Barraki and Tweezaa sobbed, almost hysterical with fright.

"Hey, settle down, guys," I said, mostly to Barraki, because he was older and Tweezaa would follow his lead. "We're okay. We're alive and we've got air." I patted Marfoglia's hand with my free left hand and then let go with my right. "You take care of them, okay? I'm going to see if I can help Ping."

She nodded.

I unstrapped and let myself float up to Ping, who was hovering over Turncrank's couch. I started rotating slowly as I moved, and as soon as I was level with them, I started drifting back "down" toward the acceleration couches and off to one side, which meant we must be tumbling, and centrifugal force was pushing me gently out toward the hull. I grabbed a railing to steady myself and took a look at Turncrank. His neck was pretty obviously broken. Ping looked up at me.

"Should we straighten his head?"

"Yeah, he's having trouble breathing. But we'll need to use something to secure it. If we get jolted again, we don't want it flopping around." I pulled the belt out of my slacks and we used that across his forehead to hold his head steady once we'd straightened it.

"What hit us?" I asked while we were working on

Turncrank. "He said it was too small for a ship. It meant something to you two. What?"

"A missile. It detonated perhaps a thousand kilometers out. It had to be that far or the collision-avoidance radar would have picked it up sooner, even something that small."

"Would the blast travel that far through vacuum?" I asked.

"There is no real blast concussion in vacuum at all, just a great deal of gamma radiation, heat, and light. The missile has a thermonuclear warhead which pumps a high energy x-ray laser—once. It is the laser that kills, not the blast. They call it a 'fire lance.'"

"So the big explosion?"

"Our hydrogen reaction mass and the ship's atmosphere all mixed up . . . that and some explosive decompression."

"What about your main power plant? Could that have gone up, too?" I asked, but he shook his head.

"If the fusion reactor had gone critical, we would not be here talking. It was already shut down; we only use it to pump the jump capacitors. Coasting like this we just use the LENR generators. Unfortunately, the explosion took out the forward generator, and we've got no live circuit to anyplace else on the ship, so we are on emergency battery power."

"How we doing on oxygen?" I asked.

"Oxygen is not our problem—heat is. We will freeze to death long before we suffocate."

That was encouraging.

"What about Mogo? We gonna hit it?" I asked.

He shrugged.

"I cannot tell how much the explosion changed our

trajectory, but the odds are it was not enough to put us in the capture zone. We will do a pass-by later today, and, without making a correction to put us in a stable orbit, we will slingshot back out. We will probably end in a cometary orbit around the primary with a period of a hundred years or more."

I thought that over.

"How long?" I asked.

"Perhaps twenty-four hours at the lowest settings which will keep us alive. Possibly a little longer if we pick up some radiated heat from Mogo as we pass it."

Turncrank woke up a little while later, but he was in bad shape. His spinal cord must have been badly damaged, and everything below the neck started shutting down. Marfoglia floated beside him and talked with him, held his hand, and after about an hour he died. She hadn't cried before, but she did then.

The control room wasn't all that big, and it just didn't feel right with Jim Turncrank's body lying there beside us. No way to get rid of him, but Ping and I moved him over to a long locker and settled him in. It wasn't a real burial, of course, but it felt a little bit like one when we closed the door and the latch clicked. Ping and I floated there for a while, just looking at the locker.

"He seemed like a pretty solid guy," I ventured after a minute. Ping nodded.

"He had a terrible life. I never saw him take it out on anyone else, though. He could not tell a joke to save his life, but I got him to laugh at mine now and then."

What do you want people to remember about you

when you check out? That you made a lot of money? That you dressed well? Or maybe that you never took your troubles out on someone else. It's worth thinking about now and then.

Jim was gone, but we were still here—for a while. Twenty-three hours left and counting. It was already cold enough you could see your breath. Barraki and Tweezaa were huddled together for warmth, we had both of our blankets wrapped around them, and Marfoglia floated with them, her arms around them as well.

Pointless. Just delaying the inevitable; just prolonging our misery, and I'm not one to pointlessly prolong misery. You may have noticed that I'm not one to give up easily, either, but I was close to stumped this time.

Think, I told myself. *Work the problem through.*

"If there's no one in orbit around Mogo, we're dead no matter what we do, right?" I asked Ping. "Because they couldn't get to us in time anyway."

He nodded.

"Okay. So we *assume* there's someone in orbit, because that's the only bet that can possibly pay off."

"Very well," he agreed. "We will assume that."

"Now, if there's someone in orbit, and they don't see us, we die anyway. How soon do they have to see us?" I asked. Ping thought for a moment.

"By now we are about ten hours out from Mogo orbit. Say another two or three hours to make a partial transit. Then, either we hit Mogo itself, or the gravity slingshot takes over, and we begin our course to exit the inner system."

"Okay, so about twelve hours, tops?"

He nodded again, and then shrugged.

"So what?"

"I'm just trying to see what we have to work with. Whatever we do, we know that we can invest half our battery power in it, right? Because after twelve hours, we're finished anyway, and it doesn't matter."

"All right," he agreed, nodding. "I do not know what good it does us, but yes. For the sake of argument, we can use up half our battery power."

"Okay. We've got half our battery power to use, and we need to attract the attention of whoever is out there in orbit around Mogo. How do we do that?"

He just looked at me.

"Come on," I insisted. "There's got to be some way."

"Well, I cannot think of any," he said, "and it is not as if I do not want to. Assuming somebody is out there, they will have sensors. They may pick up our wreckage on active radar, but there is nothing we can do to help or hurt our chances there; they either do or they do not. What we can do is try to show up on their *passive* sensors, and we do that by emitting energy."

"And we've got some energy," I said.

"Yes, but no way to emit it."

Marfoglia drifted over to join us.

"What are you two talking about?" she asked.

"We're organizing our rescue," I answered, and for the first time since the attack, Ping smiled.

"I like the way you look at things, Sasha," he said.

"Is there a chance?" Marfoglia asked, hope showing in her face.

"We're about halfway there," I answered, which was something of an exaggeration, but sometimes you need to keep people positive, just so their brains keep ticking. I brought her up to speed on what we'd figured out so far. The fact that it was a long shot there even was somebody in orbit didn't seem to occur to her. Or maybe she just looked at it the same way I did.

"So the problem is, how do we convert our battery power into an emission their passive sensors can pick up?" I finished.

"Well," Ping said, "and that is the difficulty. I already tried to transmit on the emergency sets, but according to the readouts still working, we have no antennae. Even transmitting radio white noise, without an antenna to direct the transmission, you could only pick us up for a hundred kilometers or so."

"Better than nothing, though," I said, but he shook his head.

"No, their CA radar—that's collision avoidance—would pick up our wreckage long before then. So if we get that close, we are safe, but if not..."

Yeah, and what are the odds of coming—by chance—within a couple hundred klicks of another ship while coasting past a gas giant? Not worth calculating.

"Okay. If not radio, what?"

"Thermal—heat," he answered. "But that takes more energy—too much energy. Commercial ship thermals are set to pick up stars and brown dwarves. Warships are better—they don't like to talk about it, but I've heard some of them can detect main thruster burns at a light-second or more. But what we've got here is just a *room* heater." He shook his head.

"Light," I said. "They can detect light."

He nodded. "Yes, but we cannot make it. Or rather, we can make it in here, but nobody out there can see it through the hull, and there are no portholes in the control module. It is just a solid composite sphere attached to the front of the ship. The only holes in the sphere are the access door and the circuit trunks, and those lead back into the ship, not outside. The trunks all self-sealed as soon as the main hull lost pressure, and cut the lines, or we'd all be dead."

"Okay. Can we get to the outside by going through the access door?"

He shook his head again.

"The hull is evacuated. We have two pressure suits in this compartment, but there are five of us, and there is no air lock, so if we crack that access door, the oxygen is gone and everybody dies but the two people in suits. I suppose we could draw straws."

"Nope. Not an option," I said. "Barraki and Tweezaa can't manage the job by themselves, and nobody gets in a suit unless it's them."

Marfoglia looked at me oddly when I said that. I shrugged. Way it is.

"You said there are no windows," Marfoglia said to Ping. "But I think I remember one."

"The access hatch has one, but it just shows you the interior corridor; it does not open on the outside," Ping answered.

"Well, what's that flickering light shining through it?" she asked.

The flickering light, it turned out, was the reflected glow of Mogo, blinking on and off as the wreckage tumbled and brought the planet into and out of view.

How could a planet come into and out of view of an interior window? It wasn't an interior window anymore. The control module had broken completely free from the main body of the ship and was tumbling.

When we looked, we could catch glimpses of the main wreckage of the *Long Shot* receding from us.

That was bad news, in a way. The wreckage was the biggest radar signature around. The farther we got away from it, the more chance there was that, even if someone saw *it* on radar, they'd miss *us*.

But it did give us an outside window, and that gave us an outside chance. I almost wanted to kiss Marfoglia for noticing it. But—you know—just out of gratitude.

It took the better part of another hour, but we rigged up the highest intensity light we could, secured it to the window, and backed it up with whatever reflective surfaces we could find, to direct as many photons as possible out that little circle of clear composite material. We rigged a capacitor pumped from the battery and set it to discharge and strobe once every two minutes. After about ten minutes, Ping did a battery check and some calculations.

"Eight hours," he said. "No more. Then the battery's dead. As it is, we'll start losing intensity after six hours or so."

Marfoglia looked at Ping and then at me.

"What do you think, Sasha?" she asked.

"I guess it's all our decisions, but I vote to keep the light going as long and as bright as possible. If no one finds us, what does an extra couple hours of heat buy?"

Marfoglia and Ping nodded, and that was that.

Four hours later and I wasn't so sure. I was developing a fantasy that, once it looked like there was no hope, we should crank the heat up and get warm one last time. I was so cold, I was almost anxious to run out of hope. Getting warm seemed more important.

We were floating in a big ball in the center of the control module, tethered between two stanchions so we wouldn't drift against a wall. The walls were white with frost, would suck the heat out of you if you so much as brushed up against them, and the air was chalk dry, scouring my lungs with every breath.

We had Barraki and Tweezaa in the middle of the ball, with the three of us around them, and the blankets tied around us, trying to keep as much body heat in as we could. We'd rigged a hood over our heater and run a hose into our floating cocoon, because there was no point in wasting heat on the outside. It was bearable in the middle, but the back of my head, arms, and body were so cold I'd lost all feeling in them. I couldn't make my fingers work anymore, and I was afraid to move my feet, because every time a toe brushed against the inside of my shoe, it felt as if it might come off. I wondered if they'd have to amputate my fingers and toes even if they did rescue us, and I didn't care. I didn't care whether or not they rescued us, didn't care whether or not they cut my fingers, toes, or even my cock off. I just didn't give a damn anymore, I was that cold.

What I did feel was a tug on the straps, and then I felt dizzy. It felt as if something had spun our cocoon, but that's not what it was at all. Something had abruptly *stopped* the control module from tumbling—a rescue/recovery gantry arm, as it turned out.

Then we heard the voice. The voice was all around us, filling the air. That's because it was transmitted inductively through the composite hull of the control module, using the walls as a giant speaker, but we didn't know that at the time. All we knew was we were surrounded by this booming, flat-sounding, metallic but recognizably feminine voice, speaking in aGavoosh, but in the middle of it all, there were these English words, words which seemed nonsensical and out of place.

The words were *U.S.S. John Fitzgerald Kennedy*.

EIGHTEEN

They had us in heated thermo-wraps, sitting at the small table in the crew's mess, drinking steaming soup out of big white navy mugs with no handles. I was still shivering so hard I could hardly get the soup to my mouth, but we were alive, and that felt pretty good.

The five of us sat at the table, along with the young-looking khaki-clad executive officer, while two *very* young-looking mess mates kept an eye on us—well, mostly on Marfoglia—and kept the soup coming: redroot soup for Barraki and Tweezaa, miso for the rest of us.

Barraki and Tweezaa were still pretty shaken up—maybe no more than the rest of us, but unlike us they hadn't yet acquired the adult compulsion to deny weakness. They sat between Marfoglia and me on one side of the mess table, with Ping and the executive officer on the other—which made it a tight fit on our side, but that was fine with them. More than anything, I think they needed the touch of another living being for assurance. Under the table, Tweezaa had found my left hand and was holding it. I didn't mind.

"What hit us?" Ping asked.

"Sir, we believe your ship was hit by a Type Nine-Delta torpedo," the executive officer answered.

"Is that what they call a *fire lance*?" I asked, remembering what Ping had told me.

"Yes, sir, a *Kot'pa*," he answered. Since the highest rank I'd ever managed was corporal, it felt odd having a lieutenant commander call me sir, but there was no stopping him—I'd already tried.

"Did you fire it?" Ping asked.

"No, sir, we did not. We believe it was fired by the cruiser *KZa-91*. I'm afraid that for the better part of a day, we've been in the middle of a hot war. The situation is not entirely clear, but here's what we know.

"A major famine on K'Tok brought on a series of epidemics, as well as looting and attacks against the colonial government. The death toll is in the thousands, from what we've been able to piece together, but I don't think anyone knows for sure."

"Yes, we were bringing in relief supplies ourselves," Ping put in, and the executive officer nodded and went on.

"When civil authority started collapsing down there, the Commanding General, *Cottohazz* Ground Forces K'Tok, declared martial law. That was nearly two months ago. Our task force deployed out of Fleet Base Akaampta twenty-nine days ago to support disaster relief and recovery operations. We landed three mobile field hospitals, three cohorts of military police, and one cohort of engineers, and were on station prepared to back them up with fleet Marine landing teams, if necessary."

He stopped and took a drink of his coffee. I think he was collecting his thoughts, too.

"Five days ago the task force withdrew to Mogo for scheduled refueling operations, leaving one cruiser— *KZa-91*—in orbit over K'Tok on communication watch and quick reaction alert. Our task force had five cruisers and three transports. Of the cruisers, *KZa-121* and *KZa-91* were both uZmataanki registry. That's what the 'Za' in their hull number indicates. *KHo-77* was uHoko registry, and *KBk-501* was uBakai—that's also where Commodore Takaapti flew his pennant. The *Fitz*, *KUs-222*, was the fifth cruiser."

Interesting—four Varoki cruisers, but from three different Varoki nations, three different navies. The truth was, I'd always had an outsider's view of the Varoki, had always thought of them as one homogeneous group, absolutely united in their collective desire to screw the living hell out of us Humans. Just from the way the executive officer was talking, I began to think maybe that wasn't quite the case.

Boy, was that an understatement.

"We were well along with the refueling operation earlier this morning," he went on. "The *Fitz* was tanks full and the uBakai cruiser, the pennant, was just starting its skim of Mogo's upper atmosphere when the captain of the uZmataanki cruiser came on the horn and ordered us to up-orbit and stand away. The uHoko cruiser complied, but the skip . . . Captain Gasiri refused, based on standing orders from the task force commander."

"What did your commodore say?" I asked, but Ping shook his head.

"If he was skimming hydrogen, he would be heavy in ionization—no comms."

The executive officer nodded.

"That's correct, sir. He was comm-dead when the uZmataanki cruiser made his demand."

The executive officer stopped and took another sip of coffee, and frowned, remembering what came next.

"At 0531 Akaampta Zulu, the uZmataanki cruiser launched one torpedo at the uBakai cruiser," he said.

"*At the flagship?*" I asked. This was nuts!

"At the pennant, sir," the executive officer corrected me. "Only admirals fly flags."

"Yeah, whatever. You mean you had two Varoki ships shooting at each other?"

"One ship firing on another, yes, sir. There was no return fire from the pennant. I doubt they knew they were under attack.

"We were in the high-guard position at weapons up, and Captain Gasiri immediately ordered our point-defense battery to engage and destroy the missile, which we accomplished. On or about 0535 Akaampta Zulu, the uZmataanki fired two additional missiles, one at the pennant and one at us. Captain Gasiri salvoed three missiles in reply and engaged the incoming missile with point-defense fire. We took out the missile aimed at us, and one of our missiles got through to him, but the pennant was hit at about 0540 and disappeared into the lower atmosphere. We logged it as 'Presumed Lost with All Hands.'"

I wondered if this was how he talked all the time—this flat and precise and completely devoid of color or emotion. If so, I bet he didn't get laid much.

He took another sip of coffee, and I had the sudden realization that we were getting a sneak preview—or maybe a dress rehearsal—of his testimony before the naval board of inquiry which would *certainly* be convened—assuming any of us lived that long.

Beside me, Tweezaa tried to lift her soup mug but couldn't manage it with one hand, and seemed reluctant to let go of my hand under the table. I reached over with my free right hand and held one side of the mug, really lifted it for her, but let her guide it to her mouth with her left hand, and then I put it back down on the table when she was done. She wiped her mouth with her left hand, smacked her lips loudly, and said, "Ahhh!" Then she looked up at me and we smiled at each other. The young exec across the table smiled, too, but then he remembered the thread of his story, and the smile drifted away.

I'll spare you his exact words from here on out—I think you've got the idea of how he talked. I'd already started thinking of him as Captain Didactic, and if I'd said it out loud, I bet he'd have corrected me, and said, "Excuse me, sir, but I believe you meant to say Lieutenant Commander Didactic."

It turned out their one missile hit on the rogue uZmataanki cruiser had killed it—a catastrophic kill, the exec called it. They'd convinced the uHoko cruiser to resume station and had looked for survivors, but no luck. Then about three hours later they'd gotten jumped by the other uZmataanki cruiser, the one they thought had stayed behind at K'Tok. It came up from behind Mogo and blindsided them, salvoed its missiles in a fast flyby, and hit the *Fitz* once and the uHoko cruiser twice. Three missiles went long without acquiring a target, and one of them must have hit the *Long Shot*. The *Fitz* lost main power for a couple hours, then they patched things up, rescued eighteen survivors from the wreck of the uHoko cruiser, and were about to take out after the uZmataanki ship when they noticed our improvised distress signal.

"We thank you for that," Ping said. "How badly were you hurt, son?"

His story had been emotionless, almost robotic until then, but Ping's question triggered a flash of pain across his face, gone almost as soon as it appeared.

"One of our troop-bay modules took the hit, sir. We lost seventeen fleet Marines. Other than that, most of the damage was from a power spike and cascading overloads—but we're back on line with about eighty percent function."

Eighty percent function, and that from a cruiser that—no matter how well built or well manned—was technologically no match for that undamaged uZmataanki cruiser out there. So what were they about to do? Pursue. You had to admire these guys, but to be honest, I'd have preferred to admire them from a safer distance.

"But why?" Marfoglia asked. It was about the first thing she'd said since we'd been rescued—other than a lot of thank-yous to the sailors that helped us aboard. "Why this attack? It doesn't make any sense."

"Well, like I started to say earlier, ma'am, it looks like we're in a shooting war between the uZmataanki and uBakai. The main colony enclave on K'Tok is uZmataanki, but there's a big uBakai colony down there as well. The uZmataanki say the uBakai engineered the famine and revolt so they could move in under the cover of the *Cottohazz* and take over. The uBakai say that's bullsh—Sorry, ma'am. They say that's not true.

"We don't know who's lying, and we're not really sure

who's at war with whom. The uBakai and uZmataanki, for sure, but where's the *Cottohazz* going to stand in all this, once the diplomats and lawyers try to sort things out? Who knows? We just know we were fired at while conducting lawful operations under the *Cottohazz* charter. We also know, or at least suspect, that this was not a spontaneous act by a local commander. Both uZmataanki captains acted in concert, apparently following a prearranged plan, and at the same time, uZmataanki civilian government personnel disabled most system-wide C3 facilities—that's Command, Control, and Communication."

"That must be when we lost contact with K'Tok Orbital," Ping said.

"Yes, sir," he answered. Then the executive officer glanced over my shoulder and suddenly jumped to his feet and barked, *"Captain on deck!"* The mess mates also snapped to, and I almost did as well. Funny how old habits can come back when you least expect them.

"Stand easy," the captain said, in a surprisingly lilting voice, and I turned to look.

Captain Gasiri appeared to be in her forty-somethings, short and stocky, with close-cropped black hair now turning gray. She had a dark complexion, with a long pointy chin, a nose on her like a falcon's beak, and hard black eyes to match.

"Is the XO taking good care of you people?" she demanded, her words quick. We all nodded or murmured assent.

"I apologize for the accommodations. Things are fairly Spartan on board in the best of times, and between you and the survivors of our other cruiser, we're packed in like sardines. I'd transfer you to one of our fleet auxiliaries, but I ordered them toward K'Tok several hours ago for their own safety, so I'm afraid you're stuck with us for now." She turned to the executive officer then.

"XO, take the con."

"Aye, aye, ma'am," he said, and he practically sprinted away.

She turned back to us.

"The mess mates will help get you into acceleration racks. In about ten minutes I'm going to secure the wheel and commence a long, hard delta-vee. You have my apologies for that, too."

"What's a delta-vee?" Marfoglia asked.

"A vector change, ma'am," Gasiri answered. "A hard thruster burn. It *will* be uncomfortable."

"As long as we're warm, we'll be fine," Marfoglia answered, pulling the thermo-wrap tighter around her, and I smiled. *Boy, ain't that the truth?*

"But your sensors were down for several hours," Ping said. "Do you even know which way they went?"

"Oh, yes," Gasiri answered, nodding grimly. "Our transports tracked him and coded us on tight beam a few minutes ago. I know right where he is."

"And you're going after him?" I asked.

"What's your name, sir?"

"Naradnyo."

"Mr. Naradnyo, we are indeed going after him, for three reasons. First, because as the only remaining *Cottohazz* combatant vessel in the system, it is our duty to do so, and no mother's son is ever going to say the *Fitz* didn't do its duty. Second, because I've got three missiles left and he's only got one ship, and that's math I understand. But third, and most importantly, because that son of a bitch killed seventeen of my Marines. *My* Marines, Mr. Naradnyo. May Allah have mercy on his soul, because I sure as hell won't.

"Any questions?"

"No, ma'am."

My kind of gal.

NINETEEN

The long acceleration was every bit as uncomfortable as Gasiri had promised. Well, uncomfortable is what it was for the first twenty minutes or so; after that, it was agony.

For one thing, after a while I went blind—what they call a visual blackout. It's the result of the blood being forced to the back of your head and temporarily starving the optic nerves, but there's still enough blood flowing around up there to keep you conscious—if not particularly smart—so it's not a full blackout.

It also felt like my eyes were going to collapse back into my skull, and like my ribs were going to break under the weight of the elephant sitting on my chest. Tweezaa, strapped in beside me, started crying, and I started getting mad. Maybe Gasiri had no choice but to make this long hard burn to overtake *KZa-91*, but I didn't care. I was still pissed at her, because she was making Tweezaa cry. Now, how dumb is that?

When the burn was over, I didn't feel a whole lot better. I had a terrible headache that wouldn't go away. The pain killers the mess mates gave me made me groggy, and just reduced the pain from two red-hot daggers in my eye sockets to a dull pounding ache. And these guys did this for a living? A life of crime started sounding better.

A few hours later, Captain Gasiri sent word for Ping to join her on the bridge, and he was gone the whole time the actual "battle" took place. He told me what happened later, and so here it is.

Naval combat, he tells me, is like blindman's bluff with sawed-off shotguns. Hitting someone with a sawed-off shotgun isn't all that hard, provided you know about where he is. Figuring out where he is—that's the hard part.

Gasiri knew where the uZmataanki cruiser—*KZa-91*—was: an inbound glide toward K'Tok. The enemy cruiser had a much more advanced sensor suite than the *Fitz*, and a better point-defense battery—one that could actually kill us if we got close enough. Its liabilities were that it was probably out of missiles and, much more importantly, it was convinced we were dead.

Gasiri needed to close the distance quickly, before we got in range of any orbital sensors around K'Tok, which were more powerful than anything carried by a ship, even the uZmataanki cruiser. It was also important that the burn be executed far away from the quarry, so its own passive thermal sensors wouldn't pick it up—hence a very hard but comparatively short burn to kick our speed up. Then it was just a question of coasting with all of our active sensors turned off, until we were in a firing position.

Of course, with active sensors off, Gasiri couldn't "see" the target until after they could see us, and that was too late to fire, so we had to fire blind, and hope they hadn't made a course correction. Also, once we got closer to the uZmataanki cruiser, it occluded the direct line of sight to the transports, so we couldn't get tight-beam updates from them without risking a tip-off. Gasiri could turn on the actives to make sure the target was there, but that would alert the quarry and they would go weapons up, and have a better chance of taking out the missiles. But if Gasiri just salvoed her missiles, the target wouldn't have any hint of the danger until its collision-avoidance radars picked up the three overtaking objects, and by the time they were identified as missiles, it might be too late.

All well and good, provided the uZmataanki cruiser was exactly where it was supposed to be. If not, a blind three-missile salvo would just disarm us. A more cautious captain might have held back a missile just in case. Personally—and with the clear understanding that I don't really know beans about all this stuff—that struck me as a lousy idea. If it was really as much of a hot rod as all that, then what good was one missile held back going to do? I figured better to "flood the zone" and take your single very best shot at killing him. Pay your money and take your chance.

Gasiri and I must have thought a little bit alike, because that's exactly what she did—a blind three-missile shot once her astrogation officer told her we were as close as we could get without them picking us up on passives. Three missiles was overkill, as it turned out. *KZa-91* may have been a technologically really advanced ship, but the crew wasn't all that sharp. From what Ping told me, they never did get their point-defense batteries into action, and all three missiles hit; the third one just cut wreckage. We decelerated to search for survivors, and found seven Varoki Marines still alive in a troop module that had maintained its atmosphere. They were pretty shaken up and didn't have much of an idea what was going on, other than they were at war with the uBakai, and they thought they'd won the first battle.

One thing that I'd wondered about through all of this was why they all had so few missiles. I asked about it. Missiles are big and expensive. Cruisers could carry more, but why? There wasn't anyone to shoot them at—most of the time—and the primary mission of the cruisers was to transport security personnel, so they were mission-configured for that. Most of their extra space was taken up with attached troop modules instead of more missile packs.

Here's another question: why had Gasiri asked Ping to the bridge? I figured it was just professional courtesy, but that wasn't it at all. By the time we made it to K'Tok orbit, three days later, all of us knew. You didn't need to be a rocket scientist to figure it out. As fouled up as everything had gotten, Gasiri wanted an independent witness of her decisions in that last fight—someone who knew something about how spacecraft work, and who was outside the chain of command.

You notice things about people in small places, and a guided missile cruiser is pretty small. Well, it's really big on the outside, but there's a lot of stuff that sort of fills it all up. It has a maneuvering crew of sixty-three, of which about twenty are officers and the rest enlisted personnel. There are a variable number of Marines, since the troop modules are detachable and can be configured different ways, but the *Fitz* was rigged to carry one hundred twenty at that time, of which forty-four were down on K'Tok and seventeen had been killed by the missile hit, which meant there were fifty-nine still on board. That made it pretty crowded, even though the Marines spent a lot of time on their own in their troop modules, which doubled as platoon bays.

You'd see the Marines early in the morning, running PT in formation in the big open corridor around the outer level of the wheel. That's what the open corridor was for—running. People have to stay in shape, although the Marines were more serious about it than most of the rest of the crew. The mess hall was only set up for about seventy, so they usually fed the Marines in two shifts, but now they fed them all at once. The Marines were subdued in the days following the battle—shaken, actually, but trying really hard not to show it. Marines are a pretty tightly knit group, in my limited experience of them, and the price they pay is that loss, when and if it comes, cuts deeper.

The men and women of the maneuvering crew, on the other hand, were so excited they could hardly stay in their skins. Of course, they were all professionals, and so they tried to maintain a calm businesslike façade, as if they did this sort of thing all the time. But they didn't. Nobody did. No Terran spacecraft had ever destroyed a hostile spacecraft in combat—ever, like . . . in history. And now the *Fitz* had *two* kills. When they got back home, even the Exec was going to get laid. *A lot.*

Watching the emotions fighting for control on the faces of the kids in the crew—I thought of them as kids anyway—was like watching a sack full of cats: you knew there was a lot going on inside, but it was hard to make out exactly what.

On one hand, of course, there was the thrill of the kill, and along with it the huge adrenaline rush that comes from just surviving something like that—surviving when the smart money says you haven't got a chance. Take it from me, nothing in the world feels like that. Nothing. An orgasm is real close, which I guess is why sex and violence get all tangled up so often. But I'll tell you, if you could put those two sensations—the kill, and the survival rush—together in a spike, *everyone* would be a junkie.

The day after the fight, I was in the crew's mess when the astrogator came in, and the dozen or so crewpersons around the mess tables—men and women alike—started barking like dogs, whistling, and banging their coffee mugs on the table. The astrogator had called the timing of the shot, and she'd been right on the money. She was a lieutenant, mid or late twenties, and I suppose you'd call her plain—not ugly by any means, but not someone you'd pick out of a crowd, either—and if I'd seen her in civvies and subjected to this sort of reception, I guess I'd have expected her to blush. Instead, she flashed everyone in the mess hall a big, wide, toothy grin—exactly the way a hunting cat shows you the teeth it's going to use to kill and eat you. They were killers, and they were alive, and it felt *really* good.

That's one side of it. But then there's the baggage. I'd see a couple crewmembers punching each other on the shoulders, high as a kite, and then one of them would remember something, and he or she would get this faraway look, and then the other one would get embarrassed. Some of them were remembering the seventeen crewmen who hadn't made it, and they were getting a taste of survivor's remorse. I guess some of them—not all of them, but enough—were thinking about those Varoki that had died in the two ships they'd killed, too. All the super-macho chest-beating meat puppets on the news vids, who'd never fired a shot in anger, would howl down anyone who said there was any reason to feel remorse at the death of an enemy, but military sailors through history have always had ambivalent feelings about the deaths of their opponents—probably because most of them considered their *real* enemy the sea. Well, if you think the sea's a bitch, try deep space.

So you mix that incredible high with that incredible low, and before you know it you're puking jambalaya into a little wastebasket with pictures of elephants on it—and that's if you're a heartless thug like me. These were kids.

The only point I'm trying to make is, the crew's feelings were complicated—because they were Human beings, and Human beings are complicated, and anyone who tells you all this stuff is simple is either a liar or a fool, or more likely a bit of both.

But all that having been said, the crew was pretty high most of the time. The officers were a different story. They were high the first day, too, but after that, it started looking more like an act than the real thing. What did they know that I didn't?

Were we in trouble? Maybe so. We were "bingo

missiles," as the crew put it—which meant the hard points were all empty. We were the only warship left in-system, and who knew if the next warship to show up would be friendly? Who knew what was even going on anywhere else? Gasiri had ordered one of the transports back to Akaampta to report and ask for reinforcements, but you can't just stop and turn around in deep space. Everything was already committed to an inbound glide toward K'Tok, so the transport would finish its fall, slingshot around K'Tok, head out-system again, and then jump. That would eat the better part of a week right there, and who knew how long it would take for Akaampta to respond—assuming they were even able to.

I'd rather have been on that transport bound for Akaampta, but it was about a day ahead of us inbound, and orbital mechanics are spectacularly uninterested in the affairs of people.

My problems aside, it was a potentially unsettling situation for the crew. But the officers didn't look worried. To me, they looked sort of sad and depressed.

What would make them feel that way? They were all going home heroes. Right?

So I reverse engineered the problem. I started with the assumption that they *weren't* all going home heroes and backtracked from there. If someone were going to paint this in the worst possible light, what colors would they use?

The *Fitz* had stopped the first attack on the flagship—sorry, the "pennant." The second one got through, but they'd killed the attacker. Looked to me as if they'd done everything they could. Then they'd got hit by surprise by the second uZmataanki cruiser and disabled. Once they repaired the damage, they'd rescued all the survivors there, had gone after the second cruiser, and killed it. They were in a clear state of hostilities, so legally there didn't seem to be much problem with the *Fitz*'s actions.

I went over it again. On alert, responded quickly, successfully engaged enemy, reassembled task force, searched for survivors, caught by surprise...

Caught by surprise.

Three hours after the initial attack—three hours— the *Fitz* had been caught by surprise by the second cruiser. Gasiri had known there was a second uZmata-anki cruiser in the system, and she'd been caught by surprise anyway. She hadn't known the attack was part of a deliberate, coordinated operation—but she hadn't known it wasn't, either. Could she have known for sure a second attack was coming? No. Should she have anticipated the *possibility* of a second attack?

Yeah.

And because she hadn't, seventeen of her Marines were dead, along with most of the crew of the uHoko cruiser, which she'd assumed command of—and responsibility for—when she took over the task force.

Hard telling how tight-assed the navy was going to be about this; I didn't exactly rub elbows with high-ranking navy types back on Peezgtaan—wouldn't have even if Peezgtaan *had* a navy—and every country's navy has a different organizational culture. But even if they were the most reasonable guys in the galaxy, it was hard to make this look like a completely successful command. People had died. That's why I figure Captain Gasiri wanted an independent witness on the bridge during the second fight.

Gasiri had done pretty well—in my purely amateur's opinion—as a ship's captain. As a task-force commander—not so much. So what would they do? My guess was—best case—they'd give her a nice big medal, send her to some academy to teach ship tactics, and right before she retired, they'd give her a bump to admiral, so she'd have a nicer pension. But she'd never command another task force, or probably another ship. And a lot of people would claim that was a raw deal, but I'm willing to bet she wouldn't be one of them.

Her Marines.

TWENTY

Our ears popped a lot on the way down the Needle, and the four-hour ride was time enough to gradually accustom our bodies to the higher atmospheric pressure at the surface. K'Tok was nothing like Peezgtaan. We got a good look at it, riding the Needle down, and it was beautiful—deep blue water oceans, thousands of miles of lush green rain forest, with brown and gray and white mountain ranges bursting out of the jungle canopy. There were probably deserts and savannah and badlands and all that other stuff as well, but near the equator we mostly saw open ocean and dense rainforest. Life didn't have to hide down in a crack here—it turned its face up to the sky without fear and gave it a great big grin. Made me grin, too.

Oh, yeah, one more interesting difference from Peezgtaan—there was no Human enclave. I'd scanned the planetary profile when we got the word we were heading down, and I'd been surprised to see the population breakdown by race and nationality: 61% Varoki of uZmataanki nationality, 32% Varoki of uBakai nationality, 5% other Varoki of various nationalities, 2% Zaschaan and Katami of various nationalities. Not one Human permanent resident.

You had to wonder who fenced all the stolen goods. Or stole them in the first place.

There were scattered clouds down below, thicker right underneath us, so that the Needle seemed to disappear into them. We passed through the clouds, and then rain lashed the view ports when we broke through, no more than a couple thousand meters above the surface. K'Tok Downstation was in a broad valley, surrounded distantly on three sides by jungle-covered mountains and, more closely, by sprawling habitation—industrial parks mixed with residential areas, commercial centers, and a clot of stately, official-looking buildings fairly close by Needledown.

The plantary profile listed T'tokl-Heem as the name of the city sprawling around Needledown—it was the main commercial center on the planet and also the administrative capital of the uZmataanki colony. Judging from the extent of the settlement's footprint coming down from orbit, T'tokl-Heem was a fair-sized city, for a colony world; I'd guess there were upwards of a hundred thousand folks living there. As we got lower, I couldn't help but notice that, the rain notwithstanding, there were scattered columns of thick black smoke curling upwards from a couple neighborhoods in the city. Other than that, though, it didn't look too bad.

Things look different from the air than they do on the ground.

We stepped out of the capsule's air lock and right away got a nose full of K'Tok. It was hot and wet, the air filled with that earthy smell of growth and decay that's common to the tropics everywhere. It didn't stink like I remembered Nishtaaka had, though. There'd always been a smell of sour milk, rotting meat, and something else unpleasant I couldn't put my finger on. I should have been used to it, because you get a whiff of it on Peezgtaan often enough as well, that odor of alien proteins and funky chemical reactions that your body instinctively knows just aren't right. It was funny, but I didn't get that here—maybe because the smell was laced with a hint of burning synthetics, and in my experience that's the odor of trouble.

The thing is, we weren't outside. We were still inside K'Tok Downstation, and the air conditioners should have lowered the temp and humidity as well as filtered out a lot of those smells. So that meant the environmental system wasn't working, which the big tower fans scattered around, hooked up to snaking, tangled temporary power lines, confirmed. I saw a lot of portable terminals, so the central data systems must have been down as well. The downport staff looked short-handed, sweaty, and flustered. Some of them looked worried, and a few were outright scared.

There was security everywhere—more guns than data clickers, that's for sure. Security was provided by a mix of folks—downstation corporate rent-a-cops with AZ Kagataan corporate logos on their jump suits, uZmataanki troops from the local colonial authority, and some of the imported Co-Gozhak MPs Gasiri's task force had brought. All of them were Varoki, of course, the different groups distinguishable by their uniforms and, to a degree, by their attitudes, although they were all pretty edgy looking. I wouldn't have minded seeing a bunch of Gasiri's Marines right about then—or even a platoon of Zack dirt soldiers, when you got right down to it. Zacks may not be great conversationalists, but they don't spook very easily. These guys were spooked.

Other quick impressions: overflowing trash containers. Carpet stained and sticky. Broken furniture in the waiting areas which no one had cleaned up. The faint, distant, musical tinkle of auto-fire flechettes hitting metal.

If Gasiri had known what was going on down here, I doubt she would have sent us down the Needle. Her reasoning was that the rescued civilians and ship's crew, along with the captive uZmataanki Marines, would be safer down here than in either her cruiser or one of the nearly empty unarmed transports, since there was no telling when or if more uZmataanki warships might show up. Of all the odds and ends of rescued friend and foe, only Joe Lee Ping had remained aboard the *Fitz*. His testimony might be needed on short notice. But as to the rest of us, better to ground us and let the local Co-Gozhak commander look after us.

It had sounded reasonable in orbit.

There were thirty-four of us: the eighteen surviving uHoko crewmen, seven uZmataanki Marines, four of Gasiri's Marines guarding them, the four of us from Long Shot, and Gasiri's executive officer—Lieutenant Commander Fong-Ramirez—with orders to deliver a face-only report to Commanding General, *Cottohazz* Ground Forces, K'Tok, although when they talked about the ground general, they called him COGCOG-K'Tok.

First time I heard it, I said, "And coo-coo-kachoo to you, too," but the naval ensign I was talking to just looked blank.

I guess we'd had our share of acronyms and buzz words in the Army as well. We'd have called him "the CG, K'Tok," but that didn't sound so tight-assed to me; it sounded squared away. There's a big difference between being tight-assed and being squared away.

Honest.

But ground security at Needledown didn't look like it was either of those things . . . Well, I guess you could argue for tight-assed, in the sense that the pucker factor was right up near the top of the scale.

They had already processed us at K'Tok Highstation, so the ground staff and security goons just waved us through, which I thought was pretty sloppy. A Varoki MP captain met us at the end of the concourse and explained the situation in aGavoosh to Fong-Ramirez. One of the Marines translated for the sergeant in charge of the security detail, and since we were standing about as close to her and her Marines as we could get, Marfoglia didn't need to repeat it for me.

A bus was waiting outside to take us to the Co Gozhak headquarters compound, where we'd be processed more carefully. Simple enough. We all tramped down the nearly empty corridors to the main entrance, shuffled through the security gates one at a time under the big *AZ Kagataan Welcomes You To K'Tok* banner—in aZmataan—and came out into light rain. The bus—also an AZ Kagataan corporate charter—was at the curb, with a hard gun-car in front of it and another behind it. As we hit the street, we all stopped and just looked around for a while, mouths open.

There was a lot of trash in the streets, a lot of broken windows, and I saw two burned-out ground transports, one of them rolled over on its side. When people don't bother to clean that stuff up, it's generally a bad sign.

But what really creeped us all out was the silence. There wasn't one moving vehicle in sight, not one pedestrian. Everyone wasn't dead, so that meant they were staying inside, and folks don't do that without a pretty good reason.

The Marine sergeant—Wataski was her name—broke the spell.

"Okay, people, you've had your 'oh shit' moment. Now let's get these detainees on the bus. _Pronto, muchachos._"

She was supposedly just talking to the three Marines in her guard detail, but all of us got the message.

All during the ride across the city, I kept expecting our four-vehicle convoy to be attacked, but it wasn't. A couple times we stopped and I could see the Varoki MP NCO, up at the front with Fong-Ramirez, talking by secure comm to the convoy commander. Then we'd start up again, sometimes continuing, sometimes turning at the next corner, and once backing up and turning down a side street.

Once when we turned I saw a manned roadblock down the street we'd been following—a couple spikey-bars across the street, a combat walker in an alley but with its autogun mount visible and covering the street, and four or five uniformed grunts out there on duty. The grunts didn't look like insurgents; they looked like colonial regular troops. No one was shooting, but we were avoiding them.

I'd herded Marfoglia, Barraki, and Tweezaa onto the bus and parked us in two rows of seats almost at the back and near the rear exit door, with Marfoglia and I sitting in the window seats and the kids in the aisle seats. Marfoglia and I would shelter them from any broken glass that way. I'd done all that, but my attention was on what was going on outside. Now I looked at them.

Both kids had been pretty sick from the anti-allergy and anti-viral shots we'd gotten the previous day, and they still looked rocky. They hadn't bothered me or Marfoglia that much, and as I looked around, I noticed that the Marines standing in the aisle seemed to be in better shape than the Varoki sitting in the seats. No telling with body chemistry.

I looked back at the kids. They weren't just sick; they were pretty scared, too.

"Why are we turning?" Barraki asked, once my glance let him know that I'd mentally returned to the interior of the bus.

"Are those insurgents down there?" Marfoglia asked, looking at the roadblock.

I shrugged. I didn't think so, but I wasn't sure.

"No. They are local troops," I heard a voice say, and one of the Varoki sitting in the row ahead of us turned and looked at us. He was in the plain yellow jumpsuit they'd given all the captive uZmataanki Marines, and he had a single-piece soft conforming bandage covering most of one side of his face and head—a burn-graft sustainer compress, from the looks of it.

"We trained with them, before..." His voice trailed off and he looked around, unsure what word to use. War? Unpleasantness? Sneak attack? Atrocity? Mistake?

Finally, he just tilted his head to one side—a shrug.
Before *this*.

"Hey, Curley!" one of the Marine guards standing in the center aisle said sharply, pointing to the
wounded Varoki Marine to make it clear which of
the prisoners he was talking to. "Zip it, *hombre*."

Most of the Varoki on the bus—not just the
prisoners—looked at the Marine with a mix of surprise and resentment. At least some of the uHoka
crewmen had entertained the notion that we might
all be united in brotherhood by common adversity,
regardless of race or nationality. But calling a hairless
Varoki "Curley" was not much different than calling
him a leather-head, and everybody on the bus knew
it. Sergeant Wataski shot the Marine a sharp look,
but the rifleman's defiant glare remained intact.

Hard to blame him; he'd lost friends. Hard to
blame the Varoki Marine, either. It's not as if anyone
had asked his opinion before charging off to war,
and he'd lost friends, too, probably a lot more of
them. Hard to blame anyone on the bus, or anyone
down at that roadblock. Hard to blame Gasiri, or
even the dead captains of the dead uZmataanki cruisers, carrying out orders from their government and
high command. But here we were, going down this
waterslide of blood, picking up speed every second,
and the fact that there didn't seem to be anyone
handy to blame wasn't making the ride any more fun.

aGavoosh is a heavy, guttural language, very well-
suited to angry rants. Since I don't speak it, I let
Marfoglia do all the ranting while I looked around
the deputy attaché for something-or-other's office. It

was messy, like everything else I'd seen on K'Tok. All the comforting administrative routines were crumbling, and that's probably one of the things that made the paper pushers so cranky, but it didn't explain all of it.

I mean, here this guy was, a Varoki, a cultural attaché of some sort for the *Cottohazz*, pressed into emergency refugee management, with anti-government insurgents all over the place and a nice little side war going on between the uBakai and uZmataanki. Here we were, two Humans taking care of a couple Varoki kids in trouble. And they weren't just any Varoki kids; these were the e-Traak heirs, and he knew it. Up in orbit, the only remaining functional— and loyal—*Cottohazz* warship in the star system was Human-manned. You'd think this guy would be interested in helping us, or would at least pretend to be. But no.

So I let Marfoglia do the yelling, because even though I knew yelling wasn't going to budge this guy, it let her blow off some steam, which I figured was good for her mental health. Besides, all the steam she vented at this jerk was steam that wouldn't vent my way.

I studied the guy while he sat there and took everything Marfoglia dished out, and from the way he flushed now and then, his ears back against his skull, I figure she must have been dishing it pretty good. But he wasn't moving. He didn't like being yelled at, but it was just a temporary discomfort; this too would pass.

What makes an official of the *Cottohazz* so unin-terested in apparent loyalty and/or service to it?

What makes a Varoki so uninterested in helping the scions of a wealthy and powerful Varoki mercantile clan?

The paranoid answer is that he was being paid not to help us, and believe me, there's a lot to be said for paranoia. I just wasn't buying it today. He didn't act like a guy who was on the take; guys on the take usually make excuses, or try to feed you a line of bull. This guy acted like he honestly just didn't give a damn.

How far did he think that was going to get him in his career? Not very far. So the question was, why didn't he give a damn about *that*?

Marfoglia's rant had subsided, and the official—Vice-Consul Zasa-litaan, according to the glowing name plaque on the wall behind him—had finally begun speaking again, explaining something in his bored, tired-sounding voice, maybe offering something. He and Marfoglia exchanged a few more comments, and she turned to me.

"He's offered to put us in touch with AZ Simki-Traak corporate security on K'Tok. That's about all he's willing to do until the maglev leaves for Haampta tomorrow."

I wasn't crazy about taking the maglev to Haampta to begin with. I wanted to climb back up the Needle ASAP, not head for some place over a thousand kilometers away from it, but we didn't really have an option. All of us from the *Fitz* were being shipped over to the Co-Gozhak's subsidiary ground forces headquarters in Haampta, the capital of the uBakai colony—security was supposedly a lot better there. All the *Cottohazz*'s senior commanders and staff wonks had already been flown over, but when one of the birds got knocked down by surface missile fire, they grounded all the air transports and now everything was moving by high-speed rail.

Okay. So the maglev train ride was a done deal. AZ Simki-Traak corporate security—they'd have lots of resources, and they'd be a lot more interested in helping protect the e-Traak heirs than this empty suit was.

Hmmm.

I'm told I have good verbal skills, so even when I use bad grammar, people tend to listen to me and think I'm pretty smart. Maybe you think that, too. But the truth is, I'm not as smart as I sound. I'm not stupid, but I'm no genius, either. If I were, there's something I'd have wondered about sooner.

Why hadn't Bony Jones gone to AZ Simki-Traak corporate security back on Peezgtaan? I mean, they practically ran the place. They had the Needle concession; they were the money behind the new *wattaak*. What the hell?

"Tell him thanks, but we'd rather keep the group small and low profile," I answered her.

Her eyes got big in her head, like she was getting up another head of steam, this time for me.

"Just do it," I said flatly. She'd opened her mouth to say something to me, but she shut it, looked at me with hard, angry eyes for a moment, and then turned back to the empty suit and gave him the news.

I'd explain later, when we were away from this guy. Once I spelled it all out for her, Marfoglia would agree.

Or not.

TWENTY-ONE

Flechettes slammed into the rock wall above us, flaying my back with razor-sharp chips. The building was native stone, which made it solid enough to stop all the incoming rounds except for the stuff that came through the windows, but those threw high-speed rock shards all over, and I could feel blood trickle down my back.

One of Sergeant Wataski's Marines staggered back from a window, coughing and gurgling wetly, blood bubbling out of her mouth and from around her hands where she held her throat. I was lying over Barraki, with Marfoglia covering Tweezaa closer against the wall.

"Marrissa, you've got to cover Barraki, too!"

She looked at me through a wild tangle of muddy blond hair, eyes wide with fright, but she didn't protest. She nodded jerkily and I pushed Barraki under her, next to Tweezaa, who was sobbing in terror. Barraki was shaking all over, but he was still in control. Brave little guy.

I rolled away from them, grabbed the Marine by her harness, and pulled her down onto her back. The Marines had different gear than I was used to, but there was only one thing that looked like it could be a wound kit. I ripped it open, pulled out the A-stop syringe and trachea kit, pushed the autoinserter into her mouth and part way down her throat, fired it and watched her body jerk and eyes bug out with agony as it slammed the breathing tube down her trachea and inflated it. Then I shot her neck full of A-stop, once I was sure it couldn't get down her throat and strangle her. I hit her with a shot of pain killer, too, and her eyes rolled back up into her head, but she'd probably live.

"You know what the fuck you're doing there?" Sergeant Wataski bellowed at me from another window.

"Yeah," I shouted back over the small-arms fire. "Been here."

"Then pick up her fucking weapon and cover that fucking window!"

For about a tenth of a second, I considered arguing the point, but Wataski had already turned away. My responsibility was Marfoglia and the kids, but if people came through the front door after all the damage Wataski's Marines had already dished out, they weren't going to stop shooting until a long time after everyone inside was dead.

So I picked up the Marine's weapon and gave it a quick once-over, checking its ammo and making sure it wasn't damaged. Mark 19 Rifle, Assault, Gauss— RAG-19 to its friends; four and a half kilos of light composites, with a few dense composites in critical places; 4.5mm serial flechette rifle with an integral 3cm grenade launcher; laser designator mounted on the under-slung utility bracket; four grenades and 100 flechettes internal, which added another kilo to the weight. I'd qualified on an older Mark 14, but there wasn't that much difference: aim, pull the trigger, somebody falls down.

I unhooked the Marine's ammo harness and threw it over my shoulder. Then I very carefully unhooked her helmet—tough with her still holding her throat with both hands. I needed the pot for more than just the protection, though; the gun's boresight video system dumped into the visor, so if I wanted to hit anything without sticking my own head up, I needed the helmet.

Her eyes were big and frightened, even with the painkillers in her bloodstream, and my face wasn't working right to give her a calm, reassuring expression. I just made myself go slow for the two or three seconds it took to slide the chin strap through her fingers. I cradled her head with one hand as I pulled off the helmet and then lowered it to the floor. She was still looking up at me, terrified, so I winked at her and grinned. It was hard to tell if she was trying to smile back, what with a trachea tube down her throat.

Marfoglia and Barraki were both looking at me, but their expressions were too wild to make out what they were thinking—if thinking was even how you'd describe what goes on in your head in a spot like this. I scrambled back to them, unzipped the black carryall, and pulled out the little LeMatt.

"You remember how to—"

"Fuck that!" Marfoglia practically screamed, cutting me off. *"Give me the big one!"*

Two hours out of T'tokl-Heem, the maglev current had died and we'd dropped onto the rail and slid about a kilometer along it, slowing to a halt. Nobody knew what was up, but we'd off-loaded, grabbed our gear, and started hiking toward the nearest town. There were over two hundred passengers, mostly evacuees bound for the uBakai colony, including a bunch of *Cottohazz* civilian officials and their dependents.

There was no well-planned ambush waiting for us. We just started getting some small-arms fire about a klick from the town—scattered single shots at first that didn't hit anyone, but they put everyone down in ditches and behind hedges. There wasn't anyone in charge, so no one to tell people to get up and move. Our group was lucky—Wataski and Fong-Ramirez both kept their heads and figured out we needed to get to some hard cover. A few people followed us, but most of them stayed out there in the ditches.

The firing got hotter as we got closer to the town, and we took our first casualties, but we made it to this stone house on the edge of the built-up area. Then things got very exciting for a while, but whoever was shooting at us decided the pickings were easier elsewhere. There was still scattered small-arms fire from down the road, where everyone else took cover. There were a few armed MPs back there, but if the bad guys—whoever the hell they were—decided it was massacre time, there wasn't going to be much to stop them.

After about fifteen minutes, the firing died away, and

once it looked like it wasn't going to start up again, Wataski made a head count. She had two Marines down: the Marine I'd patched up—Private Lashia Coleman, I found out—was still hanging on, but the guy who'd called the prisoner "Curley" took a head shot and was gone. That's one of the things about firing from behind hard cover—the cover protects most of your body, but the exposed parts are real important, and if you get hit there it's usually pretty bad news.

We'd lost four of the uHokos getting to the house, and two of the uZmataanki Marines had slipped away in the confusion. About a dozen other passengers had attached themselves to us, along with five Co-Gozhak MPs, four of whom were still standing. Including injured civilians, we had eight wounded, of which Coleman was the worst, but three of them would have to be carried if we were going anywhere.

Wataski reported the count to Fong-Ramirez, since he was the senior officer present—not that this sort of thing was covered by his training.

Wataski finished her report to Fong-Ramirez and then turned away and threw up in a corner. When she was done, she wiped her mouth and glared around the room, daring anyone to say something.

"Those bologna sandwiches on the train really sucked," I said.

"You think you're funny?" she demanded, eyes hard as steel.

"Yeah, a laugh a minute. You want an ammo count?"

She glared at me for a second or two, and then nodded.

"Yes. You dry?"

I shook my head.

"Nope. I got four mags left in the harness and seventeen rounds in the system. Two grenades still in the pipe, too, but I haven't checked your Marine's pack to see if she has any more."

"*Four mags?* You shy about shooting people?" she asked.

Behind me, I heard Marfoglia laugh humorlessly. I nodded over my shoulder.

"My fan club doesn't seem to think so. I just don't know when we're likely to see any more ammo, that's all, so I kept it on selective fire and used a light touch."

She scowled at me for a couple seconds, as if to intimidate me. The thing was, I wasn't drawing Marine pay, so she could give me all the *Real Bad Glares* she wanted to. My concern was three people, and if anybody here was going to live, they were. Period. So glare away, Wataski.

"Well, this is the situation," Fong-Ramirez said, a half hour later, to the semicircle of "shooters." He spoke in English, but one of the MPs muttered the translation into some Varoki language I didn't recognize for the two MPs that didn't understand English. The six Varoki each stood about a head taller than most of us Humans, so we made a ragged-looking huddle. The shadows were already long as Prime crowded K'Tok's horizon. Maybe I should have known the star's name, but nobody uses the star catalogues but astronomers and astrogators. What matters are the inhabitable worlds; the primary stars in most systems are just "Prime" to average guys like me, or "the Star," the way folks back on Earth just talk about "the Sun," not Sol.

Aside from Fong-Ramirez himself, there were nine

shooters: four Varoki MPs with sidearms, two Marines still standing—Wataski and Aguillar—the ranking uHoko officer, Lieutenant Palaan, who had picked up the other Marine assault rifle, a Varoki private security guy with his own gauss pistol, and me. Four RAG-19 combat weapon systems and five gauss pistols or light carbines—six with Fong-Ramirez's own sidearm: not much of an arsenal.

"We have a functional TBC—tight beam communicator," the exec went on, "but the satellite comm system is off-line, so we can't contact the *Fitz*—that's *KUs-222*—until we have line of sight, two hours from now. Even then, I'm not sure what the captain can do, but at least she can figure something out if she knows our situation."

"She can put the Mikes down, sir," Wataski said.

Fong-Ramirez nodded.

"That's correct, Sergeant, provided she hasn't already had to commit the Mike Force elsewhere, or there isn't a potential situation which requires her to keep it as a force in being. Remember, if we don't have access to the Needle, and the bad guys have any sort of air-defense capability, once she drops the Mike Force, it's down. The landing barge won't be an option for recovering them."

Fong-Ramirez went up a bit in my estimation right then. I mean, he'd seemed like a decent enough guy back on the *Fitz*, all that Captain Didactic stuff aside. But now he was showing some brains and perspective. It's easy to just see your own problems; he was stepping back and looking at the big picture. We had no sure indication that the Needle was compromised, but security was deteriorating in T'tokl-Heem, the attack on the maglev suggested that things were getting worse instead of better, and it was a pretty good guess that we at least shouldn't *count* on the Needle for a while. How did that shape Gasiri's options?

Not in our favor, that's for sure. Well, if she couldn't drop the Mike Force, maybe she could drop a couple containers of ammo. Not everyone had been as careful as me, and I'd already had to give up one magazine just to give Lieutenant Palaan a reload. I still had more rounds left than anyone else, so unless these guys got really light on the fingers, we had one more fight in us, and then we were dry and it was all over.

"Commander, I got a couple questions," I piped up, and he nodded for me to go on.

"First off, just what the hell is going on? I mean, maybe everyone in uniform got a briefing or something, but there are a few civilians here and we're all pretty much in the dark. Who's shooting at us, for starters?"

"Good question, Mr. Naradnyo. Unfortunately I don't have a firm answer for you. A few days ago and I'd have said they were certainly insurgents. Now that the uBakai and uZmataanki are at war, and shots have been exchanged between uZmataanki and *Cottohazz* naval forces, we aren't really sure what the situation is."

"You mean those might be local colonial troops shooting at us?" I asked. Fong-Ramirez looked uncomfortable with the question.

"I don't think we can rule that possibility out," he answered reluctantly.

Great.

"Okay, next question. When we get word to orbit, why don't they have the troops back at T'tokl-whatever send some transport aircraft to pick us up?"

"Another good question. But the reason we were moving by rail is this is all non-secured air space. No atmospheric aircraft, and certainly no orbital shuttles, are safe coming down here. If there's going to be a relief column, it will have to come overland."

If? I didn't much like hearing that.

"Okay. Last question. Wataski, can you patch our embedded comms into your squad tacnet?"

She shook her head.

"I need a platoon terminal to do it. No got. We'll have to go with audibles."

Audibles—a polite word for "shout over the noise of battle." Well, it had worked for cave men, so I guessed it might work for us. Of course, a tacnet could have translated English to aGavoosh, or aHoka—or aPig Latin, whatever those MPs spoke. Absent that—and figuring that a running translation under fire wasn't all that practical—tactical hand signals were probably going to be the order of the day.

I was a little rusty. Now, what was the tactical hand signal for "FUBAR"?

I crawled back and sat down next to my three charges and, because nothing gets by me, noticed right away that the group had grown to four. There were also four other Varoki youngsters clustered at a cautious distance, sizing up Barraki and Tweezaa—probably waiting until the grown-ups got their stuff over with so they could make contact between the two tribes.

Marfoglia was kneeling, sitting back on her feet, back straight, with both hands on her knees. She lifted one hand, turned the palm up, and gestured gracefully to the middle-aged Varoki sitting between Barraki and

Tweezaa—the Gavaan-Varoki formal presentation of an important guest in one's home.

"This is the Honorable Bok e-Kavaa," she said.

The guy was late middle-aged, I'd guess, with a thick torso—the Varoki equivalent of a pot belly—and the reflective sheen of the skin on his head and hands was beginning to dull with age. He wore a torn and muddy civil uniform—closer to a suit, really, and with no insignia, but a common cut and color, in this case dark green.

"Hey, *TheHon*," I said. "How you doing?"

Marfoglia frowned at me, but the Varoki paper pusher smiled faintly.

"I am reminding myself how much better I am than so many of my colleagues. I am afraid that a good many of them out along the road are dead."

I nodded. Good chance of it, although maybe the guys hitting us—whoever the hell they were—took some of them as hostages. Hostages for *what*, though?

The Varoki private security guy who formed part of our small combat force walked past. He and *TheHon* exchanged a look, *TheHon* nodded and smiled to him, and the guard walked on and settled down next to another Varoki, also in civil green. That guy was a bit older than the security guy, near as I could tell, with alert eyes and an unmistakable air of authority. Apparently he rated his own bodyguard.

"Mr. e-Kavaa is the assistant to the *Cottohazz* Executive Council's special envoy plenipotentiary for emergency abatement on K'Tok," Marfoglia elaborated.

"That's nice. That your boss over there?" I asked, nodding over at him, and *TheHon* looked at me oddly, but nodded.

"You . . . have met him before?"

"Just putting two and two together. I'd say you and your boss are in the right place, pal. Any time you guys feel like abating *this* emergency, be my guest."

He smiled ruefully, humor sparkling in his eyes.

I checked out my three people of interest. I already knew they'd come through the fight without a scratch, and by now they'd settled down as well as could be expected.

Marfoglia still had my Hawker 10—"the big one"— stuck in the waist band of the white Navy slacks which—along with a white short-sleeved shirt with insignia removed—the *Fitz*'s astrogator had given her. Well, an hour ago they'd been white; crawling through muddy drainage ditches had left all of us pretty earth-toned, but she'd wiped off her face, pulled her hair back into a ponytail, and tucked her shirt in, so she actually looked tidy—at least by the standards of current company.

I was getting to know her well enough to figure she was shaking like a leaf behind that façade of manners and duty, so I didn't begrudge her the frowns of reproach. She hid her fears behind the niceties of form; I hid mine behind wise-ass remarks. Whatever gets you by.

Barraki must have been scared, but he was doing a great job of pretending nonchalance. Marfoglia had dug a couple kotee-nut bars out of her pockets, and Barraki was eating one of them, looking around with curiosity but no apparent concern. When I looked close, though, I could see his eyes were darting back and forth from place to place, never staying put for more than a second or two, his ears twitching and turning restlessly. He was keeping it together, though, and that's what counted. Maybe he'd taken some panic-control lessons from Marfoglia. He could have done worse.

Whatever gets you by.

Tweezaa had the other kotee-nut bar, but she was just holding it. She was eyes-wide scared, and although she wasn't making a big deal about it, it was pretty clear she didn't really care if anyone knew it, either. Strange little girl. So far as I could tell, she never said or did anything—or failed to say or do something— just to make an impression. It wasn't that she didn't care what other people thought or felt; she just didn't seem to care what they thought or felt *about her.* In my life, I have met a handful of people whose self-image had nothing to do with the reflection they cast in the eyes of others. All of those people were very old, except for Tweezaa.

Strange little girl.

It was up to me to say something to put them a little more at ease, but I wasn't comfortable saying everything was going to be swell when I couldn't be sure it would be. They'd have to take what comfort they could from the plain old truth.

"Okay, here's the deal. We don't know who's shooting at us or why, but we're secure for now in this house. So far all we've seen are AWiGs—*assholes with guns*—and we can handle them. If they bring up an armored vehicle or a tac missile or something, it might get interesting, but I doubt they've got anything that heavy—or that we're important enough to them to commit it—but if they do, we'll have to improvise. But for now, we're snug. In about two hours we'll be able to contact Captain Gasiri in orbit, and we'll see what she can work out."

"Are they insurgents?" *TheHon* asked.

I shrugged.

"*Ya nya znayu. Ya toureest.*"

He looked at me blankly.

"*I don't know; I am a tourist,*" I translated. It was a wonderfully useful phrase, the perfect answer to almost any question. Other than yes, no, and obscene insults, it was about all I knew of the Old Language.

"Have the soldiers been able to contact any *Cottohazz* ground elements?" *TheHon* asked.

I shook my head. What was his real name? I'd already forgotten, so *TheHon* would have to do.

"Nobody has a broadcast transmitter along, just tight beam. Thing is, all the relay towers are down and the communication satellites are off-line, so we're stuck with line of sight."

"But what can they do to help from orbit?" Marfoglia asked.

I didn't want to oversell this, so I thought about it for a second or two before answering.

"Well, the big thing is they can copy the ground forces—those three MP cohorts—on our location and situation, and then hopefully those guys can arrange an overland rescue. They can also drop us supplies, which we'll need if we're going to be out here for a while."

"You did not mention the Mike Force," *TheHon* said. So he knew at least something about what was what, which was understandable given his job description. I mean, when it comes to "emergency abatement," not much tops a shit-load of Marines dropped from orbit.

"I wouldn't count on Captain Gasiri dropping her last reserves for a rescue mission," I answered.

"What is a Mike Force?" Barraki asked.

"Mike stands for *Meteoric Insertion Capable*," I answered. "The Mikes come down from orbit red-hot in individual reentry capsules."

His eyes lit up with recognition.

"Oh, yes, the *Azza-kaat*! I have seen vids of them. Have you ever dropped from orbit, Sasha?"

I laughed.

"Not a chance, pal. Not on a bet."

TWENTY-TWO

What is the essential prerequisite of leadership?

Is it brains? I don't think so. I've known some real dumb-asses that folks would follow anywhere, and I've known brainy guys that could hardly get their shadows to tag along. Don't get me wrong; anyone I follow I'd rather be smart than stupid, but it's not smart that makes them a leader, is it?

Being honest with your people, giving them a fair shake, sharing their load, looking out for them—those are all great qualities to *have* in leaders, but they don't *make* leaders.

Courage.

The essential prerequisite of leadership is courage.

Any situation which requires leadership—as opposed to management, which is an entirely different animal—is by its nature fraught with fear. That's why people need leadership—to get them through a fearful situation. And nothing messes with your ability to make clear, rational decisions like fear. So anyone who in a fearful situation can stare down that fear, and keep their mind clear enough to make good decisions, is a leader. Those folks aren't leaders because I say so; they're leaders because that's who people follow.

Of course, what goes along with that is that people who have the sort of delicate egos and fragile self-images which make them yearn to be hailed as great leaders naturally spend a lot of their lives drumming up business by trying to make people afraid.

Once the *Fitz* came over the communication horizon that evening, Gasiri had about ten minutes to make a decision, unless she wanted to wait until the next transit to do something, and a lot could happen in those extra hours. Ten minutes—and that was stretching it. Wait any longer and the Mikes would overshoot us.

Even though the Mikes are supposed to be ready to rumble on a moment's notice, even though all the ammo and gear was preloaded, even though you could get them in the capsules, pop them out, then do a quick briefing with downloaded intel and maps while they were in the early part of their descent, ten minutes still doesn't leave you any Murphy-margin. There was no way for Gasiri to know whether she could even recover her Mikes once they were down, given how fluid the situation was getting, and there was no time to gather more information, think things through, or even get anyone else's ideas.

Eighteen minutes after the *Fitz* broke the comm horizon, we could see the first bright streaks as the Mike capsules hit atmosphere.

That's courage.

✧   ✧   ✧

Not that we had time to leisurely enjoy the overhead light show. Once we got the word that the Mikes were coming down, we were, as the saying goes, "all asses and elbows." Up until then, we'd been hunkered down in the house. Now we needed to move our shooters out and either secure a drop zone for the Mikes or, failing that, at least figure out how hot the reception was going to be.

We left the two linguistically challenged MPs behind as rear security and moved out in two squads of four shooters each, each squad with one of the two Marines as a comm link and one of the two officers for adult supervision. For firepower each team had two of the RAG-19s and two gauss pistols. My team was Fong-Ramirez, Wataski, the envoy's bodyguard, and me. SOP was for the command and control element—Fong-Ramirez and Wataski—to bring up the rear, with us two expendable guys up front to trigger ambushes and booby traps and stuff like that. It made sense; I was just ten years out of practice at being expendable.

How expendable was I? Well, Wataski relieved me of two more magazines and all of my grenades, if that tells you anything.

In return, she gave me a snooperball. You roll it into a room, and its cameras, mikes, and seismics capture everything in all those different directions as it rolls, while its internal locomotor keeps it rolling in programmed patterns, like a purposeful Mexican jumping bean. The smart feed sorts all that wildly moving, spinning imagery into a stable 3D video display in the helmet visor of the scout. I still had Private Coleman's helmet, but had the feed patched into Wataski's display as well. All those images ghosted onto the visor can be disorienting unless you're used to it, and I was definitely rusty. I fell on my face twice trying to walk while the snooperball display was running, and cracked my shin hard enough to bring tears to my eyes.

You get away from something for a while, you start feeling nostalgic about it. It's good to be reminded that, fond memories and colorful tattoos notwithstanding, the Army really did suck. Not the guys I served with; I loved them, still do—even the assholes, maybe especially the assholes, because they needed it more, and if you've been there, you understand that. So I love those guys. But the Army—the thing itself—that's a different story.

The two teams moved in opposite directions, moved out one block, cleared and secured the buildings along the way as quickly as we could, and then swept counterclockwise, so the two teams were always going in different directions. Once we each did our half-circle, we moved out another block and then swept around again, making wider and wider sweeps each time. It was a good quarter-and-sweep routine for as few people as we had, and it had to be Wataski's brainchild. I doubted that either Fong-Ramirez or Palaan had much small-unit tactical training, but the exec was smart enough to recognize good advice when he heard it.

The sweep gave me a chance to size up Borro, the Varoki security guy I was paired with—the envoy's bodyguard. He knew his stuff, and he was sizing me up, too. I could tell, and he could tell I could tell. It's one of those deals where, after a while, you'd start laughing if the situation wasn't so bizarre and dangerous. I chuckled anyway. He looked at me for a moment as if I was nuts, and then he shook his head and smiled, too.

"You girls having a good time up there?" Wataski yelled from the other side of the alleyway we were working.

I turned back to face her, touched two finger tips to my lips, and then pointed at her.

Quiet.

That pissed her off, but she didn't say anything else.

We found local inhabitants—a lot more frightened of us than we were of them. We also found survivors from the maglev who were hiding in some outbuildings, and once we got out into the open, we found some more hiding in patches of brush. We sent them back toward the house we'd made our temporary base of operations.

We found bodies, as well, a lot of them. It was as if God were a little girl, and her rag dolls rested in the tangled heaps they'd fallen into the instant She'd lost interest in them.

Did I mention that some of the officials on the train had brought their dependents with them? I think I did. We found some of them out in the ditches, too. Seeing those little, motionless bodies scared me—bad. Right then, I needed to look over and see Barraki and Tweezaa—yeah, and Marfoglia, too, I guess—sitting in the corner, safe. But I couldn't, of course. They were back being guarded by two Varoki MPs who got the job because they'd be more of a liability than an asset in a fight. You can imagine how that put my mind at ease.

The local animal life looked to be crustacean—lots

of sizes and shapes, but most of them with exoskel-
etons. Multi-legged "bugs" anywhere from two to
ten centimeters across were crawling over some of
the bodies, but none of them were feeding. Just as
well—it was bad enough without that.

So we found a lot of things, but one thing we
didn't find was trouble; the bad guys had pulled
back. Wataski and her Marines had left some marks,
that was sure. The bad guys had taken all of their
dead and wounded with them as well, except for
a couple bodies hidden in ditches or behind walls,
either overlooked or too dangerous to get to. I'm no
expert on local fashion, but uniforms are uniforms.
These looked a lot like the colonial troops I'd seen,
but with some personal variation in minor kit. Maybe
insurgents were using some captured gear, but these
guys looked more standardized than any insurgents
I'd ever seen, and a bit less than regulars.

"These are contractors—mercenary strikers," I said
to Borro when we paused to look at one of them, and
he nodded. The colonial government was fighting an
insurgency, and often as not you hired specialists to
do that. So why were the hired goons shooting at us?
The local government being at war with uBakaa had
sort of complicated things, but this was more than just
a "complication." I had other things to worry about
right then, but I knew that *somebody* higher up the
food chain had better be worrying about this.

Less than half an hour after we started, we saw the
upward-bound streaks of half a dozen SAMs—surface-
to-air missiles—launched from no more than a dozen
kilometers away. Then we saw the big intercept flashes a
few thousand meters up, and a second or two later heard

the crackling explosions of the multiple seeker heads. That'll turn your stomach inside out, let me tell you. Of course, it's not as if SAMs were a shock. SAMs are part of the expected threat envelope, and so the Mikes always come down in the middle of a swarm of decoys, and they have pretty good ECM action going, too.

Still . . . it was tough to stand there and watch those strings of explosions up in the sky. And fixed-site SAMs weren't just some contractors gone nutty; this was the local government's way of saying there were people—namely us—who needed killing.

Not long afterwards, the first of the Marine parasails began gliding down into the open fields we'd secured and marked with IR strobes. Quite a sight. They came down with a sharp angle of descent, then at the last second they flared the sail and slowed almost to a hover. As soon as their feet touched the ground, they released the sail harness, and it shot up and drifted for twenty or thirty more meters before collapsing. They were clear, down on one knee, and with their RAG-19s up and level before the shadows of the sails had glided away—blocky and angular, sexless and vaguely inhuman in their segmented body armor.

Everything about the spectacle was impressive in a graceful, lethal way, particularly the silence. There were tactical hand signs, but no voices. They didn't need voices; they were all on the same tacnet, their embedded comms picking up low-volume subvocalized speech, enhancing it, and putting it in whichever ears needed it.

Possibly they had a platoon terminal, and so we could all get on the same net. But more likely—and much better in my opinion—they'd just tell those of us non-Marines playing expendable point guy to go back to our day jobs. Fine by me. I had my four hours in; I was ready for retirement.

I should have figured the Mikes were coming down. Why?

TheHon's boss—if he really was his boss, which I was beginning to doubt. But think about it—the *Cottohazz* Executive Council's Special Envoy Plenipotentiary for Emergency Abatement on K'Tok. Anybody with a job title that long rated a V.I.P. rescue effort. And that's what he got—a full platoon of Mike Marines, under a captain named Rosetti, the top-ranking Marine officer left on the *Fitz*. Thank you very much, Mr. Naradnyo, and your services are no longer required.

But they had me keep the RAG-19 for now, and in its way that was a sign of changing times. The dozen or so Varoki MPs were under Rosetti's authority, and all of them were still armed with gauss pistols or carbines. Why not give the extra RAG-19 to one of them, instead of leaving it with a civilian?

Because they were Varoki, and I was Human. That's a distinction which would not have been so openly drawn a week ago. Maybe it was because Wataski gave Rosetti a thumbs-up report on me—she may not have liked me, but she knew I wasn't either trigger-happy or gun-shy, and that counts. But neither was Borro, and he didn't get a RAG.

Times change, and sometimes they do it in the blink of an eye.

As I started to leave, Fong-Ramirez saw me and held up his hand to stop me, and then made his way over to me.

"Mr. Naradnyo, I wanted to thank you for your help," he said. "Commodore Gasiri downloaded your service jacket."

"*Commodore?* When did she get the bump?"

"Standard procedure is for the senior surviving line captain in a task force to assume the acting rank of commodore upon taking command. I noticed that you're still carried on the A.C.G. inactive reserve rolls."

"Yeah, I guess so," I answered.

"Well, I just wanted you to know I made sure the commodore logged you as reactivated. That way, if you're taken prisoner while armed, there will be no legal question concerning your combatant status."

That was thoughtful. I wasn't sure it would make any difference, but I was impressed he'd thought to do it.

"Thanks, Commander. So now I gotta call you sir, instead of the other way around, huh?"

He smiled, I think maybe to cover his embarrassment, and shook his head.

"I believe we can dispense with that."

Not a bad guy.

When Borro and I got back to our "people of interest," *TheHon* was hanging around my guys again, sitting down and playing with the kids, tickling Tweezaa, which I wouldn't have dared—the Dark Princess had too much *gravitas* for me to tickle her. But she was screeching with laughter and writhing in his arms now, and he teased her with rough, guttural aGavoosh phrases.

I stood next to Marfoglia, watching them. She was smiling at their play; I was a little less enthused. Something about the guy wasn't quite square. I don't mean he was a *wrong* guy—he just wasn't what he let on.

"I don't like it," I said to Marfoglia, and she knew what I meant right away, and shot me a hard, angry look.

"You should be more polite to him," she told me. "He's a good man."

"Yeah, I like him a lot," I answered. Her expression got even more sour at that.

"Look, for once I'm not being a wise-ass. I actually *do* like him. But here's the thing—I'm not here to make new friends; I'm on the clock, and you need to remember that. If I thought being nicer to him would get you and those two kids to Akaampta safely, I'd give the son of a bitch a blow job . . . or, you know, whatever they do. But as it is, I'm not sure it's safe to be anywhere near him."

"You don't think he'd hurt the children."

"Nope. Not what I meant."

Later I cornered him, away from the others, although I could feel Borro's eyes on me the whole time.

"What's your interest in those kids?" I demanded.

"I have no special interest. I just like children," he said.

"Bullshit."

He looked at me for a moment, trying to tell if another lie would work.

"It is complicated," he answered reluctantly, looking away.

"That answer doesn't exactly make me feel all warm and fuzzy inside, either," I said. "In my experience, things are never really complicated; they just look complicated when you don't have all the pieces of the puzzle. Once you do, though, it always gets simple. So I'll ask you again, what's your interest in those kids?"

"I knew their mother," he answered after a moment.

Really? But we hadn't told him the real names of the kids, which meant either he was stringing me along, or he knew who they were without us having to tell him.

"How long have you known who they are?" I asked.

"Since I saw them on the train. I recognized them from pictures Laraana and I exchanged of our children. They have never met me, however."

I didn't know their mother's name, so I still wasn't sure, but I was getting pretty strong truth vibes.

"You travel in those circles?" I asked cautiously.

"No. Well...yes. Sometimes," he answered, frowning. "But I knew her before she was the Lady e-Traak."

Bingo.

"Oh. She married up, huh?"

He straightened and looked down at me, then, and there was a hardness in his look I hadn't seen in him before.

"I do not view it that way. She married for passion, not position. The children—particularly Tweezaa—have more of her than their father in them. Much more. Aside from his money, Sarro was not really worth very much, you know."

I thought about what Barraki had told me about the last year of his father's life, what he was trying to do, and I wasn't so sure about that, but I didn't argue the point.

Did I say nothing is complicated? Nothing really is, except for people.

TWENTY-THREE

Captain Leona Rosetti's Mike Marines were awfully good. By good, I mean they killed a whole bunch of uZmataanki mercenaries and didn't have a single fatality of their own that first morning. There were three casualties, one of them pretty serious, but no KIA or Died of Wounds.

My hunch was confirmed by now—we were up against uZmataanki counterinsurgency specialists: mercenary strikers, not regulars. In theory, they could have been as good, or better, than the colonial regulars. Since I didn't know how good the local grunts were, it was hard to make a comparison. What was clear, though, was they weren't in the same league as the Mike Marines. Why they were trying to kill us was a little less clear.

Seeing all those dead hostiles was supposed to make me happy, I guess, especially since the uZmataanki strikers were trying to kill us. Part of me definitely felt more secure. A deeper part of me felt kind of sick. No part of me actually felt "happy."

Sure, I know, *better them than us*. And you may have noticed that I'm not at all squeamish or hesitant about actually dropping the hammer when necessary—nor particularly narrow-minded about deciding when that might be the case. But I'll tell you what might have made me genuinely happy—putting my fingers around the throats of the sons of bitches who made our choices come down to *them or us*.

Good luck figuring out who that was, though.

I'm willing to bet that half those young Marines had never heard a shot fired in anger before, but you'd never know it from watching them, that's how good their training was. Training is everything, by the way. Experience is highly overrated. If your training is good, you learn what you need to know there. Combat experience—"seeing the elephant"—doesn't tell you much more about surviving and winning. It tells you a *lot* about yourself, but that's a different matter.

Now, if your training is only half-assed—like the strikers the Marines were fighting—then combat experience can help fill in the blanks. The trick, though, is living long enough in combat to figure that stuff out. For example, if you don't know any better than to stick your head over the top of a wall—instead of finding an edge or break you can look around to the side without skylining—you're probably not going to learn a valuable combat lesson; you're probably just going to get your brains blown out.

I speak from some experience on this subject—the training part, not getting your brains blown out.

The training we got in the old Piss-can Rangers was half-assed at best, and we learned the hard way. I survived, but not because I was smarter than anyone else; I was just lucky. Very lucky.

I read once that when Napoleon was picking guys to promote to Marshal of France, he looked for two characteristics: suicidal bravery and luck. Not brains, interestingly enough—I guess he figured he had brains enough to go around—just suicidal bravery and luck.

So I'd have made, like, half a Marshal of France.

"Sammies want a parley," Rosetti told Fong-Ramirez in her booming voice. "Figure they want to surrender?" She laughed, and she said it loud enough to carry all the way through the warehouse we were using for a shelter. I imagine she intended it to. Sammie, I'd learned, was Marine slang for the uZmataanki. I'd also learned it wasn't exactly polite slang, so no one had used it when the uZmataanki colonial troops were "partnered" with *Cottohazz* forces. Of course, all that had changed a few hours ago.

There were muttered translations of Rosetti's words into aGavoosh, aHuka, aDakai, and other languages I didn't recognize, by the civilians spread out through the open area, mostly sitting on low stacks of pallets. Then there were nods and smiles—mostly. A couple Varoki didn't seem thrilled at the thought of Human Marines kicking Varoki ass, even if the Humans were on their side and the Varoki out there weren't. I kind of knew how they felt. Back on Nishtaaka, I wasn't always sure which side I wanted to root for... and I *was* one of the sides. Nothing's complicated but people.

"Parley? Really? Okay, should we see what they want?" Fong-Ramirez answered.

"I'll go, sir," Rosetti said. "If we need more brass to close the deal, I'll send a runner."

So Captain Rosetti went to see what they wanted. She was gone for maybe twenty minutes when the runner showed up and gave a message to Fong-Ramirez, who then called over the tall, distinguished-looking Varoki special envoy. They spoke briefly, heads nodded, and then Fong-Ramirez left. The envoy came back and spoke to the bodyguard and to *TheHon*, who didn't seem all that happy about the situation. He looked up and noticed me watching him. He said something to the other two and then walked over to join Marfoglia and me.

"Hey, *TheHon*, what's the latest bulletin from the High Command?"

"The uZmataanki colonial district military commander has arrived. He has relieved and arrested the commander of the striker cohort which has been in action against us, has apologized profusely for the 'misunderstanding,' and is supposedly arranging ground transport for us to T'tokl-Heem."

Two words I didn't particularly like hearing: *supposedly* and *T'tokl-Heem*.

"Not to Haampta?"

TheHon looked at me significantly and shook his head. "The commander says he cannot guarantee our safety near the uBakai border, as there are ongoing military operations there."

"Has he heard of a temporary cease-fire to allow passage of neutral refugees?" I demanded.

He dipped his head to one side.

"But if they take us back to T'tokl-Heem, that's better," Marfoglia said. "We'll be able to get back up the Needle."

Only one word in that I didn't like hearing: *if*.

"So, is Fong-Ramirez going to straighten them out?" I asked. That didn't seem very likely to me. The lieutenant commander was a good, solid naval officer but didn't strike me as a hard-nosed negotiator.

"I do not know. They wanted the commanders of all of the national contingents to personally certify the good conduct of their troops while in uZmataanki territory—apparently a prerequisite for allowing our troops to retain their arms while in transit. He and Lieutenant Palaan have both gone to do so."

"Uh-huh," I said.

He just looked at me again. He definitely smelled a rat, but he didn't look scared. Both of those facts were interesting.

Instead of heading back to rejoin his crew, he hung around with us for a while, but with me instead of the kids, which was also interesting.

"What would you do, were you in the place of Commander Fong-Ramirez?" he asked me.

I shrugged.

"Maybe exactly what he's doing now. He's playing the hand he was dealt. I think if I were him, I'd be getting ready to run a bluff, though, because it's not nearly as strong a hand as I think he thinks it is, if you know what I mean."

"I am not sure," he answered, "but I believe so. You are talking about the card game poker? I have watched it played once or twice, but I did not really understand it."

"No? Well, some day we'll sit down and I'll teach you. Bring your money."

"I would like that," he said, and I caught the briefest flicker of a smile, swept back into hiding as soon as it appeared. So, among other things, *TheHon* was a hustler. I think I liked the guy a little more, then.

"What bluff?" he asked.

"Well, the *Fitz* is only overhead a few hours a day, because it's got other responsibilities, and it's the only armed ship up there, right? But there are those transports. Suppose Gasiri put deadfall ordnance on one of them and parked it in a synchronous planetary orbit overhead. We're still close enough to the equator to pull that off. So then there's a looming presence overhead always ready to drop hot spikes on anything that we paint with a laser down here. That would make them think twice before hitting us again." Of course "deadfall" was a bit of a misnomer, as you had to give the spikes a pretty good shot downward or they'd just hang around in orbit with you, but that's what everyone called them, and *TheHon* knew what I was talking about.

"But it would take time to modify the transport for this new ordnance, would it not?"

I looked at him for a second.

"You really *don't* understand the concept of a bluff, do you?"

"Ah!" he said, as the light came on in his little lizard head.

Twenty minutes later, the Marine runner returned and headed for *TheHon*'s two pals. He was still standing with us, asking about what I'd do if I were in Fong-Ramirez's place—just idle talk, of course. The Marine talked to the other two guys for a minute, and then they both looked over at *TheHon*, who stood looking silently back at them for a few seconds.

"I was expecting this," he said, his voice heavy. "I have to go."

"No," I said. "*He* does," pointing to the tall, distinguished-looking Varoki standing next to Borro the bodyguard.

"I think I should go instead," he said quietly.

"Let that man do his job," I answered. "You do yours. What, did somebody tell you this was going to be easy?"

He looked at me and shook his head. Then he walked over to the group.

Marfoglia was standing right next to us as we spoke, but she had no idea what we were talking about.

"What's happening?"

"I guess the uZmataanki district commander wants the special envoy to come to the talks, too."

"Why?"

"Probably so he can kill him. I doubt that's the reason he gave, though."

"*Kill him?* My God, that's horrible," she said, eyes wide with shock. "Would they really do that?"

I shrugged.

"And Mr. e-Kavaa wants to go in his place. That's very noble of him," she said.

"Yeah. Noble and stupid," I replied. She shot me an angry glance, but she didn't say anything.

The three Varoki spoke quietly but earnestly amongst themselves for a minute or so, then *TheHon* and the tall guy embraced, and the tall guy went off with the Marine runner.

"You shouldn't have talked Mr. e-Kavaa out of going," she said. "They wouldn't know which one was which, and if something did happen, at least the special envoy would still be here alive."

"Dr. Marfoglia, don't give up your day job for a career in security. If *TheHon* went, and something happened to him, we wouldn't still have the special envoy—we'd have his *two* bodyguards."

She looked confused, but just for a moment, because she wasn't stupid.

"*Oh...*"

We didn't have access to a broadcast transmitter, but of course they did, so the proceedings were televised. We had vidscreens; they made sure of that.

They had them kneeling, hands bound behind their backs, and an officer walked behind them with a gauss pistol.

First was Captain Leona Rosetti, the Human "gangster" who had ordered her men to shoot down uZmataanki soldiers trying to surrender. All bullshit, of course, but what difference did that make?

SNAP!

Down she went, to twitch on the pavement, this odd little fountain of blood bubbling up from the gunshot wound in her skull for the last two or three beats of her heart.

Next was Lieutenant Palaan, the uHoka "turncoat" who was in league with the uBakai, and who had participated in the unprovoked attack on the uZmataanki cruiser at Mogo.

SNAP!

e-Lotonaa, the *Cottohazz*'s special envoy, who was actually a paid agent of the uBakai and whose actions had corrupted the institutions of *Cottohazz* governance. That's not who was kneeling there, of course. The tall, distinguished-looking Varoki was actually a security specialist named Bammatats. I'd made it a point to find out his real name. Mr. Bammatats made no effort to correct the record.

SNAP!

Last was Lieutenant Commander Edward Fong-Ramirez, the "criminal" who helped mastermind the attack on an unsuspecting and peaceful uZmataanki cruiser. Fong-Ramirez, young for his rank and responsibility because he was so smart, and a really good kid, even if he was way too serious about stuff, who should have gone home a hero and got laid a lot, and maybe he'd have loosened up some, but he never got to.

SNAP!

An hour later, the Marine NCOs were still arguing. Because they'd lost their platoon sergeant on the way down, there were four buck sergeants and as many corporals, but a couple privates were getting in on the act as well. Eloquence and passion carried as much weight in this council as stripes.

The uZmataanki had sent Private Lee, the platoon runner, back to us as a gesture of good faith. The executions had settled any scores, they said. Now they were ready to ship the rest of us back to T'tokl-Heem.

This time they really meant it. Honest.

Some of the NCOs wanted to take the deal, because they didn't see any other way out. Others wanted to go after the uZmataanki and get payback for what they'd done. There were variations on the theme, but those were pretty much the two options—at least as they saw things.

I could follow the argument closely because I was digging through the pile of supply canisters—stocking up.

"What do you need, Mr. Naradnyo?" one of the Marines asked. I looked up and recognized him as the other Marine still on his feet from Wataski's original guard detail. What was his name . . . ? Aguillar.

"Just topping off with ammo, Aguillar. Never know when we'll need it."

He looked at the two rucksacks I was carrying, and his eyebrows went up a bit.

"And some ration packs," he said.

"Yeah. Gotta eat."

He nodded but didn't say anything else.

In everything you do throughout your life, people are the critical variables. You got to pay attention to people, every one of them, not just the big shots. Most people don't. Every server in every restaurant you've ever been in starts by telling you their name, and most people have forgotten it halfway through the list of daily specials. I remembered Aguillar's name, because I pay attention to people.

Now think about this for a second: what can *you* tell me about Aguillar? Here's what I can tell you. He knew I was bullshitting him about topping off with ammo, because I was taking rations, too, but he didn't make a fuss about it. Why? Maybe because he was hearing the same dead-end crap from the NCOs I was hearing, and thinking along the same lines . . .

stock up on ammo and rations and make a break for it on your own.

The thing is, I wasn't exactly looking for travel companions, but I also needed Aguillar as at least a neutral. Not that I was really worried Aguillar wanted to tag along—he was a Marine, and he'd probably cut his nose off before he'd bug out on his unit.

I reached down into the supply canister, pulled out a ration pack, and looked at it.

"You like *pad Thai* with shrimp?" I asked.

He smiled and nodded, but it was a sad smile. It was the smile of a twenty-year-old who didn't figure on making it to twenty-one, but couldn't see anything to do about it but take it like a man.

I tossed the ration pack to him, and I felt like a worm. Here was a kid who wanted his life, and instead I gave him maybe his last meal.

And he smiled in melancholy gratitude.

I sat down beside Marfoglia, both of us with our backs against the concrete wall. I offered her a drink from an energy bottle, and after she shook her head I took a long pull myself.

"How bad is it?" she asked.

That was the big question, wasn't it? And I was back to that same problem I always seem to bump up against—how much to tell? I needed her thinking, functioning, if we were going to get out of this alive, so I didn't want to shock her into depression. But what did that leave me with? I was tired of trying to second-guess how much truth other people could take.

"It's about as bad as it gets," I said.

"Is there any chance they'll . . . just let us go?"

"Nope."

And then I felt the tingle in the back of my neck, the sweat break out on my torso and face, as panic's long bony fingers closed around my chest, made my heart race and my breathing come faster. They were coming to kill us, every one of us, and I couldn't stop them. What the hell good was I? What did I know? *How to blend in? How to make it on the city streets?* See how far that gets you on a boonie-rock where you're the only Humans. I was about as useful here as an Eskimo in the desert.

"Do you have any idea what to do?" Marfoglia asked.

"Of course," I answered.

I had no idea.

"We're going to get out of this," I told her. It was a bluff, but it would have to do until I came up with something better. "Right now, you're going to go back to the kids. Keep them together in case we have to move quickly. Keep them calm, too. Can you do that?"

I looked at her and she nodded. There was determination in her eyes—determination and hope. She looked frightened, but not as frightened as I felt. That's because she had someone to count on. Sasha would get her and the kids out of this. However bad things got, Sasha could handle it.

Sasha wasn't so sure of that, which was why Sasha was scared shitless.

Ten minutes later I was still sitting with my back against the wall when *TheHon* sat down next to me.

"Who is winning the dispute?" he asked, gesturing to the arguing Marines.

"Doesn't matter," I answered. "Go for revenge or trust to mercy—either way they're dead."

"Yes," he agreed. "What does Commodore Gasiri think? Do you know?"

"Near as I can tell, she said she'll back any decision the ground makes. No choice, really; she can't micromanage things from orbit."

He nodded in agreement.

"I would like revenge for my friend Bammatats," he said. "Perhaps you would as well, for Commander Fong-Ramirez. He was one of those who saved you, was he not? But my duty is to all of these people here. Yours is as well, I think."

I didn't say anything.

"You agree?" he asked after a while.

"No."

"I am surprised. Surprised and disappointed that you would put revenge ahead of your responsibility."

I turned and looked at him. I knew that Borro was watching us, so I didn't make any threatening moves, because there was no point in risking a gunfight here in the warehouse, and I needed stuff from *TheHon* anyway. But aside from that, I wasn't in a very good mood.

"Listen, you fat fucking lizard, I liked that kid Fong-Ramirez a lot, but I know what my responsibilities are, and they aren't to 'all these people' around here. They are to exactly three people, and you aren't one of them, so don't waste your time trying to play me.

"I'm getting those kids out of here. There are some things I need if I'm going to pull it off. Are you going to help me get those things? Yes or no."

A lot of emotions struggled for control of his face as he sat there, but eventually acceptance triumphed over resentment.

"What is it that you need?"

"A good set of maps, and the best current intel on the local military situation. And I need it downloaded into this." I held up Private Coleman's helmet.

"Is that all?"

"Nope. The Marines have Picketwire sensors scattered all over the town—I put a couple of them out myself. The Sammies will have a transport park somewhere in the town, and the Picketwire system should have identified it. I need to know where it is."

He studied me for a moment.

"You have a plan?"

"I got a notion, which I think I can parlay into an idea, that with luck I can bootstrap into a plan."

He nodded thoughtfully.

"Very well. I will get you what you need. Borro and I will accompany you."

"Nope."

I started to tell him why, but he beat me to the punch.

"Of course not," he said. "Why would you endanger your lives by traveling with me, when I am possibly the most sought-after target of the local officials? And why make your party any larger than it needs to be? Better to travel in a small group, and attract less attention. I could tell you that I won't get you the information you need unless you take us along, but that would be a lie—an obvious bluff. Instead I will say three things.

"First, the local officials do not know that I am alive. They will likely find out eventually, but they do not know yet, and that will give us some time.

"Second, although I may be of little use to you,

Mr. Borro is quite capable. You will need another experienced... operative, I think.

"Third, it is my understanding that while Dr. Marfoglia speaks aZmataan, she is not as conversant with it as she would like. Both Borro and I are fluent, and Borro's accent is good enough to pass as native.

"Finally, your small group will *not* go unnoticed, because there are no Humans on K'Tok. You and Dr. Marfoglia will be jarringly out of place, no matter where you go. Two adult Varoki will make your party less conspicuous, not more so."

"That's four things," I said, "not three."

He tilted his head to the side.

I thought about it for a little while, but there wasn't that much to consider. Everything he'd said had been right on the money, and I'm not one to cling to a losing hand out of stubbornness or pride.

"Have you talked this over with Borro? I asked.

"No. I had not even considered it until I realized you had an escape plan in mind."

"Well, he's going to shit bricks when he hears this. Even if the deal makes sense from my point of view, it really stinks at his end. In terms of keeping you alive, we are nothing but trouble."

"Mr. Borro will follow my orders."

"Yeah, that's why I shudder at the thought of VIP security as a career. You people hire guys like Borro and me to keep you alive, then you do whatever you feel like and leave it up to us to keep all the balls in the air, as if we're supermen. Marfoglia may be a pain in the ass, but when it comes to security, she does what I tell her."

"Then you are a fortunate man," he said, and smiled.

"You think this is funny? Okay. Here's *my* condition. If you two come with us, I am in charge, one hundred percent. Borro is number two if something happens to me. Then Marfoglia, then the *kids*, then you. You understand? You have resigned as potentate, effective immediately."

"Plenipotentiary," he corrected me.

"Well, you're just baggage now, pal. If we get you out of this alive, you can get back to the noble calling of screwing up entire planets, but meantime, you're the cook and dishwasher."

He frowned at that.

"That is an unfair assessment," he said. "My responsibility is to correct difficulties, not create them."

"Sure. You're from the government and you're here to help. And let me tell you, you're doing a hell of a job. While you're sitting here, there's something I've been meaning to ask you. The war between the Sammies and the uBakai—you got a dog in this fight?"

He frowned in confusion.

"I do not understand."

"What nationality are you?"

"Ah. I see. Yes. I am uKootrin—in that sense I do not have a dog in this war."

"In *that* sense," I repeated. "But in some other sense?"

"In some other sense, we all—even you—have a dog in the war."

Trust a government guy to give you an answer which was probably truthful, but definitely not very satisfying. I let him off the hook, though, and shooed him away so I could go back to figuring out our next move. I had the start of a plan that at least had a chance of not getting us all killed. Turns out, I wasn't the only one. Jarheads can surprise you once in a while.

"We're going to pretend to go along with their deal, but when they send the trucks, we're going to hit them instead. Hit them hard, then grab the trucks and head west."

It was an interesting plan—flawed, but interesting. I thought it was even more interesting that Wataski was explaining it to me.

Wataski had never developed what you'd call a fondness for me in our brief association, and yet here she was, explaining the plan. Remember what I said about paying attention to people? What does this tell you about Wataski's state of mind? She didn't need my permission, but she wanted my opinion. Why?

Because decapitation attacks work. That's what this had been—a nice, surgical decapitation of the unit. The NCOs weren't dummies, but they were NCOs. What NCOs do is execute a mission. That's their job. Give them a mission, they'll execute the hell out of it. But deciding what the mission ought to be—that's not their job. And if you make them change mental gears this quick and this hard . . . well, that's why decapitation attacks work.

So the NCOs had a plan, but they were uncertain about it—uncertain enough that one of them was floating it past me, a civilian—and as far as she knew, my only claim to fame was that I kept my head when the flechettes started flying. So that's the first thing it told me about Wataski's state of mind—she was uncertain.

But the second thing it told me was she wasn't insecure about her own authority. If she had been, she wouldn't have asked my opinion, because it might have looked like weakness. But she knew who she was, she knew who I was, and she didn't really give a damn what I thought of her. She just wanted to know what I thought of the plan.

I brought up the map *TheHon* had snagged for me on my helmet display. We were about three hundred klicks west of T'tokl-Heem, and almost twice as far from the uBakai colonial border due north, quite a bit farther from Haampta, the uBakai colonial capital almost due west of us. The map showed a lot of jungle-covered mountains to the south and to the northwest, some prairies and scattered hills to the west, and jungle-covered lowlands most other directions. Jungle, jungle, jungle. Didn't these people have farms? What the hell did they eat? Then I remembered the bubble-covered greenhouses I'd seen out the window of the maglev, that and the buildings with all the plumbing fixtures that shouted hydroponics. The leather-heads were growing all their stuff artificially. It was a good thing the maglev conked out where it did—this settlement was in one of the few fairly good-sized prairies around—ideal drop zone for the Mikes.

When I cranked the magnification on the map, it showed a thin trace of roads and trails through the jungle, connecting a handful of small, scattered settlements. Not only was there a lot of jungle, there were a lot of little rivers and streams, too—not big enough to navigate, but big enough to be a pain to get across, and I was willing to bet that a lot of the jungle lowlands were swamps with overhead canopy. Swell. There weren't a whole lot of different ways to skin this particular cat, it was beginning to seem. I'd looked at it a dozen times already, before Wataski buttonholed me, but it gave me something to look at while I came up with an answer.

"Sounds better than anything else I've heard," I said, and that was—strictly speaking—the truth. After all, I hadn't *heard* my own thoughts.

She looked at me, and I think she suspected that there might be more to that statement than just the obvious meaning.

"So. No suggestions?" she asked, eyes boring right through me.

If the Marines went due west, they'd be a great diversion for us, because we sure as hell weren't going that direction. They'd take the other civilians along, and there was a good chance the bad guys wouldn't spring to the crowd being a little thin. No one would notice us, because the Marines would keep making lots of noise—until they were all dead. All we had to do was break away in the confusion and head the right direction. Piece of cake.

I hadn't told the kids the plan yet. I looked over at Tweezaa talking with four other Varoki children, survivors of the massacre. I'd met them... hadn't meant to, hadn't wanted to, but had. Two of them were missing their folks—probably dead out in a ditch by the road. Tweezaa looked up, from ten meters away, looked in my eyes, and from that serious, accusing stare I could tell she knew exactly what I was thinking. She reached out and took the hand of the little girl next to her, her eyes still locked on mine.

And then I closed my eyes and sighed, because I am foolish and soft and unprofessional, and I know it, but I can't seem to do anything about it.

"You taking all the civilians with you?" I asked Wataski.

"That's the job," she answered.

I nodded.

"Okay, here's my opinion. Actually, three opinions for the price of one.

"First opinion: there's no magic solution that's going to bewilder the bad guys and get us all out of this in one piece. No matter what we do, most of us are going to end up dead, and you may as well get your head around that. There are too many of them, and they're trying too hard to kill us."

I paused, and a flicker of fear danced across her eyes. She hid it well, but she wasn't some emotion-less killing machine, any more than any of the other Marines were. They were kids—well-trained kids, but still kids. They had nice long lives still ahead of them, and none of them were ready to lie down and die just yet. Unfortunately, it wasn't really up to them, and Wataski was starting to realize that.

"Second opinion: north is better than west. The jungle closes in tight and the roads have triple canopy overhead cover. It won't make it impossible to track you, but it will make it harder. And it's closer to uBakai territory and their air-defense umbrella."

There was another advantage of heading north, but she didn't need to know it yet.

"Third opinion: if you stick together, you will all die very quickly."

"You're talking as if you won't be with us," she said right away.

"That's right. My people and I are going our own

way as soon as possible. You better start thinking along those lines as well."

"Bullshit," she spat back. "We're trained to fight and survive as a team. That's our best asset."

"Then do it," I answered. "No skin off me. But the Sammies have tac air and artillery rocket systems with area kill submunitions. Right now we're in too close to their strikers for them to hit us. But once we all break away, if you guys stay together as one big target, they will flatten twenty hectares of jungle just to make sure you are good and dead."

She thought about that for a minute or two, scowling and chewing on the inside of her cheek, and I could tell it was sinking in. Then she looked back at me.

"And you think you're just going to sneak away while nobody's looking?" she asked, her voice heavy with sarcasm.

"Nah. I figure I can count on you Marines for a violent and noisy diversion. Break things and hurt people, right? It's sorta in your DNA."

"Oo-rah," she growled, and she smiled a little, although as smiles go it was a pretty sour one.

Then without another word she turned and walked back toward the other Marines. After all, she had what she wanted from me, and I got the feeling Wataski wasn't really big on idle chitchat.

TWENTY-FOUR

A different Marine sergeant came around to fill us in on the final plan. He introduced himself as Marty Gomez—short, dark, stocky, and broad-faced, with a lot of Native American blood showing in him. I got the feeling that he'd emerged as the group leader, just the way he talked to us—respectful but confident, serious but relaxed and friendly, all the things that make people comfortable with listening and following.

There were four squads of Marines down, although one of them was banged up and they'd folded Wataski's detail into it, with her taking over. Wataski's improvised squad was going to make a lot of noise— "duplicate the fire signature of a platoon" was how Gomez put it—while the other three squads hijacked enough transport to lift us all out. Then everyone would disperse, the basic unit being a single vehicle and its occupants. Gomez looked square at me when he explained that part, which I guess was his way of saying they'd decided I wasn't a total asshole.

When the Mikes came down, the *Fitz* also dropped seven loaded RTM "twelve-packs." The RTMs— Remotely Triggered Munitions—were short-range artillery rockets. They were dropped in modules of twelve rockets—hence the nickname—and they went inert as soon as they landed and deployed, hopefully hidden by the surrounding jungle and brush. The Marines could call them in singles, pairs, or pretty much any multiples up to a twelve-rocket salvo, and they'd either fly a pre-plotted course to a fixed target point or home on a laser reflection. They were the closest thing the Marines had to artillery actually down here on the dirt, and Gomez planned to fire all of them in a box barrage around the settlement as soon as we cleared the perimeter. That should slow up the pursuit.

"We'll try to make sure there's at least one Marine or Varoki MP in each vehicle," he went on. "That way there's a helmet uplink communicator with every group, and the *Fitz* can track each party on the ground, feed us instructions and updates."

"I still got Private Coleman's helmet," I put in. "No need to send a Marine with us, although I wouldn't mind an MP."

Gomez looked back at me, and his eyebrows went up a little.

"Nothing personal," I added. "It's just that a Varoki in a uniform—any uniform—will blend in better."

"Okay, fair enough," he agreed. "We're stretched thin as it is. Your Excellency," he said, turning to *TheHon*, "I'll have two Marines ride with you, including one of our surviving NCOs. That's all I can spare, and any more would probably just attract attention."

"Thank you, Sergeant Gomez," *TheHon* answered, "but it is not necessary. Mr. Borro and I will be traveling with Mr. Naradnyo's party."

Gomez looked at *TheHon* for a second or two, then he turned and looked at me, then back at *TheHon*. He didn't say anything, though. He had other fish to fry, and we'd just made his staffing decisions a lot easier. But I bet he was dying to ask what the hell was going on. *TheHon* and I were not exactly two guys you'd expect to find bumming around together.

Once Gomez moved along, we huddled up to make sure everyone knew the plan. The Marines would grab as many trucks and cars as they could, we'd take one vehicle as a group, load as many civilians in back as we could manage, and haul ass.

"Who can drive?" I asked.

Borro nodded right away, which figured. Wheel man can be a pretty important skill in executive security.

"I can drive, too," Marfoglia said.

"Yeah, so can I," I said. "I learned in the service, but I'm a little rusty. Nobody drives in the Crack. And whatever driving we do here probably isn't going to be all that sedate, so let's leave the wheel to Borro."

"That's fine," she said and nodded to Borro. "I'm sure he's an excellent driver. But if necessary, I can manage difficult driving as well."

"Take a course or something?" I asked, imagining some kind of weekend survival driving retreat, complete with lots of controlled pyrotechnics and actors in bad-guy costumes.

"No," she answered coolly. "But two years ago I finished seventh in the Monaco Grand Prix."

Across the circle of faces *TheHon* looked at me and smiled. I almost said that wasn't the same thing as combat driving, but I decided to shut up and just nod instead. After all, I hadn't done any real combat driving, either, and I hear European drivers can get pretty rude.

The "fire diversion" and raid for vehicles had all gone as well as anyone had a right to expect. Waiting in the alleyway behind the warehouse with all the civilians and MPs, I didn't see a lot of the actual fighting, but we could hear it, and once the vehicles showed up we saw its evidence in flechette holes and blood spatter.

"In the trucks! In the trucks!" I yelled, and the Varoki MPs shouted the same in a couple different languages. The Varoki civilians ran, fell, crawled, dragged, and pulled themselves up into the truck beds. All of a sudden there were rounds coming into the alley from every direction, and a grenade exploded against a concrete wall, throwing fragments everywhere. Screams, sobbing, cries of pain all mixed up with the snap of flechettes and a babble of Tac chatter over my helmet limk. Another grenade went off closer. I instinctively put my head down and tucked in my hands, and felt the concrete chips and wire fragments pepper Private Coleman's helmet and body armor. In the distance, I heard more explosions, short zips of flechette bursts, and the deep, rhythmic hammering of a Marine two-fifty-four thud gun in autofire mode.

I looked around and tried to see who was firing

down the alley, and I saw an MP slump back against the wall and slide to the ground. Gauss weapons are flashless, but I saw a flicker of movement in a window in a storefront down the alley to my right and across the street, a window that all of the glass was gone from. I selected the grenade launcher on the RAG-19, lased the window and got a solid reflection off the back wall of the store, backed the detonation point five meters back, and hit it with a can of nails. Then I switched to the serial flechette system and unloaded twenty rounds into the smoke and dust.

I banged on the truck cab's door and pointed down the alleyway, and the truck started moving. A couple more had already pulled out—just three left, one for my folks and two for Wataski's crew.

"Okay, last serial, haul ass!" I shouted. The warehouse back door had been ajar, and now it flew open and Borro came out with his gauss pistol up, checked my orientation, and covered the opposite direction. Marr came next, her arms around Barraki, and The-Hon ran behind her with Tweezaa in his arms. There were about two dozen Varoki civilians in the group as well, scrambling and stumbling out of the doorway and piling into the three light trucks. I checked the Varoki MP who'd gone down earlier. He was bleeding from a chest shot that had punched his armor, and bright red blood bubbled up out of his mouth, but he was still alive and conscious.

"You two, get this soldier into that truck."

The two Varoki civilians piling into one of Wataski's truck didn't even break stride, and thinking back I'd say the odds are they didn't hear me—very common in the stress and confusion of combat—or probably even understand English, but at the moment I got really mad. The Marines and MPs were dying to get these people out of this alive, and by God they were *not* going to leave this guy all alone to drown in his own blood in a dirty alleyway. I grabbed one of them by the belt as he was trying to climb up into the truck, pulled him back hard, and almost threw him toward the wounded MP.

"HELP THAT MAN UP, YOU MOTHERFUCKER, OR I WILL KILL YOU MYSELF!" I bellowed.

For a moment, I thought the guy might have a heart attack staring down the barrel of my RAG, or at least wet himself, but after a second of terror paralysis he bent over to pick up the MP, and all of a sudden three more Varoki civilians piled out of the truck to help.

"Borro, get in the cab and fire it up. I'm going to cover Wataski's back."

He nodded and climbed in without argument, pushing the MP driver to the side. I saw Marfoglia's face look back from the back of the truck, alarm mixed with outrage that I wasn't right there protecting them. Couldn't be helped.

"Marfoglia, get your head down! Everybody down in the bed of the truck," I shouted.

"Wataski," I called over the helmet's tacnet, "the last group's loaded. Have you dropped their recon drone yet?"

"Affirmative," she answered. **"Their drone is down."**

Good. We needed to blind them if we were going to get away with this.

"The train is at the station. Pull the plug and haul

ass!" I told her. It wasn't my call—I was just some guy in the alleyway, but there didn't seem to be anybody else hanging around.

Then there was more fire from the other end of the alleyway. I heard the *snap-snap-snap* of a flechette burst, and then another, as they ripped through the length of the light trucks, shattering some of the windshields in front. People inside cried out in pain and terror. I felt panic claw at my throat—who had those rounds torn through?

I turned and let a long auto burst rip down the alley on spec. I didn't hit anything, but somebody dove for cover and dropped his rifle. *Dropped his rifle!* Part of me wanted to run down there and shoot the stupid bastard just as a lesson, but more bad guys were showing up, and I knew the alley was turning into a death trap. If anyone put a grenade into the trucks sitting there, we weren't going anywhere except on foot.

"Wataski, where the hell are you?" I called on the helmet's tacnet.

"Coming. Five seconds."

"Be advised, alleyway is red hot—AWiGs everywhere," I transmitted back.

I changed magazines on my RAG. I hadn't done much shooting until the last couple minutes, when everything started going to hell, so I still had half a dozen magazines, but I was out of grenades, because I'd been a dumb ass and hadn't taken any reloads. I was a civilian, after all, and smart civilians don't get themselves into dirty little firefights like this.

Then a round punched me in the chest and slammed me back against the concrete, and my head whipped back and cracked the wall. The helmet did its job, but it still left me seeing stars, and the blow to my chest left me gasping for air. I slid down the wall to sit in the alleyway as more rounds tore chunks out of the concrete above me. I checked my chest; there was a frayed furrow in the cloth covering of Private Coleman's body armor, but the composite plate underneath was intact, and there was no blood. The round must have been either spent or hit a very glancing blow, because the body armor wasn't designed to stop a clean hit from a smart-head flechette at close range. Who was shooting at me? Where the hell was he now?

The door opened and one of Wataski's Marines came out carrying a missile director in one hand and a RAG-19 in the other, and as soon as she took a step out, her face just exploded in gory red mist and she dropped lifelessly to the ground. Who shot her? I scanned right and left in near panic, and then a four-round burst sent another Marine tumbling back through the doorway. Two rounds must have hit the Marine, but one round hit the doorsill at about a meter up and one hit the floor right inside. How was that possible? Then I got it.

I looked up, and the son of a bitch was on the roof of the building across the alleyway. I raised my rifle, aimed, and when he showed himself to take another shot I killed him. I scrambled to my feet and looked over at the doorway. Wataski had been looking up, her own rifle raised, but now she looked at me.

"Nice shot!" she shouted.

"Get your people in the truck before we're all fucking dead. NOW!" I emptied my magazine down the alleyway to suppress as much fire as I could and then sprinted for my own truck. Borro had it accelerating as my hand yanked open the right-side door and I pulled myself in, with the Varoki MP sandwiched between Borro and me as we took the corner out of the alley almost on two wheels.

I triggered my embedded commlink, the sound of flechettes tearing through vehicles and the screams of pain a few moments earlier echoing in my head.

"Marrissa! Are you okay?" I practically screamed over the link.

She was okay, and so were the kids, although she was so frightened and excited she started hiccupping.

It's funny how under stress you sort of abbreviate things. I meant to say, "Are you *and the kids* okay?" It was really the kids I was most concerned about, but the words came out different. She knew what I meant, though.

We sped out of town and headed northeast, because that was the shortest road to thick jungle. We didn't pass any disabled vehicles along the way, but I lost sight of Wataski's trucks in all the confusion. We needed to get some vegetation overhead as soon as possible, hopefully before they got another drone airborne. The RTM rockets made a moaning scream as they passed over, and I heard the rippling crumps as they detonated all around the town.

We made the jungle edge without even seeing any sign of pursuit. Then we entered the dark tunnel of the rainforest road. There were roads going in a couple different directions, a few vehicles on each of them. There was a car and three other light trucks in our little gaggle of fugitives. My pulse rate slowed down enough that I got some of my higher brain functions back, and I took a good look around.

The jungle road was pretty interesting. The roadway was very hard, almost glass-like, but with a flexible composite covering four or five centimeters thick over the top. You could see that the roadway was buckled and uneven in places, maybe because of tree roots or erosion of the ground nearby, or just settling under the weight of traffic. I'd seen roads like this before—directed-fusion burned, with the heat probably used to incinerate the undergrowth as well as form the roadbed from the soil underneath, melted in temperatures that you usually find inside a star. The composite layer came later—you needed it to protect the vehicles from the roadway, because once that solid sheet began to break—and anything that long and that rigid would start to break right away—the edges would slash your tires to ribbons. But it was a cheap and fast way to cut a road.

I wondered how they kept the rainforest from burning down while they were cutting it; maybe they did their fusion work in the rainy season. Dirt was not very dense, so you needed to fuse a lot of it to get a solid roadbed. As a result, the road itself was sunken in a shallow ravine, which meant the road would be a canal in the rainy season if it weren't for the drainage ditches to either side. Maybe it was a canal anyway when it rained hard enough.

After an hour of exciting driving, I spotted a wide spot in the road and told Borro to pull over. Another truck came even with us and stopped, and a Marine corporal I didn't recognize stuck his head out the cab window.

"Why are you stopping?" he yelled.

"We got wounded," I yelled back, and hooked my thumb over my shoulder toward the cargo bay.

"We need to keep moving!" he answered.

"Go ahead. We'll catch up."

Sure, when pigs fly we would.

He hit the accelerator and sped down the road. The car ahead of us had already vanished around a bend, and the two following trucks disappeared after it in seconds.

"They still have difficulty accepting the need for dispersion," Borro observed.

"Yup."

We had some very frightened people in the back of the vehicle—all Varoki, of course, except for Marfoglia. Aside from our original group, we had the MP, four Varoki men, two women, and a little girl. None of the adults were the little girl's parents.

One of the men had taken a flechette in the side of his head, and it apparently went in and then bounced around inside for a while. We had plastic body bags, so we bagged and sealed him, slid him under the bench seat with as much dignity as the situation allowed, and gave him a moment of silence.

Another man and one of the women had combat dressings as well. The wounds didn't look that serious, but both of them were carrying on and making a lot of noise. That was typical; really serious wounds don't hurt as much as light wounds do, strange as that sounds. It's partly because serious trauma tends to put you in shock—nature's anesthetic.

The little girl shivered with fear and pain, her left hand badly mangled by a flechette burst. Someone had already dressed her wound and given her something for the pain, so she was probably a lot better off now than half an hour ago. Tweezaa sat beside her, holding her good hand, and I think that might have been as effective as the anti-shock drug.

TheHon was sitting on the other side of Tweezaa, and Barraki next to him. *TheHon* had his arms around the two kid's shoulders, and it made me feel jealous, in a stupid sort of way. After all, I was the one supposed to make them feel safe, right?

Wrong. I was supposed to actually make them *be* safe, which was what I was doing. It still felt like he was stealing my job, though.

"You guys okay?" I asked Barraki. He gave me a shaky smile and nodded. Tweezaa looked calmer. She had someone to comfort—the wounded girl—and that can make a big difference.

Marfoglia was inventorying our consumables. Maybe she was doing it to keep busy and take her mind off her fear, or maybe she was doing it because that economist part of her brain just needed to count shit and make lists, but either way, it needed doing.

Borro and I did a quick material assessment next. The truck was a pretty standard outback rig—all-wheel drive, each wheel powered by its own electric motor in the wheel assembly, juiced from a central battery pack spread along the bottom of the chassis. The batteries recharged from an LENR generator—Low Energy Nuclear Reaction, what they used to call cold fusion. Not a lot of energy output, but it's continuous, clean, and cheap, provided the generator had a good fill of deuterium—heavy water—and a fill might last a year or more. The generator didn't kick out enough juice to actually run the truck continuously, which is why the batteries were there—the generator was charging them all the time, and you could get maybe eight or ten hours driving in every twenty from them.

There were solar skins on the cab roofs as well, and they would get you extra mileage if you were out in the sunlight a lot. But since we were avoiding open skies, the LENR was it.

"We need to disable the vehicle transponder right away," I said to Borro. Every vehicle has a unique transponder code, an electronic vehicle-identification number that makes stolen vehicles fairly easy to track. We were facing counterinsurgency goons, playing at soldier instead of cop, but sooner or later they'd remember their basic police procedures. Borro shrugged.

"In some ways a vehicle without a transponder signature is as much of a problem as a vehicle with a high interest code," he answered. "Let us contact your people in orbit and have them download a modified transponder code."

"Uhh . . . I doubt they can do that," I answered.

"Mr. Naradnyo," he said, "I understand that you have some experience at this. Trust me that I have some experience from the other side of the . . . contest. They have the means to alter the transponder codes from orbit, provided your helmet downlink is within a meter or so of the transponder itself."

Really? Now, that was interesting.

We added up the firepower next. We had my Hawker, the little LeMatt, and the Marine-issue RAG-19, with twelve magazines and eight grenades. Borro and the MP each had a gauss pistol, and that was it. We were okay on rations—Marfoglia's inventory showed we had enough to last a week, and if it took any longer than that to get to safety, we were screwed anyway.

The truck had enough battery charge for about six more hours of driving, given the fact that the roads weren't all that good back here in the jungle. I didn't want to run us absolutely bone dry, though, so Borro and I decided on four more hours of travel and then we'd stop for the night to let the generators recharge the batteries.

Tomorrow I'd spring part two of the plan on everyone.

TWENTY-FIVE

"Jungle Bird Seven, this is Orbital Six. Why have you turned northwest?"

"Commodore Gasiri!" I answered. "Good to hear you again."

"Maintain comm protocol and answer query: Why have you turned northwest?"

"Take it easy, Commodore. We're on tight beam. They can't listen in unless they got a hover-plat almost right between us, and one of us would notice that."

"Goddamnit, Naradnyo, if you think I do not know what you are up to, you are sadly mistaken. Now get back on that northbound road or I will have your ass."

"You talk pretty tough from orbit, Gasiri. Why don't you come down here and we'll see whose ass gets kicked?"

I could tell her self-control was starting to slip. She was under a lot of pressure, after all, and I wasn't making her life any easier. Well, too bad. That wasn't my job.

I had the feed switched to the uplink helmet's speaker so we could all hear, but for a half minute or so there was just silence. Beside me, Barraki's ears started quivering with alarm. I killed the mike for a second and winked at him.

"Don't worry, pal. I'm pretty sure I can take her."

Borro covered his eyes with his hand and shook his head. The Varoki MP, a lance corporal named Tuvaani, broke into a big grin. Marfoglia just looked off into the jungle. She was wearing viewer glasses and cramming like crazy on the data dump I'd given her a couple hours ago.

When Gasiri spoke again, her voice was level and controlled. She was sharp enough to know that screaming wasn't going to get her anywhere. More to the point, she understood the implication of what I'd said—as long as we were the ones down here with our asses in the grass, she was just another backseat driver with a dime-a-dozen opinion.

"What does your special passenger think of this new plan?"

"I don't know. I didn't share it with him. I got him out digging a latrine for us, but when he gets back, you can ask him yourself."

Gasiri probably figured that last bit was a wisecrack, and it was, but it was also the truth. I *did* have the *Cottohazz* Executive Council's Special Envoy Plenipotentiary for Emergency Abatement on K'Tok digging a latrine. I'd told him before that I was in charge and he was strictly coolie labor, and so I'd given him a couple crappy jobs just to drive the point home.

"You really do amuse yourself, don't you, Naradnyo?"

"Well, Commodore, somebody better. Nobody seems to like it much when I get mad."

A half hour later we were on the road again, and this time I rode in back, while the Varoki MP rode shotgun up front with Borro. We had the sideflaps of the cargo bed rolled up to get more air, but it didn't help that much. The jungle closed around us like a prison, made more oppressive by the solid overhead canopy of vegetation. Sweat poured off me, and everyone else for that matter. I swatted a flying bug that stung me on the neck—no more survival instinct than the bugs on Nishtaaka, but at least they were smaller.

"Okay, so now you're my political expert," I said to Marfoglia. "Educate me."

We were sitting all the way in front, right behind the cab, with a little space between us and the other passengers. It wasn't much privacy, but it was all there was.

She ate as she frowned in thought, working through an answer. She was eating a ration pack, and just the way she held the pack in one hand and her fork in the other looked balanced, comfortable, and somehow elegant, as if it were the only right way to eat rations in the field. How did she do that? Was it some gimmick they taught in charm school or something? I found it impressive and irritating at the same time, and that's a good trick.

"How much of the briefing did you read?"

"Enough to give me a headache," I answered. "That's when I turned it over to you. Imagine I'm an investor. What's the prospectus?"

She gave me a look that said she didn't like being patronized, but she was used to it coming from assholes like me.

"Don't invest a *Cotto* here. Terrible risk-to-reward ratio. Everybody's banking on the ecoform working."

"Problems with that?" I asked.

"Well, the old Many-Eggs-One-Basket problem to begin with. They have had a Needle in place a long time, and it's not exactly paying for itself. A lot of governments and merchant houses have money sunk into the world, and they all believe the money has earned them the right to decide what happens here. But the people who live here have their own ideas."

"Is that what this revolt is about?"

She frowned again as she took another bite and cocked her head to the side in thought.

"Ultimately, yes. There are complaints about corruption and incompetence in the uZmataanki colonial government, but the political agenda of the insurgents isn't simply reform or a power change; it's union between the two colonies to become an independent member state of the *Cottohazz*."

"That's why they're called Unionists?" I asked, and she nodded. "Well, hard to see the *Cottohazz* making them a member when they're shooting up *Cottohazz* security forces."

"I didn't see any record of hostilities against any *Cottohazz* forces in the briefing," she said. She didn't see any because there weren't any—*that* I'd checked. Interesting that she'd noticed.

"Okay, one more question. Later I'll have a million, but this is the big one. I didn't run across any clear records of atrocities. What did you see?"

"Quite a few charges by the uZmataanki colonial government—assassinations of government officials, firing at people who were under flags of truce, executing prisoners after a battle..."

"Yeah, yeah," I interrupted. "Shit happens. Half of it's lies and the other half everybody does when no one's looking. Here's the acid test—any mass graves?"

She shook her head.

That's what I'd figured, but it was good to have it confirmed. I leaned back, took a drink of water from my load harness, and let my mind wander. Sometimes a wandering mind finds useful places to go.

"I wonder if Wataski made it out," I said.

"You like her, don't you?" Marfoglia asked.

"Yeah. She reminds me of a Zack. Don't ever tell her I said that; she'd probably take it wrong."

"You like Zaschaan, too."

"I do. Great senses of humor."

She frowned at me, unsure if I was making fun of her or just being a wiseass. For a change, none of the above.

"When I was on Nishtaaka—seems like a lifetime ago now—right after we made planetfall they trucked us to the front. We drove past a Zack ADA battery deployed to defend Needledown. ADA, that's air-defense artillery, mostly high-energy pulse lasers and masers, but backed up with a few missile rails. The directed-energy weapons will knock down just about anything aircraft-sized that pokes up over the horizon, unless it's really well shielded—say a superconducting reflector skin. If so, that's what the missiles are for. This Zack outfit we passed was a missile battery.

"I didn't speak or read Szawa yet, but my squad

leader did, and when he saw what they'd painted on one of the sealed launch canisters, he laughed.

"*What did it say?*" I'd asked.

"*Reflect This.*"

I smiled again just remembering.

"That's why we headed north originally, isn't it?" she asked. "To reach the uBakai, so their air defenses can protect us from uZmataanki aircraft."

"Yup."

"But if so . . ."

She was looking at me oddly, like she was thinking real hard. Then her eyes narrowed, but in triumph rather than anger, and she smiled.

"I know your new plan, too," she said, and she leaned back against the truck railing and folded her arms in triumph. "It will probably get us killed."

"Open to suggestions," I offered, but she didn't have any, so the conversation petered out.

It sounds odd, but I don't remember much of the next two days. I do remember almost getting lynched once.

We'd pulled into a jungle settlement—a dozen or so buildings and maybe half again as many vehicles. There were two small stores—one specializing in dry goods, hardware, and food, the other for technical stuff: vehicle parts, comm gear, etc. There was a hostel that served hot meals to the locals, one official-looking building, and a bunch of private residences. Not a very big town, but it had a purposeful look to it. There might be a famine and a war going on, but these people had food, work, and a mission, whatever that was.

Marfoglia stayed under canvas in the truck with *TheHon* and the kids, and Lance Corporal Tuvaani stood guard to keep the curious away. Our five adult Varoki civilians had broken up into two groups to shop for supplies, one group per store, but their real purpose was to poke around and see what they could find out.

Meanwhile Borro, wearing parts of my body-armor rig and the corporal's fatigue cap and shoulder brassard as a half-assed MP uniform, pushed me at gunpoint down the street. I had my hands tied in front of me, and I was wearing some body armor and the helmet, but with the visor up so folks could see Borro's Human "prisoner." Maybe staging a one-man POW parade wasn't the smartest part of my plan, but none of us could think of any other way to get me and the helmet close enough to all those vehicles one at a time.

See, it occurred to me that changing our transponder code wasn't much of an answer. If it was a phony code, that would show up in their database. If it was a duplicate code, it would also show up, and although they might not know which code location was the phony, they could at least narrow it down to two target points. No, the answer was to go into a town and change *all* of the vehicle transponder codes there to match ours. Then let them figure out which one was which. Of course, a stranger in an uplink helmet hanging around everyone's vehicle might attract attention, so instead we staged our little passion play.

"Do you believe that this plan of yours will work?" Borro asked.

"You gave me the idea."

"No, not this business with the transponders; the other part. How can you be sure the Unionists have an effective air-defense network?"

"So you figured that out, huh? Well, I guess it's pretty obvious what I had in mind. As to their ADA umbrella, I'm not sure what they've got, if anything. All I know is they've survived under Sammie-controlled skies for months, so whatever they're doing, it's working."

"How will we contact them?" he asked. "You know, you cannot simply drive into the jungle and say, 'Take me to the rebels.' Were it that simple, the government forces would have done it long ago."

"Yeah, but they didn't have the *Cottohazz* Executive Council's Special Envoy Plenipotentiary for Emergency Abatement on K'Tok as a bargaining chip."

I watched him carefully then. A lot of this depended on how he reacted to the idea. If he had any reaction, I couldn't pick up on it. His skin color and ear movement remained just about the same as before. Borro was good.

After a few seconds, he simply nodded.

"Yes, that will probably work."

"You're okay with it?"

"Yes, within some parameters as to the envoy's physical safety."

"No guarantees," I said.

"There are no guarantees anywhere," he answered. "It is a matter of comparative risks and likely outcomes. Not all decisions are easy, but they must be made. I believe that this is the safest course."

"You gonna get in trouble from your boss?"

"Undoubtedly."

"If it will help, I'll talk to him," I volunteered.

Borro smiled at that and then shook his head.

"The Honorable e-Lotonna is my assignment, not my employer."

"Oh yeah? Then who—"

But just as the conversation was getting interesting, pain flashed through my left upper body as a fist-sized rock bounced off my shoulder.

I looked over at the locals who had been following us, watching our little act, and they were buying it, maybe better than we'd figured on. Four or five spectators had grown to over a dozen, and they were getting uglier as they got stronger, iridescent skin flashing the dark red-orange of rage and danger-buzz, ears splaying out like Chinese fans and then snapping back tight against the head.

"Borro . . ."

"I see them," he said.

"Well, you better do something. I'd say you're about thirty seconds from either having to shoot people or feed me to them."

"Which would you suggest?"

That probably sounded a lot funnier to him, he being the guy with the gun and me being the one with my hands tied. He didn't wait for an answer. Instead he turned and started talking to them in Sammie. He didn't yell, and he didn't point the gauss pistol at them. He just talked, softly and quietly. I picked up most of it. Do not do anything foolish, I am responsible for this prisoner, that sort of thing. Blah blah blah. The words didn't really matter as much as how they were said. Borro said them without bluster, without trying to intimidate or frighten. He said them the way someone tells you something just for due diligence, not really caring what you do with the warning, because once the warning was given, his hands were clean, and he was going to do whatever the hell he wanted to next.

Later I figured out that these little settlements had seen their share of hard people lately, between rebels, government soldiers, and mercenary strikers. If not, things might have gotten uglier, but these folks knew the signs and what they meant. That particular moment on that particular street, the signs meant go home and live. So they did.

"I owe you one, pal," I said as they dispersed.

"I doubt it will be the last one," Borro answered. "I will be sure to keep track."

"So what did we learn? Anything?" I asked.

Borro translated into aGavoosh as I looked at the little circle of faces—the five Varoki adults who had done our "shopping." They talked to each other a bit, ears expanding and contracting in agitation, comparing notes I guess, trying to figure out what was important and what was just meaningless background noise. Then one of the two females spoke to Borro for a while, gesturing out at the jungle as she did so, her ears very large and gracefully expressive.

"Kavaani-la says the town is an agricultural research station. They are force-changing the jungle flora. That is why it looks so wilted here; microorganisms in the soil attacking the local plant life, trying to replace it with Varoki-compatible protein forms."

"Yeah? How's that working out?"

Borro repeated the question to her, the group compared notes again, and Borro turned to me.

"Not well, Sasha. They are managing to kill a great deal of local plant life, but they have not been successful in getting the replacement stock to take root. Mr. Hoozhu," he said, gesturing to an elderly male

Varoki, "believes that is why there is so much hostility. They are afraid for their future."

"Is that the way you see it, Borro?"

"I see no reason to doubt it. But I was interested in the extreme hostility they showed you, a Human."

"Yeah, I was interested in that, too. So interested I almost wet myself."

It was weird. Humans were not real popular anywhere, but the mob scene was over the top, especially with no Human enclave on-planet to cause background friction. Very weird.

Well, nothing else seemed to make much sense on K'Tok so far, so why should this be an exception?

I thanked the five civilians, excused myself, and walked over to where *TheHon*, Marfoglia, and the three children were eating.

"How's the chow?" I asked, and swatted a bug on my cheek.

Barraki translated the question for Tweezaa and she looked at me and said, "It sucks!" She beamed with pleasure, ears spread wide and then twitching up and down at the tips. Then she went back to eating. While the adults looked at each other, momentarily speechless, Barraki started laughing.

"You been giving your sister English lessons, Weasel Boy?" I demanded.

He just cocked his head to the side, but his grin told the story.

"Just out of curiosity," I asked, "what does Tweezaa think *it sucks* actually means?"

"I do not know. Well . . . she may think it means *quite good*." Then he looked down at his ration pack to keep from giggling, but it didn't do any good.

"Barraki!" Marfoglia exclaimed, but the rest of us started laughing, and then Marfoglia did, too.

"Be advised, though, Weasel Boy," I said, and pointed at him for emphasis, "if the word *fuck*, or anything like it, comes out of her mouth, you're going to start riding standing up, and it won't be because anyone makes you—it's just going to be the only comfortable position. You read me?"

"You are going to kick my ass," he translated.

"In a cold-blooded fashion."

Marfoglia said something to Tweezaa, who gave Barraki a look of irritation followed by a punch in the shoulder.

"Ow!" he said, and then Tweezaa went back to eating, the ledger apparently balanced to her satisfaction.

"You should probably eat something, too, Mr. Naradnyo," Marfoglia said, but frowning and not looking at me. "Have you had anything today but energy water? It's stupid not to eat."

Hard to turn down such a gracious invitation.

"Yeah, maybe later. I need to report to Gasiri."

I pulled on the uplink helmet and opened the oomm channel.

"This is Jungle Bird Seven . . . or Eight, I forget which. But it's Naradnyo and company, okay? We got clear of the town without much trouble, and it looks as if Operation Chameleon was a success. How does it look from up there?"

"Jungle Bird Seven, this is Orbital One. Acknowledge your transmission. Our telemetry shows 100 percent success with Chameleon. Hold for Orbital Six."

Orbital Six was Gasiri. Commanders are always

"six." There was probably a good reason for it once, but damned if I knew what it was. In a few seconds she came on the circuit.

"Good job, Seven. We have matched all other transponder codes to yours and the decoys. We are also sending word for the other ground parties to locate settlements and duplicate the operation if feasible."

"Swell. So now we'll try my other little plan, and if we're still alive to chat tomorrow, you can tell the other ground parties to follow us there, too."

"Negative, Seven. You are categorically forbidden to contact the Unionist resistance. Do you understand?"

"Yeah, I understand. I just don't care."

TWENTY-SIX

About twelve hours later, I stood quietly in the middle of the road, looking down a sewer pipe. Well, actually, it was the barrel of a medium-gauge shotgun, but it looked big as a sewer pipe from where I was standing.

There were three Varoki in front of us, all of them armed, no more than three or four meters away, and since the shotgun was cut down short, it would be pretty hard for the guy in the middle to miss, no matter how much his hand was shaking—and it was shaking a lot. It must have been from buck fever, because Marfoglia and I were both unarmed.

The undergrowth to our left parted and four more Varoki with rifles showed themselves, all in civilian hunting clothes but wearing the same yellow armband on their left sleeve. Then one more guy with a submachine gun showed himself on our right and kind of behind us.

"Well, this is working out better than I thought,"

I subvocalized to Marfoglia on our dedicated comm link. *"Now that we're surrounded, if they open fire they'll shoot the hell out of each other."*

She looked at me with a look of mixed terror and anger. No wonder—I'd gotten her into this mess, and now I was making wise about it. Served her right for being a jerk.

*"**To hungding!**"* she transmitted back, her eyes desperate. Her subvocalization technique left a lot to be desired, but I was pretty sure she was trying to say *"do something."*

Yeah. Good idea.

"Any of you guys speak English?" I asked out loud as an icebreaker, and I threw in a big grin so the natives would know I was harmless.

They looked at each other for a few seconds, and then one of them lowered his assault rifle and answered.

"I speak English. You are a long way from home, Earthman."

"I'm from Peezgtaan, actually, but that's still far enough," I said, smiling as politely as I knew how. I'm not all that good at either smiling or polite, but extraordinary circumstances demand extraordinary efforts.

"You are the ones who have the Special Envoy prisoner?" he asked.

"Not prisoner. Guest."

"You will turn him over to us and leave."

"Nope. He stays with us. We all go with you or nobody does."

"We can take him," the spokesman said.

"His dead body, maybe."

The guy that spoke English looked at me for a few

seconds and then withdrew a few steps to talk things over with the others, but he left the guy with a giant shotgun to cover us. Actually, now that the shotgun wasn't pointed directly at my face, it had shrunk down to real-world size.

While they talked, I looked them over. They had an interesting mix of gear. They were wearing civilian outfits, but they were very well-made outdoor clothes in jungle green with a broad dark tone camo shatter pattern diagonally across them. I figure they were hunting smocks of some sort, but they were similar enough they could almost be uniforms—or at least all from the same supplier. The weapons were a mishmash of civilian hunting rifles and shotguns along with a few civilian low-end copies of military small arms, and—I was pretty sure—one genuine uZmataanki Milspec RAG. The webbing was all the same sort of hunting stuff, and again all the same pattern, as if somebody made a mass buy. Headgear was varied and soft, and what body armor they had was all light civilian grade. And they were clean. It just wasn't how I'd envisioned a hard-core guerrilla insurgency.

The huddle broke up, and the mouthpiece walked back to face me.

"Why should we let you camp with us? The puppet council forces will follow you here. That will mean trouble for us, perhaps deaths. Why should we?"

"That's a yes," I transmitted to Marfoglia, because she needed some good news, but also because it was true.

"Because it's too big an opportunity to pass up."

"Nell me gen why uh hell I'm here." she transmitted back. Was that supposed to be *"Tell me again* *why the hell I'm here"*? I decided to take that as a compliment and hid an honest smile under my phony one.

"I will have to consult with my commander," he said.

Sure, go ahead, pal. Talk to your commander. Get a witch board and talk to Che Guevara if you want. We're in!

Marfoglia almost fainted once things settled down, and that surprised me. I mean, I knew she was scared by all those guns, but she was *really* scared—teeth-chattering, knee-wobbly, sweat-soaked scared. She'd held up under a lot the last few days, but it's really different when you can look in people's eyes and see the guns pointed at you. I had to hold her up for a minute or so, and I thought she was going to start crying on me, except almost every drop of spare water she had in her had gone out her sweat glands in about two minutes. Then I thought she might take a swing at me, but she didn't, she just pushed me away. She almost fell again then.

"Marrissa, you're dehydrated."

She glared at me through wet, tangled hair plastered to her face, her expression a mixture of anger and fear. Then she slowly sank down to sit in the road cross-legged. As she did, I realized that I was feeling dizzy myself. I hadn't eaten much in the last few days and had built up a pretty impressive sleep deficit. Well, pretty soon I could catch up.

I pulled the water bladder out of the back of my load harness, squatted down, and handed it to her.

"Dehydration makes you physically weak, but it also triggers anxiety, even panic attacks. It's not real fear you're feeling—it's just your brain chemistry out of whack. So drink—sip if you want, but drink, keep drinking, and just sit here and rest for a while."

She took the bladder with trembling hands and started drinking. I sat down at arm's length and waved to Borro back in the truck cab and gave him a thumbs-up.

"Feeling any better?" I asked her.

She shook her head.

"Look, I wouldn't have put you through that if I didn't think it was necessary," I said.

"You call that an apology?" she demanded, her voice weak and trembling, but angry.

"Nope."

I think she almost hit me then, but she thought better of it—probably lacked the strength. Instead she just turned away and looked at the jungle, still taking regular sips of water. I stood up, waited for another spell of dizziness to pass, and walked back to the truck to give her some space. I told Lance Corporal Tuvaani to go hang out with her until she felt better—and keep his sidearm handy. I didn't think the insurgents would give us any trouble, but this was untamed wilderness either side of the narrow ribbon of the road, and the jungle started about five meters from where Marfoglia was sitting. No telling how hungry the big toothy things lurking in there might be, and if they weren't any smarter than the little bugs, they might eat her first and get sick later.

But if some giant crab-thing didn't eat her, she'd be okay. She'd almost packed it in, but not during the crisis, only afterwards. That was important. She might be a spoiled, rich pain in the ass, but she wasn't worthless.

They kept us waiting on the road for a couple hours in the mid-afternoon heat—either so they wouldn't look too anxious, or to give them time to clean up their HQ compound. After all, they probably didn't get a lot of guests way out here in the mountains.

On the surface, I figured this insurgency was about what they were all about—gross government mis-management, crooked elections, corrupt judges, and a growing sense that whoever the hell was running things didn't give a damn about the common folks anymore—didn't even think that giving a damn ought to be part of their job descriptions. Underneath it all, it was about the arrogance of power, and how after a while that really pisses people off, on a very basic gut level. Once that ember starts smoldering, it doesn't take much to fan it into a roaring blaze.

And I figured that somewhere in all that mess, there was probably an uBakai spoon stirring the pot. The whole Union thing meant uniting the two colonies under a single government, and I bet uBakaa figured to come out ahead in that, since their people weren't in open revolt.

That's who I really wanted to talk to, the uBakai. I'm not crazy about governments, but there are times when there's just no substitute for them. Or so I thought.

Once things started moving, they moved fairly quickly. An hour driving behind a hard-gun car got us to the cliff base that was the staging area to their base. Was it their main base? An alternate base? A satellite base? I had no way of knowing. It was just a base.

The entrance to the compound was a nearly sheer cliff side, and it opened into some very impressive underground chambers. Some of them looked natural, but there had been a lot of additional work done— some excavation, some reinforcement, and in places it was hard to tell what was original and what was new. The artificial lighting was good, and it was cooler than outside—probably naturally cool. Ventilation was just okay—the air wasn't heavy with CO_2, but it didn't smell very good, either: mold, rotten garbage, feces, and body odor all mixed up together. Of course Varoki shit, urine, and BO smell different than ours, because of the different protein groups, but they are still unmistakable odors.

I carried Tweezaa, who was sleeping, and Marfoglia held Barraki's hand. A fair number of Varoki watched us—all of them in fatigues except for one guy in a suit who stayed in the shadows. Groggy as I was from fatigue, I still noticed things like that, maybe on some subconscious level.

We got everyone settled in a storage area they had thrown some bedding into, and got our three injured folks to their infirmary. Then it was time to go meet the head guys. I wasn't crazy about leaving Barraki and Tweezaa, but I also didn't want to draw attention to them, so we left them with Corporal Tuvaani, along with the clear understanding that if he let anything happen to either of them, cohorts of heavily armed Sammie mercenary strikers intent on hunting him down and killing him would be the least of his troubles.

The mouthpiece and another guy led Marfoglia, *TheHon*, Borro and me down concrete-walled corridors damp with condensation. While we followed them, I reset the transmit gain on the dedicated link to Marfoglia to its lowest setting, and I subvocalized instead of speaking out loud.

"Testing One Two Three. Don't respond verbally. Just nod if you hear this."

She looked at me and then nodded.

"Crank your power on this channel all the way down. Unless their receiver is in the same room as us, odds are it will get us some privacy."

The commander was a slender Varoki with a long, narrow face, darkly iridescent skin, and intelligent eyes. He wore hunting camies like the others, but his looked older, more worn, and they bore no rank insignia. His office was large but simply furnished. He rose from behind his desk to greet us, and there were two officers already standing beside him. They both wore sidearms—unlike the commander—but there were no sentries anywhere. No sidearm, no sentries—here was a guy who trusted his people.

A fourth Varoki sat in the shadows, deeper in the commander's office, and he looked like he was in a business suit rather than camies. Same guy I'd noticed earlier.

Bingo, I said to myself.

We got introductions all around, although the three Varoki insurgents went by their titles, not their names—the commander, the security chief, the political officer. Then the guy in back stood up and emerged from the shadows, and the commander introduced him as Mr. Katchaan, their technical advisor.

"Katchaan is aGavoosh for 'nobody,'" Marfoglia transmitted to me. Her subvocalizing was getting a lot better.

"So probably not his real name, huh?" I suggested.

"Ha ha," she answered without a trace of mirth.

He was the youngest of the four, and was short for a Varoki—maybe a whisker over two meters—and very slender, which just made him look younger than he was, and he was probably pretty young. He had a look of earnest commitment about him which I wouldn't normally associate with a covert operative, but then again, maybe we Humans were just getting too jaded and cynical about this kind of stuff. There was probably a time when almost all spies had been young idealists. I just wondered what their survival rate had been.

The commander spoke English, and his security chief translated it to aZmataan for the political officer. I thought the choice of language was interesting.

"Let me make it clear that I am here unofficially and against my expressed wishes," *TheHon* began.

"I understand, Excellency," the commander replied. "You and your companions will be treated with consideration. Notice that we have allowed you to retain your weapons. Since we do not consider ourselves in a state of hostilities against the *Cottohazz* itself, you will be treated as neutral noncombatants until your status is . . . clarified. I hope that will be acceptable."

TheHon actually bowed his head a little as a sign of assent. So far this was going about as well as I could hope. Then the commander turned to Marfoglia and me.

"I apologize for the delay at the perimeter. My soldiers are alert to tricks by the colonial puppet forces, but they should have known to act with more dispatch. We have been monitoring the colonial military communications, as much as we could, to follow your progress. Once the fighters at the rendezvous point made it clear that two Human civilians were present, we ordered them to bring your party here at once. We have been hoping you would seek sanctuary with us."

He looked sincere, but lots of people can look sincere when it suits their purpose. But what was so important about two Human civilians? Unless...

"You knew our identities before we contacted you?"

"Naradnyo and Marfoglia, yes. Other than Marines, you were the only Humans with the group on the train. It was a simple deduction."

"Yeah...but how did you know to begin with?"

"Mr. Katchaan has been tracking your movements, to the extent we have been able. Since the train accident, he has been particularly anxious concerning your safety," the commander finished, glancing sideways at the technical advisor, and all of a sudden I believed him. There was just enough concealed irritation in his voice to tell me Mr. Katchaan—*Mr. Nobody*—had been a pain in the commander's ass, and for more than just a couple hours.

Katchaan blushed but nodded.

"It is true," he said in very good English, and the security dude murmured a translation for the political boss. "We do not normally have the honor of guests of this stature and importance, so naturally we have been anxious. I wished the commander to contact you directly, but he...persuaded me that such an attempt would endanger you more than it would help."

Stature? Importance? I looked at Marfoglia, and she returned my look of mostly concealed surprise. He might be spreading it on thick to flatter us, but I could tell she didn't think so, and I sure as hell didn't. I also didn't think he was talking about a few

Marines and some refugees. I felt Marfoglia's hand on my forearm, a warning gesture.

"Who is he talking about?" I asked Marfoglia over our net.

No answer. She was as puzzled as I was. Okay, time for Plan B.

"Forgive me for asking, but why is the uBakai government interested in two Human travelers?" I asked.

He and the officers exchanged a glance of surprise.

"No, there is a misunderstanding. I am not uBakai," he said.

"Oh. My apologies. Okay...who *are* you with?"

That was not a polite question, I know. The deal in a situation like this is that if someone wants you to know who they're with, they'll tell you. Normally I'd have been more circumspect about that question, but when you think you know what's what, and then you get the rug pulled out from under you, you act instinctively and without subtlety.

"Why, AZ Crescent Technical Systems," he answered, as if it were obvious.

"Okay, consigliere, this is why you're here. Who is this guy and what is this all about?" I demanded of Marfoglia over our net.

"AZ Crescent is a majority-owned subsidiary of the e-Traak holding group," she answered. **"Maybe they're the ones behind the revolution."**

"Not uBakaa?"

"Apparently not."

e-Traak holding, huh? Suddenly I had a pretty good idea why they were interested in us, but I wanted to hear him say it.

"Okay. Why is AZ Crescent interested in us?"

"Because you guard the children of Sarro e-Traak, of course! The twin diamonds, the heirs of our future."

Twin diamonds? Heirs of our future?

"Uh . . . yeah, guess we do," I answered cautiously. Interesting as this was getting, there was more pressing business.

"Commander, I need to cut a deal with you. There are a bunch of trucks wandering north out there in the jungle, full of Marines and Varoki civilians, trying to get away from the uZmataanki security forces."

"Yes, the others from the maglev. We are aware of that."

"Well, they can run north for a while, but pretty soon they're going to run into the rear security detachments of the uZmataanki front-line combat troops engaged against the uBakai. Then they're in real trouble. I can communicate with the cruiser in orbit, and the cruiser can direct those trucks here, or to whatever safe enclaves you have closer to them."

He shifted uncomfortably and frowned, ears folding and unfolding.

"Yes, but then those enclaves will become somewhat less safe. You understand this?"

"Yup. But it's worth the risk to you."

"Oh? Why?"

"I think you know the answer to that. Helping us is a card—and a damned good one—to play at the peace negotiations. You had the *Cottohazz and* the colonial government against you before. Now, with this war, the uZmataanki are on the *Cottohazz's* shit list, and that moves you into the neutral-but-dangerous column. That's an improvement, but you need something else to move you over into the neutral-but-useful-and-possibly-friendly column, and those trucks out there are it."

"Helping you, and the Special Envoy, will not be sufficient?"

"No. We came to you, Commander. We made the overt act. Now it's time for you to step up and make an overt act of your own."

He looked at his two officers briefly, and I could pretty much tell how they stood on the subject. The security guy was against it, because it was terrible security. The political guy was for it, because it was great politics. I couldn't tell where Katchaan stood, and the commander didn't seem to care about his opinion on this one. After a moment, the commander nodded.

"There is no time to waste in arguments over this," he said, as much to his security guy as to us. "Several of your trucks have already been disabled and their occupants captured and executed. My security deputy will give you the land grid rendezvous coordinates for the surviving parties. A number of them will be routed here. We already have an uplink communication antenna focused on your cruiser, but we have not yet activated the link. It is time."

So I managed to broker a deal between Gasiri and the commander for the other trucks to come in under their protection. After that we were escorted back to the area they'd set up for us. They lined up a hot meal, showers, and some clean clothes, and then let us get some rest.

I hadn't realized how depleted my reserves were until I'd almost collapsed during the walk back from the commander's office. I really hadn't been eating or sleeping since we hit the jungle, and without the adrenaline pumping to keep me upright, I almost didn't make it back. I skipped the shower for now, made myself eat a couple mouthfuls of something from a ration pack, and then crashed. I used my black carryall as a pillow, and I was out as soon as my head hit it. If I had any dreams, I don't remember them.

The next day I showered, ate, and felt a little better. I used a razor to scrape away the beard that was coming in pretty thick, and while I did I got a good long look at myself in the mirror. I was a little shocked at how much weight I'd lost, how gaunt my face looked. I looked _old_, especially around the eyes. I wasn't used to that.

By now we were all in clean jungle camouflage fatigues provided by the commander. They were pretty long in the waist for us, and Marfoglia's were absurdly large, but with the sleeves rolled up almost to the shoulders, the waist belted tight, and the enormous baggy trousers tucked into the tops of tall boots and bloused out, she managed to pull it off as a look—sort of _Rebel Gaucho Chic_.

Humans might not be able to win a revolution, but by God we could dress for one.

So later that day, Marfoglia and I were asked to meet with Mr. Katchaan, and things started getting weird.

IIIIIIIIIIIIIIIIIIIIIIIIIIIIIIIIIIIIIII TWENTY-SEVEN

Katchaan was young and lonely, and he had a need to talk to someone. Marfoglia and I were excellent listeners—once we'd each gotten some rest. We were also both very sympathetic, and in her case, the sentiment was genuine. I, on the other hand, am a heartless bastard, but I can fake a lot of things if the situation requires it, and in this instance it clearly did. I could be Nobody's best pal if it served my purpose—and believe me, the irony of that linguistic *double entendre* did not escape me.

Since Marfolglia and I were *Saviors of the Heirs*, and the two little squirts confirmed it by calling us *Boti*, Mr. Nobody was probably more forthcoming with us than he would normally have been with Humans—or even Varoki. Maybe especially Varoki.

One of the things Katchaan spilled to us—in private—over the course of the next two days was that he was a member of a Shadow Brotherhood, called *Tahk Pashaada-ak*, which Marfoglia later told me was old aGavoosh for *End of Empty Dreams*. Over the next couple days I'd find out that this Shadow Brotherhood stuff was a lot more important to the Varoki than most people ever realized. Katchaan was partly here on orders from AZ Crescent, and partly on orders from his brotherhood, and he wasn't really sure to what extent the one was influenced by the other, but they were entangled, no doubt.

What he was sure of was that AZ Crescent wanted the Unionists to succeed, so uBakaa would come out on top. *Tahk Pashaada-ak* wanted the forced eco-forming ended immediately. Why? That was about the only thing he was reluctant to tell us. I started thinking maybe he didn't know.

Turns out, the "Twin Diamonds, Heirs of our Future" business had been a bad slip on his part, and he was a little nervous about it. Those phrases were *Tahk Pashaada-ak* lingo, not the company line, and it let anyone else in the commander's room that day know which brotherhood he was with—provided they were high enough up to know something about another brotherhood. The good news was that *Tahk Pashaada-ak* wanted the kids alive—practically seemed to worship them, for reasons I never figured out. The bad news was Katchaan had no clue who was trying to kill them or why, no idea what other brotherhoods were active in the insurgency headquarters, or what their motives might be.

I'd known Varoki all my life, grew up next to them, worked with them, stole from them, palled around with a few of them, and not one of them ever even *hinted* at the existence of the brotherhoods. And now I know that almost all of them belonged to one, or were aligned with one, or were under the protection of one, the whole time. And here's the really creepy part—they *all* know about them, but they *never* talk about them—at least the working-class folks don't.

Marfoglia had mixed more with the rich and powerful and had heard rumors of the Shadow Brotherhoods. Very rich people feel more secure—nothing really bad has ever happened to them, and they believe that nothing really bad ever can—so they are less careful about things like that. It was still a secret, of course, but what is a secret?

Something you tell to only one person at a time.

You see two-and-a-quarter-meter-tall Varoki, long torsos, smooth, hairless, iridescent skin, great big ears, and you think, "Oooo! Look! *Aliens!*"

Then you get to know them, watch them wear silk robes with embroidered Chinese characters, see them hang Rembrandt and Chagall prints in their dens, and listen to classic rock with the audio cranked up high . . . see their government structure so much like ours, their economy, their approach to science and technology, and you figure, "Hey, these guys are just Humans in lizard suits."

But then you find out about the Shadow Brotherhoods, and you start to wonder again.

That guy Henry lined up for the e-snap data mine back on Peezgtaan—what had he said? That he was in the wrong "club" and so wasn't getting promoted? I was willing to bet now he wasn't in it for the payoff *or* the payback; he was acting under orders from his brotherhood to mess up AZK, for whatever reason. And I'd thought *revenge* was a bad motive!

Peeling back this layer of the onion was like looking

at a small town someplace, studying it for years, thinking you knew all about it and the people in it, and then one day discovering that everyone in the town was actually a giant cockroach disguised as a Human.

Another thing I picked up on was why Katchaan trusted us more than he trusted any Varoki—more than he *could* trust any Varoki.

To Katchaan, Marfoglia and I were like Henry's great-great-grandfather back in that Nazi POW camp. The Americans back then had a word for those Black flyers, maybe the ugliest word in the English language by the time they got done with it—*nigger*. Say it to yourself. Go ahead. Let the word roll around in your mouth. What does it taste like? It's not enough to say it tastes like hate; hate is where it ends up, but it starts with contempt, and then drifts into fear—the fear taste is really strong. Only after those two—contempt and fear—cook together for a while do you get genuine hate.

Katchaan had no idea which of the other Varoki in the insurgency belonged to a rival brotherhood, but he damned well knew we didn't, because to the Varoki, we were niggers. We had jazz and blues and disco and *gangsta'* rap—cubism and impressionism, existentialism and nihilism, *auturism* and post-modernism and the little black dress, and they ate that shit up with a spoon—but come closing time, as far as they were concerned we were still just niggers, and all the money in the galaxy wouldn't have made us anything more than *rich* niggers.

He actually believed we would be flattered by this gift of his special trust.

❖   ❖   ❖

About a third of the trucks had been lost—that was actually fewer than I'd expected. They straggled in over the next couple of days, and Wataski's truck was the second one in.

Her truck was shot up, the composite flexi-cover in back all shredded and with a couple flechette holes in the cab. Wataski swung down from the shotgun door on the left, her face swollen, discolored, and showing stitches, but it didn't keep her from talking.

"Well, you look like shit!" she said. I guess I wasn't the only one who'd noticed.

"I call that big talk from some broad with twenty stitches in her face."

She made a sound, like gravel rattling around in a metal bucket, it took me a second or two to identify as laughter.

"This little party your doing?" she asked, the sweep of her arm taking in the Varoki insurgents hustling to unload her truck and get IR damper shrouds over it.

"Yeah, pretty much."

She nodded slowly, looking around.

"Come on, help me unload."

"The Sammies can handle it," I answered, but she shook her head.

"Not this. Aguillar took a flechette in the shoulder, so he can't help." She walked around the back of the truck and I followed, not sure what I'd find.

A body bag.

"Who's this?"

"Swanson, Corporal Francis X. We ran into a contractor convoy about three nights back. Things got pretty hot, and he went down, but we managed to recover his body and get away. They got some place we can keep him until we can get him back up to the *Fitz*?"

I nodded.

"The Sammie doc's got a cooler."

I carried one end and Wataski carried the other. Swanson had been a big guy, and I was still feeling a little weak, so by the time we got to the infirmary my knees were wobbly. The Sammie medical orderly on duty knew me by sight and waved us into the morgue holding area, and we hoisted Swanson's bag up onto a polished metal table. Wataski took off her forage cap—she called it a "cover"—and scratched her pale straw-like hair that looked as if it had been barbered by a goat missing half its teeth. She looked at me from under heavy brow ridges. The deep cut she took to her cheek back on the trail looked like it was going to make a puckered scar that would go really well with her broken nose and lantern jaw. In a lot of ways, she did remind me of a Zack, and her expression was particularly sour and Zack-like right then.

"I need to open the bag and pull his ID tag."

"Want me to?" I asked.

She looked at me as if I was an idiot, put her cap back on, and unzipped the bag.

"SON OF A BITCH!" she yelled and jumped back, and I saw a flash of movement as something scrabbled out of the bag and dropped to the floor. It was one of the local crustaceans, about twice the size of my fist, and it scrabbled a meter or two across the floor before Wataski's heel came down on it hard, crushed its shell, and sent green and red guts and fluid squirting out.

"Goddamned thing scared me half to death," she said. "We must have scooped the sonuvabitch up in the dark when we bagged Swanson."

I looked at the open body bag, and half of Swanson's face had been eaten away.

It took about one second to sink in, and then the adrenaline rush made my hair stand up. I just stood there with my mouth half open.

So *that's* why the Varoki back at that ag research station had been so hostile to Humans: guilt often manifests itself as rage. A lot of other things started to come together, too many to sort out all at once, but the first thing that popped to the surface was Survival 101. I scooped up the dead crustacean, threw it back in the bag, and zipped it up.

"What the hell?" Wataski hadn't put the pieces together.

"Look... just let me think for a minute." I took a deep breath and rubbed my forehead, momentarily overwhelmed. "Okay... I'm gonna get word to Gasiri, but until I do, don't mention this to anybody."

"How come?"

"Because all the time the Sammies were chasing us, they weren't trying to kill *TheHon*. They were trying to kill us."

"You and the kids?" she asked.

"No, not the children. *Us.* Humans."

I found *TheHon* sitting by himself, watching Tweezaa play with three of the other children from the convoy, and I lowered myself down to sit by him. We watched the children play in silence for a while before I spoke.

"You people are really sick," I said.

He didn't react at first, didn't turn to look at me, but after a few seconds he sighed.

"I gathered from Dr. Marfoglia that you have learned about the . . . fraternal associations which form a part of . . . our social lives."

"*Social* lives? Kiss my ass."

He turned and looked at me, ears flared out, anger in his eyes.

"I'll get back to that in a minute," I said before he could reply, "but there's something more pressing. Your *other* little secret."

He frowned and looked at me, confused.

"What, do you have that many secrets that you don't know which one I'm talking about? Well, I already passed the word on to Gasiri in orbit, so the cat's out of the bag, and no way to get it back in. I did it so casual that the duty commspec didn't even realize what I was saying—just mentioned the body of one of the Marines being half eaten by a local crab—and I'm not sure the commspec even understood what it meant. Guess he's not high enough up the pecking order to be in on the secret."

"What are you talking about?" he asked, frowning in irritation, but his ears began to flutter nervously. Since he was a politician—some would say a guy who lied for a living—that reaction let me know this was as big and ugly as I'd been afraid of.

"What am I talking about? Let me ask you a question, *TheHon*. How come there's no permanent Human enclave here? Most worlds with this many air-breathers living on them have Humans, even if it's just some dirty little ghetto. What's the deal here?"

"Perhaps the locals are xenophobic—people on colonial backwaters . . ."

"Bullshit. Answer me this: How'd you react to those shots you had to take before you hit dirtside here? Pretty rough, was it? Funny, didn't bother me at all. None of the other Humans, either. The local bugs sting the shit out of us but don't seem to bother you. Why is that? Well, maybe the bugs are xenophobic, too.

"So here's the real question: *Why didn't the fucking crab die?*"

I waited, but he just looked away, ears sagging in surrender. What could he say?

"I'll tell you what I think. I think that if Humans lived here, or even visited here on a regular basis, they'd figure out the truth. The indigenous protein chains on K'Tok are Human-compatible. That's why the scavengers don't touch Varoki dead. That's why the shots don't bother us—we don't need them. And that's why the local government types, even in the middle of this giant shit-storm of a war, were so desperate to wax all us Humans before we ate something—or something ate us—and we put the pieces together."

I waited for him to deny it, but he didn't.

"You lousy, no-good bastards! Every so-called habitable world in the stinking galaxy we've found so far has protein that kills us. You've got Akaampta and a couple other places that are Varoki-friendly. That's not *enough*? Other people find worlds with protein chains compatible with a different race, you broker the exchange. But when you find a world that could actually be a garden for *us*, what do you do? Keep it a secret and start force eco-forming it so someday it'll kill us, too."

He looked at me for a moment, then tilted his head to one side.

"I had nothing to do with this decision," he said at last with a sigh. "It was made long ago and far above me. It was a foolish decision, but that is not something you can say to certain people. Industrial concerns believed that the environment could be—altered, made more hospitable . . . to us. A terrible decision, in many ways."

"Yeah, up to and including the fact that it doesn't seem to be working. What made your eco-science guys think they could pull this off in the first place?"

He looked away and said nothing. And then I got it.

"Son of a bitch. You've done this before . . . with a similar protein group."

"Nearly identical," he said softly. "But *I* did not tell you that."

"Where?"

He turned and looked at me but again said nothing. *"Peezgtaan?"*

"It was before we contacted you, before we knew the strain was remotely compatible with that of any intelligent race. The eco-form template was developed in the Peezgtaan project. By the time we had contacted you, discovered the similarities, the original project was complete."

"Yeah. But K'Tok was just ramping up."

"Considerable funds had already been invested."

"Money talks and bullshit walks."

His ears twitched in reluctant agreement.

"But that means . . . aw, hell. That's why AZ Tissopharm moved a shitload of humans to the Crack, isn't it? To work the black farms. That was the plan all along. The mold spores are original form; if they were genetically altered, they'd be no good to you. So the mold proteins won't kill us; we just die a little later of chronic pulmonary disease, or malnutrition, or just despair."

He returned my look and answered carefully, ears motionless.

"As to that, I cannot say with certainty, but it is a reasonable conclusion."

I looked at him for a while and then shook my head in disgust.

"Reasonable from people who, instead of belonging to the Elks or Moose or KC, join the Mystic Order of the Eternal Blood Jellyfish, or whatever the hell."

"Do not confuse the one with the other," he snapped. "Your own world had the Skull and Bones, Illuminati, other secret societies to which men of wealth and power belonged. Is it not so?"

"Yeah, but where I came from, those were the *bad guys*."

His eyes flickered away, his shoulders and ears sagged.

"Yes," he admitted softly.

"So, which little sicko club do you belong to?"

"I cannot say . . . will not say, at any rate. None of the things I have done concerning her"—and he pointed to Tweezaa—"or her brother, Barraki, have been at the command of any will but my own. These children are . . . not important to my brothers, only to me."

"Why should I believe you?" I asked, and he immediately turned and looked me in the eyes.

"You should not. You are responsible for their safety. Believe no one. Trust no one," he said firmly, and he meant it. It sounded like pretty good advice.

"What do you know about this *End of Empty Dreams* outfit?" I asked.

"Nothing," he answered, turning away and shaking his head. When I didn't say anything, he turned back and looked at me, saw I didn't believe him.

"Do not be stupid, Sasha," he said. "I know only that it is a Shadow Brotherhood. It is neither allied with nor an enemy of mine. Beyond that, I have only even heard its name once—perhaps twice—before. I know nothing else about it . . . because it is *secret*. You understand? *Secret*."

"Well, he says they're mostly centered inside AZ Crescent, and there's some sort of messianic prophecy about end-times and the e-Traak blood line, and there's a computer projection or something . . ."

"You should not be telling me this," he said, turning away. "It violates the privacy, the sanctity, of his brotherhood."

"Yeah, like I give a damn," I answered.

He turned and looked me in the eye, and there was fear way back there behind everything else.

"If anyone learns you know this," he said slowly, softly, and carefully, "or that you have told a member of another brotherhood, we will all die, Sasha. You and Dr. Marfoglia and the children will die quickly; that young fool and I will die slowly, but we will all die. Knowing that K'Tok is Human-friendly is a terrible thing, but if the truth is out, there is nothing to be done but face the consequences; knowing the name of his brotherhood is next to nothing; but knowing this other thing is death. Please, *never* speak of this again if you value the lives of the children."

Most of the time, all you can do is guess at what's

going on in somebody's head, but once in a while, the clock face falls away and you can see every gear and spring and flywheel, all going round and round, clear as high noon in the Crack, when the sun breaks the canyon rim way up there and the light floods everything, bouncing and sparkling off the turbulence of the river below the first spillway.

Right then, for just that moment, I could look inside of *TheHon* and read him.

He needed to know whether I would tell anyone else, because if I did, it would almost certainly lead to the death of Barraki and Tweezaa, and so if he thought that I would tell, he would try to kill me himself. He didn't think he would succeed, but he would try, because their survival meant more to him than his own life.

That was interesting.

"Dr. Marfoglia and I will never tell anyone else what we know," I said. "I'll make sure she understands."

He studied me for a few seconds, and then he nodded, satisfied.

"You people are really sick," I said.

He sighed and nodded, and looked away.

"Yes."

We watched Tweezaa and the others play for a while in silence before I spoke again.

"What's your interest in those two children?" I asked.

"You asked that once before, and I told you—"

"Yeah, you told me shit," I said, cutting him off. "The children of an old flame? I believe it; I just don't believe it's enough to die for."

"My interest in them is exactly the same as yours, Sasha."

"Not likely," I answered. "I'm getting paid."

"Of course you are!" He laughed that creepy honk of a Varoki laugh, just like Arrie would have. "Both of us are," he continued. "Both of us are *desperate* for our payment, my friend, are we not? And when they are finally safe, we will receive it in the only coinage for which we both truly hunger—redemption."

I could have said something like *Speak for yourself, Bud*, but I didn't. Instead we just sat together in silence for a while, watching the children play.

How and why did *TheHon* know about all those old secret societies back on Earth? The Black Hand holovids.

That was the how. The why was more interesting. Leaving aside for a moment why anyone would make those pictures, why would a man of the education, sophistication, and stature of Special Envoy Arigapaa e-Lotonaa rot his brain watching them? Maybe more to the point, why were those holovids so popular as exports? Why did Varoki—apparently all of whom belonged to one secret society or another—love watching holovids where the good guys were trying to bring down the evil secret society?

You people are really sick, I'd said.

And he had agreed.

Maybe deep down inside, most of them agreed. Well, so what? Tell a junkie the junk's bad for him, like as not he'll agree. Doesn't mean he can walk away from it.

Funny, those pictures always had the stock "good cultist" character—maybe a woman who falls in love with the hero, or a man who can no longer face the evil of his actions—who helps the characters escape, and who always dies in the end. That's one way to find redemption, I guess. Was that the character the Varoki audiences related to—the one who turned against his or her own and found salvation in the grave? Or did they relate to the hero, who got to do all the righteous killing in the bloody ballet of slaughter which always consumed the last ten or twenty minutes of the story?

Or maybe they related to the villain, who usually died as well but at least got most of the good lines. I guess it depended a lot on the viewer. Different strokes and all that.

But here's a good question for you—had those Black Hand filmmakers just *stumbled* onto the winning formula? Had the forces of the marketplace showered riches on the first filmmaker who simply got lucky, and then everyone else followed the money and the herd? Or did the filmmakers know something? Were they trying to tell their audience something? Maybe prepare them for something—their Human audience as well as their Varoki ... perhaps prepare each of them for something different?

See? This is exactly how you start thinking after a couple days of being around a headcase like Katchaan. Everything is a conspiracy. But you know what Freud said: sometimes a cigar is just a cigar, and so by extension I guess you'd have to say sometimes a bad holovid is just a bad holovid.

But when Katchaan disappeared the next day, I had to wonder.

TWENTY-EIGHT

Marfoglia and I were supposed to meet Katchaan for breakfast, but he didn't show up. Well, sometimes people are late, and sometimes things come up unexpectedly when you're trying to keep a revolt ticking along smoothly. We were done eating and ready to leave when one of the Varoki insurgents came over to our table, introduced himself as a maintenance specialist—no name given—and asked to sit down. Katchaan, he explained, had been called away to oversee an equipment transfer and pickup near the uBakai colonial frontier. He didn't volunteer who the equipment was coming from, and we didn't ask. I gathered it was fairly high-tech stuff, which is why the technical advisor had to be present.

Okay, swell. Thanks for the heads-up.

But he lingered for a while, wanting to pose a question but hesitant to do so. Finally, he overcame his reluctance.

"I hope that you will not find me forward in asking this . . . but I am very curious about something Mr. Katchaan spoke of . . . an organization known as *Tahk Pashaada-ak?*"

I'd already given Marfoglia the warning concerning loose talk, and so she looked at me as if she'd never heard of it before. But this didn't feel right to me. Time for *maskirovka*—admit the little thing to cover the big thing. I looked back at her, and then I "remembered" something.

"Wait . . . yeah. Didn't he say something like that when we were in the commander's office two days ago?" I looked straight at Marfoglia when I said it, and she met my eyes for a moment, got it, and nodded. She wasn't stupid.

"Yes. *Tahk Pashaada-ak* . . . it means the End of Bad Dreams, doesn't it?" she improvised, turning to the maintenance man.

"Empty Dreams," he corrected her. "Or so I have been told," he added hastily after a moment. "Did he tell you anything about the organization?"

We looked at each other, shrugged, looked back at him and shook our heads. *Ya nya znayu, pal. Ya toureest. Know where we can get a bacon cheeseburger around here?*

After another ten minutes of us playing dumb, he eventually wandered away, satisfied that we were no threat to anyone. The secret was safe; no further action required.

After he left, we just sat there for a while, not saying anything, and I could feel prickly sweat collect on my forehead and upper lip. Marfoglia got the shakes pretty bad, and got this desperate, haunted look in her eyes for a moment until her defenses came back up like a drawbridge.

The following day the security chief called Sergeant Gomez into his office and told him that, sadly, Mr. Katchaan had been killed in a government ambush. From that point on, Joe Security Chief would be his liaison.

Right.

There wasn't much to liaise, really. We had a section of the underground compound all to ourselves, and we pulled our own security—or the Marines and MPs did. I was retired again. Rations were as good as could be expected, the wounded were doing okay, and we had free communications with Gasiri and the transport overhead, provided it was by tight beam and so didn't give away the position of the compound. Just to make sure, their comspecs controlled the uplink, and I'm sure they recorded all our conversations, but I could live with that.

That didn't leave us a whole lot to do but worry about how the war was going, wonder how long we'd be welcome here, and try to figure out just what the hell was really going on. That was Marfoglia and my department.

After another day of fruitless speculation, it finally occurred to me that maybe we were letting this Shadow Brotherhood thing mess with our brains too much. After all, if every brotherhood was that secret, then its influence on events had, by necessity, to be very subtle. You couldn't act overtly without exposing the organization. So most of what happened had to happen for what we'd call rational reasons—if there's ever anything rational about politics and war.

Okay, so pretend the whole *End of Empty Dreams* thing didn't exist—which everyone else in the compound seemed pathologically intent on doing. Why was Katchaan even here in the first place? That was no secret; the commander had told us right at the start—he was their technical advisor. I figured out pretty quick what that meant—factory sales and service. He came along to make sure all the weapons worked, the comm gear was on line, spare parts and ammo were in the pipeline—in short, all the things that I'd figured an uBakai government liaison guy would handle, but he wasn't from the uBakai government.

He was from AZ Crescent.

"Okay, *consigliere*, explain how this makes any sense at all," I asked Marfoglia the second day after Katchaan's disappearance. Mostly I really wanted to know, but partly it was to give Marfoglia's brain something to chew on instead of itself. She'd been jumpy, looked frayed around the edges, except when she had something to concentrate on.

We sat at a table in their mess hall, but we'd run late for the midday meal and so had it almost to ourselves. Of course, even though they had a complete mess facility, most of their food was inedible to us, so we were still eating self-heated Marine ration packs—but at least we had plates and silverware.

She sat looking at a poster on the wall, elbow on table and chin in hand, for all the world like August Rodin's *Thinker*, but better looking. A lot better looking, despite the lines in her face that hadn't been there—when had I first met her? Was it really only about a month ago?

As I looked at her, I remembered somebody telling

me once that sex with someone you don't like can sometimes be as good or better than sex with someone you do like. Interesting notion. I didn't have any first-hand experience to go on. It's not that every time I'd ever had sex it had been a deeply meaningful emotional and spiritual experience. I'd had my share of one-night stands—someone I met casually, ended up in bed with, and said good-bye to the next morning. But regardless of how little I'd known about them, what I had known, I'd liked. It just never occurred to me to sleep with someone I *didn't* like. Until right then.

Interesting notion.

I watched her think while I picked at my zucchini *etouffee*. It was okay, but I'd had a lot better.

After a couple minutes she stirred and frowned. Well, her frown deepened. She frowned all the time these days.

"What?" I asked.

"How long has AZ Simki-Trak Trans-Stellar had the Needle concession on Peezgtaan?"

I thought for a minute. Before this trip I hadn't been up the Needle since getting back from Nishtaaka, but I remembered some news stories.

"Since Independence, I think. About four or five years. Why?"

She nodded thoughtfully.

"That's interesting, because AZ Kagataan has the concession here. Remember the big welcome banner at Needledown?"

I remembered, along with all the AZK logos on the ground staff's uniforms. I looked at her and shrugged. *So what?*

She still had a thoughtful, faraway look as she took

a bite of the zucchini, and then looked down at it and made a face.

"Yeah," I said, "it needs a little something... I think saffron."

She poked at it with her fork, as if to see if it was really dead, and then nodded her agreement, but her mind was still a dozen light-years away. Then, as if a puzzle piece fell into place, her head came up suddenly and the lights came on behind her eyes.

"Premier e-Tuvaanku keeps an excellent table," she said, nodding to herself, "spices as well as fresh ingredients imported from all over, some all the way from Earth. It would be considered an extravagance, but the taxpayers don't foot the bill—it's all compliments of AZ Kagataan."

"That's nice," I said. "Who's Premier e-Tuvaanku?"

"The premier of the Republic of uZ'mataan, and also its *ex officio wattak*—from back on *Hazz'Akatu*."

"Okay," I agreed amiably, "he eats better than this, thanks to being in bed with an interstellar shipping line. You're saying that's what got AZ Kagataan the concession here?"

"No," she answered, "I doubt that it's that simple, but I'm thinking that the Republic of uZ'mataan and AZ Kagataan are... intertwined. I've heard the uZmataanki elections are particularly expensive, very media-heavy."

"Yeah, well, whose aren't? But sure, I get it. The government's bought and paid for by AZK, just like the *wataak* from back home..." but then I stopped, because it wasn't *just* like it, was it? My guy's election was financed by AZ Simki-Traak. It was my turn to frown in thought.

"Now, wait a minute," I started. "How does that work? Peezgtaan is an uZmataanki colony."

"*Was* an uZmataanki colony," Marfoglia corrected me. "Now it's independent."

And that's when the little lightbulb above my own head finally came on.

"Yeah. And you remember what Ping called AZ Simki-Traak Trans-Stellar?" I asked.

She nodded. *uBakaa Incorporated.* But he had it backwards, didn't he?

"And this whole stupid war between uZ'mataan and uBakaa...," I started, but let the words trail off.

She shook her head.

"I don't think it's between uZ'mataan and uBakaa," she said.

No, it wasn't, was it? Not really.

Two days later, the First K'Tok Campaign ended when a three-ship squadron of uBakai warships jumped in-system and began their glide toward the planet. If that seems like something of an anticlimax to you, get used to it. Life sometimes plays out that way; the real trick is living long enough to benefit from it, and we had.

The arrival of the uBakai squadron by itself wasn't the end of the war, not by a long shot, but it was effectively the end of the campaign. Those uBakai warships were packing canister after canister of deadfall spikes. Once they got in orbit, the Sammies were cooked, and they knew it. They could have gone guerrilla, except they were already fighting guerrillas and had done so with enough callous stupidity to thoroughly alienate the population out in the countryside, so it was pretty much throw in the towel and ask for terms, or find a hill, shoot the horses, and save the last bullet for yourself. The local Valley District commander, I learned later, was the main holdout for continuing the fight—probably because he figured that the way the colonial government could get the very best terms would be to turn his sorry ass over to the *Cottohazz*'s Provost Corps for court martial and summary punishment.

Turns out, he was right.

I saw the transcript of the closed tribunal later. He was the guy who cut the power on the train and then sent troops to kill everyone. He'd sent contractors because the colonial regulars might have gotten all touchy and legalistic about wholesale murder. Even the contractors had been less than enthusiastic until the Mike Marines had waxed a bunch of them; then it got personal. The order had been to kill all *Cottohazz* personnel, but that was just a cover. We Humans had been the real target all along. He was one of the handful—aside from the agtechs out in the field actually running the show—who knew the ecoform secret, and he decided he couldn't risk letting us live for a few months over in uBakaii territory. Too much exposure.

Justice was swift; all of us who survived the trek north from the maglev witnessed the execution, three days after the ceasefire was signed and about an hour before we processed back up the Needle.

All we had time for was a quick good-bye to *TheHon*. With an armistice in place and martial law reestablished in Sammie-land, he'd become the *de facto* governor, so he had a full plate. He made time to witness the execution, though, and he made time to see us off, especially the two kids. By now he was their *boti*, but not *Boti-Ar*, for *Arigapaa*—he was *Boti-Hon*, for *TheHon*. I'm not sure how crazy he was about that, but you don't get to pick your *boti* name—the kids do.

After he finished with the kids, and hugged Marfoglia awkwardly, he faced me. I held out my hand and he shook it, but with a rueful grin. I had calmed down a lot from my first peak of rage—none of this nightmare was his doing. He was just trying to find his way through the dark woods, same as me.

"A very strange road we have traveled together, Sasha," he said. "Stranger than ever I would have imagined."

"Amen, brother," I agreed. "But we went the distance. How's the payoff feel?"

He looked at Tweezaa, and nodded, the smile softening on his face.

"Better than I deserve. And for you?"

I shook my head.

"I haven't gotten them home yet. I'll let you know after I do—if we ever see each other again."

He turned and looked down at me, and put his hand on my shoulder.

"I hope that we do, my friend. I sincerely do."

He meant it. I guess I did, too. There were a lot of things messed up about *TheHon* and the world he was part of, but I wasn't in much of a position to judge, when you got right down to it. I liked him, and once you got past all the lies, he was a pretty honest guy. Does that sound like double-talk? Maybe. Here's the thing, though—he was honest with himself about himself, and without that, nobody can be really honest about anything.

I got a chance to say a quick good-bye to Borro as well.

"Take care of yourself, Sasha. Perhaps we will see each other again."

"Maybe so. Maybe some day I'll get you to tell me who your real boss is."

"That would be an interesting conversation," he said, and smiled.

Yeah, I bet it would be.

But I was happy that justice was swift and the leave-taking brief, because I was ready to get the hell out of Dodge. Nothing I'd heard had convinced me that an uZmataanki squadron couldn't show up in-system just as suddenly as the uBakai ships had and swing the balance back the other way. Was I right about that? Well, the fact that this miserable little fight, mostly out in the jungles along the colonial frontier, with fewer than a dozen combat cohorts in action per side, is called the *First* K'Tok Campaign might give you a clue. The fact that Humans now knew that there was something worth fighting for on this world—something really remarkable—might give you another.

But somebody else could fight those wars. We were gonna be down the road and see you later.

So we said our good-byes and boarded the Needle for transit to orbit, the four of us and about half the healthy Marines—the other half would come in the next capsule, and the wounded had already gone up. The capsule climbed above the city, and then every-thing disappeared as we hit the clouds, and when we emerged from the clouds, saw the planet spread below us like a relief map, and knew that we were no longer a part of it, something finally gave way in

Marfoglia. She sort of got smaller, seemed to collapse in on herself, bent forward, covered her face with her hands, and began sobbing, her shoulders heaving with the release of all that carefully contained fear and grief and horror. Both the kids put their arms around her and laid their faces on her back. I felt like reaching out and touching her myself, but wasn't sure if it would help or make her feel worse, so I just sat there and let her cry.

I heard someone sniff behind me, turned, and saw tears on Sergeant Wataski's face.

"What are you lookin' at?" she growled.

I just smiled.

TWENTY-NINE

I sat in Commodore Gasiri's cramped day cabin and hurt.

My head throbbed and still felt fuzzy, despite the anti-tox I'd taken when I got up, and I was pretty sure blue mezcal was going to be on my list of things to avoid for a long, long time. The pain in my left upper chest was sharper, better defined, under the 10 cm square bandage that covered the two puncture wounds made when a fist hammered in the brass posts of the globe-and-anchor insignia. Eighteen-year-old kids probably thought that part of the ceremony was swell; I thought it was pretty stupid. Like somebody once said about being ridden out of town on a rail: if it weren't for the honor of the thing, he'd rather have walked.

Gasiri came in eventually, moved quickly to her desk, and would have sat except she saw I hadn't stood up. She frowned.

"You're still an activated reservist in the A.C.G. It is considered proper courtesy and discipline to stand in the presence of a superior officer until told to stand easy."

"I'm a disgrace to the uniform," I answered, nodding, "or would be if I were actually wearing one. If I were you, I wouldn't take this kind of crap. I'd fire my ass—and right now."

"All in good time," she answered, and then she sat down and gave me a reproachful look. "Hurt yourself last night?"

"Little bit."

"Serves you right," she growled, her expression darkening. "They sent us here to put down an insurgency, and instead of suppressing it, all of a sudden the *Cottohazz's* in bed with it, thanks to you. Some small-time hood playing at spy and diplomat—what the *hell* were you thinking?"

"Hey, kiss my ass. And that goes for everybody else who was supposed to keep us alive and safe down there. They can all line up and kiss my ass. I did *exactly* what you needed me to do, and because it was me instead of someone in uniform, you and *TheHon* and the *Cottohazz* all got to keep your hands clean. You got to bark orders for the record, knowing I'd disobey them. But look me in the eye and tell me you'd have given the exact same orders if you thought I'd have gone along with them."

She sat back in her chair, the scowl still in place, but after a moment she shook her head.

"Okay, then," I said. "Neither one of us had a lot of great options. We did what we had to."

She studied me for a few seconds, and then looked

at a photograph on the wall—an old-style black-and-white print of an officer in a uniform I figured was over a century old—and after a while she nodded.

"Yes, I know," she said with a sigh. "I think Slim was right, Mr. Naradnyo. Do you know what Field Marshal Slim said at the start of his Burma Campaign?" And she gestured to the print.

"Never even heard of him, and *never* trust a guy named 'Slim.'"

She smiled at that.

"This is how he said he wanted to run that campaign: no details, no paper, no regrets."

"Guy after my own heart," I said, and she nodded in agreement.

Fair enough...done is done, and no regrets.

"And this ugly business with the protein chains down there...," she said, but let the words trail off and just shook her head.

"You get the word out?"

She nodded.

"It's embedded deep in a burst data dump that's gone out with every outbound craft that's left system since we got the word. By now it's in a couple thousand different data cells, what with retransmissions in other systems."

"It's only been a few days," I said, but she shrugged dismissively.

"We have some rapid departure courier drones which aren't exactly public knowledge. We burned one to get the news of the war back to Akaampta, which is why the fleet showed up so soon. Your news about the protein chains earned another, aimed in a different direction."

"Well, consider warming another one up. I found out more, and it gets worse. This stuff is technically rumor, but it will be easy to confirm in a lab."

So I told her the news about the Peezgtaan eco-form, leaving out the part about who told me. Her expression didn't change through any of it, but when I was done she touched a soft panel on her desk and when it chimed said, "Burn previous five hundred seconds for secure comm, BUNAVINT, sprint departure. List source as X-ray two one, previous reliability one zero zero. Hold launch for my voice authorization."

She looked back at me.

"In case you've got any more good news," she explained.

I shook my head. "You think the *Cottohazz* will try to stop it, once they figure out what's going on?"

"No. The Varoki are ahead of us in most scientific fields, but cryptography is as much art as science, and they aren't very good artists. They've never broken any of our naval codes. Down on K'Tok they know we know, and they've communicated to the squadron in orbit, but it's too late. The drone is long gone, already in another system. The word is spreading by electron transfer, and they'll never catch up with the information wave front now. I think it surprised the new squadron commander as much as anyone...and left a bad taste."

"Not everybody with big ears is an asshole."

She grunted a humorless laugh. "Enough are. Now everyone's pissed at everyone else. Allah only knows what will happen when this news gets to Earth."

"Not our job," I said, and she nodded in agreement, but without any real enthusiasm.

"If the big brass back home decides to sit on the news—you think someone's gonna come looking to shut us up?" I asked.

She looked up at me, and a wry look came over her face.

"If anyone thinks they can shut you up, Mr. Naradnyo, I'd pay cash money to watch them try."

I think that might have been a compliment.

"So, did the jarheads treat you rough last night?" she asked after a moment, smiling wickedly, but a little friendlier, too.

I touched the shirt over my upper left chest, feeling the bandage there, and winced.

"Yeah. Well...you know what it's like."

She shook her head.

"No, I'm afraid I don't. It's a rare tribute, being made an honorary lance corporal in the Corps, one I've never experienced."

"Well, they'll..."

I started to say they'd get around to it, but I shut up, because it occurred to me they probably wouldn't. Not after what happened out by the gas giant. The Navy might give her a medal, and the Marines on board undoubtedly respected her, but all of a sudden I knew they wouldn't make her an honorary Marine. I shook my head.

"It's not...," I started, but I just trailed off.

"Fair?" she finished for me with an ironic smile, and it sounded as stupid spoken out loud as it had in my head.

"Dammit, Commodore, they've gotta know how much you care about them." I remembered the way she'd said *my Marines,* like a lioness about to tear apart someone who'd murdered her cubs. But she just shrugged.

"Caring isn't enough, Mr. Naradnyo. Not nearly enough. You've also got to bring them back. You did, and whether it was due to skill and cunning, or just blind dumb luck, I will always be deeply grateful."

Then she stood up and offered her hand, and I rose and shook it.

"Mr. Naradnyo, I also offer you the sincere, if unofficial, thanks of the Department of the Navy of the United States of North America. I doubt that anything more public will be forthcoming."

"The handshake means more to me, Commodore."

"Well... that's very kind of you to say, Mr. Naradnyo, and I appreciate the sentiment." She was momentarily embarrassed, but recovered quickly. "I doubt that it will end up mattering as much as someone nailing that Marine brass to your bare chest last night. Who did the honors?"

"Sergeant Wataski."

She shook her head and laughed.

"You poor bastard! Oh... and *now* you're fired."

It was terrific seeing Ping again, and he got pretty choked up when the kids ran to him and engulfed him in those long, bony lizard arms. He'd gone practically crazy with worry, just sitting on the *Fitz*, unable to do anything to help, following our cross-country odyssey of fire and misdirection by recorded comm traffic, as well as a daily update from Gasiri's Smart Boss—that's what the Navy guys called their intelligence officer.

Ping made us tell him an overview, and then promise we'd tell him the detailed story later. But for now, 'it was just great to see him again. We really hadn't known each other for very long, but we'd gone through so much together, shared so much, been prepared to die together, that there was a bond between us now that—even if we didn't see each other for another ten years—would never disappear.

We'd have time to catch up, in any case. Gasiri was sending a transport back to Akaampta, carrying the Varoki wounded, as well as the ship crew survivors from the Hoka cruiser and the five uZmataanki Marine prisoners that had stayed in custody—and alive—through all that hell down below.

And we were riding along as well.

It was an uBakai troop transport—*ABk-401*—so we were something by way of celebrities. If they had wind of the coming shit-storm over the K'Tok eco-form project, none of them seemed to understand what it might mean. As far as they were concerned, we were all still pals. There was a lot of space on the *ABk-401*, since its troops were deployed down on K'Tok, and so the five of us had a troop module all to ourselves. All of the lockers with the troops' personal possessions were moved into six of the module's ten dormers and secured, but we had the use of the common space and the four remaining dormers. Ping, Marfoglia, and I each had our own, and Barraki and Tweezaa were in the fourth. Our first night outbound from K'Tok's orbit, Marfoglia softly closed the door to their room.

"They're both down. Exciting week, but exhaustion finally got the better of them."

"Great kids," I said, and meant it.

"They love you," she answered. "You treat them

like people, not like little animals or cute decorations. That's rare."

"Well, you know. It's not like I don't have . . . Varoki friends." It was pretty interesting how *leather-head* didn't come comfortably to my lips anymore.

"Like Mr. Arrakatlak," she said, smiling, "who would be sad if he had to kill you."

I grinned back and shook my head. "Arrie would be sad if anyone killed me; he'd be brokenhearted if he had to do it."

We both started to laugh, but Marfoglia put her hand over her mouth to muffle the sound and waved me away from the door. We stepped away and then stood there for a moment, friends—maybe for the first time.

Ping was reading in the common room, but he looked up and smiled.

"Tell me something. How long have you two been protecting those kids now?"

Marfoglia and I looked at each other and thought.

"Something like fifty-one or -two standard days, by the calendar," I answered. "But that includes slide time when we went through J-space. I think forty-seven days without the slide."

She nodded.

"Well, a couple days longer, for you," I added. "You were on your own—until I broke into your apartment."

"You saved our lives that night, and I never thanked you."

I shrugged it off.

"Forget it, Doctor. That was a . . . pretty horrible night. Sorry you had to see it. You know, all you guys."

"I know. But at least call me Marr."

"Okay. Marr."

"The reason I ask," Ping said, "is that it occurs to me that in those forty-seven, or fifty-two, or however many days, neither of you has had a day off. You've been watching those kids all day, every day. Why don't you take the night off? They're both asleep. Leave their safety and security to me and the crew of *ABk-401*."

"Take the night off?" I asked. "And do what? We're on a military transport in deep space, coasting to a jump point."

"I don't know. Go see what kind of dinner they can put together for you in the galley. Take a walk around and see what a transport looks like from the inside. The main thing is, take a night off from *worrying*. Nobody on this ship is here to hurt those two children."

Well, he was right about that. I looked at Marfoglia— Marr. She shrugged and gave me a funny, lopsided smile. I'd never seen that smile from her before, and I had the feeling I was seeing her real smile—not the practiced, cultivated one.

"Want to go exploring?" she asked.

"Sure. Why not?"

The troop modules were attached to the outer rim of the big wheel, so you had to climb up a spiral staircase to get to the main hull. We climbed up into the interior of the transport and wandered around for an hour or two. I enjoyed looking at things without having to assess them as potential threats or hiding places.

Not that I didn't do that—I just did it out of habit, not necessity, and that was a luxury by itself.

So we wandered awhile, figuring out what the various equipment spaces were for, sometimes asking the crew questions—at least Marr did. My aGavoosh wasn't up to it yet. aGavoosh is a guttural language—lots of hard sounds in the back of the throat along with those clicks—but it sounded nice coming out of Marr's mouth. I liked listening to the questions and answers, and watching the expressions dance across her face as she spoke, her eyes lighting up, her lips...

Oh, now, wait a minute. Wait just one goddamned minute. This wasn't gonna happen. No way. Fantasizing about casual sex was one thing, but this was an entirely different animal. There were reasons—really good reasons—why it absolutely *could not happen*.

The crewman we were talking to pointed to an observation port one deck up, and Marr put her hand on my shoulder.

"Oh, let's see what kind of view there is," she said.

I didn't say anything, because my shoulder was tingling, and a shiver of pleasure had gone through my entire body when she touched me. Even the goddamned hair on the back of my neck stood up from the adrenaline surge—and that wasn't the only thing standing up. I followed her, but was careful not to brush against her. I didn't know what would happen if I did, didn't know what to do or what to say or what was coming next. I am not awkward around women—I'm actually as comfortable with them as with men—so this was uncharted territory for me. All of a sudden I felt like a sixteen-year-old kid again, and I didn't much like the feeling.

Well...that's bullshit. I loved the feeling. It felt terrible, but it felt great, too, and all of a sudden I had to fight to keep a goofy grin off my face—that or a look of sheer panic.

From the observation port we could see back along the spine of the ship to the fuel tanks and drive module, and behind us was K'Tok—all pale blue seas and gossamer white clouds.

"It's beautiful," she said.

Yup. Sure was.

"You're pretty quiet all of a sudden," she said and looked at me. I smiled.

"I think I'm getting hungry," I answered. "What do you say—should we find the galley and try our luck?"

ABk-401 was an uBakai transport, so the crew was all Varoki—Marr, Ping, and I were the only Humans onboard. But it was a fleet transport, and that meant it could put meals on tables for any and all of the six races anytime it had to.

That didn't mean they were necessarily *great* meals, and there probably wasn't going to be a lot of variety for the next few days, but what they served that night tasted pretty damned good.

"How's the chicken *katsu*?" Marr asked.

"Terrific! I think it's better than back on the shuttle."

"Really?" she asked, surprised. "I thought that was the best chicken I'd had in a long time."

"The flavor was good, but I thought the texture was odd—sort of stringy."

She looked down at her plate, suddenly interested in her food, and I could see she was trying to hide a smile. But it was a gentle smile—not unkind at all.

"What?" I asked.

She raised her face and looked at me fondly. "Sasha, back on the shuttle—that was real chicken."

"Really?"

"Yes, really."

"Huh! You mean they killed a *real* chicken?"

She laughed softly in simple delight, the sound of a tinkling wind chime.

"Well, somebody did, somewhere, yes. And it was flash frozen until they cooked it for you that night. That was a deluxe flight, and that meant real food, not flavored protein imitations—except for that Paleo Special."

"So...if I'd ordered the veal..."

"Yes," she said, and then looked at me oddly. "I don't believe it! It bothers you." Her face broke into the broadest grin I'd ever seen on her.

"No, of course not...It's just a chicken."

"Yes, a chicken. But it *bothers* you. It does! I can tell. The big tough bodyguard is squeamish about a little dead chicken!" She covered her mouth with her napkin to smother the laughter, and I could feel my ears turning hot.

The idea that it bothered me was absurd, of course, but there wasn't any point in arguing with her about it. I'll admit I was glad the transport just used flavored soy protein, but not because I felt sorry for the chicken—that would be stupid. The thought of all the blood and feathers and internal stuff just didn't seem...sanitary, that's all.

"Oh, Sasha! I think you may be the most complicated man I have ever known," she said, laughing, and her voice gave me a strange thrill...a thrill which I knew right away was dangerous and very, very bad.

"Nah. I bet there are a dozen guys waiting in line to have their hearts broken when you get home to Earth."

She looked down, her smile still there but sort of melancholy, and she picked at her salad with her fork.

"The truth is, Sasha, I'm not very good at...connecting with people. I don't form bonds, or at least not strong bonds."

"Why not?" An hour ago I'd never have asked that, because it wasn't any of my business, but somehow it had become my business, and that was interesting, wasn't it?

"Some sort of attachment disorder from childhood, I suppose. That's what my therapists said, anyway. My parents were gone a lot. Then they were dead—killed in a plane crash. My aunt and uncle gave me financial security, and a home, sort of—a room of my own for the summer, and boarding schools the rest of the time. Wonderful boarding schools...not the sort of life anyone has any right complaining about."

"But not a lot of love," I said.

She smiled wistfully and shook her head. "I was... very promiscuous when I was younger. I suppose I was looking for something, someone, anyone really... but it didn't help."

"Your 'bad boy' phase," I said, and she nodded. She blushed, too.

"I miss out on all the fun."

She laughed. "You'd have liked me even less back then, I think. What was your childhood like?"

"You sure you want to know?"

"Why not? Was it very bad?"

I nodded. "Yeah, looking back on it, it was pretty awful. But the truth is, when you're a kid, you don't know what's normal and what isn't. One thing we've got in common: we're both orphans."

So I told her the story of my younger days, how

my father, mother, and older sister had gone out one day—one of the bad days, during the food riots—and only my mother had come back, her clothes torn, face bleeding. She'd never said anything to me, hadn't even seemed to see me standing there. She'd just gotten undressed and gone to bed and never got up again. She wouldn't eat, wouldn't even drink water, no matter how much I begged her. She'd pissed and shit right in the bed, and laid in it, and eventually died there, I guess from dehydration.

"The bitch," Marr said, and the anger in her voice surprised me.

"She was ... I don't know ... sad ... ," I started.

"How old were you?"

"Seven, near as I can remember."

"She left a seven-year-old boy to fend for himself because she couldn't face the world."

"She'd lost everything."

"No, she hadn't. She still had you, but you weren't enough to keep her alive, were you? How did that make you feel?"

"I never thought about it."

"I don't believe you. Did you have relatives?"

"No. And there were stories going around about the orphanages—how they chopped little boys and girls up for food. You know the kind of stories kids tell, but I was a little kid myself, and I believed it, so I hid. I stole food for a while, until the local merchants started getting wise to my hiding places. Then I hooked up with what's called a bezzie pack. Bezzie is short for *bezprizornye*; it's what the old-timers from Ukraine used to call wild orphans. There were a lot of us there for a while. A few of us survived."

She didn't say anything for a while, but her eyes looked so sad I thought she might start crying. But she didn't, and while I was watching her, I understood why she had agreed to take care of Barraki and Tweezaa, risk everything—even her life—to help two orphans she'd never met before. They weren't even the same species as her—not that that had slowed her up.

Or me, either, come to think of it.

She shook her head after a minute.

"Here you had a childhood that was a...a nightmare, and you don't have a problem bonding...connecting with people. There's something really wrong with me."

I laughed, and she looked up sharply. I shook my head.

"Marr, I'm not laughing at you, honest to God. It's just the idea that *I'm* the normal one...I mean, that's pretty rich. Let me tell you something. That day before I met you, the woman I lived with tried to have me murdered."

"Did you...?" she started, but couldn't finish the question. I shook my head.

"No, I didn't hurt her...I'd lived with her for six years—six really good years; I couldn't hurt her. I sent her away with some money.

"Here's the thing, though; I don't miss her. I never missed her, not for one second. I don't hate her. I don't have any bitterness, or anger. I don't feel anything. Six years, Marr. Six years of the most intimate relationship of my life, capped with an attempted murder, and I don't feel a goddamned thing, one way or another. So you think *you've* got attachment issues?"

This was not exactly turning out to be the romantic dinner I had half hoped and half feared it might.

Instead it was devolving into true confessions of the emotionally halt and lame. I put down my fork and leaned back in my chair, no longer hungry. Marr sat looking off to one side, lost in thought. After a moment she turned and looked at me, and her expression was odd—serious, curious, but not sad like before.

"Sasha, this lady friend of yours . . . in the six years you were with her, were you ever scared you'd lose her?"

"What do you mean?"

"You know . . . really frightened. Down here," she said, and touched her stomach with her hand.

"No," I answered, after thinking about it for a moment, "never."

"Has there ever been anyone you were frightened of losing? Someone that . . . the thought that they might not go on being a part of your life . . . really terrified you, drove you almost to panic?"

I looked away.

I looked away because suddenly I couldn't speak. Since my family had died, I had never been scared of losing anyone, ever in my life. Ever.

Until right then.

Then I felt her hand on mine, and when I turned, there were tears glistening in her eyes.

"Me, too," was all she said, her voice husky with emotion.

I looked at her and then shook my head.

"Son of a bitch! You're the cigar that'll ruin me for everything, aren't you?"

She looked puzzled, so I told her the story of that perfect imported cigar, and how I'd never smoked another local cigar or cigarette again. She got sort of a dreamy look when I described how perfect everything was about it. When I finished, she sat there for a long time, just looking at me. It gave me an odd feeling, because I was looking right back at her, and I had no idea what was going on behind those green eyes.

"Sasha," she finally said, "do you ever miss those other cigars?"

I thought about that for a while, really thought about it, because the truth was, I had never considered it before. Finally, I had to shake my head.

"No," I said, a little surprised at the answer. "Not really."

She smiled that soft, lopsided smile, and gave an elegant shrug.

"Well, then," she said.

THIRTY

There is something surreal about falling through silent star-speckled space, falling in love, and all the time knowing the world is falling apart around you. Some worlds deserve to fall apart; maybe this was one of them. But deserve it or not, it was crumbling, that much was sure.

It's not as if there hadn't ever been shots fired in anger before in the *Cottohazz*, but this was different. All the stuff before was low-level fighting between different countries over borders, water, minerals—the usual stuff. That's how a lot of Human mercenary units made their living, fighting these little brushfire wars on the peripheries. But this was a full-scale war between two of the most powerful Varoki nations, and they weren't just fighting it out on the colonies with surrogates—they were using their own armed forces and taking it into space—even shooting at the forces of other *Cottohazz* members if they got in the way.

We got both sides of the story over the course of the next couple days. The uZmataanki Marines had the parole of the living spaces, and they were more willing to talk to us—and to the uHoko—than to the uBakai military personnel. Once the uZmataanki talked to us, the uBakai wanted to as well. Everybody wanted to tell us their side. All of their stories were bullshit—not that they knew it. They just repeated what they'd been told, what they believed, but it was all bullshit.

I don't know that I'd have figured it out on my own, or that Marr would have, or Ping, but the three of us together—that was different. We'd seen this world from three different perspectives—seen its gears turning, its wheels going round and round—and seen the different machinery from up close: law, crime, finance, trade—home worlds, colonies, deep space—rich, poor, and everything in between.

And it stunk.

Pretty much everyone knew that all the sputtering little brushfire wars were struggles between the major powers but by proxy. This colonial administration, that guerrilla group, the trade union over there—all were masks of one sort or another for one of the principal Varoki nations. But somewhere along the line, even the Varoki national governments had become masks—masks for money.

Peezgtaan had been an uZmataanki colony. After all the trouble on Nishtaaka, Peezgtaan had gotten its independence, and its own legislators. And who had elected them? Simki-Traak money. That was the real political shift—not from colony status to independence, but from AZ Kagataan—the money behind the legislative majority in the uZmataanki national territory—to AZ Simki-Traak, a lot of whose board members were "closely associated" with the uBakai senior executive. Different puppets, same show.

And down in the basement of the puppet theater, which Shadow Brotherhoods were plotting to gain control of AZ Simki-Traak? And for what?

Maybe it didn't really matter. The big money was fighting again, and they'd stepped the violence up another notch. I didn't figure the *Cottohazz* was strong enough to hang together through all of this, and whoever ended up controlling the floor of the *Wat* might find it deserted except for discarded masks. Why?

Because there really wasn't anything else to it.

It was *all* masks, *all* proxies, all smoke and mirrors and greed, and it was probably all coming down. Everybody was used to having it around, but nobody loved it—not the way you need to love something to lay your life down for it. Nobody was willing to die for somebody else's greed.

Unless you fool them, of course, and make them think they're dying for uBakaa, or uZmataan, or some other flag. Of course, when they figure out they're fighting for AZ Kagataan's bottom line instead, they'll be really pissed. A lot of them never will figure it out—not because they're stupid, but because they'll lose someone they love, and they love them so much they'll never be able to accept the possibility that they lost them for nothing.

But a lot of them *will* figure it out, because greed is arrogant and cocksure. Greed can't keep a secret—can't help bragging about who it screwed and how. There's no such thing as "enough" for greed, so it will never step away from the table. It will just keep rolling those dice, double or nothing, until it busts.

Greed is stupid.

We always forget that. We put greed in charge of the farm, because greed says it will run it more efficiently, and then greed cuts open all the geese to get the eggs quicker.

Pile all the creepy secret-society crap on top of the naked greed and the bad-to-the bone government corruption, and the one thing I knew for sure was that we—Humankind—had to get the hell out from underneath these guys' thumbs.

I wasn't the only one who'd figured that out—Sarro e-Traak had as well, and he'd sure done his bit to make it a better world—for the Varoki, too, to my way of thinking, but obviously not everyone saw it that way. He'd at least purged the poison from his own blood, and given the two kids in the next room a shot at freedom from this madness as well. Maybe it would work for them. I'd come to love those two kids—Weasel Boy and the Dark Princess—and I hoped they could stay clear of this nightmare, but I'd done about all for them I could at this point. Pretty soon their family would be back in the picture, and God help them then.

I wondered about *Tahk Pashaada-ak*, then. Had old Sarro e-Traak swung it so there was a Secret Brotherhood just watching out for his kids? What had Mr. Nobody called them? The Twin Diamonds? Maybe. But the brotherhood wanted to spill the beans on the whole K'Tok eco-form as well. What was the angle there? Were they part of Sarro's bigger plan?

The truth was, I'd probably never know. That's the

thing with secret societies: you can't just call them up and ask what's on their mind. And with Sarro gone, who knew who would take over—assuming he'd been kind of in charge anyway—and what they'd decide their *real* mission was now? No telling. After all, the Knights Templar had started off as a bunch of guys running a church or something.

We didn't see much of Ping after we broke J-space in the Akaampta system. Once the naval brass on Akaampta got the decoded versions of the burst transmission from *ABk-401*, Ping and a couple senior officers from the transport had spent most of their waking hours answering questions over tight beam to Naval HQ. With Lieutenant Palaan dead back on K'Tok, Ping was the surviving go-to guy on the space battles. Late one night when he got back to the module, I'd asked him how the brass was taking it.

"The tops of their little heads are coming off," he'd answered.

Yeah, I imagine so. Everything was sliding down the mountainside, and these were the guys who were supposed to stop it. I was glad I didn't have their jobs, because they were going to fail, and they could see the train wreck coming, and they didn't know how to stop it, or how to get out of the way. No matter what they did, it wasn't going to be right, it wasn't going to be enough, and they'd go to their graves thinking that a smarter guy, or a more determined guy, or a more ruthless guy might have prevented what came next—whatever the hell that turned out to be. Here's the epitaph they'd write for themselves: *A better man would have held back the night.*

"Don't lose any sleep over them," Ping advised that same evening after a couple stiff rums. "You have to remember...these *Cottohazz* admirals and flag captains are Navy guys who never fought a war, never even really saw a war. You know what sort of top leadership you get in the military when you go a generation without a war? Bureaucrats. Empty suits. Most of them are more concerned with covering their own asses than preventing a disaster—because they have no concept of disaster. They've never seen disaster, never been in disaster. Disaster is just a report that needs to be explained so they don't get down-checked on their next performance review."

"Some of them, probably," I agreed. "But there will be some who get it. They'll try the hardest, and fall the hardest, probably."

"Stubborn bastards," Ping said, and raised his glass of rum to them. He took a drink and then settled back in thought.

"All my life," he said, "I've seen some people try while others just go through the motions. What makes them different, do you suppose?"

I shrugged. No clue.

"I don't think they're smarter—the ones that try," he said. "I don't know that they're better people, deep down inside. I don't think they're less frightened when things get tough."

I looked over at Marr, who was curled up on the couch and reading Adam Smith—again—and I smiled. What she'd done...I had no idea where she'd found the courage, and courage is exactly what it took, because she'd been absolutely terrified every step of the way. Terrified—but not petrified. She'd always taken that next step, no matter what. Where does that come from?

I looked back at Ping, and he was looking at Marr, too. He looked at me, smiled, and nodded.

"Everyone has intentions—good and bad, noble and base," he said. "Everyone wants to fight the good fight, but also wants to run away and hide and be safe. Everyone wants to stand out and wants to blend in. Everyone wants to lead, and wants to follow. Makes you wonder sometimes who we really are."

"We are what we choose," I said.

"*Argh*, I think you're on to somethin' there, matey."

Five days after we broke J-space, we started our deceleration burn for orbit around the inner gas giant. We'd grab the shuttle in-bound from there—or at least Marr, the kids, and I would. Ping and a couple others were leaving by priority military shuttle. So that meant a good-bye.

Tweezaa cried; Barraki almost did. They both kissed *Boti-Joe*, and Tweezaa gave him a long hug. He said his good-byes in aGavoosh to them, and then English to us.

"Take good care of that lady of yours," he said as he shook my hand.

"Take care of yourself, Cap'n."

"*Argh*," he said, nodding.

And then he was gone, and it felt quiet, and odd. We'd become like a family, and now someone was missing.

Like a family. But we weren't a family.

That evening, after the kids were in bed, I led Marr into my room. She was smiling—we'd been taking turns sleeping in each other's rooms, whichever one we felt like when the urge struck us—which was usually right after the kids were down. But tonight I sat her down on my bed and pulled my black carryall out from the closet.

"There's something you need to see," I said, and I opened the carryall. I still had our travel documents there, and my traveling cash, but there was something else. I took it out and handed it to her. She read it, then looked up, confused.

"A return voucher? From Akaampta to Peezgtaan? I . . . I don't understand."

"Once you and the kids are safe, I'm going back, Marr. Unfinished business."

"It's because of Dr. Zhan, isn't it?"

"In a way, but . . . not that way. Look at the date on the voucher."

She looked down again.

"You were *always* going back?"

"Yes."

"To her?"

I shook my head. She thought for a moment, then understood, her eyes growing wider in surprise.

"Why . . . that was the plan all along, wasn't it? Pretend to run, get the three of us away . . . and then go back."

"Yes."

She frowned in renewed confusion.

"But *why?*"

"Like I said—unfinished business. Not mine, Kolya's. He won't let this rest until it's settled between the two of us. Killing June was just a start. He'll destroy the clinic, the soup kitchen, the agency, everyone who worked for me, everyone who ever helped me, everyone I ever helped. He'll do it slowly, as he gets around to it, when the mood strikes him, but he will do it. He'll figure if he keeps at it long enough, eventually he'll strike a nerve, make me want to come back and take my revenge."

"But you don't kill people for revenge," she said.

"No."

"You kill people to keep them from doing things."

"Yes."

She sat there, staring at the wall, her expression bleak and hopeless in a way I'd never seen on her before. Then she shook her head.

"But . . . you thought you'd have surprise, Sasha, that you'd go back before he started killing anyone, before he expected you. Mr. Washington would make peace, you'd be gone . . . then you'd come back. That was it, wasn't it?"

I nodded.

"But you *haven't* got surprise, Sasha, not now! He killed Dr. Zhan, and he'll be expecting you—maybe not for the right reasons, but that doesn't matter. He'll be *waiting* for you."

"I know."

"Doesn't that change anything?"

"No, Marr. Unfinished business—that has to be finished, one way or another. And it has to be me. Nobody else."

"Why?" she asked, voice trembling.

"I told you I ran with a bezzie pack when I was a kid. Kolya was part of it, too. I'm a few months older than him, and when we were kids, I was bigger, looked out for him, kept him alive a couple times.

"There were other gangs, older kids—bad news. One day a half dozen of them caught Kolya and me foraging out of our normal run. We weren't that afraid of them when we were close by our nests, since we knew all the small holes and narrow passages we could get though and they couldn't, or would slow them down more than us. But out in unfamiliar streets... all we had was speed, and Kolya's leg was banged up from a fall a couple days earlier."

I stopped for a moment and closed my eyes, and I remembered the smell of old mold and garbage and cook fires, remembered the metallic taste of my own blood from the glancing blow one of them had landed on my cheek before we broke away and started our long, desperate run. I heard the echoes of their howling pursuit.

Marr touched my arm, and I opened my eyes and looked at her, but the ghost images of the street remained all around us.

"We made it a block before Kolya went down. His leg gave out. I stopped to help him up, but he yanked his arm away, just sat with his back against a trash can, and smiled up at me. 'Run, you stupid fucker,' he said. 'I'll hold them off.'

"So I ran, because that's how we survived. And they got Kolya. I think he must have figured he'd slow us and we'd both get caught, so he went down on purpose, to make me go on alone. Payback for the times I'd saved him."

"They beat him up?" Marr asked quietly. I laughed softly, probably not a very nice sound.

"Some. Then they kept him for a couple weeks, passing him around as their group bitch."

"A little boy?" she asked quietly, horror in her voice.

"Boy, girl, didn't much matter. Whatever was handy. Ever watch young baboons?

"Well . . . Kolya got a sharp piece of metal from somewhere. One day he used it on one of them when no one else was around. Cut his throat. I guess that was the second thing on him he cut. He got away, and we joined up again."

"At least he survived," she said.

"No he didn't," I said softly, and I felt like crying—crying for my old pal, trapped inside a nightmare all those years, until the only way he could go on living was to become the nightmare.

"So . . . it's between him and me," I said. "I owe him that. I'm sorry, Marr. Believe me, I am so sorry. I thought maybe we . . ."

Well, there was no point in finishing that thought. But she looked at me, and after a moment she just reached over and took my hand and held it to her cheek, and I felt the dampness of her tears.

Take good care of your lady, Ping had said. Yeah. And the first thing I did was break her heart.

The next day the four of us got on the inbound shuttle and started the final stage of our journey together. What I didn't know—couldn't have known—was that only two of us would get off that shuttle alive. Some things you're better off not knowing.

THIRTY-ONE

Four days inbound, Tweezaa and I were walking from our quarters around the big wheel to the club deck when I felt myself become a little heavier for a moment, then a little lighter, like being in an elevator when it starts up. Tweezaa felt it, too, and she giggled.

I didn't.

If birds stop singing...

Either I was nuts, or we'd just done a docking maneuver, way the hell out in the middle of nowhere. I tried to activate my comm link to find out where Marr and Barraki were, but all I got was a high-pitched screech. Somebody was jamming the comms. If they were jamming, they might be tracking, too, so I ordered my link to power down cold.

"Tweezaa," I said and knelt down so we'd be face-to-face. She looked at me and stopped smiling. I held up two fingers. *"Gikaa-doe,"* I told her—*hiding place two.* Her eyes were suddenly enormous with fright, but she nodded. She turned to go but then stopped, turned back, and put her arms around my neck and hugged me. I held her close for a second, then said, "*Nktu!*" Hurry!

Then she was gone, running back up the wheel toward the quarters area.

Good girl. There was a place near housekeeping where she could wriggle into a life-support feed trunk, get way the hell back, where they'd never see her. A bio-sniffer could find her, but this would at least buy us some time.

The captain of the transport had made a point of giving me back the Hawker 10 when we left—he'd said he'd had particular orders from Commodore Gasiri to make sure I got it. I'd started carrying it again, and I was glad, but now I wished I'd given a little more thought to ammunition. I had ten in the grip and two more magazines in my pocket—that had seemed like a lot more this morning, when any threat was potential and abstract, not right here in my face. I could go back to quarters for more ammo, or I could look for Marr and Barraki. Not that tough a choice. I drew the Hawker as I started running toward the club deck.

I made a mental map of the shuttle as I ran, and tried to get a step ahead of whoever was coming after us. Anyone who docked had to dock with the shuttle's spine, since it wasn't spinning. Then they'd go E.V.A. and enter the maintenance trunk of the big wheel. Once inside, they'd head down (away from the spine) into the wheel and out in different directions, trying to cover as much ground as possible before anyone knew what was going on.

The shuttle's command crew had to know this was

going on; the collision-avoidance sensors would have been going off like crazy. So either the command crew was dead, or they'd gone along with the docking maneuver. But if the command crew were dead, the docking maneuver would be unnecessary: without control, everyone on the shuttle was already dead but just didn't know it yet. So the command crew was alive, and had gone along with the docking maneuver without alerting the passengers.

That meant that the docking was either official or it was pretending to be official. Maybe right now the command crew was on tight beam to Akaampta Orbital trying to check their bona fides, but the time lag would be—what?—an hour or more. That was plenty of time for the bad guys—if they *were* bad guys—to get in and get out.

And if they weren't bad guys, why jam the comms? Better to just monitor the comms and take your time.

I got to the door of the club deck, and half a dozen diners looked up in a mixture of surprise and annoyance at the drawn Hawker. I did a quick scan, but there was no sign of either Marr or Barraki. The purser saw me and headed toward me, anger clouding his face.

"Put that away!" he ordered, pointing at the Hawker. "You know the rules in the dining compartment."

I lowered the pistol but didn't holster it.

"Has Dr. Marfoglia or Barraki been here?"

"Put that away, I said!"

"Tell me why we just docked with another ship, and I will."

That stopped him, and he looked uncomfortable.

"I . . . don't know. There must be a good reason."

"They didn't *tell* you? *The purser?* Tell me where Marfoglia and Barraki are, right now."

He looked around nervously and licked his lips, starting to put the pieces together. When it came to smarts, this guy was no Walter Wu.

"I . . . I think they were going down to Observation."

I headed for the elevator, but it opened just before I got to it, and the two guys inside, still suited up but without their pressure helmets, took one look at me and started shooting.

In the confined space of the club deck, the pistols had roared like thunder and had left my ears ringing. I dropped the empty magazine from the Hawker's pistol grip and loaded magazine number two. I have a vague memory of people screaming and china breaking behind me. Both of the dead guys in the elevator were packing identical Rampart Auto-10s with the serial numbers burned off. On the elevator ride down, I stuffed one of the Ramparts in my waistband, and half a dozen magazines into my pockets, and I felt a little less naked. I checked the rounds in one of their magazines—simple hollow points, not poisoned pills. That was *really* good news, since I was bleeding from a glancing shot to the left side of my rib cage and a shallow through-and-through to my right thigh. The ribs hurt worse right now, but the thigh was probably going to slow me down more. But the bullet missed the bone and the artery, so I was still in business.

I have no memory of actually shooting the two guys.

I looked at them, really looked at them for the first time, and got a funny chill down my back. I *knew* one of these guys—I didn't know his name, but he'd run Lotto cash for Kolya, back on Peezgtaan. What was a Piss-Can Lotto runner doing fifteen light-years away from home?

Okay. Think, Sasha, think! What does this mean? Everybody thinks that trained assassins grow on trees or something, and that any time anybody with a pocket full of money wants somebody gotten rid of, it's easy—just call the Assassin's Hotline or whatever and there will be all these unbelievably deadly killers just waiting for a job. But it doesn't work like that.

Not that there aren't incredibly deadly professional killers; the opposition had hired two of them, brought them in from off-world, but Bony Jones—praise his memory—had dropped them. That meant that whoever was behind this had to improvise. Kolya was all there was available, and once they hired him, he had to move fast. No time to bring in additional help from off-planet. When it turned into a chase, it was still better to chase with the people you knew—no way to keep a lid on things if you start broadcasting what's going on and what you need done. Hence, this Lotto runner—and who knows what his buddy did for a living—filling in as killers, all with their matching untraceable Ramparts, probably from the same production lot.

Not that I was some unstoppable killer myself, understand. I was just a guy ran a lotto and loan operation to fund a soup kitchen and a clinic. But at least now I knew I wasn't up against a dozen Co-Gozhak silencers, with some government agency behind them and death in their black lizard hearts. So I had maybe a little chance.

The elevator stopped on the observation level—the

outer deck of the big wheel—and opened. I came out
with the Hawker leveled and braced with both hands,
checked right and then left, and didn't see any movement at all. No sign of a struggle, either. I listened, and
didn't hear anything, but I wasn't really sure how good
my hearing was after all the shooting on the club deck.

I started aft—because I had a hunch I'd get a look
at the ship that had docked from the aft windows—
and started checking the private rooms off the main
lounge. One turn, twenty yards, and I was at a window looking aft, and sure enough, there was a ship
docked on the spine, just going out of view as the
wheel turned, but I saw enough to recognize it as a
Blackbird. It's long and tapered for a purpose—very
low radar signature from the front, which is the aspect
it presents when overtaking or approaching. It also had
big liquid nitrogen-cooled damper hoods to kill most
of its thermal signature—again, from the front. From
the side or rear it would show just as hot, but this
was a ship to get you in secretly and then out fast.

The good news was there weren't any extra quarters
modules attached. It only had internal room and life
support for maybe eight or ten guys. Also, no spin
habitat. If they'd been out here waiting long, they
might be out of shape.

And if that sounds like I was grasping at straws,
what's your point?

There were two ways to work this.

I could try to run out the clock—delay and annoy
them until they had to get out of Dodge before getting
intercepted by the real Co-Gozhak—but the longer I
let them wander around, the more chance there was
they'd stumble across Marr and the kids.

Or I could hit them hard. They were spread out searching, they didn't know the shuttle's interior as well as I did—looking at floor plans is no substitute for walking the ship—and they weren't trained killers. At least some of them weren't. Kolya had a couple of pretty dangerous guys on the payroll, and he'd have them along for sure. And Kolya would be here, too. You could count on that.

But no choice, really. Hunt 'em and hit 'em.

My hearing must have been bad, because I came around a corner and there were two of them, not five meters from me. I almost pissed myself, but the Hawker was pointed in the right direction. I fired three times, and one of them fell down, two slugs having gone in the back of his head and exited the front. The other guy ducked through an open door into one of the side rooms, and I recognized him as Charlie Nguyen, one of Kolya's real killers. He'd had a Rampart in each hand, and I dropped down to one knee, the Hawker trained on the doorway.

Charlie had a signature move that always worked, because he was crazier than most people he came up against. He'd stick both guns out and start shooting as fast as he could, aiming about where he knew the target was but with the pistols spread side to side, spraying bullets, and then he'd come out, following the guns, and adjusting his aim onto the target. When the shooting started, sane people ducked, and that gave Charlie his chance to get out in the open alive. Once he saw you, and he was shooting while you weren't, he had you. That's why I knelt down. He stuck out his pistols and started shooting, but the rounds all went over my head. I waited, and when he came around the door, I shot him in the forehead and he fell down.

My ears were really messed up now. They actually hurt from the noise, and I tried saying something just to see if I could hear it. I could, but my voice sounded tinny and distant. I looked down at Charlie and the other dead guy, and I felt nothing. I'd felt sick when I'd killed Ricky, but that was different. Ricky was just trying to kill me, and he had his reasons. These bastards were trying to kill two little kids, and Marr, none of whom had ever done a single thing to hurt these guys, or anyone else for that matter. If there really were a hell someplace, then these two monsters were already there. Pretty soon they'd have some company.

Since the observation deck was on the outside of the wheel, it was the biggest deck, and we'd figured out a number of places where the kids could hide. But Marr was with Barraki, and lots of those places she couldn't fit, so I started with the big ones. I found them the second place I looked, in the equipment spaces for the hydraulic pistons that closed the solid shutters on the aft observation ports. They were down behind and underneath the pistons, and you couldn't see them unless you knew just where to look.

"Hey, are you okay?" I called down.

"Sasha! Oh, thank God it's you!" Marr cried out.

"Come on, let's get you out of there."

Easier said than done, it turned out. They were down below deck level and had to climb out over the pistons, and we hadn't figured on all the lubricants. After they slipped and fell back a couple times, I ended up hauling them up by sheer muscle power, which also was easier said than done, since both of them were pretty greasy by then.

"Oh my God, you're hurt!" Marr said as soon as she saw the blood on my shirt and pants.

"Little bit," I answered. No point in trying to bullshit her at this point. "Nothing serious, though. Have you seen any of them?"

She nodded her head.

"We saw the ship dock but didn't know what it meant. I tried to call you, but something's wrong."

"They're jamming the comm links."

She nodded.

"We heard the security alarm and the announcement that there had been shots fired on board. We didn't know what to do, so we hid."

"You did exactly right. You okay, sport?" I asked Barraki. He looked up and nodded. He'd been staring at the wound in my leg, and he was trembling.

"Sasha, are you going to die? Like Mr. Jones did after they shot him?"

"Look at me. No, I'm not. It's not that kind of bullet, Barraki. It's just a plain old slug, and it made a plain old hole. Here, I took the guy's gun. Look."

I pulled out the Rampart, dropped the magazine, and let him see the top bullet—not that he'd necessarily know a poison pill if he saw one, but he could see there was nothing special about these. I put the magazine back in and laid it on the carpet. I pulled the Hawker and its spare magazine out and held them out to Marr. I preferred the Hawker, but I had more rounds for the Rampart.

"Remember how to use this guy?"

She nodded. "I had a good teacher."

"Yeah? What did he teach you?"

She looked me in the eye and took the Hawker.

"He taught me to just shoot."

"Okay. I've dropped four of them so far. I'm not sure how many there are, but there can't have been more than a dozen, outside, to start with."

"There were nine," Marr said. I looked at her in surprise. "They had to go outside their ship, in pressure suits, to get in the shuttle," she explained. "We could see them. Barraki and I counted them."

I grinned.

"Good work! Good thinking. Okay, that helps. Four down and five to go. But they'll be more alert now that they've lost guys, so it'll get harder. Tweezaa's in hiding place number two. You remember which one that is?"

Marr and Barraki both nodded.

"First thing, Marr, power down your comm link. Not sleep mode, dead cold. Second, we go get Tweezaa. Then we figure out if we bunker up or keep moving, depending on what we see between here and there. If...if we get separated, get to Tweezaa. Clear?"

They both nodded.

We started down the circumference corridor, me in the lead, Barraki behind me, and Marr bringing up the rear. I told her to stay ten or twenty paces back so she wouldn't be in the line of fire if there were trouble. That wasn't me being protective. Tactics 101: don't get both of your guns pinned down by the same shooter. What difference would ten or twenty paces make? In a regular building maybe not a lot, but we were walking the inside circumference of a wheel. The deck rose ahead of and behind us, and you could see people's feet coming before anything else. With a little luck, trouble ahead wouldn't know Marr was there at all.

Oh, yeah. Tactics 102: keep your best gun back. I suppose taking the lead *was* me being protective—so sue me.

The observation deck is almost mazelike in the variety of paths you can take from here to there, although it is very simple in basic design. Think of the deck as a long, endless corridor. In the center is a spine of rooms—meeting rooms, and a lot of dead machinery spaces with no access from this level. The three elevator foyers were spaced around the wheel in this center strip as well. There were parallel corridors to either side of the central spine, and then observation lounges outboard of those. Some of the lounges were linked, and most of the meeting rooms had access to both corridors, so there were lots of ways to get from point A to point B, if you knew what you were doing.

That also meant there were lots of places for bad guys to hide. Speed and caution are always a trade off, and this was no exception. If I wanted to be cautious; I'd have checked each room as we came even with it. I'd checked them all coming this way, but someone could have come up behind me and slipped in, or come by way of the other corridor. I didn't bother, because it was a big ship, there weren't many of the bad guys left, and we'd never get to Tweezaa if we checked every door we came to. At a certain point, speed is a better defense than caution, and I figured that's where we were right then.

I wasn't entirely wrong—I was actually about half right, as it turned out. My decision to move fast was a calculated risk, and in any calculated risk, there's a chance things will come out wrong.

We were about thirty yards down the corridor when I heard a door open behind me, and I heard a familiar voice say, "Hey, Sasha. Long time." Then there was the explosion of a gunshot behind me, and a slug buried itself in the wall beside me. I went down and rolled to the side, the Rampart coming up, and I saw Bear Bernardini stagger forward and fall face-first to the deck. Marr was half a dozen meters behind him, the Hawker up in both hands. It was her slug that had hit the wall, after it had gone through Bear.

So the gamble on speed hadn't paid off, but trusting Marr with my back had.

Barraki crawled out of another open doorway, where he'd gone for cover.

"Are you safe?" he asked.

"Yeah, I'm fine, thanks to Marr."

She lowered the automatic and tried to smile, but she was shaking from reaction.

"He's moving!" she said, and started to bring the Hawker up again, but I waved it down.

"I've got him. Let's get into that room."

I got up and limped over to Bear. He was conscious and moving, but obviously hurting. I kicked his Rampart away from his hand, then scooped it up and tucked it in my waistband, grabbed his collar with my left hand, and dragged him into the conference room, although it took some doing. My right leg throbbed with pain, and the knee was starting to get wobbly and watery feeling—and Bear wasn't called Bear for nothing.

"Marr, watch the corridor at this door. Barraki, watch the other. Heads down low, at floor level, so you'll see feet coming and they won't see you."

I pulled Bear against a wall, propped him up, and had a look. The bullet had entered his lower back and come out the front.

"Who shot me?" he asked, confused and in pain. I nodded toward Marr, and Bear made a face.

"Son of a bitch! Well, I'm out of this hunt. I never had much stomach for it anyway."

"It's worse than that," I said. I ran my finger through the blood oozing out of his abdomen and held it up for him to see. The blood was nearly black. "You took one through the liver, Bear. You're not going to make it."

"Aw, Jesus!" he said, his face wrinkling up like we was going to cry. "Aw, Jesus."

"Bear, you're dying, and you owe me. You tried to kill me back in the Crack, and you tried again here."

"Kolya made me," he protested, but I shook my head.

"Kolya didn't make you—you chose your side. And now here you are, blood leaking out and poison filling up your body. And you owe me."

He licked his lips, and I could see panic starting to take hold, but he fought it down and nodded.

"Yeah. Yeah, Sasha, I guess I do owe you. What do you want?"

"How many total?" I asked. Marr and Barraki had counted, but he didn't know that, and I wanted to see if he would lie to me.

"Nine, counting me and Kolya."

So Kolya was along. I felt a chill, a shudder of dread. I'd been sure he would be here, but being sure and having it confirmed are two different things.

"Any other good shooters?"

"Charlie Nguyen. He's down here someplace. And Abe Cisco's supposed to be down soon. Abe's been a pal, Sasha. Can you maybe cut him a break?"

"What's the plan?" I asked.

"You know—in and out quick. We head out, sweep the outer two levels first, four guys per level in two-man teams—then move up as quick as we can, leap-frogging levels, so if you run up, we have guys above you. Kolya stays up top in case you run for the spine and try to get to the command module. If the sweep comes up dry, Kolya starts with a bio-sniffer. He got some of the kid's blood from the crime scene—don't know how—but the sniffer's tuned to their family-common DNA."

So everyone but Kolya was headed this way, sooner or later. I'd already taken out Charlie Nguyen and his teammate, and another team on the elevator—probably headed for the level above this one. Abe Cisco and his teammate would be working that now. That left Kolya and one more unaccounted for.

"Where's your teammate?" I asked. He shook his head.

"I don't know. Carlos Li—he's a fuckup. Son of a bitch should have been backing me up, but after we heard the shooting down this way, he disappeared. Said he was going through the other corridor, but I think he just bugged out."

Bugged out? It was a possibility, I guess, but I wasn't going to put a lot of eggs in that basket.

"Okay, now the big question. Where's the money coming from?"

Bear looked down at the black blood still oozing

from his abdomen. He was sweating, was probably already feeling sick—not just injured, but dying. He looked back up. Answer this question, and Kolya would kill him for sure. But now he was sure he was dying anyway—he could feel it.

"Was it someone in the e-Traak family?" I prompted him. He shook his had.

"Simki-Traak management. Not even top management. Some mid-level suits with their own silencers, and some secret-identity shit . . . the leather-heads got secret societies in their corporations, did you know that? With handshakes and stuff, I guess. Maybe decoder rings. Fucking whack jobs. It was guys looking to take over down the road, wanted to make sure there was still gonna be something left to take over."

I looked at him, and I could tell he was telling the truth, at least as he understood it.

"Was it something called *Tahk Pashaada-ak*?" I asked.

He frowned and shook his head.

"Nah, nothing like that. Something like Future Sunrise . . . I don't remember exactly. Honest. Anyway, Kolya went kinda nutsy about the whole thing, thinks killing these kids will start some sort of civil war, split us Humans off from the *Cottohazz*. Something like that. Anymore, he sounds crazy to me." He shook his head and then looked down at the spreading black stain on his shirt and trousers, and again I thought he was going to start crying, but he still didn't.

Profit and loss? Was that all there was to it? I doubted it. Why go after the kids, then? Was it one brotherhood sending a message to another? Was it a response to another creepy prophesy-*cum*-computer projection? Or was it something that made even less sense? Profit and loss was a motive we Humans understood, so that's what they'd have told Kolya, but who the hell knew?

"Okay, Bear, we're square." I held out my hand. For a moment he just looked at it, then he shook it, not sure if I meant it. I stood up and grabbed him by the collar and dragged him out the door, across the corridor, and into the observation lounge. I propped his back up against a chair, so he was looking out the big floor-to-ceiling window, and I put a cushion behind his head.

"Best I can do for you, Bear."

His chin quivered with emotion, and he didn't say anything, but he nodded in gratitude. I left him there, staring at the stars.

"Is that man really dying?" Marr asked when I came back into the conference room. Her skin was pale and clammy looking, and she was perspiring. I picked up a wastebasket from beside the conference table, and handed it to her.

"He is. Puke in that if you have to. I've done it plenty of times."

"No," she said. I looked at her, and she was okay. Really okay.

"Sasha!" Barraki whispered insistently. Marr and I looked, and he pointed down the corridor he was watching, and made the sign of a man walking with his fingers. I held up one finger, then two, then three, and held my hands out and shrugged as a question. He stuck his head back out, down by the floor, and watched for another two or three seconds. He pulled his head back and held up two fingers. Then he made a gun with his thumb and forefinger.

Two armed men. That would be Abe Cisco and his partner, coming to see why the two teams from down here hadn't passed through them to leapfrog up to the next level—and maybe wondering what happened to his other two guys, also.

This was everyone except Kolya, who was up in the spine with his bio-sniffer, and Carlos Li—wandering round loose somewhere out of everyone's traffic pattern. I had about two seconds to make a decision, and I did.

"Marr. I'm going to deal with these two guys. You go out this other door and head down the corridor, away from them. Run, but keep your eyes open for Carlos. If you see him, shoot him. Get to the elevator and get up to Tweezaa. We'll meet you there when I finish with these guys. But if I don't show up, bunker up someplace, and use the Hawker. You keep Tweezaa alive."

She nodded jerkily, her eyes wide with fright but with adrenaline, too.

"Should Barraki come with me?" she whispered. I looked at him and then shook my head.

"I'll take care of him," I said. She looked at him, looked at me, and she got it. I was spreading our risks. This way, one bad break wouldn't kill both of the kids. But it also meant that if . . . something bad happened to either of us, the other one wouldn't be there. She touched my cheek with her hand, kissed me, and then she was gone, through the door and down the corridor.

I took a breath, steadied myself, and carefully turned over one of the conference tables on its side. Then I found a shadowy spot beside a chair by the wall, as far away from either door as I could get.

"Barraki," I whispered, and he looked at me and nodded. "When they get close, stick your head out and look at them, so they see you, and then duck back in and run out that other door across the room. Hide in one of the observation lounges, but not the one with blood by the door. Can you do that?"

He nodded, and then I heard gunfire. It was from the other corridor, the one Marr had gone down, and it was from the direction she'd gone. There was a single shot, a pause, and then two more shots. For a second I thought I was going to pass out. I got light-headed, and saw white flashes of light in the dim room, but the voices of Abe Cisco and someone else I didn't recognize brought me back to reality.

"Hey, what the hell?" I heard.

"Hey! Who's shooting?" Abe shouted.

Concentrate on the here and now, Sasha. Barraki was still alive.

Barraki was staring at me, unsure what to do. I pointed toward the door and nodded. Barraki stood up, stuck his head out the doorway, looked down the corridor, cried out in alarm, and then streaked across the room and out the other door. The first guy came through the door at a run. I wanted to wait until they were both in the room, but when he saw the overturned table, he smelled a rat. He stopped in the middle of the room and raised his Rampart, and there was no sign of his partner, so I shot him in the head and he fell down. It wasn't Abe. Tactics 102.

Abe came around the corner and put three rounds right through the conference table. That was the natural move, and it was what I was counting on. I fired, but he was too damned fast for me—gone before my hammer fell, and the round went through the open doorway and into the wall beyond. Now he knew where I was.

I would have rolled to a different firing position, but my right leg was like a sack of wet sand—all weight and no strength. Instead I pushed the chair over against another chair. Abe came around the doorway again, but he came around low this time, and I'd been aiming high, so my shots went over his head. I dropped my aim and fired again, but he'd already ducked back. He hadn't taken a shot, because he'd seen right away that I wasn't where he'd expected me. A lot of guys would have tried to adjust their aim, set up a second shot—and I probably would have nailed them. Abe was smarter than that.

Well, no, he wasn't all that smart, when you got right down to it. He'd just been trained by old Harry Slaughter, one of the best gun men I'd ever seen. Great name for a shooter, huh? Abe had learned every trick old Harry had to teach, learned them by rote, by heart, made them a part of his physical reactions. I started to sweat then. *Think, Sasha.* This guy's better than you, but he's not smarter than you. In fact, he's as dull as last year's gossip.

Okay. Anything I could do in a gun fight, Abe could do better. Therefore, Abe would win the gun fight. Therefore . . .

I fired three rounds in rapid succession at the doorframe where I knew he was standing—an obvious desperation move. I waited about five seconds and then fired two more rounds at the doorframe, but after the second round the slide on the Rampart locked all the way back, because that was the tenth round in the magazine and it was dry.

"Son of a bitch! Barraki! Run for it!" I yelled, and threw the empty Rampart as hard as I could through the open doorway. It hit the corridor wall and bounced on the floor. Abe sauntered slowly around the doorsill with a huge grin on his face, and I shot him with Bear's Rampart. I shot him six times, which I don't normally do, but Abe had me spooked, and I needed to be sure he'd actually fall down. He did.

I could hear Barraki running away down the corridor, so I shouted to him that it was okay, and to come back. I got up and hobbled to the door and met him there.

"You are safe?" he asked.

"You bet. I may need your help walking, though. My leg's starting to give out on me." It was awkward, but he helped me, and we made our way down the corridor Marr had taken, trying to hurry but not really wanting to get there.

I got to the elevator foyer, knowing what I'd see, but I was wrong. It wasn't Marr on the floor, but Carlos Li, the missing eighth guy, and I felt my heart lift, as if someone had been sitting on my chest and then just turned into a bird and flew away. Carlos had been winged in the shoulder and then kneecapped, twice, near the elevator doors, judging from the blood trail he'd left pulling himself over to the wall. His face was twisted with pain, and then fear when he saw me.

"Jesus, Sasha, you gotta help me! I'm bleedin'!"

I punched for an elevator and then turned to Carlos. "Where'd she go?" I demanded.

"The lift," he answered, pointing to the elevators.

"Yeah. What floor?"

"I don't know! How the hell would I know?"

There was a bank of illuminated numbers by the elevators that showed the level they were at. If he'd paid attention, he'd have seen where her elevator stopped. I raised the Rampart and aimed at his forehead.

"What fucking floor?"

"Okay! Five—level five!" he answered.

The elevator car door opened, and I shot Carlos in the head.

"Let's go," I said to Barraki, and we got in. I hit the button for level three, dropped the magazine out of the Rampart, and put in a new one. Barraki was just looking at me—confused, afraid, and I guess disappointed.

"Why did I kill that man?" I asked.

He looked down and shrugged.

"Because he wanted to kill us," he answered listlessly.

"No. He was unarmed and immobilized, and couldn't kill us. Why did I kill him? Think."

Barraki looked up. "Because he lied about where Boti-Marr went?"

"No. He told the truth. She went to level five. Think, Barraki. Use your head."

Then his eyes got wide. "Because he knew what level Tweezaa was on! That's where Boti-Marr went, and he saw. He would tell Mr. Markov."

I nodded.

"And that's why we're only going to level three," he went on, excited to have figured it out. "Mr. Markov could be watching the elevator lights."

I nodded again, and smiled, and he smiled back. Smart little weasel boy. I'd make a crook out of him yet.

I remember thinking that, that I'd make a crook out of him yet. I remember it very distinctly. But I never did.

You can't hear the bird songs end when your ears are full of thunder.

I'd fallen down. I wasn't in the elevator anymore, but I don't remember where I was or how I got there. I was sitting, leaning back against a wall, and I could hardly move. When I breathed in, I made this whistling, sucking sound, and when I breathed out, bloody bubbles oozed out of my chest and ran down my shirt. The cheap little Rampart was still in my hand, but when I started to raise it, Kolya shot me again, in the upper right arm. I felt the bone break, and my fist dropped back to the deck like a limp rag.

There was so much blood! I looked to my left, and Barraki was lying next to me. A lot of the blood was his. Most of the back of his head was missing, and there was bloody bone and gray matter all over. I started crying then. It wasn't supposed to end like this, not with Barraki dead. Me maybe, but not him. I could feel my life ebbing away as Kolya walked over and stood looking down at me. He had a bio-sniffer on his belt and a smoking Rampart in his hand. His voice came to me faintly, from another world.

"You got lucky, Sasha, taking out Charlie and all the others. But you know what they say? Luck can't last your whole life unless you die young. Before you go, I want you to know that after I finish off the other leather-head, I'm going to find that blonde piece of ass and take her with me. I got a long coast back to the C-lighter, and I promise I won't push her out the airlock until I've really used her all up. You know what I mean?" And he gave me a big wink.

I couldn't lift my right hand, could hardly move it from side to side, but he was standing right in front of me. Even trying to pull the trigger made my upper arm feel like the bone was coming right out of the meat, but I pulled anyway. The first bullet shattered his ankle, and he came down, his face twisted with pain and shock and rage. He shot me twice while he was falling, somewhere. I felt myself move with the impact, but I didn't feel anything else. When he hit the deck, he was at the level of my Rampart, and I shot again, and again, as fast as I could pull the trigger. I saw bullets rip up through his neck and chest. I was slipping away now, but I saw a big arterial spurt rise up in the air from him, and it sort of dissolved into flowers—roses, I think. They were beautiful.

Dying wasn't really so bad. You know things when you're dead, things live people don't. I knew that Marr and Tweezaa were okay, and that they were going to make it to Akaampta just fine, and that made me feel really good. Then it got very bright. I always loved sunlight.

And I got to meet Bony Jones.

THIRTY-TWO

I woke up in heaven. I knew it was heaven, because there was this angel that looked just like Marr. I got to say, though, I was surprised that heaven looked so much like the inside of a hospital room.

"He's conscious," I heard someone say, and the angel looked up. Her hair was oily and matted, tied back in a half-assed ponytail, and her eyes were sunken and red.

She looked great. Even when her face got all scrunched up and she started crying, she looked great.

More people came in—all of them Human—and they started looking at readouts and poking me and stuff. I couldn't take my eyes off of the angel.

"This ain't heaven, is it?" I asked eventually, and I was surprised how weak and hoarse my voice sounded—more of a croak than anything. Marr started laughing through the tears, and shook her head.

I'd never let on to this, but I was a little disappointed

about that. Heaven had been nice, if that's where I'd been. Wherever I'd been, it had been *really* nice. But it was pretty great seeing Marr, too. No denying that.

Eventually the head doc got there and chased away some of the others and we talked. He asked me how I was—hell, I didn't know. He was the doctor, right? I'd thought I'd died.

Well...it turns out, I had.

The shuttle doctor pronounced me. No cardiovascular activity, no neural activity—dead. But Marr still had my Hawker and I love this—at *gunpoint* made them load my corpse into a cold-sleep capsule.

My kind of gal.

So they de-oxygenated and froze me for shipment back here to...where was this?

Earth.

No shit! I was actually on *Earth*.

But what about all that brain-dead stuff?

"It's true," the doctor answered, nodding. "When your heart and lungs failed, and the oxygen flow to your brain was cut off, you suffered considerable brain damage. You were, technically, brain dead."

Now all of a sudden this wasn't sounding like such a great deal. My mind felt slow and groggy, but I'd figured it was just the drugs.

"You mean I'm gonna be a dummy?" I asked. "I think I'd rather have gone out clean."

Marr squeezed my hand, and that felt good, but how long was a smart woman like her going to hang around some guy with half a brain? And did I even want that? I wanted a partner, not a nanny. But the doc was shaking his head.

"We're pushing neurocine as fast as your system

can handle it, and it's re-growing the damaged tissue. If it wasn't working, you'd never have regained consciousness."

"So I'm going to be good as new?" I asked.

"For the most part," he said.

"For the most part? What does that mean?"

"Neurocine is a very powerful nerve regenerative. You'll regain all of your cognitive skills; you may end up better in some areas than you were before. It's not uncommon for patients to discover an increased aptitude for mathematics, for example. But the neural damage also took out some of your memories. Your capacity for remembering new material will be unaffected, but growing new nerve tissue doesn't get back old memories. I'm afraid some of those are gone forever."

I thought about that for a while. I wondered what it was that I didn't remember. It's hard to figure out something like that, you know?

I didn't remember the end of the gunfight on the ship. I mean, I remembered the *very* end where I killed Kolya, but how had he shot me to start with? And Barraki. I didn't remember him getting shot, just him lying there dead.

Barraki!

"This neuro stuff—did you put Barraki back together with it, too?"

The doc and Marr exchanged a look, and then he shook his head.

"No, the trauma was too massive for a drug to repair. There wouldn't have been enough intact structure to work with. Besides, neurocine is a Human-specific drug. We haven't developed anything that effective for Varoki nerve tissue."

Poor little Barraki. Well, I'd never remember the shot that killed him, and that was fine with me. I started crying, though. Poor little weasel boy.

I could tell Marr was pretty worn out. It didn't look as if she'd slept much since the fight on the shuttle, but she must have, since it turns out that had been ten weeks ago. Long time to lie here with tubes and shit stuck in me. Well, four or five of those weeks I'd been frozen, but still.

Marr had gotten Tweezaa to her family—what there was of it—on Akaampta. She was safe now, and word was the provosts were getting ready to make some arrests, maybe already had—news travels slow between worlds, especially with a war going on.

Marr had gotten me to Earth. I guess Tweezaa's family helped with the long priority jump from Akaampta to Earth, high-burn express shuttles at both ends, and the hospital, too. *Serious* buckage, Bernie the Rat would say. I wasn't crazy about where all that money came from, but thinking it was kind of Tweezaa's made it seem less . . . dirty. Maybe that was just my damaged brain not working right. I don't know.

One thing was sure: there had been no need to kill Barraki or Tweezaa, except maybe to make a point. Sarro e-Traak's dream had died with him. No one guy owns a whole family's fortune. He'd been the principal heir, but he was still in a minority position. He'd spent that last year of his life persuading seven other family members to sign over their proxies to him—personally. That gave him the votes necessary to push through his reorganization—to make his revolution. Once he was dead, the proxies meant nothing, and it didn't look as if those particular stars would line up that way ever again.

Three of the seven proxy signers were already dead: one suicide, one professional silencing, and one murder by the signer's own son when he found out what his mother had done. There was a mental competency hearing pending against another, and all of them were being vilified in the press—the Varoki press, anyway. If they'd had any dreams of being remembered as benefactors, those dreams had been shattered. Instead, they were the monsters—either evil or mad—who had decided to sell out their race to the Humans. Nobody was going to go down that road again.

And there had been anti-Human riots on Peezgtaan because, after all, it was our fault. Now there were anti-Varoki riots here on Earth, since the ugly business about the K'Tok and Peezgtaan eco-forms had come out. People were waiting for things to calm back down again—I wasn't so sure they were going to.

While I was recovering, I got a formal letter of thanks from the United States Navy for helping to save the ground personnel on K'Tok. It was a handsome thing, signed by the Secretary of the Navy and the Chief of Naval Operations. My first instinct was to wonder whose head Gasiri had held a pistol against to get this pushed through, but then it occurred to me that keeping the *Cottohazz* happy just might not have been as high a priority these days as it had been before.

Too bad. Not about the letter, about the riots—about everything. Sarro e-Traak had figured out a way to get us from yesterday to tomorrow, and it was a pretty good way—for everyone. Call it a "soft landing." But they killed the goose to keep all the golden eggs, and as I lay there in my bed day after day, my brain slowly healing, the pieces coming back together, I knew they had made a terrible mistake.

Tomorrow was still coming, but now it wouldn't come like a lamb.

After a week, I was up out of the bed and doing physical therapy. Marr was looking healthier, too. My right arm was in really bad shape, with a synthetic bone replacing the original, and the muscles didn't feel like they were grabbing hold of it right, but the docs said I just had to keep working on it. It hurt like hell, but sometimes pain can be good—like atonement. The truth is, I wasn't doing all that well with Barraki's death. Then I got a couple of visitors.

My first visitor was that cutthroat Arrie. I hardly recognized him without the rose-tinted glasses, or tee-shirt, or Nehru jacket, or some other ridiculous outfit. In black and red, with the three jingling gold chest gorgets of a Co-Gozhak provost major, he looked like a completely different guy, which I guess he was.

He still had that same sly little shit-eating lizard grin, though.

"Sasha, my friend," he said without preamble, "you have no idea how much trouble you have caused. In fact, I am not certain even I know where this will all end, and *I* know a great deal."

"I'll bet," I said. "How'd you get here?"

"When a senior official of the Provost Corps expresses a desire to travel somewhere quickly, the major passenger lines are very cooperative. It is most gratifying."

"Yeah. So, you here to read me my rights?"

He just laughed that creepy, honking lizard laugh.

"*Rights*?" he repeated. "Oh, Sasha! What quaint ideas you have."

My brain was starting to work a little better these days, and a couple more pieces fell into place.

"It was always about Kolya, wasn't it? Until this thing with the kids came along, I mean. But that's how you found out that Kolya had mined my comms. You'd already mined *his*, hadn't you?"

He smiled and nodded.

"Correct."

But then I remembered some other pieces, and I started getting angry.

"What the hell were you thinking, Arrie? You *had* them! Barraki and Tweezaa were in your hands, safe and sound, and you put them out there as targets for . . . for *what*, Arrie? What was so goddamned important you'd put those kids in front of a dozen guns, and nobody to keep them alive but me?"

He wasn't smiling anymore, but he wasn't looking tough, like I figured a cop was supposed to, either.

"I am sorry, Sasha, but I had no choice. The bodyguard—Mr. Jones—came to me thinking I was a criminal. His employer had certain . . . tastes, which could not be satisfied through legal channels, and so I had developed a business relationship with him, through Mr. Jones."

"Laugh?" I asked, but he shook his head.

"Nineteenth Era French impressionists—the famous ones, the ones which are not normally for sale. So Mr. Jones came to me precisely because he thought I was *not* the authorities, and although he was wrong in that belief, his logic was quite sound. With the two killers carrying provost credentials, I could not trust anyone in my own agency. It would take time to find out if the agency really had been compromised, and if so, how high up the poison went. But I did not have time, so I sent them to the *only* person I could count on—you."

"Yeah? Well, if the only guy you could count on was some two-bit crook like me, then that's a pretty sad commentary on the people you work with, isn't it? So, *was* there a problem in your shop?"

His eyes got a distant look, and a little of his smile came back.

"If I told you that, then I would have to kill you. And you know how much that would distress me, Sasha."

"Yeah, blow it out your ass, Arrie. And the so-called brotherhood you said you reported to—was that a cover, or was it your own personal Double-Secret Order of the Purple Honking Ivory Back Scratchers?"

He frowned a bit then, maybe in surprise, and tilted his head to the side.

"Again, to tell you would necessitate dire and unfortunate acts."

"Uh-huh. So, are you going to cuff me and make me do the perp walk?"

He actually giggled with delight, ears fanned out wide to the sides.

"I *love* the way you talk, Sasha! I really do. I am tempted to do exactly that, just so that years from now I can tell people that I once made Sasha Naradnyo 'do the perp walk.' But instead, I would settle for you signing this paper."

He took a paper out of his tunic's side pocket, along with a narrow blue piece of official-looking plastic. He handed me the paper and a stylus.

"Is your arm up to signing?" he asked.

"Maybe. What's this I'm supposed to sign?"

"It is a receipt for this bank draft," he answered, and waved the blue plastic.

"A bribe, Arrie? To shut me up? Here's an idea. Why don't you just go fuck yourself instead?"

He laughed and shook his head.

"I love the way you talk! No, it is not a bribe. I cannot imagine shutting you up with *any* amount of money, Sasha, and certainly not *this* pathetic sum." He looked at the draft and shook his head in disgust. "It really is appalling how little we pay our undercover operatives, considering the risks they take."

"What's the deal, Arrie? I'm no spook; I'm a crook. A drug dealer at that."

"Oh, I'm sorry to disappoint you, Sasha, but you are not *really* a drug dealer, at least not so far as I know. None of the merchandise you sold me ever reached the streets."

"Well, at least that's good news. I never liked that stuff."

"I know, Sasha," he said, and he was serious for a moment. "Believe me, if you had, this conversation would be entirely different. Even as it is…well, you did a great service saving Tweezaa, and I do not forget that sort of thing."

"I didn't do it for you, Arrie, and I sure didn't do it for a paycheck, so let's just forget about it, okay?"

"No. If I do not pay you, then you were not really working for me when we conducted our…business.

Sooner or later, some bureaucrat will notice that, and then you will receive a very different sort of visit, from someone much less congenial than I. So please sign the paper, deposit the bank draft, and send it to your clinic if you like. Take some enjoyment in the irony of the Co-Gozhak Provost Corps financing your charity work."

Well, that made sense, so I signed.

"But just so we understand each other," I said as I handed the receipt back to him, "I didn't do it because they were rich, or important to you guys; I did it because they were just two kids in trouble."

"Just so we understand each other," Arrie answered, looking me in the eye, "that is exactly how I felt, also."

Okay. Fair enough.

"That trick with the travel covers—you do that, too?" I asked.

"Yes, of course. I learned your covers from my data mine on Mr. Markov's communications. Since Markov and his friends already knew the truth, I sent a burst transmission to *K'Pook* with an updated set of travel covers—yours. It gave your enemies no additional information, and I hoped it would ease your path."

It damned near got us killed, but that wasn't his fault. Now there was something I needed from him.

"Henry Washington . . . he's taken over my operation back in the Crack."

"Yes, I am aware."

"He didn't like dealing Laugh, either. And now that Kolya's gone . . ."

He nodded.

"I understand. I will see what I can do."

"Thanks, pal," I said. "For *that*, I'll owe you."

He smiled.

"You know, Arrie," I said, "I like you—a lot. But I got this feeling that the times they are a-changing, and that uniform of yours...well, just don't get too comfortable with us being on the same side. You know what I'm saying?"

He looked down at the insignia on the cuff of his tunic and nodded, the smile gone.

"I know," he said softly, but then he looked up and smiled again, ears erect. "I suspect the day really *will* come when it would have been wonderful to have been able to tell people that *I* once made Sasha Naradnyo 'do the perp walk.'"

"Someone else would like to see you," Marr said, smiling from the doorway. She stepped aside, and Tweezaa peeked in, looking around at all the monitors, ears turning and twitching like little radar antennae. Actually, there wasn't that much stuff around anymore. A week earlier and she'd probably have been pretty frightened by all the mad scientist crap they had me hooked up to.

She came in, walked over to where I was sitting in my chair, and held out her hand. I took it, and she looked at my hand for a moment. She said something in aGavoosh, and Marr translated.

"She says, 'I always remembered you are real.'"

"Oh, Tweezaa...I'm so sorry about Barraki."

I started crying again, but she crawled up on my lap and put her arms around my neck, just like she did the last time she saw me, back on the shuttle. We held each other for a long time, then she patted my head, as if to make me well, and she slid down.

She turned and looked at me, and said in what was probably carefully practiced English, "Sasha get well, so take care of me. Please."

"You bet, Sweetheart," I said, and nodded, not really able to say anything else.

Later I asked Marr what she'd meant, about me taking care of her.

"You're going to be the head of her personal security detachment—provided you accept the job."

"That's a lousy joke," I said, "considering what a bang-up job I did protecting her brother."

"You died for them," she said. Well, not much I could say to that.

"Whose idea was this?" I asked.

"Her court-appointed guardian thought it would be an excellent choice, because of your proven loyalty, the bond that's developed between you and Tweezaa, and your credentials."

"What credentials? Numbers and loan-sharking?"

"You have no actual criminal record, Sasha, since your one arrest was expunged after your military service. In fact, your official recommendations are quite impressive. There's the letter of thanks from the United States Navy, and don't forget what Major Arrakatlak said—you were an elite covert operative of the Co-Gozhak, not to mention a decorated combat veteran of the Nishtaaka campaign."

"*What* decoration?"

"I believe a Meritorious Service Citation."

"Yeah, a perfect-attendance award!"

"You don't really understand resumés, do you?" she asked.

All this was happening pretty fast, and I was worn down from the physical-therapy session, so all of a sudden I felt dizzy. I sat back down in the chair by my bed and leaned back, and I felt the sweat break out on my face and upper body. Marr sat down next to me.

"Are you okay?" she asked.

"I don't know. I don't know what I'm doing or where I'm going. But things are going to start happening, Marr—and when they do, I don't know that Tweezaa's security detachment is where I belong."

"I think it is," she said softly, her hand on my shoulder. "See, there's this guy I've fallen in love with, and you know why? Because he's going to change the world, but not over the bodies of children. You know, in a few years, Tweezaa's going to have to decide what she's going to do with her share of this fortune."

"You think I should try to brainwash her?"

"No, her brain's just fine. But she lost her father and her brother. She needs a male in her life—even if he *is* Human—that she can look to for an example. Someone who's not . . . just . . . *worthless*. Like the rest of the useless parasites in her family. Believe me, I've seen them. Just *be* there for her, Sasha. She'll figure out the rest."

I thought about that for a while, and it made some sense, except for one problem.

"What about you and me . . . where does that leave us?" I asked.

She smiled.

"The Varoki have some really odd customs and laws. I knew some of them, but the proceedings of the uBakai Guardian Court on Akaampta make for interesting reading. The three judges were really *unim-*pressed with the rest of the e-Traak family, especially the fact that everyone seemed more interested in being named Tweezaa's fiduciary guardian than really taking care of her."

"Yeah, well," I said, "rich assholes are rich assholes, wherever you find 'em, and they always seem to get all the justice they can afford. What's so unusual about that?"

"Nothing. But the uBakai seem to take the idea of an independent judiciary a lot more seriously than we do—at least in their guardian court system. I think they were really impressed with what Tweezaa had to say as well. That's not something many Human courts would have given as much weight to. And afterwards, they did something I can't imagine that any Earth court would have done, especially with a family that influential."

"What?" I asked. What was the big deal? She looked at me for a moment and smiled that soft, lopsided smile of hers.

"Sasha, *I'm* her court-appointed guardian. *I'm* offering you the job. So, what do you say, sailor?"

I took a deep breath.

"You know how I've lost a bunch of memories?" I asked her. She was surprised by the question, but she nodded.

"I've been trying to figure out which ones I've lost. Mostly they don't matter, but there's one . . . there's one that's breaking my heart, Marr. You remember that night on the transport, when we had dinner in the ship's mess, just the two of us?"

She nodded.

"That night was the first time we made love, wasn't it?"

She nodded again.

"I wish . . . I really wish I could remember that first night."

"Oh, Baby," she said softly.

Then we kissed, and I guess I'll remember that.

Later, as I drifted off to sleep, Marr sat in the chair by my bed.

"This thing between you and me," I said sleepily, "you know it's a hundred-to-one shot."

"I know," she said, and she patted my shoulder and smiled.

"You're the perfect cigar, gonna ruin me for everything else in life."

"Get some sleep, Sasha," she said, and she left her hand on my shoulder. It was warm, and the warmth gradually spread down through my chest into my heart, and from there it filled my whole body. It was a feeling of contentment that I suppose lots of people know, but I'd never felt before, at least not when I was alive.

I was home.

The following is an excerpt from:

BALANCE POINT

ROBERT BUETTNER

Available from Baen Books
April 2014
trade paperback

ONE

The pilot on my left tapped my shoulder as his voice crackled in my headset. "Captain Parker? There, sir!"

I looked where his gloved finger pointed. Twenty degrees right of the tilt-wing's nose, five miles distant, an oily black rope writhed between the ground and the sky. The smoke tied together the South Georgia swamp below us and the low cloud ceiling beneath which we raced.

"Fire? Why the hell is there fire?"

"Flame thrower, sir. Apparently the animal doesn't like 'em."

I shook my head and swore. Of course "the animal" didn't like 'em. No being in its right mind liked burning alive. "What idiot thought that up?"

"I just fly the bird, sir." The pilot banked the tilt-wing toward the smoke. He had never overflown this place before and knew only what he'd been told through his headset during the last two hours. His tilt-wing was a regular Army trainer that had been diverted in flight from Ft. Stewart, a couple hundred miles northeast, because it was the only available vertical take-off and landing aircraft near enough to pick me up in a shopping center parking lot, then drop me off, that was also clearable into restricted airspace.

The pilot leveled the ship and settled it toward a landing pad. The pad was just a rectangle where the scrub had been scraped back to expose bare soil. At one corner an orange wind sock flapped from a pole. A ground level breeze now carried the smoke from the fire across the pad like a shroud four hundred yards long.

Two turret-variant hellcats idled at the pad's edge. Each 'cat's roof was stenciled "OCWTRS," an acronym for "Okefenokee Chemical Weapons Test Range Security." Of course, the eighty-three square miles of muggy Federal scrub woodland and restricted airspace that surrounded the pad had never seen a chemical weapon, unless you counted that flame thrower.

But the skull and crossbones signs on the barbed wire fencing and the overflight restrictions advisories on aerial maps discouraged the curious. The 'cats with their turret guns, and automated triple-A 'bot batteries along the range perimeter, discouraged the more-than-curious.

Half hidden in the trees bordering the pad a boxy command and control hovertank hunched like a plasteel porcupine, its roof bristling with swept-back antennae.

On the pad another tilt-wing, like the one that was delivering me but spook-black, already squatted on its landing gear alongside the vehicles. A command and control communications pod bulged from its back like a tumor.

"Looks like there's some brass on the ground already, sir. Guess you could ask them about the fire."

The tilt wing's props were still blowing at landing pitch when I dropped through the belly hatch and ran, eyes slitted against the dust and smoke, to the command slider. The air smelled of seared wood and jellied gasoline.

As the tilt wing that had hauled me in lifted off, a personal security detail corporal, posted alongside the slider's rear hatch recognized me, saluted, then jerked his head at the command vehicle. "The Old Man's waiting for you in the slider, Captain Parker."

Inside the red-lit command slider only one person sat, back to me, hunched at one of the flatscreen consoles.

The rest of the consoles were dark and unattended. "Where is everybody, Howard?"

General Howard Hibble, AKA The Old Man, AKA The King of the Spooks, didn't turn around, but in the reflection of his face off the screen I saw his gray eyebrows flick up. "Inauguration Day's a Federal holiday. If you hadn't been moping around for the last week you'd know that, Jazen."

Howard Hibble was the longest-serving general officer in the history of the United States Army, but not because he was conventional. He had been a professor before the Slug War, was commissioned as an intelligence officer during the Blitz, and had run his spooks his way ever since. His way included being called by his first name by everybody, and an every-day-is-casual-Friday dress code that would choke any drill sergeant. Howard's way also included knowing more about the personality balance point between the two individuals who made up each of his officer pairs than a marriage counselor knew about her clients.

In fact I *had* taken accumulated leave to mope after Kit left. Not just because I missed waking up beside her. Case officer pairs, whether het or monogender, typically bond closer than married couples, but separation is a job requirement of military life. The trouble with this particular separation was that Kit's job required her to spend two weeks in Paris without me, because the man in charge of the trip preferred I disappear from her life. And he happened to be her father.

I said, "It's my leave. I can mope if I want. I've still got more time accumulated than I can use."

With a bony hand Howard twisted the handlebar of the little scooter he rode around on— they didn't call him "The *Old* Man" for nothing—and faced me. "It is, you can, and you do. I assume you're seeing her this weekend."

"If I can still rent an outfit. You kidnapped me in the Tux shop parking lot before I got in the door."

He adjusted the old-fashioned wire rimmed glasses that hung on his wrinkled face and stared at my jeans. "Wear your dress whites instead."

I eyed his wrinkled flannel shirt. "What do you know about the dress code for black-tie parties?"

"As little as a man who's survived four decades in Washington can. But I know you. You'll be less intimidated in your own skin." Howard shrugged as he spun back to the console and tapped up the screen image. "I didn't send that tilt-wing so I could give you relationship counseling."

I peered over his shoulder.

The screen showed a crowbot overhead, real time, visible light, displaying two hundred by two hundred yards. Dismounted infantry, probably the squad that normally patrolled the range's perimeter aboard the two parked hellcats, were deployed on line, prone behind the cover of a shallow ridge at the screen's left, west, edge.

I guessed that when things had gone bad they had been pulled off perimeter patrol. The command slider probably had been rolled out from The Barn on auto and rendezvoused with Howard's hunchback when it landed.

The infantry were all armored up in full

Eternads, and two of the GIs had flamer tanks strapped on their suits' backs.

Fifty yards to the squad's front brush and scrub burned. The smoke plume now drifted south, forming a concealing barrier at ground level between the squad and anything beyond the smoke that depended on visible light to see. The Okefenokee is damp terrain, even around its edges, and the fire looked to be burning itself out.

On the other side of the smoke screen the hovering crowbot's feed highlighted three biologics among the trees.

The first biologic, twenty yards beyond the fire, was another GI in Eternads, lying face up. Fifteen feet from him lay a twisted metal lump that had once been the tanks and hose of a back-mounted flamer. Just beyond the trashed flamer were two larger lumps. They remained barely recognizable as a utility variant hellcat and its flatbed trailer, both now mangled and overturned, impellers to the sky.

The GI lay motionless, and at first I assumed he was dead. But his suit vitals shimmered in orange digits displayed on the screen alongside his image. They were normal, except for elevated heart rate and respiration, which were hardly surprising considering his circumstances.

I nodded to myself. Playing dead was a logical strategy.

His circumstances were defined by the other two biologics on the screen. The first, according to the vitals displayed alongside it, was a newly dead, but still warm, truck-sized animal carcass. One of its six legs had been torn off and lay alongside the limp body, and its neck had been wrenched so that its rack haloed its head like a spiked wreath.

I pointed at a shredded harness that had tethered the recently deceased animal to the trailer. "I assume that's his Christmas turkey woog?"

Howard nodded, then frowned. "Normally, that makes his day."

I nodded back.

Woog were more-or-less antelope, but six legged, bigger than elephants, and not native to South Georgia. Very not native. Downgraded Earthlike 476, known to everybody except its tourism bureau as Dead End, was about as far from South Georgia as the human race had gotten so far.

Dead End harbored a Carbon 12 based fauna so biochemically dissimilar to Earth's that feeding an Earth animal's flesh to a Dead End carnivore was like feeding sand to a lion. So, in order to nourish OCWTRS' one and only guest, Howard's xenobiologic nerds had bred, here on Earth, a herd of woog.

The nerds found that the docile, Earth-bred woogs provided dandy nourishment, but failed to offer the "robustly combative dining experience" provided to a grezzen when he chased

down a natural-born wild woog back home on
Dead End.

The Army has its faults, but it spares no
expense to give remotely deployed GIs a taste
of home. You may get your Christmas turkey
dinner in a bunker, but you *will* get it. So, on
each Federal holiday, one of which was the
inauguration day of the United States President,
the Army, driven by force of habit, imported
one live free-range woog, all the way across
the ten jumps between Dead End and Earth,
as a dietary change-of-pace for South Georgia's
most voracious tourist.

I squinted at the third organic on the screen,
which was the intended beneficiary of the Army's
generosity. Unlike the possum-playing GI game
warden who had delivered the woog, the grezzen was very much in motion. As I watched, the
grezzen uprooted a thirty foot cypress with a paw
swipe that spun the tree through the air as if
an eleven ton, six legged ochre grizzly bear had
swatted a salmon out of a stream. The grezzen
spun like a dog chasing its tail, sprang twenty
yards in a single bound to another cypress, then
splintered it, too.

"Howard, what's got up his ass?"

Howard shook his head. "Don't know. That
warden lost his helmet audio before he could
elaborate."

"He's lucky he didn't lose his helmet and
the head in it. He knows better than to use his

flamer. Does that relief squad know enough to hold *their* fire?"

"Well, I hope so."

I blew out a breath. A dithering professor *hoped* his students knew what to do. A four-star general made *sure* they knew, then motivated them to do it. Intelligence was an unconventional business, and Howard's resume' spoke for itself, but there were times when running a military organization like a Socratic method graduate seminar was idiotic.

I stepped to the hatch. "I'm going over there, Howard."

"Take the hellcat on the left. There's an Eternad suit in your size in the right hand seat."

I had already slid behind the hellcat's control yoke when I realized that, for a dithering professor, Howard Hibble excelled at motivating people to risk their lives without even asking them to. At least the gullible ones. Who never seemed to learn.

"God *damn* you, Howard." I shifted the 'cat into drive and steered toward the smoke.

—end excerpt—

from *Balance Point*
available in trade paperback,
April 2014, from Baen Books

The Looking Glass Series
Into the Looking Glass
(pb) 1-4165-2105-4 • $7.99

Vorpal Blade with Travis S. Taylor
(hc) 1-4165-2129-1 • $25.00
(pb) 1-4165-5586-2 • $7.99

Manxome Foe with Travis S. Taylor
(pb) 1-4165-9165-6 • $7.99

Claws That Catch with Travis S. Taylor
(hc) 1-4165-5587-0 • $25.00
(pb) 978-1-4391-3313-2 • $7.99

Master of Hard-Core Thrillers
The Last Centurion
(hc) 1-4165-5553-6 • $25.00
(pb) 978-1-4391-3291-3 • $7.99

■ ■ ■

The Kildar Saga
Ghost
(pb) 1-4165-2087-2 • $7.99

Kildar
(pb) 1-4165-2133-X • $7.99

Choosers of the Slain
(hc) 1-4165-2070-8 • $25.00
(pb) 1-4165-7384-4 • $7.99

Unto the Breach
(hc) 1-4165-0940-2 • $26.00
(pb) 1-4165-5535-8 • $7.99

A Deeper Blue
(hc) 1-4165-2128-3 • $26.00